WHEN THE MOON IS LOW

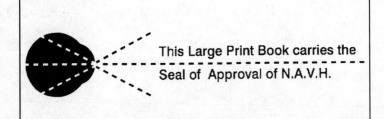

This Large Print Book carries the
Seal of Approval of N.A.V.H.

WHEN THE MOON IS LOW

NADIA HASHIMI

THORNDIKE PRESS
A part of Gale, Cengage Learning

GALE
CENGAGE Learning

Farmington Hills, Mich • San Francisco • New York • Waterville, Maine
Meriden, Conn • Mason, Ohio • Chicago

GALE
CENGAGE Learning·

LIBRARY OF CONGRESS CATALOGING-IN-PUBLICATION DATA

Hashimi, Nadia.
    When the moon is low / by Nadia Hashimi. — Large print edition.
    pages cm. — (Thorndike Press large print core)
    ISBN 978-1-4104-8605-9 (hardcover) — ISBN 1-4104-8605-2 (hardcover)
    1. Afghan War, 2001- 2. Refugees—Afghanistan—Fiction. 3. Large type books. I. Title.
PS3608.A78975W47 2016
813'.6—dc23   2015034938

Published in 2016 by arrangement with William Morrow, an imprint of HarperCollins Publishers

Printed in Mexico
1 2 3 4 5 6 7 20 19 18 17 16

*For Zoran, who made me the luckiest girl
in the world when he
promised to always be my best friend*

The small man
Builds cages for everyone
He
Knows.
While the sage,
Who has to duck his head
When the moon is low,
Keeps dropping keys all night long
For the
Beautiful
Rowdy
Prisoners.

— "DROPPING KEYS" BY HAFIZ,
A FOURTEENTH-CENTURY SUFI POET

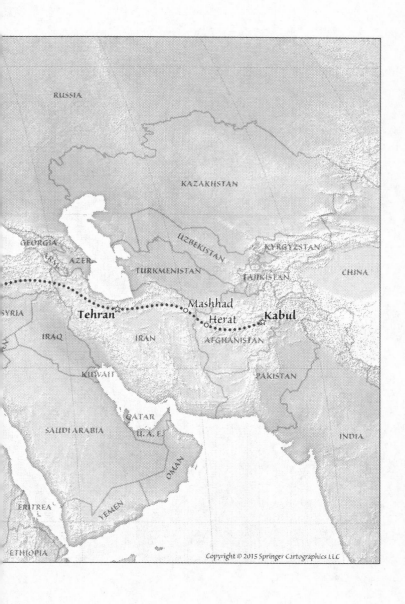

PROLOGUE:
FEREIBA

Though I love to see my children resting soundly, in the quiet of their slumber my uneasy mind retraces our journey. How did I come to be here, with two of my three children curled on the bristly bedspread of a hotel room? So far from home, so far from voices I recognize.

In my youth, Europe was the land of fashion and sophistication. Fragrant body creams, fine tailored jackets, renowned universities. Kabul admired the fair-complexioned imperialists beyond the Ural Mountains. We batted our eyelashes at them and blended their refinement with our tribal exoticism.

When Kabul crumbled, so did the starry-eyed dreams of my generation. We no longer saw Europe's frills. We could barely see beyond our own streets, so thick were the plumes of war. By the time my husband and I decided to flee our homeland, Europe's allure had been reduced to its singular, sexiest quality — peace.

I am no longer a new bride or a young woman. I am a mother, farther from Kabul than I have ever been. My children and I have crossed mountains, deserts, and oceans to reach this dank hotel room, utterly unsophisticated and unfragrant. This land is not what I expected. Good thing all that I coveted from a youthful distance is no longer important to me.

Everything I see, hear, and touch is not my own. My senses burn with the foreignness of my days.

I dare not disturb the children, as much as my heart wishes they would wake and interrupt my thoughts. I let them sleep because I know how exhausted they feel. We are a tired bunch, sometimes too tired to smile at one another. As much as I'd like to sleep, I feel obligated to stay awake and listen to the nervous banging in my head.

I long to hear Saleem's determined footsteps in the hallway.

My wrist is bare. My gold bangles and their melancholy clink are gone. It was my plan to sell them. Our pockets are too empty for us to brave the rest of our journey. There is still a long road ahead before we reach our destination.

Saleem is so eager to prove himself. He's more like his father than his adolescent heart could realize. He thinks of himself as a man, and much of that may be my doing. Too many times I've given him reason to believe he is one. But he is not much more than a boy, and the unforgiving world is eager to remind him of it.

*I'm going, Madar-*jan. *If we hide in a room every time we are nervous, we will never make it to England.*

There was truth to what he said. I bit my tongue, but the gnawing feeling in my stomach condemns me for it. Until my son returns, I will stare at the sickly white walls, paintings of anchors, faded artificial flowers. I will wait for the walls to collapse, for the anchors to crash to the floor and the flowers to turn into dust. I need Saleem to come back.

I think of my husband more now than I did in those days he stood by my side. What foolish and ungrateful hearts we have when we are young.

I wait for the doorknob to turn, for my son to enter, boasting that he's done for our family what I could not. I would give anything for him not to risk as much as he does. But I have nothing to barter for such a naïve wish. All I have is spread before me, two innocent souls lightly stirring in their own troubled dreams.

I can touch them still, I remind myself. Saleem will return, God willing, and we will be as close to complete as we can hope to be. One day, we will not look over our shoulders in fear or sleep on borrowed land with one eye open or shudder at the sight of a uniform. One day we will have a place to call home. I will carry these children — my husband's children — as far as I can and pray that we will reach that place where, in the quiet of their slumber, I, too, will rest.

PART ONE

CHAPTER 1
FEREIBA

My fate was sealed in blood on the day of my birth. As I struggled to enter this twisted world, my mother resigned it, taking with her my chances of being a true daughter. The midwife sliced through the cord and released my mother from any further obligation to me. Her body paled while mine pinked; her breaths ceased as I learned to cry. I was cleaned off, wrapped in a blanket, and brought out to meet my father, now a widower thanks to me. He fell to his knees, the color leached from his face. Padar-*jan* told me himself that it was three days before he could bring himself to hold the daughter who had taken his wife. I wish I couldn't imagine what thoughts had crossed his mind, but I can. I'm fairly certain that had he been given the choice, he would have chosen my mother over me.

My father did his best but he wasn't built for the task. In his defense, it wasn't easy in those days. Or in any days, for that matter. Padar-*jan* was the son of a vizier with local clout. People in town turned to my grandfather for counsel, mediation, and loans. My grandfather, Boba-*jan,* was even tempered, resolute, and sagacious. He made decisions easily and didn't waver in the face of dissent. I don't know if he was always right, but he spoke with such conviction that people believed he was.

Soon after he was married, Boba-*jan* had come upon a substantial amount of land through a clever trade. The fruits of this land fed and housed generations of our family. My grandmother, Bibi-*jan,* who died two years before my tragic birth, had given him four sons, my father being the youngest. Her four sons had all grown up enjoying the privilege their father had secured for them. The family was respected in town, and each of my uncles had married well, inheriting a portion of the land on which they each started their own families.

My father, too, owned land — an orchard, to be exact — and worked as a local official in our town, Kabul, the bustling capital of Afghanistan tucked away in the bosom of central Asia. The geography would become important to me only later in my life. Padar-*jan* was merely a faded carbon copy of my

18

grandfather, not penned with enough pressure to imprint strong characters. He had Boba-*jan*'s good intentions but lacked his resolve.

Padar-*jan* had inherited his piece of the family estate, the orchard, when he married my mother. He devoted himself to that orchard, tending to it morning and night, climbing its trees to pluck the choicest fruits and berries for my mother. On hot summer nights, he would sleep among the trees, intoxicated by the plush branches and the sweet scent of ripe peaches. He would barter part of the orchard's yield for household staples and services and seemed satisfied with what he was able to garner in this way. He was content and didn't seek much beyond his lot.

My mother, from the bits and pieces I heard growing up, was a beautiful woman. Thick locks of ebony fell below her shoulders. She had warm eyes and regal cheekbones. She hummed while she worked, always wore a green pendant, and was well known for her mouthwatering *aush,* delicate noodles and spiced ground beef in a yogurt broth that warmed bellies in the harsh winter. My parents' short-lived marriage had been a happy arrangement, judging by the way my father's eyes would well up on

19

the rare occasion he spoke of her. Though it took me almost a lifetime to do it, I put together what I knew of my mother and convinced myself that she had most likely forgiven my trespass against her. I would never see her, but I still needed to feel her love.

About a year after their marriage, my mother gave birth to a healthy baby boy. My father took a first look at his son's robust form and named him Asad, the lion. My grandfather whispered the *azaan,* or call to prayer, in Asad's newborn ear, baptizing him as a Muslim. I doubt Asad was any different then. Most likely, he didn't hear Boba-*jan*'s *azaan,* already distracted by mischief and ignoring the call to be righteous.

Asad seemed to be born feeling he owned the world. He was, after all, my father's first son, a source of immense pride for the family. He would carry our family name, inherit the land, and care for our parents in their golden years. As if he knew what was to be expected of him later in life, he consumed my mother and father. He nursed until my mother was raw and exhausted. My father scrambled to construct toys for his son to play with, planned for his education, and became even more intent that he bring home enough to keep his wife, a new mother, in good health and well nourished.

My mother was proud to have given her husband a son, and a healthy one at that. Fearful that the neighbors or family members would be jealous and cast an evil eye on him, she sewed a small blue stone, an amulet, to the baby clothing her sister-in-law had given her to ward off the evil eye, or *nazar*. That wasn't all she did. She had an arsenal of tricks to combat the many faces of *nazar*. If Asad felt heavier in her hands or if a visitor commented on his pink, fleshy cheeks, she would look to her nails. She punctuated their compliments with whispers of *nam-e-khoda*, praising God's name. Arrogance attracted *nazar* with the ferocity of lightning on an open field.

Day by day, Asad fattened off our mother's milk, his face taking shape and his thighs thickening. Forty days after his birth, my mother breathed a sigh of relief that her son had survived the most dangerous time. My mother had seen a neighbor's baby, two weeks after its birth, stiffen and shake desperately as if overcome by a wave of evil. The newborn's spirit was taken before it could be named. I learned later that cutting an umbilical cord with a dirty knife probably seeded toxic bacteria in the baby's blood. True or not, we Afghans are firm believers in not counting our chickens until forty days after they've hatched.

Like so many mothers, Madar-*jan* called upon the powers of wild rue seeds, called *espand.* She let a handful of the black seeds smolder and pop over an open flame, the smoke wafting above Asad's head as she sang

It banishes the Evil eye, it is espand
The blessing of King Naqshband
Eye of nil, Eye of folks
Eye of allies, Eye of foes
Who ever wishes ill, let burn in these coals.

The song traced back to the pre-Islamic religion of Zoroastrianism, though even Muslims trusted its powers. My father watched, pleased that his wife was taking such care to safeguard his progeny. And, oh, how it must have worked! My mother's death didn't affect my brother's life the way it did mine. He was still my father's first-born, still managed to be successful in life, usually at the expense of others. His care-less doings hurt those around him, often me, and yet he always seemed to emerge unscathed. In the two short years my mother nurtured him, he had gained enough strength to secure his place in the world.

But my mother died before she could pin an amulet to my gown, before she could whisper *nam-e-khoda,* before she could look at her fingernails, and before she could lovingly waft the *espand* over my head. My life became a series of misfortunes, a product of unthwarted evil eyes. My birth was haunted by the death of my mother and, while Boba-*jan* mournfully whispered the *azaan* in my ear, a very different prayer was being said over my mother's depleted body. The *azaan,* spoken in my grandfather's voice, wove its way through to the fabric of my being, telling me to keep faith. My salvation was that I listened.

My mother was buried in a newly dedicated cemetery near our home. I didn't visit much, partly because no one would take me and partly because of my lingering guilt. I knew I had put her there and people would remind me of that.

My father became a young widower with a two-year-old son and a newborn daughter. My brother, unruffled by our mother's absence, crankily went about his toddler business, while I naïvely sought my mother's bosom. With two children now in the nest, my father buried his bride and began looking for a new mother for his children.

My grandfather hastened the process, knowing a newborn would not fare well in the unintuitive care of a man. As vizier, he was familiar with all the families in the neighborhood. He knew a local farmer who had five daughters, and the eldest was of marrying age. Boba-*jan* was sure the farmer, burdened with providing for five girls until they wed, would be agreeable to his son as a suitor.

My grandfather went to the farmer's home and, praising his son as a noble and trustworthy person who had the misfortune to be widowed early in life, he negotiated the engagement of the eldest daughter to my father. Gently emphasizing that the welfare of two small babes were to be taken into consideration, the process moved quickly. In months, Mahbuba entered our home where she was renamed, as most brides were, with a "house name." It's meant to be respectful, not calling a woman by her familiar name. I think it's more than that, though. I think it's a way of telling the bride not to look back. And sometimes that's a good thing.

KokoGul, as the eldest of five sisters, had cared for her younger siblings from an early age and was fully capable of tending to two children. She decided quickly not to live in my mother's shadow. She rearranged the few decorative pieces in our home, discarded my mother's clothing, and erased all evidence of her existence, save my brother and me. We were the only proof that she was not the first wife, an important distinction even if the first wife was dead.

It was more common then for men to take on multiple wives, a practice that stemmed from times of war and the need to provide for widows, I'd been told. Practically speaking, this created a certain undercurrent of tension among the wives. The status of the first wife could not be matched by those that followed. KokoGul was robbed of the opportunity to be the first wife by a woman she never met, a woman she could not challenge. Instead, she was forced to rear the first wife's children.

KokoGul was not an evil woman. She did not starve me, beat me, or throw me out of the house. In fact, she fed me, bathed me, clothed me, and did all the things a mother should. When I stumbled upon language, I called her Mother. My first steps were toward her, the woman who nursed me through childhood fevers and scrapes.

Yet all this was done at arm's length. It didn't take long for me to feel her resentment though it would be years before I could give it a name. My brother was the same but different. Within months, he transferred the title of "mother" to KokoGul and forgot that there had been another woman in her place. She tended to his needs with a bit more diligence, knowing that he was the key to my father's heart. My complacent father, when at home, was satisfied that he had found his children a suitable mother. My grandfather, more astute with years, knew to watch over us. He was a constant presence.

I wasn't an orphan. I had parents and siblings, a warm home and enough food. I should have felt complete.

But being without a mother is like being stripped naked and thrown into the snow. My biggest fear, the dread that grows alongside my love for my children, is that I may leave them in the same way.

I wonder if that fear will ever pass.

CHAPTER 2
FEREIBA

KokoGul was a pleasant-looking woman, but someone you wouldn't notice in a crowded room. She was nearly as tall as my father, with thick black hair that just grazed her shoulders. It was the kind of hair that would fall limp just minutes after the curlers came out. She was too buxom to look dainty and too thin to appear commanding. KokoGul had been painted with a palette of average colors.

Two years after she married my father, KokoGul delivered her first child, a daughter, a disappointment she promptly blamed on my mother's ghost. My half sister was named Najiba, after my deceased grandmother. Najiba had KokoGul's round face, and dark eyes framed by thick, arched brows. KokoGul, following tradition, lined her daughter's lids with kohl so she would have healthy eyesight and striking eyes. For the first two months, KokoGul spent hours

27

trying to make some concoction of fennel seeds and herbs that would soothe Najiba's colic and stop her howling. Until her temperament calmed, mother and daughter were a sleep-deprived, ornery duo.

KokoGul's patience with her stepchildren wore even thinner once her own daughter was born. Even more aware than before that we were not her own, she was quickly exasperated and lashed out at us with the swift strike of a viper. We were disciplined by the back of her hand. Meals were laid out with disinterest and inconsistency when my father was away. We ate as a family only when he came home at the day's end.

With Najiba's birth, KokoGul's womb warmed to the idea of carrying children, and over the next four years she delivered three more girls. With each pregnancy, her patience shortened and my father, preferring peaceful days but unable to demand them, grew more distant. Sultana was born a year after Najiba. KokoGul did not make any effort to hide the fact that she had been hoping for a son, unlike my curiously disinterested father. With her third pregnancy almost two years later, she prayed, reluctantly gave alms to the poor, and ate all the foods that she heard would guarantee her a male child. Mauriya's birth disappointed her and she believed that my mother's spirit had placed a powerful curse on her womb. When Mariam, my fourth sister was born, KokoGul was not in the least disappointed or surprised. Feeling thwarted by my dead mother, she bitterly resolved not to have any more children. Asad would be my father's only son.

My earliest memory should have had something to do with school or a favorite doll, but that was not the childhood I had. KokoGul lay on a cushion in the living room, a newly born Mauriya nestled beside her, tightly swaddled in a prayer shawl. I was five years old.

"Fereiba!" KokoGul bellowed. Mauriya's tiny face grimaced. She was too tightly bound to react in any other way.

"Yes, Madar-*jan.*" I was only steps away. KokoGul, still recovering from childbirth, was to do nothing but nurse the baby. I knew this because she'd reminded me of it often.

"Fereiba, your aunt left some chicken stew still simmering on the fire. There's hardly enough for all of us. Why don't you get some potatoes from outside so we'll have enough to feed everyone."

This meant two things. One, that my

father and brother would be the only ones eating chicken tonight and the rest of us would have to settle for stewed potatoes. And two, that I would have to go out into the frosted backyard to dig out some spuds. Earlier in the season, we had buried a stash of potatoes, radishes, carrots, and turnips behind the house where they were refrigerated in the earth.

"Madar-*jan,* can't you tell Asad to get them?" It was cold out, and I could already imagine myself struggling with the shovel.

"He's not here and we need the potatoes now or they won't be ready in time for dinner. Put on the coat and mittens your father bought you. It'll only take you a few minutes."

I didn't want to go.

"Go on, sweetheart. Help your mother, will you?"

Her endearments were like powdered sugar on burnt bread. I bit into it.

I remember struggling with a shovel that was as tall as me, then giving up and finding a trowel that I could actually manage. My breath seemed to crystallize in the icy air and my fingers were numb despite my mittens. Hurriedly, I picked out four potatoes and was about to rebury the rest when I saw a few radishes. For no real reason that

I can recall, I brought the radishes in as well, stuffing them in my pockets since my hands were full.

"I got them, Madar-*jan,*" I called out from the kitchen.

"Good girl, Fereiba. God bless you. Now wash and peel them and toss them into the pot so they can cook in the tomato sauce." Mauriya had started to whimper.

I did as KokoGul instructed and cut the potatoes as she'd taught me, careful not to slice my fingers in the process. On a whim, I washed and cut the radishes as well, tossing them into the pot as a bit of culinary creativity. I stirred once, re-covered the aluminum vessel, and went to check on my other sisters.

"What is that awful smell? Fereiba! What have you done?" KokoGul's voice traveled through our home as if it had legs and a will. I'd noticed the smell earlier but dismissed it with the carelessness of a five-year-old.

I didn't think I had anything to do with the smell until KokoGul pulled herself to her feet, walked into the kitchen, and lifted the aluminum top. A pungent cloud of steam filled the room. I covered my nose with my hand, surprised I'd missed this smell.

"Fereiba, you fool! You fool!" She repeated those words over and over again, shaking her head and huffing, one hand on the small of her back.

The red flesh of my cubed radishes had told KokoGul exactly what I'd done. I learned that day that those hard, fuchsia bulbs let out a horrible stench when cooked. It was a smell I would never forget and a feeling I would always remember.

After each birth, the routine KokoGul used with Najiba was repeated. The babies' eyes were lined with kohl, sweets were purchased when they'd survived forty days, and their heads were shaved to give them full, thick locks. I was left to mourn the miserable eyesight, fortune, and hair I would have since none of that had been done for me.

When it came time for me to attend school, KokoGul convinced Padar-*jan* that she needed my assistance at home with the younger children. My father, unable to afford help, agreed to have me stay back a year. Though I was young, I was useful — able to fetch things and do small chores. But even as my sisters grew, the same argument prevailed.

Thankfully, Boba-*jan,* my grandfather, kept a close eye on us. He dropped by frequently, and KokoGul's behavior was notably different in his presence. He would call Asad and me to walk with him, his pockets jingling with coins and candies; there was no visitor we looked forward to more than Boba-*jan*. He would ask us to recite our prayers while he inspected our clothing and pinched the fat of our arms. KokoGul would watch him out of the corner of her eye, resentful of his mistrust.

But Boba-*jan*'s visits didn't change much for me at home. As my sisters got older and KokoGul busied herself caring for them, I shouldered more and more of the household chores. I fed the chickens and tended to the goat. I beat the carpets daily and watched the younger girls. When Najiba reached school age, KokoGul argued that there was more to do than she could manage alone. My father conceded and I was relegated to home for another year. My younger sisters trotted off to learn the alphabet and numbers while I learned how to cook. My hands were chafed and cracked from scrubbing food stains from dirty clothes. Still, it stung more to stay in the kitchen while everyone else busily dressed for school in the morning.

KokoGul's mania for superstitions made the situation even more maddening. Superstitions abound in our culture, but KokoGul took them on with a special zeal. We could not sleep with socks on, lest we go blind. If anyone dropped a piece of silverware, I was tasked with cleaning the house from top to bottom in anticipation of guests. If she coughed while eating or drinking, she cursed those who were undoubtedly speaking ill of her somewhere. I think that was her favorite, the conviction that others were jealous of the relatively privileged life she had.

As if popular superstitions weren't enough, KokoGul created plenty of her own. Two birds flying overhead meant she would get into an argument with a close friend. If her onions burned on the fire, someone was bad-mouthing her cooking, and if she sneezed more than twice, evil spirits were toying with her. Padar-*jan* said nothing to KokoGul but would quietly tell us which interpretations she had invented so that we wouldn't share them with others. He shouldn't have bothered. KokoGul wasn't the type to keep her thoughts to herself, and all the neighbors were familiar with her fantastic theories.

In one corner of our orchard stood a cluster of striking mulberry trees, their overgrown branches draped down, bringing tiny fruits within arm's reach. The trees were mature with heavy, rooted trunks. One tree in the center of the group had bark so knotted and gnarled that KokoGul swore she could make out the face of an evil spirit in its woody convolutions. She was petrified of the bark-carved face but loved the mulberries that came from the branches above. Whenever KokoGul fancied mulberries, she would summon me.

"Fereiba-*jan*," she would call sweetly, pulling a ceramic bowl from the cupboard. "I need you to fetch some berries from the orchard. You know no one else can pluck those little fruits as delicately as you. I'll get nothing but jam if I send anyone else to pick them."

Her cajoling was unnecessary, but knowing KokoGul was too frightened to come out herself made me smile. As a skinny, stringy-haired twelve-year-old, I feared KokoGul more than the mysterious maze of trees in the orchard. In fact, in the light of day, when the house was full of people and demands, the orchard was my refuge.

One weekday night, with my sisters hunched over homework assignments, KokoGul was struck with a craving for mulberries. Obediently, I crept out the back door with an empty bowl and made my way to the familiar tree, the twisted bark snarling in the amber moonlight. Without daylight to help me, I let my fingers float through the leaves and guide me to the berries. I'd plucked no more than two or three when I felt a soft breeze behind me, as gentle as a whisper.

I turned around to see a luminous figure, a man, standing behind me. I dared not breathe as he placed his hand on my shoulder, so lightly that I hardly felt his touch.

I followed his long tapered fingers to his arm until I could take in all of him. He was old; a short, white beard covered his chin and crisscrossed wrinkles lined his face. Thick, white brows hung heavily, leaving just slits of his blue-gray eyes. He was a friend, I knew instantly. My racing heart slowed at the tender sound of his voice.

"Fereiba-*jan.* In the darkness, when you cannot see the ground under your feet and when your fingers touch nothing but night, you are not alone. I will stay with you as moonlight stays on water."

I blinked and he was gone. I looked around, expecting to see him walking away through the trees, but there was nothing. I replayed his words in my mind, hearing his voice echo. I whispered them to myself to make them linger. Seldom had my name been said so lovingly.

"Fereiba!" KokoGul called out to me from the house. She had grown impatient.

Hastily, I grabbed as many mulberries as I could, my fingers purple with their ripe juice. I scurried back to the house, shooting an occasional glance over my shoulder lest the old man reappear. My hands trembled as I put the bowl down in front of KokoGul, who sat overseeing my sisters as they worked diligently in their notebooks. She started on her snack. I stood before her, unmoved.

"What is it? What's happened to you?" she snapped.

"Madar-*jan,* I was outside — under the mulberry tree."

"And?"

"It's that, while I was there . . . I saw an old man. He came from light, from *roshanee.* He said my name and he told me that I was not alone. He said he would stay with me." As I said the words, I could hear his voice in my head.

"An old man? So where did he go?" KokoGul squinted and leaned forward pointedly.

"He disappeared. He came so suddenly; I felt his hand on my shoulder. As soon as he finished what he had to say, he disappeared. I didn't see where he went — he just vanished! I don't know who he was." I was breathless but not frightened. I waited for KokoGul to interpret what I'd seen.

"*B'isme-Allah!*" KokoGul exclaimed, praising God. "You have seen an angel! That's who he was, you simpleminded girl! Oh, not to recognize an angel when he taps you on the shoulder and promises to watch over you!"

An angel? Could it be? Grandfather had told us stories about angels and their celestial powers when he recited *suras* with us. How blind I had been not to recognize an angel before me! KokoGul went on, ranting that I did not appreciate this unearthly encounter. My sisters looked on wide-eyed. Her sharp voice faded as the angel's words echoed in my mind.

He would watch over me. My guardian angel would bring *roshanee* to the path ahead. I would never be alone.

The following *Jumaa,* Friday, we waited for my father to return from the *masjid.* KokoGul had instructed my father to pray that she and her daughters would also receive a visit from a guardian angel. My father hadn't said much about my encounter. I didn't know what or how much he believed.

KokoGul and I believed together. In this,

38

we were united. She saw small changes in me, and I saw what those changes did to her. I walked taller. I followed her instructions but didn't quiver before her as I once had. I wandered in and out of the orchard boldly, day and night. I half expected my angel to reappear and offer soft words of comfort.

KokoGul was beside herself. To her friends, she boasted that I, her daughter, had been visited by an angel. The visit was a herald of good fortune, and she hoped to absorb some of that light. She began to examine her dreams with more diligence, looking for clues that the heavens were communicating with her too. I heard her newly charged supplications when she prayed at home. She spoke to me a little more sweetly, with a gentle hand stroking my hair.

My sisters were curious about the whole matter but unable to grasp KokoGul's yearning to meet the man I'd seen in the orchard. Najiba, closest to me in age, was most puzzled by KokoGul's reactions.

"What did the angel look like, Fereiba? Were you scared of him?" she asked curiously. We were sitting cross-legged on the floor, shelling peas from their pods.

"He just looked like an old man, like somebody's grandfather." My words felt far too simple, but I didn't know how else to answer.

"Whose grandfather? Our grandfather?"

"No, not anyone we know. Just a grandfather," I paused, wanting to do him justice. "He glowed and he knew my name." I tossed a handful of peas into the bowl between us.

Najiba was quiet, considering my explanation. "Well, I'm glad I didn't see him. I think I would have been scared."

I might have said the same had I not been there to see his blue-gray eyes. His gentle voice had filled the darkness and left no room for fear. Still, Najiba made me feel brave.

KokoGul didn't quite see it the same. She began to absorb my encounter as her own, vicarious experience. I heard her talking to two friends over tea one day.

"And then he disappeared? Just like that?"

"Did you expect a horse and carriage would come and carry him off?" KokoGul said in her trademark snappish way. Unless they were the target of the sarcasm, her friends were typically entertained by it.

"God must be watching over her to have sent an angel to her," said one.

"You know, the poor thing, her mother's spirit in heaven watches over her. Must have

40

had something to do with it," said the other sympathetically.

The reference to my mother inspired KokoGul's imagination. "I asked Fereiba to go to the orchard that night. I rarely get such cravings for the mulberries, but something mysterious had come over me. My tongue began to tickle for those sweet berries. I tried to ignore it but I couldn't help myself. As if something in those trees was beckoning me, I wanted to run out there. But I was busy helping the girls with their homework so I asked Fereiba to pick a few for me. She's such a good daughter, she went off into the orchard for me. So I'm not sure who the angel was supposed to meet. Maybe that craving was his way of calling me. But I sent Fereiba-*jan* in my stead, so we'll never know."

The women didn't seem too impressed with KokoGul's theory, but they didn't challenge her. I entered the room, carefully balancing a tray with three hot cups of tea in one hand and carrying a bowl of sugar in the other.

"Afghan carpets were made with Fereiba-*jan* in mind," KokoGul announced. "Thanks to their red color, you would never know how much tea gets spilled on them." There was light laughter, and my head

41

stayed lowered. I smiled politely as I placed a cup before each woman and offered sugar cubes. I could feel myself being scrutinized.

"*Afareen, dokhtar*-jan," KokoGul commended. *Well done, dear daughter.* I retreated to the kitchen with the empty metal tray. Today I was her daughter.

In truth, most days I was her daughter. Because I wasn't attending school, I spent a lot of time at home with KokoGul. Indeed, the weight of the household fell mostly on my shoulders, and she reprimanded me severely when things weren't done to her liking. But I was with her the most. We spent hours together preparing meals, cleaning the house, and tending to the animals. Her sharp tongue needed an audience — or a target. I loved going to the bazaar with her. Inspecting a pile of bruised tomatoes, she asked the vegetable vendor if his hefty wife had mistakenly sat on his produce. At the housewares shop, she asked if the overpriced dishware was from the king's private collection. KokoGul's wit either rubbed the wrong way or scored a chuckle and a discount.

We were allies when we bargained our way through the things we needed: the meats, the vegetables, the shoes. I mimicked KokoGul's brazen demeanor and negotiated the best price I could. She would nod approvingly. In the market and the chores, my younger sisters could not do anything as well as I did.

"Najiba, look at this," she would complain. "This shirt still turns the water brown. How can you think this is clean? Have you seen how your sister makes a good lather? How many times have I told you — you can't expect a shirt to clean itself! Thank goodness I at least have one daughter who can actually help me around the house."

These were moments when I felt connected to her, this woman who was my mother, without being my mother.

CHAPTER 3
FEREIBA

Each night my brother and my sisters worked on their school lessons, pencils in their right hands, erasers in their left. They sat with elbows propped up on the table, chins in their palms while they read, memorized, added and subtracted. At first, they stumbled over the letters, learning how each character was connected to its neighbor with curved strokes. The dots, the dashes carefully placed, bringing words to life. Then came phrases, short simple sentences describing the daily activities of obedient boys and girls. When they started to learn the complex Arabic of the Qur'an, I grew even more envious. I'd learned to recite these prayers under my grandfather's tutelage, but I hadn't been taught to read the text itself.

They played with numbers. In singsong chants, they learned multiplication tables. I listened. On paper, they manipulated numbers and symbols. They learned to calculate, to make sense of digits.

They learned stories. The history of our country. The rise of kings and their sons. How our country was carved from the mountains. My brother was first to learn the national anthem and would sing it, a hand up in salute. My sisters learned play songs from their classmates, the rhythm and lyrics putting a hop in their carefree gait as they walked hand in hand.

Coo coo coo, leaf of a plane tree
Girls seated in a row neatly
Plucking pomegranate seeds
If only a pidgeon I could be
In the skies my wings soaring free
Sifting through river sand slowly
And drinking of waters so holy

In the mornings, I watched my sisters put on their uniforms, steel gray and modest. They would hike their socks up and hastily buckle their shoes, afraid of being late but even more afraid of appearing unkempt. The teachers took both issues very seriously. Every day I resented seeing them rush off while I stayed home. I envied their bags full of papers, pencils, and stories. I knew I was just as smart as my sisters — maybe even smarter.

My brother had always done well, maybe not top of his class, but well enough that my father and grandfather did not complain. I'm sure he could have excelled if he'd tried, but he rushed through homework assignments to get on with other business — soccer with the neighborhood boys, climbing the orchard trees, and bicycling down the streets near our house. As a teenager, he endured his most awkward phase, with his spotty skin and unpredictable voice. Once on the other side of puberty, his voice was that of a confident man who wanted to be out in the world.

I had broached the topic of school with my father in the past. His tired answer was always that KokoGul needed my help at home with the younger children but now this excuse was wearing thin. Mariam, my youngest sister, was seven years old and in primary school herself. There were no babies in the house.

We'd cleared the dinner dishes when I approached my father again. I was thirteen years old and determined. I knew girls who hadn't gone to school usually married earlier, and I did not want to be married. Every year put me further away from a chance at schooling and one step closer to becoming a wife.

"Padar-*jan*?" He looked up at me and smiled gently. He turned a dial and shut off the radio, his evening news program over. I placed a cup of hot green tea next to him, two sugar cubes quickly dissolving. He always took his evening tea sweet.

"Thank you, my dear. Just what I needed after such a good dinner," he said, patting his stomach and exhaling deeply.

"*Noosh-e-jan*," I replied, a wish his appetite be satisfied. "Padar-*jan*, I wanted to ask you something." My father raised an eyebrow as he took a cautious sip of his tea.

"Padar-*jan*, I want to go to school like my sisters."

"Oh, this again," he said, sighing. KokoGul, bent over her crochet needles, paused at my mention of schooling.

"I can still help at home, since it's only for a few hours. All the other girls go, and there are no little ones left in the house now. I want to learn the things they are learning." That was as much as I could get out before the cascade of tears. I lowered my head, cursing myself for not being able to get more out without my voice breaking. I waited for the knot in my throat to release or for my father to speak. I wasn't sure which would come first.

47

"Fereiba-*jan,* I thought that by now you didn't care about schooling anymore. Your sisters all started when they were younger. You're now a young woman and you've not attended a single day of classes." He grew pensive, his brows furrowed. I pursed my lips, focusing my frustration.

"I know that," I said simply. KokoGul resumed her needlework at full speed, satisfied that the outcome of tonight's discussion would be no different from any other.

"Is it that you want to read? Maybe Najiba can spend some time with you to help you learn how to read. Or even Sultana — she's doing very well in her writing and loves to read poetry."

I'd never before felt so angry with my father. I was hurt by his patronizing suggestion and resented his warm smile. I didn't want my younger sisters to teach me how to read. My sisters came home quoting their teachers daily. Their voices reinforced all that I was missing out on.

Moallim-sahib *says that my penmanship is improved. Moallim*-sahib *says we should drink a glass of milk every day to stay strong and healthy.*

I didn't want to look at my younger sister as my *moallim.* She might have been able to instruct me on the basics of the alphabet

48

and sounding out words but she couldn't be a true teacher, standing in the front of the classroom, pushing me to memorize multiplication tables, monitoring my progress. I wanted more.

"No, Padar-*jan.*" I could feel my windpipe reopening, my voice returning with new resolve. "I don't want to learn from a student. I want to learn from a teacher."

My response must have surprised him. He must have thought my aspirations were childish, fanciful ones. He must have thought I wanted to don the school uniform and escape some of the housework. But I wanted much more than I could put into words, and I knew only that I was running out of time. My father considered me carefully, the corners of his mouth turning down.

"It would not be easy for you. You would have to start from the beginning, in a class with children."

"He's right. You'll be a giant sitting among babies. It's a terrible idea. Like a chicken trying to climb back into an egg!" KokoGul cautioned.

"It won't bother me," I promised.

A necessary lie. This was the first time I'd seen my father consider my wish in a real way.

"Let me talk with the principal of the school. Let's see what they say. Although I'm sure your mother will miss you being around during the day."

"Isn't this all a bit silly? Why would she want to bother with school now? She has everything she needs here at home." KokoGul was clearly surprised at the direction this conversation had taken.

"I'm not promising anything. Let me talk with the school and see if they'll consider it," he said. Ever noncommittal, my father left both KokoGul and me feeling hopeful.

Much to his surprise and KokoGul's disappointment, the school agreed to enroll me provided I start from the beginning. I entered the first grade six years behind schedule. The night before my first day, I ironed the austere skirt and blouse, wanting to make a good impression on Moallim-*sahib*. Mauriya and Mariam, my two youngest sisters, were tickled to see me in uniform for the first time as we left the house together in the morning.

Najiba and Sultana, the older two, seemed a bit more concerned about what others would say to see an adolescent walk into a first-grade class. On the walk to school, Najiba tried to prepare me.

"Moallim-*sahib* will check to make sure

that you have a pencil and a notebook. And she will probably ask you to sit in the back of the room, you know, since you'll be taller than the other students."

I appreciated the delicate way Najiba phrased her prediction. Sultana nodded in agreement, but less diplomatically.

"Yes, no one would be able to see over your head." Najiba shot her a look and Sultana focused on her shoes, her steps slowing.

"You'll be moved soon. You mostly know the alphabet already. You'll be reading quickly."

I gave Najiba a grateful smile. My sister and I were not very close, but there was sincerity in her words and on this particular day I needed it.

"If Sultana could learn it, then I'm sure I'll have no problem."

Sultana huffed, glared straight ahead, and quickened her steps. I hadn't meant my comment to be biting. Ashamed, I turned around to check on Mauriya and Mariam trailing behind us. They walked hand in hand, bags slung over their shoulders.

My sisters distracted me from the trepidation of my first day of school. Najiba pointed me in the direction of my classroom once we passed the school's wrought-iron gates.

Sultana quickly disappeared into her own classroom. Mauriya and Mariam waved me off cheerfully.

I entered slowly, my eyes scanning the room. I wasn't sure if I should find a chair or walk to the front and introduce myself to the teacher first. The other students were filing in and busily taking their seats. I decided I'd best make my presence known, rather than have the teacher notice me and make a scene. I was almost more a woman than a girl, yet here I sat beside children. In another setting, I could have been their caretaker. Here, I was their peer.

"Welcome, dear. I had heard you would be joining us. You'll sit in the last row, on the end. It's the last empty seat we have. Here, take this book. This is what we're learning from now. Do you know your letters?"

My first teacher was a firm but kind-hearted woman who took an instant liking to me, thank goodness. She spoke to me differently than she did to my classmates and did not make me feel as awkward as I must have looked to sit among such young children. Grateful and determined, I worked fervently. I had listened while my siblings mastered the alphabet, so the letters rolled off my tongue easily enough.

Within two months, I moved into the second grade. I was happy to be advanced but sad to leave my teacher behind. And that was before I'd met my next *moallim.* My second-grade teacher seemed put out to have such an oversized pupil in her class. She called on me often to read aloud and took great pleasure in watching me fumble the words. When my classmates snickered, she would facetiously chastise them.

"That's enough! Remember, students, don't be fooled by Fereiba's size. She is new to second grade."

I worked even harder and, after passing the competency exam, she had no choice but to move me along to third grade. Every afternoon, I came home from school and got started on the chores I couldn't escape. Since I'd promised that I would still help KokoGul and I didn't want her to complain to my father that I was lagging in my housework, I still beat the dust from the carpets, laundered, and tended to the animals in the backyard. Only after the chores were finished and the family had eaten did I sit down to my studies. I toiled into the late hours. Padar-*jan* noticed.

"Fereiba-*jan,* you've been studying harder than your sisters ever did. The proof is in the marks you're getting. Are you managing well enough?"

"Yes, Padar-*jan*. I just want to catch up to where I should be."

"And what of your classmates? Are you getting along well enough with them?" I knew what he meant. He was asking if I, the teenaged third grader, was drawing too much negative attention.

"They're fine. They don't bother me and, anyway, I'm hoping to move out of this class soon."

Satisfied, he left me to complete my assignments. We would repeat the conversation every so often until I'd moved into the fifth grade and sixth grade, when the subjects required more focus and learning. Reading had come easily to me, but mathematics was different.

Simple math I'd learned from the marketplace. If the man on the corner quoted me a price for a single yard, I knew how much it would cost us for five. I could figure out the price of a quarter or a half kilogram of raisins given the price of a whole kilogram. Geometry and algebra were tougher but I managed.

I memorized by candlelight. I recited as I dusted the living room. My finger traced invisible words and paragraphs onto my leg as we ate dinner. I stole moments where I could to absorb all that I needed to learn.

I managed to catch up. I was sixteen years old in eleventh grade, with girls of the same age. I would be graduating in only one year. I was proud, as was my father. He read each of our school progress reports carefully. He leafed through the numbers and comments and looked up at me. I saw in his eyes what he couldn't put into words. The corners of his mouth turned up in a sly smile, although he tried to sound nonchalant in his assessment.

"Well done."

My grandfather listened in from the corner, with a pillow propped under his elbow and his back against the wall, nimbly moving the beads of his *tasbeh,* his rosary. The look on his face told me he wasn't in the least bit surprised.

CHAPTER 4
FEREIBA

Despite the fasting from sunrise to sunset, Ramadan was a joyous month. I was typically so consumed by schoolwork and chores that the hungry days passed quickly and painlessly. During the day, stomachs growled, but after sunset, we indulged in foods we'd spent all day preparing, special dishes to reward our stoicism.

My brother, Asad, often became grouchy and spiteful in Ramadan's afternoon hours. One afternoon, Asad had come into the living room where I was propping a pillow behind Boba-*jan*'s back. Without a word, he had thrown one of his shirts at my back. I turned around, surprised.

"Asad! What are you doing?" I said. It was a long-sleeved shirt that I had recently laundered.

"Asad, *bachem*. Why would you do such a thing?" Boba-*jan* admonished.

"Boba-*jan*, I need this shirt cleaned, but it

still has a stain on it. She was supposed to get the stain out!"

"What stain?" he asked.

"It was the juice of mulberries."

"Ah. So it is understandable then. You should not expect to wash the mulberry juice from the shirt. And do you know why?"

"Why, Boba-*jan*?" I had no idea either.

"Sit down so I may tell you. It is a good way to pass the hours until *iftar,* when we can break our fast and the restlessness that comes with it. So there was and there wasn't, under a battered sky . . ." And with the "once upon a time" line of Afghan storytelling, Boba-*jan* began his tale.

"There was a fair young maiden . . ."

He told us about the girl and archer who met by chance in the jungle. When the beautiful maiden heard the guttural growl of a tiger from the trees, she panicked and her nose began to bleed. She fled immediately, leaving her bloodied head scarf behind. Her beloved, finding her crimson-stained head scarf and spying a tiger crouching in the distance, assumed the very worst. Heartbroken and wanting to avenge his love's murder, he charged after the tiger who killed him effortlessly. When the young maiden worked up the courage to return to the jungle, she cried at the sight of her mauled and lifeless hunter. She collapsed beside a bush of poisonous berries and, in her abysmal grief, reached over and brought a toxic handful to her mouth, willing her soul to reunite with her beloved's in the next world.

"Since then that mulberry tree and every other mulberry tree has borne fruit that stains the color of the blood that united those two hearts, a stain that nothing can wash away."

Asad had listened intently but, when Boba-*jan* finished his story, looked disappointed to have no one to blame for his permanently stained shirt. With a huff, he picked it up from the floor near me.

"It's old anyway. I have better shirts."

I was thinking of Boba-*jan*'s story as I strolled through the bazaar a year later in search of plump dates for our *iftar*. There was a lightness to my step as I was eager to get home and share my good news. I'd been awarded the second-highest marks on a mathematics exam. Loud enough for all to hear, my teacher had announced, "Fereiba, nearly perfect score, second only to Latifa. Very good."

I knew Boba-*jan*'s eyes would twinkle with pride in that way that spoke more than words. I wanted to get the dates and make it home early enough to see my grandfather.

Sheragha owned a store packed with barrels of spices and dried goods: whole walnuts, fragrant cardamom, rock salt, brilliant turmeric powder, and fiery peppers. Though I found his store to be the most colorful and pleasing to the senses, Sheragha seemed less taken by it. He walked with a slow and heavy step. The width of two men, his forehead glistened with sweat even in the frigid cold of winter. I was rarely successful haggling down this particular vendor, but today he seemed to be in a generous mood. I kept my head bowed and took the sack of dates from him, careful not to brush against Sheragha's thick, hairy fingers.

Before I headed home, I adjusted the *chador* on my head and counted the coins I had in my pouch. KokoGul would be impressed. Content with my own triumph, I didn't notice the shadow following me into the narrow side street. Two coins fell from my hands into the dusty road. I crouched to pick them up when I heard footsteps and words so filthy my face burned red. The coins slipped through my fingers as I leaped to my feet and turned. Just inches from me stood one of the leering boys from the marketplace. I took a step back and scowled.

His long hair hung over his forehead. His eyes were dark and closely placed. He smirked, baring a yellow, gap-toothed sneer.

"Where are you off to? Why not stay awhile? I've got some *nakhod* in my pocket. Go ahead and take some," he said, sneering as he held his pant pocket open enough for a few dried chickpeas to fall out.

"Be-tarbia!" Brute, I yelled. I turned and fled, willing the warped leather of my old sandals to hold together as I hurried to the main road. The boy laughed behind me.

I exploded into the kitchen, sweating. KokoGul was cutting chunks of raw meat and tossing them into a pot of sizzling onions.

"Oh, *dokhtar!*" She called out, shooting me a look of surprise and warning. She pointed the tip of her knife at the corner of the kitchen where a bundle sat against the wall, wrapped in a coarse green blanket. KokoGul was making yogurt and it needed absolute stillness for the culture to take. "You have the grace of an elephant."

"Forgive me," I panted.

"What's going on? You look wild."

I was too embarrassed to recount what had happened.

"I was afraid I would be late to help with dinner."

"You *are* too late. It's almost ready. Wash up and make a salad at least. My back is beginning to ache. Did you bring the *khormaa*?" she asked, remembering the task she had given me in the morning.

"I did." I pulled the sack of dates from among my school supplies and handed her the change that remained. She counted the coins, short the few that I had left behind in my hasty escape.

"They look fresh. Whose store did you go to?"

"Sheragha. His mood was even worse than usual," I said, hoping to explain how much money had gone toward the dates. KokoGul clucked her tongue and put the sack to the side.

"From that bear's paws, nothing escapes. Go on into the living room. Your grandfather's been waiting to see you."

I sidestepped the living room and went to wash up. I was convinced my grandfather would see right through me in a way KokoGul never could. I couldn't look at him with the flush of embarrassment still on my cheeks.

Another day, I thought and put my exam in my room.

CHAPTER 5
FEREIBA

In my last year of high school, the orchard drew me in more than ever, the fruit-laden branches like curled fingers beckoning me to enter. In the cradle of peach trees, sucking on the gummy, amber-colored sap I'd peeled from the trunk, I considered what I might do after my graduation. Some girls were going on to university. Others were becoming teachers. Many would be married. I wasn't sure what I wanted, but I had no interest in marriage and the household that would come along with it.

When my chores were completed, I would slip into the orchard with a book. The grass felt cool against my feet, its soft blades tickling my toes. I would read with my back against a mulberry tree or sometimes lying on my stomach. My sisters asked me why I was so drawn to the mulberry trees and I told them it was there that I dreamt best.

"What do you dream about?" they would ask.

"I dream about tomorrow."

"What will happen tomorrow?"

"I don't know. I can't remember what happens, but I wake feeling that it is amazing. A story worth telling."

It was that summer that my grandfather fell ill with a bitter, relentless cough. He lay in bed for days, nursing cups of herb tea meant to exorcise disease from the body. I watched his heavy breathing, perspiration on his upper lip. Padar-*jan* summoned a doctor who gave an injection and then left two bottles of pills. I held the cup of water to his lips to wash the chalky tablets down.

I went to see him almost daily, hoping for signs of improvement. But his face paled even as his fever spiked red and hot. On my fourth visit, I made him soup and sweet tea. He took no more than a few sips before begging me to let him rest.

We called for the doctor again. Boba-*jan* looked so frail and small in his bed. I longed to see him stand up, reach for his cane, and walk to the kitchen. My father and I were at his side most of the time, but neither of us spoke of just how weak Boba-*jan* looked. Padar-*jan* did not say much at all but that was his way, as if he was afraid of his own voice.

"Fereiba-*jan*," my grandfather called out.

"Yes, Boba-*jan*?"

"My sweet granddaughter. You're nearly finished with high school, are you not?"

"Yes, Boba-*jan*. Just this year left."

"Good, good. And what will you do after you have completed your high school studies?"

"I'm not sure, Boba-*jan*. I was thinking of college but . . ." His eyes were half closed. I let my voice trail off, thinking he'd fallen asleep. He hadn't.

"But what?"

I had no answer for him. I shrugged my shoulders and wiped his forehead with a cool cloth.

"Fereiba, you have watched your father in the grove, haven't you? His talents come alive there. I taught him what I could when he was a boy, but before he became a man I could see there was more he could show me. He is a master at cultivating and grafting trees."

This was true. One winter, I'd watched my father strip a carefully selected scion from an apple tree. I followed him to the edge of the orchard where he had picked out a well-rooted apple tree of a bright red-skinned variety. Humming, he'd stroked the bark and circled the trunk, looking for the perfect place to introduce the graft. With surgical precision, he sliced into a branch at an angle, creating a lip that he pulled back. Into the opening, he slid the tapered end of the scion, placing the two raw faces in direct contact, an interface of two species. He continued to hum as he bound the scion to the host with long strips of cloth that circled the joint. He covered the tip of the scion and its three buds with a paper bag, shielding it from the drying air. By spring, we had a new kind of apple from a sapling branch that should have withered and died. Instead, two living, breathing species were made into a new fruit unique to our orchard, a fruit of my father's creation.

"I wish your father could carry his talents into his home, but they seem to dry at the threshold. That leaves things in your hands, Fereiba-*jan*." Boba-*jan* shook his head. I wanted to disagree, to tell him my father was nothing like KokoGul, but he continued.

"Even your brother has found his way, without obligation to anyone. I do not know who is to blame. He has the body of a horse but the mind of an ass."

"But you have always looked out for me,"

I said, holding his hand.

"Maybe I am hard on your father because he is too much like me. You, you are different. More like your mother, may Allah give her peace. She could see beyond her nose. With her, your father was better. It's too bad. She would have made a man out of him."

My legs were going numb, sitting beside Boba-*jan,* but I dared not move. I wanted to remember every word of what he was saying.

"No use speaking of such things. You are an intelligent girl. Trust yourself to know what's best for you."

"You always know what's best for me, Boba-*jan.* I can always turn to you."

"It's best not to depend on the gray haired. We're too close to God to rely on," he warned with a tired sigh.

He was exhausted, so I changed the subject and talked to him about the rosebushes growing outside his home. I told him about the chicken vendor who had to chase his clucking hens down the market street when a child opened the latch on the cage. He smiled and nodded, his eyes drifting off as sleep overcame him.

I kissed his hand and promised to return in the morning, but some time between then and sunrise, Boba-*jan* left to be with God and my mother. I wondered if the angel from the orchard had come to claim him. I wept for two weeks, away from my father and KokoGul and my siblings. I wanted to be as alone as I felt, and the only place I could do that was in the thick of the orchard.

Forty days after my grandfather's passing, I went walking among the fruit trees. Boba-*jan*'s death made me think of the angel from my childhood again, though I was fairly convinced he was nothing more than my youthful imagination toying with me. Still, I had the fleeting thought that if I saw him, I'd like to ask him about my grandfather and mother.

Behind a row of mulberry trees was our neighbor's orchard, separated from ours by a high clay wall. As I spent more time in the shade of the mulberry trees, I began to feel I wasn't alone. It was different from the time I'd seen my guardian angel. This time the presence felt earthly. This time the presence sneezed.

I sat up straight, suddenly very self-conscious. I closed my book and straightened my skirt, looking all around me for the source of the sneeze. There was not even a bird in sight. I was walking around the trees when I heard a rustle of leaves from just beyond the perimeter wall and a thump, followed by the sound of running feet. Someone had been watching me!

In the following days, I wasn't sure if I should return to that corner of the orchard. But, in my heart, I knew the mulberry tree had always brought me good fortune, so I wandered through the brush again, walking quietly and listening closely. A week later, I crept along the wall and looked up into the neighbor's trees. I was surprised to see a pair of legs dangling from a heavy branch.

It was him, I was certain. I tried to get a better view of the rest of him but I could only see his pant legs. Leather sandals hung loosely from his swaying feet.

This had to be the son of the neighboring family. He was a few years older than me, but I had never seen him before. Had my academics not been so delayed, we might have met in school. What was a boy, a young man, of his age doing perched in a tree?

Feeling a bit brazen, I stepped purposefully on small branches and kicked at a rock as I made my way over to the mulberry tree, taking my usual place in its generous shade. With an upward glance, I noticed the legs had disappeared from view. He was hiding!

I took out my book and stared at the page, the words blurred together as I asked myself why I'd come out here. After an interminable period of silence, I got up and walked back into the house, hoping I didn't look as panicked as I felt.

Nothing is foolish to the adolescent. The adolescent acts, without questioning the wisdom of the action. I returned every day after that, slinking through the trees, spying the familiar leather sandals, and taking my place under the mulberry tree. It became routine: school, housework, and orchard. I would stay awake late into the night to work on homework since I couldn't concentrate in the orchard. After two silent weeks, I decided to let the stranger know I was aware of his presence. The stalemate was driving me mad.

I spent the walk home from school working up my nerve. By the time I snuck into the orchard that afternoon, I was feeling so bold I barely recognized myself. I walked loudly and approached the wall. When I was sure I was within earshot, I said loudly, but not too loudly, "It's not polite to stare. It would be more respectful to say *salaam*."

I heard nothing in reply. Not a single word. Had I imagined the whole thing or was he not here today? Worse yet, perhaps he thought me shameless to speak this way to a stranger. I spent all my time either in a classroom of girls or at home. The only boys of my age that I knew were my cousins. To have any interaction with a boy outside was taboo and I knew it. I was at that age where I needed to be mindful of my comportment, but it was the orchard and I was invisible. I allowed myself some latitude.

That he ignored when I had crossed a line to interact with him disappointed and angered me. I stormed off.

I returned the following day, curiosity getting the best of me. Defiant, I sat beneath the tree for a few moments when I heard a voice.

"Salaam."

My back straightened and my face reddened with the affirmation that I'd overstepped my limits. I was suddenly ashamed and scared. I stood up, blurted *salaam* in reply without looking up, and scampered back into the house.

These were awkward days for me. For two weeks, KokoGul had hinted cheerfully that a well-to-do family wanted to pay us a visit. They had a son, a handsome young man who was likely to follow in his father's accomplished footsteps. My father had met the young man's father, Agha Firooz, in the course of official business, here and there. Agha Firooz now saw potential in forming a union with my father, who had inherited Boba-*jan*'s influence in the community. Aspirations of local prosperity and influence brought Agha Firooz's wife to our door.

I felt anxious. Like any other girl, I'd dreamed of having suitors, of having my family turn down a few persistent families before we settled on one that was good enough. The courtship was enticing, the feeling of being wanted by an entire family, not to mention the lavish celebrations and gifts that came with engagements.

But something didn't feel right about this. The interest felt conniving and mercantile. KokoGul approached me on a Friday, while my father was at *Jumaa* prayers. She was wearing a freshly pressed dress and her most delicate *chador,* mauve chiffon with lace trim one shade deeper. She hummed cheerfully as she entered the kitchen where I was making a snack of flatbread and walnuts.

"Agha Firooz's wife and daughter are stopping by this afternoon. Why don't you go brush your hair back and wear something nice — maybe your purple dress? When they come, you can bring tea and the salted biscuits. No sweets, mind you! I don't know exactly what this visit is about but we don't want to embarrass ourselves."

Sweets were given to a suitor's family as an affirmative signal, a nod of agreement to give the daughter's hand in marriage. It would be shamefully forward to serve candied almonds or chocolates to guests on the first visit.

"If you hear me call out for *tea,* then it means I want you to bring it into the room and serve the guests. And that's all you'll do. This is not their chance to strip you down and see it all; it's just to give them a little taste. You'll set the cups down, offer the biscuits, and then politely go back to the kitchen. Now, if you hear me call out for more *biscuits,* have one of your sisters bring the tray in. Do not enter the room at all."

It was a game of strategy, and KokoGul didn't want to show her hand until she knew what her opponents were holding.

My appetite spoiled, I went off to make myself presentable. I rummaged through my wardrobe, trying to imagine a way to escape this orchestrated visit and not sure why I was diffident about something every girl should want. I wanted to disappear into the orchard.

At the knock on the gate, Najiba ran outside to welcome our visitors. She led them through our modest courtyard and garden. KokoGul waited at the main door, eager to receive them. I watched from the upstairs window as the two women folded their embroidered shawls and draped them over their arms, almost synchronously. KokoGul and the women kissed cheeks and exchanged pleasantries before she led them into our parlor. I tiptoed to the upstairs landing to eavesdrop.

Agha Firooz's wife was a short, stout woman with gray hair and an inauspicious mole over her left eyebrow. Her lower lip puckered out in an unintentional look of displeasure. Her eyes roamed about, taking stock of our home and measuring it against her own. KokoGul led our guests to the hand-carved sofa Boba-*jan* had given my parents as a wedding gift.

Agha Firooz's daughter shared her mother's comportment but was very different physically. She stood six inches taller and measured half her mother's width. Heavy, penciled-in brows arched over kohl-rimmed eyes, and her bright fuchsia lipstick matched her dress perfectly. She almost looked pretty until I saw her smile politely at KokoGul. Even from my hidden view, her teeth looked jagged and unsightly. I felt my stomach reel at her smile, though I wasn't sure why I had such a visceral response.

I knew KokoGul well enough that I could imagine her sizing up Agha Firooz's daughter and deciding how I would compare to her. Her eyes moved quickly, as did those of Agha Firooz's wife, as she calculated what the family would think when they saw me. Far from stunning, I did have my mother's fair, even skin and her dark hair. I knew KokoGul was already calculating the effects of Agha Firooz and Padar-*jan* joining forces. If my father helped Agha Firooz expand his textile commerce into new areas, both would surely reap the benefits. KokoGul was restless, her mind spending money she eagerly anticipated.

"Fereiba-*jan,* please bring some *tea* in for our dear guests! You ladies must be parched, traveling in this weather. It's been quite warm the last few days, hasn't it?" KokoGul said with great poise.

I made my way down the creaky steps and went to the kitchen. I arranged KokoGul's china teacups and plates onto a silver tray and brought them into the parlor. My face burned as I felt all eyes on me. I kept my gaze on the tray, gripping the handles so tightly my knuckles blanched.

"Salaam," I said softly as I set a cup of tea before Agha Firooz's wife.

"Wa-alaikum, dear girl," she echoed with a greedy smile. I let my *chador* fall across my cheek, hiding my flushed face. Doing my best not to tremble, I placed the second cup in front of her daughter and then held the tray of biscuits out to them. Agha Firooz's daughter grinned as she plucked two from the plate. Up close, her smile again sent shivers through my body, but this time I was conscious of why.

She had the same gap-toothed grin as the lewd boy from the market.

Had I not already set the teacups down, I'm sure they would have rattled right off the tray. I kept my head lowered and made a quick escape from the parlor. I could hear Agha Firooz's wife casually suggesting to KokoGul that I join them for tea. KokoGul waved off the suggestion and began to extol my virtues. Najiba was in the kitchen gulping down a glass of water — ever neutral, ever oblivious to what was going on around her.

"Najiba, can you stay here and listen out for Madar-*jan?* Wait a few minutes and then refill their teacups, please. My head is spinning and I need to lie down."

Najiba looked at me as she tucked a lock

of hair behind her ear. "Okay, Ferei," she replied affectionately.

I kissed her cheek and went out the back door of the kitchen, creeping up the stairs as noiselessly as I could.

I leaned against the upstairs wall, my heart pounding. I prayed Agha Firooz's emissaries would soon take their leave.

CHAPTER 6
FEREIBA

Courtship and gifts lost their romantic appeal as I was slapped with the reality of marriage. I could not imagine becoming part of Agha Firooz's family. How could I tell Padar-*jan* how I felt? Through KokoGul's oblique comments I learned that Padar-*jan* was exploring Agha Firooz's business propositions. I couldn't confess my worries to my sisters or my brother. I had much to hash out and no one to talk with.

KokoGul eagerly anticipated a second call from Agha Firooz's wife. A respectable courtship was a slow, deliberately coy dance between two families. KokoGul rehearsed for that call, her chance to feign surprise and hesitation. With me, she was especially lenient in the next few weeks. I was excused from many of my duties around the house, a pampering that made me feel more suspicious than grateful.

"Fereiba-*jan,* do not bother with the pots

today. Too much scrubbing will roughen your soft hands. Let your sister help you," she called out. I put the washcloth down and turned my palms up. Years of hand-washing the family's clothes, sifting dry rice, and scrubbing burnt cookware had callused my fingers. I wiped my hands dry. The orchard called.

As I neared the mulberry tree, the sandaled legs abruptly stopped swinging. I did my best to steal a glance at his face, but the rest of him was hidden, as usual, by the foliage. He could see me from his vantage, which I thought very unfair but dared not protest. I had to consider my modesty.

"Salaam." A cautious greeting.

"Salaam," I returned. I breathed easier in the silence that followed. I was more comfortable in this unknown, protected by the orchard walls. I waited as my neighbor pondered his next words. There was, today, a tranquil tension between us.

"You haven't brought a book today."

"I haven't felt much like reading lately," I confessed.

"Something troubles you."

How much could I reveal? But I was lonely. Not one person in my family knew how I felt. Not one person knew why. My distress was trapped in my throat like something I could neither choke down nor spit out.

"I come to the orchard when there's something I want to avoid. Or when there's something I want to think about . . . something private." His voice dropped off at the end. I kept my eyes on the grass. I didn't want to see his face or any other part of him. In this moment, the unsure rises and falls of his voice were all that I needed.

"My father loves the orchard enough to do his dawn prayers here. He believes his prayers nourish the trees, but it's probably the other way around," I said. "He empties his heart to these trees, to their branches and roots, and in return they sweeten his mouth with their fruits. In the afternoons, the orchard is mine. My siblings are too afraid to come this far out into the trees."

"Some people fear what they cannot see."

"I have seen and there's nothing to fear here. It's beyond this orchard that frightens me." Again, there was a pause.

"You were reading Ibrahim Khalil last time."

I was surprised. Indeed, I had been. My reading skills had improved tremendously, and I was now studying the writings of contemporary Afghan poets.

"Yes, actually."

"Why?"

Why? A question that I couldn't eloquently answer. There was something powerful about the clarity and conciseness of the lyrics. How amazing to condense the profoundest of thoughts into a few lines, to boil them down and mold them into an enchanting rhyming package. I loved picking those packages apart, like unwrapping a gift meant only for me and deciphering the lines.

"He is a compass," I explained, finally. "There are days when I sleep and wake with a dilemma. I can think and think on it and not know up from down. But more than once, I've read his words and then . . . I don't know how to say it. It's almost as if he has written answers to questions I never asked him."

"Hmm."

Did he think me ridiculous?

"That's how I see it," I added. I felt my face blush.

"Can I tell you one of my favorites?"

I nodded. He cleared his throat and began to recite. I recognized the poem as one I'd bookmarked and underlined.

As you tread to the temple of your supreme
    pursuit

A hundred peaks may hinder your route
With the hatchet of persistence, conquer
    each
And bring your aspirations within your
    reach

Yes, I thought, looking at the skyline and seeing the hundred mountain peaks that separated Kabul from the rest of the world. There was quiet as the simple words made the distance between us thin and meaningless. The verse he'd chosen made me feel he knew every thought I'd dare not share with others. He had put a gentle arm around me. It was my first experience with intimacy, both rousing and frightening.

"That is a beautiful poem," I said finally. "Thank you." I wished him a good day and slowly returned to the house, feeling my throat thicken and not wanting to cry in his presence. I'd revealed enough today.

I ran back into the house, passing KokoGul on my way up the stairs. She was hemming a skirt and barely looked up.

"Fall and break your leg and see who will carry you around. Act your age!"

A few days later, KokoGul received the call she'd been awaiting. The Firoozes had made their intentions clear and official. KokoGul was delighted, as if she herself were being courted instead of me.

"I knew. I knew they would take one look at my daughter's face and see the loveliest *aroos* a mother could want for her son! That woman would be lucky to have you as her daughter-in-law and they know it now. You're far more beautiful than anyone in their family, and our family has a good name. Your padar is as well respected as Boba-*jan* was, may God give him eternal peace. Agha Firooz will have to show *us* that *they* are worthy of our daughter. And we won't make it easy . . . no, no, no. I'll make that woman call on our home so many times, she won't be able to dance at your wedding for the calluses she'll have on her feet; I don't care how much money they have."

I knew that wasn't true. She'd estimated, in the days after their first visit, just how much the fabric of their dresses had cost. She'd taken stock of the stitching and the design, commenting that only Kabul's most capable seamstress could have crafted a dress that made such a stocky figure seem womanly.

I was relieved to hear KokoGul's plan for the day of their return. She and I both wanted me out of sight for their second visit.

"Your sisters will bring the tea and biscuits. They saw you last time — let's let their mouths water a bit."

"Madar-*jan*, a girl should have multiple *khastgaar*, shouldn't she? You've said many times that one *khastgaar* attracts a second suitor and a third. That would look better for us, wouldn't it? Maybe you should turn this family away."

KokoGul balked at my reasoning.

"A second and a third *khastgaar*? Look who thinks very highly of herself! Agha Firooz's son is not good enough? An educated boy from a wealthy, respected family like that is not good enough? Listen, girl, just because one family has come knocking does not mean that anyone else will! Kabul is full of girls."

Her demeanor had changed completely.

"I just thought . . ."

"You should be thankful that anyone has come knocking on your door at all! A girl raised without her mother is not exactly the kind of wife a family welcomes with open arms."

Without a mother. Her words should not have stung as harshly as they did. I'd lived my life as KokoGul's stepdaughter, aware with each breath that I was not Najiba or the others. I was inherited, an outsider in

83

my father's home. That I'd laughed at her jokes, that I'd learned to cook the foods she loved, that I'd rubbed her back when it ached, that I'd spent my life calling her "Madar-*jan*" — I wanted to take it all back. KokoGul's heart was a fixed space, a container with finite dimensions, and every inch of it had been spoken for by my sisters and my father. I stared at her and through her. Once again and even more unexpectedly this time, I was motherless.

"Such ridiculous notions. This business is for me to manage. You're too young to know what is good for you."

I watched her lapis ring tap sharply against her teacup. She was a fiery woman, with strong feelings about everything. But in every embrace, every conversation, every glance with me she was lukewarm. I imagined my home without me — my sisters laughing in the hallways, my brother at my father's side, and KokoGul, hands on her hips, proudly presiding over it all.

Why did my mother have to die?

Nothing exceptional happened on this afternoon. It was a few words, not much different from any other day but it was a private, cataclysmic moment when I saw the woman before me through unclouded eyes.

"They're coming back sooner than I

expected," KokoGul said, thinking out loud. "But I'll find a way to keep them baited."

KokoGul made her own mouth water.

I saw the peaks of a hundred mountains rising before me.

CHAPTER 7
FEREIBA

Agha Firooz's family approved of me. I should have been flattered.

Instead, I wondered if I could have done something in that first visit to turn their attention away.

But the mother returned, and this time she brought her son along with her. Forbidden from appearing, I kept hidden. I snuck down once only to catch a glimpse and confirm my suspicions. Sitting next to his mother and appearing as proper as a prince was the boy from the market. I slinked away without anyone noticing.

Repulsed, I sat on my bed. My head fell against the wall.

I could hear KokoGul speaking in the singsong voice she used to tell witty stories. She was masterful at telling tales, creating suspense with the cadence of her words. Her eyes would brighten under the attention. She disarmed people in that way, mimicking voices and facial expressions in a way that had listeners doubled over in laughter.

People loved her. I loved her.

Since Boba-*jan*'s passing, my father had grown ever more distant. I'd once placed a bowl of dried apricots and walnuts at his side while he was reading. He'd looked up from his newspaper startled. A quiet mumble and a shake of his head told me it wasn't me he'd seen when he looked up. He still grieved my mother, as did I. He wouldn't say a word about her, but his melancholy eyes hid nothing. He barely bothered to ask about my classes. We exchanged but a few words in the course of the day.

I wanted to ask him to forgo this suitor.

My father would see things KokoGul's way. He always did. Not so much because she was looking out for his financial interests, but because it greased the cogs of our home. Life was easier on him when he agreed with KokoGul.

I spent more and more time in the orchard. Being in a house full of people betrayed the solitude I felt. KokoGul was exceptionally cheerful. She spent mornings in the fabric store and afternoons with the seamstress. Her closet celebrated with new lacy hems, a delicate head scarf, and a white wool shawl brilliantly embroidered in gold and emerald stitching.

The courtship continued, the ladies now expressing frankly that they were seeking a wife for Agha Firooz's son. They did not want to be kept waiting. He was an educated young man who was in line to inherit his father's business. KokoGul was not pleased that they would ask for an answer so quickly. For her, the dance had only begun.

"Fereiba-*jan* is a very hardworking girl, you know. My husband has offered time and time again to bring servants to help with the housework, but Fereiba and I, we manage everything together. And I'd rather not have strangers in my home, so I've refused."

I shook my head. It was hard to keep straight truth from lie with KokoGul. I doubted she knew the difference herself.

"Good for you that you've been able to raise a hardworking daughter. I've never had my daughters do any of the chores around the house. I was afraid they would end up as servants in the homes of others if I did. But to have an *aroos,* a bride, who can run a household — that would be a welcome change!"

"Yes, indeed. My other daughters are not as involved for the same reason."

KokoGul danced on, her lapis-ringed finger twirling in the air as she choreographed their exchange.

"Ferei, are you really going to get married?"
A giddy Sultana whispered as I tried to
focus on my literature assignment.

I ignored the curiosity of my younger
sisters. I spoke, ate, and slept very little.
Schoolwork was the only effective distraction. When I had time, I returned to the
orchard to sulk in privacy.

KokoGul was quietly gathering what she
needed to make my *shirnee,* a symbolic tray
of sweets to be presented to the suitor's
family as formal acceptance of their proposal. A silver-plated serving tray, gold tulle,
and a box from Kabul's confectionery store
had been tucked into her dresser drawer.
Despite the beguiling dance she did with
Agha Firooz's wife, KokoGul was eager to
dress me up with ribbons and send me off
to a new home. I stared at the things she'd
bought. I put her freshly laundered under-
garments in her drawer and fought the urge
to rip the tulle to shreds, to smash the
sweets and leave KokoGul nothing but a
tragic pile of gold foil wrappers.

"Why are you unhappy?"
Lost in thought, I hadn't noticed the
sound of leaves crunching under my neigh-

bor's approaching feet. So long as my splotchy face remained hidden, I didn't mind the anonymous company. I touched the wall. As my fingers traced its roughness, a slip of clay lifted. I rubbed a bit harder and more crumbled to the ground. I turned and leaned against it. The khaki dust lingered on my fingertips.

"There is a family . . . with a boy." I tried different combinations of words but choked on a real explanation.

"Your suitor?"

Though he could not see me, I nodded.

"You know?" I asked.

"My mother and sisters were talking about it. They've seen the family come and go, and KokoGul mentioned something when she stopped by this week."

"She stopped by your home?" I'd paid no attention to KokoGul's whereabouts in the last two weeks.

"Yes." The voice spoke quietly. "I can't say I think much of that boy."

"You know him?" He confirmed my judgment.

"Not very well. Here and there and from a distance. But we attended the same high school."

"And even from a distance you have this opinion of him."

"Some things are clearer from a distance. I don't know if I should say more."

"Whatever it is, you should say it. No one else is saying anything worth hearing."

He told me about the boy's mischief. Teasing girls, fighting with classmates, poor marks in school. Rumors circulated about him, things that my orchard confidante refused to disclose. Since the Firooz boy had graduated from high school, his parents were hoping marriage would mature him in a way age hadn't.

I sank to the ground, pulled my knees close to me, and let out a defeated moan.

"I'm sorry. I don't mean to scare you, but I thought you should know. Your family should know."

How could I tell my family? It wasn't as though I could repeat things I'd heard from a strange boy I'd been meeting in the orchard.

"I don't know what to do," I whispered. "My mother thinks their family is a good match for us. And my father . . . even when he's in the room, he's not around. He's happy to leave things to my mother. I tried to tell her I didn't want to be married now, but she's not interested in what I want. She won't believe anything I tell her about this boy. She'll just tell me not to listen to rumors."

"I see."

My behavior was unforgivable. I'd revealed my private thoughts and our family affairs to our neighbor's son, a faceless voice behind a wall. Where was my honor? And how could I trust him to keep our conversations to himself? I was suddenly flustered.

"Please excuse me. I shouldn't have said anything. I don't know why I troubled you with this. Please forget everything," I said, straightening my shoulders and trying to shake the emotion from my voice.

"You are upset. You haven't done anything wrong . . ."

"But I have. Please do not repeat any of this. I wasn't expecting to . . . to be so . . ."

"You have my word. I will not say anything to anyone. But I will tell you something as well. I'm as troubled as you are with the news of this suitor."

The orchard held its breath. His words hung in the air above the wall between us, lingered there far enough out of reach that he could not pull them back and I could not claim them. I didn't want his words to float away.

"Why are you troubled by this suitor?"

He did not reply. I repeated my question and still heard nothing.

"Are you there?"

"I am here."

"You did not answer."

"No, I did not."

The air grew thick with his reticence. I held myself back, not daring to fill the silence with my own inventions. I wanted only his words. In a flash of honesty, I knew why I'd come back to this spot day after day. I touched the wall, my hands trembling.

"I am going back to the house."

"Fereiba-*jan.*"

He knew my name? I froze in my tracks. My skin tingled with anticipation.

"For today, just know that the news of your suitor distresses me. Come tomorrow so we can think of how we may be able to change matters. God is merciful." I heard his footsteps as he walked away, pictured the grass bending under his leather sandals. My eyes stayed fixed on the wall between us, the barrier that kept us apart but not as much as it kept us together, for without it, I would have fled in shame long ago. The wall was my *purdah,* my cover.

My father came home that evening and saw me in the kitchen, peeling purple carrots he'd harvested from his garden. I stood up and said hello to him, kissed his cheek. He nodded quietly. He looked conflicted, as if there were much he wanted to say but couldn't.

"Where is KokoGul? Has she gone to rest?"

"She went into the market with Najiba and Sultana. I think they'll be back soon."

He took two steps out of the kitchen, hesitated, and turned back.

"And you, how are you?" He sounded concerned.

"Me, Padar-*jan*? I am well."

"You are?"

"Yes," I said meekly. From the tone of his voice, I knew there was more he was asking me. I knew he loved me as much as he loved my siblings. Had I not taken my mother from him, he may have loved me more.

"You know, you are a great help to everyone in this home. You have always worked very hard."

I listened, my head bowed respectfully.

"Allah keep you alive and well, my daughter."

"And you too, Padar-*jan*."

"Every day, you have more of her in you. Every day." Like the words I'd left suspended in the orchard, these words hung in the air. They'd been unsaid in each conversation with my father, implied every time he looked at my face as if it hurt him to do so.

These were the kind of tender words KokoGul would scream to hear.

If I hadn't known better, I would have thought it would be hard to grieve a stranger. I would never have thought it was something I could do my entire life.

How I wished I could pull up a chair and beg my father to go on, to tell me every detail of my mother so I could at least know the woman I mourned. I wanted him to tell me about the first time he saw her, the sound of her voice, her favorite foods, and the shape of her fingers. I wanted to close my eyes and have her appear before me, to hear her call my name just once. But trying to conjure my mother was like trying to hum a song I'd never heard.

Padar-*jan* walked away quickly, as if he knew what I would ask if he lingered. I heard his hurried footsteps go into the next room as I stared blankly at my hands, stained a despondent violet by the carrots that my father had nurtured from seedlings.

Certainly, KokoGul had talked to my father about Agha Firooz's son but, from his actions, I could not decipher how he felt. I didn't expect my father to speak to me directly about the courtship — such matters were not discussed between fathers and daughters. Mothers were liaisons in these purposes, shuttling information back and forth and coloring it to fit their needs. In my case, KokoGul had been singing the praises of Agha Firooz's son as if she were his mother.

Did Padar-*jan* want me to be married off? Was there a chance he might reject their proposal?

I was left to wonder.

I returned to the conversation in the orchard. I'd been unnerved to hear the voice speak my name. The anonymity of the orchard had been lost. I was left feeling excited but exposed. I wanted to know him.

I returned to the mulberry trees the following afternoon. I felt my face flush even before my feet touched the grass. I was playing a dangerous game. But we were no guiltier of flirting than two kites whose strings were crossed by a wayward wind, were we?

The sound of whistling carried through the breeze. I smiled to myself and breathed it in. It was him. I cleared my throat to announce my arrival. He noticed.

"*Salaam,*" he said.

"*Salaam.*"

"How are you today?"

"I'm well. And you?" I was growing bolder

in my conversations with him.

"Fine."

Sunlight filtered through the mulberry branches, warming my face. I squinted but stayed where I was. The radiance soothed my nerves. I wondered if he felt the same.

"I saw your suitor this morning."

He caught my attention with those few words.

"You did? How did that happen?"

"By the bakery. I'd taken some dough for my mother. He was walking nearby with friends, passing time in the way they usually do." His words were measured, cautious. His tone said what his words left out. "It's fortunate you started your schooling when you did. Nothing the teachers said could rein him in. I heard they all celebrated when he finally left."

He knew about my schooling. How did he know so much about me when I knew nothing about him?

"You seem to know my story well. And I know nothing about you, except that you like to spy on your neighbors and read poems in the trees."

He chuckled.

"The height gives me perspective. But you're probably right. What would you like to know about me?"

"What are you studying?" I plucked at blades of grass, trying to imagine his face.

"Engineering. I'm nearly done with my university studies. Maybe that's why I like to sit where the birds sit. From a distance it's easier to see how things work, how water flows from high to low."

"You sound like you enjoy it very much."

"I do, yes."

"I would like to go to university too."

"What would you like to study?"

Months ago, I'd been giving that very question a good deal of thought, though I hadn't come up with an answer. It occurred to me that in the last few weeks, I'd stopped imagining my tomorrows. I'd stopped thinking about what I wanted to do. Boba-*jan* would have been disappointed. My angel from the orchard, if he'd really existed, would have shaken his head. What did I want to do?

An answer rolled off my tongue as if I had made up my mind years ago. And it was the most natural decision.

"Teaching. I think there is nothing more important than teaching. Of course, engineering is important too, but even engineers need teachers."

"You are right. Teachers are the yeast that makes the dough rise. You would be a great teacher."

"I don't know if I'll have the chance," I said, my voice lowered.

"Has your family said anything about it yet?"

"No. I don't think I'll hear anything until it's already been decided. I almost feel like I'm already not part of this family. My mother and my sisters, they're so wrapped up in guests and gifts and celebrations. It's all happening around me and I'm invisible, the girl who used to live in this house." My voice cracked with my last sentence.

"You're not invisible. I can close my eyes and picture you. I can be alone and hear your voice. You're anything but invisible."

In those words, the voice made a declaration that could not be misinterpreted. His was the only voice I wanted to hear, the only person who spoke to me about me. It was as if he'd scaled the clay wall between us and let my head rest on his shoulder.

"You shouldn't say such things," I said quietly. My reaction was reflexive, protective.

He understood.

"Let's do something then, shall we? Maybe we should say a prayer? What do you think?"

I was no stranger to prayer. When the

azaan beckoned from the nearest minaret, I felt a calm. Five times a day, I had a chance to share my thoughts with God. I had a chance to ask for forgiveness and pray that Allah keep my mother and grandfather in His peaceful gardens. Maybe God would hear two voices together better than mine alone.

"Okay," I agreed. I let him start.

"Bismillah al Rahman al Raheem . . ."

"Bismillah al Rahman al Raheem . . ."

He recited a simple prayer and I echoed the words softly, my eyes closed. He closed with a simple plea.

"Please, Allah, bring a solution to my neighbor's situation. Please help her avoid the path that others are choosing for her and this suitor. She's not been able to take a peaceful breath in these weeks and surely things would only be worse with this suitor, as You know better than any. Please find a way to bring her to a home that will not take her for granted. Please find a way to give her a hand in making this choice for herself and help her family to make the decision that is in her best interests. Please free her to pursue her studies in teaching so that she can, in turn, help others. Please do not let anyone hold her back from her goals."

He paused.

"And please help me to achieve my goals, both in school and in life. Please bring us both a brighter future."

If I could have seen into the future and known just how our prayers would be answered, I wonder if I still would have prayed along. I wonder if he would still have uttered those words. It frightened me to think that we would have. It frightened me more to think of what might have happened had we not done so.

My head on my pillow that night, I thought of Rabia Balkhi, Afghanistan's legendary poetess from the tenth century. Rabia, a true princess, lived lavishly in a palace with servants at her feet. When her father died, her brother became her guardian. Rabia lived in extravagant solitude, filling her empty days with verses of her own creation.

But love can grow even in a place where there is hardly air to breathe, and Rabia fell in love with a handsome young man, Baktash. Their affair, a hidden exchange of love letters and poems, was discovered by Rabia's brother, who ordered his sister to be taken to the bathhouse. Her wrists were slashed as she lay in the steamy waters.

Rabia, in her own blood, wrote her last

poem on the walls of the bathhouse and declared her undying love for Baktash.

Love was not something we could talk about. We explored the phenomenon only in poems and song lyrics or imported Bollywood movies, where as the story became more tragic and the lovers more star-crossed, the love between them became more profound. This was what we were taught, though only incidentally. The dead mother, the unwanted suitor, the boy in the orchard — the requisite elements were coming together to make my life an epic love tale. My adolescent heart churned with the nervous anticipation of tomorrow.

With eyes tightly closed, I tried to recall Rabia's final poem but could only remember the last two lines:

When you see things hideous, fancy them neat.
Eat poison, but taste sugar sweet.

CHAPTER 8
FEREIBA

KokoGul was at the front door when I came out of my room. Her voice carried through the hallway, her volume rising. Within seconds, she'd reached a frantic pitch.

She ran past me. I reached over to steady the teacups she'd sent rattling on the glass nesting table.

"Stay here. Watch your sisters and pray that this news is not true! I am going out to make sense of this. I've never heard such a story . . . if this is a lie, I'll curse that busybody. Dear God, this cannot be!"

She threw her *chador* over her head and whipped the end over her shoulder. The door slammed behind her before I could ask where she was going or what the terrible news was. I went about my chores with an uneasy feeling in my gut. My sisters were busy with their school lessons and would know nothing more than I'd already overheard. I would have to wait for KokoGul to return.

When two hours passed, I grew more apprehensive. I went through the courtyard and opened our front gate. Our quiet street offered no clues. A few children chased a feeble mutt, pelting it with scraps of trash. An older man walked by with a cane. Nothing looked out of the ordinary.

Padar-*jan* came home earlier than usual and found me beating the dust from the pillows in the living room. I couldn't sit still.

"Where is your mother? Don't tell me she's gone out to the market again."

"No, Padar-*jan,* she went to call upon a friend, I think. She didn't say much — just that she'd heard some terrible news that she hoped wasn't true."

"Terrible news?" He looked alarmed, both by KokoGul's sudden departure and by the anxiety in my voice. "Did she say what the news was?"

I shook my head.

"She was in a hurry. She flew out the door without explaining."

My father sighed heavily and asked if I'd prepared dinner. He decided we would not get worked up before we knew what we were talking about. My father would swallow a spoon of salt smiling if it meant keeping the house in peace.

Padar-*jan* was hungry so I summoned my siblings and set the table, wondering if KokoGul would make it back before we started to eat. Cumin steam swirled from the platter of hot rice I was carrying when she swept into the room. KokoGul threw her *chador* onto the back of a chair with a huff. Her voice boomed in the small space.

"Ooohhh God, our merciful Allah! What horrible news!" Her head swayed from side to side as she sat next to my father. "What tragic and unexpected events have befallen us . . . I still cannot believe such a thing would happen!"

Padar-*jan* furrowed his brow, impatient with her dramatic prelude.

"Just say what it is, KokoGul. What happened?"

KokoGul ignored his frustration and went on with her story at her own pace.

"I was home today making sure these girls were doing their homework and on top of that there was a lot of laundry and cooking to do and I had my hands full, as usual," she added. Padar-*jan* sighed heavily and I wondered when KokoGul had last washed so much as a sock or stirred a pot.

"Habiba-*jan* came knocking on our door to borrow some flour — sometimes I think

105

we could make a healthy living supplying her with all the ingredients she's forgotten to pick up from the sundries store — anyway, I gave that foolish woman what she needed and she started to chatter about the unfortunate family arranging for a *fateha* in two days for their young son and what a sad story it was. I asked her who it was that had lost a son and she told me that it was that wealthy family from across town, Agha Firooz."

My fingers gripped the edge of the table tightly. I could feel the blood drain from my face. I waited for her to continue.

"When she said that, my head spun and I just about fainted right there at her feet but I pulled myself together and asked her if she knew which of their boys it was and how it had happened. She was more interested in getting home with the flour and she didn't know much else anyway so I told her to run along. I went to Fatana-*jan*'s house since her brother-in-law lives next door to Agha Firooz's family.

"Fatana's better informed than the KGB and she told me everything! My God, how this changes things for us! Just two days ago . . ."

"Dear God, wife, please! Just say what happened!"

"Unbelievable, truly unbelievable! The whole story is just unimaginable! Agha Firooz's boy was walking from the movie theater to home with his friends. You know, they said he was studying engineering, but Fatana tells me he hadn't been to any classes since high school and he wouldn't have even graduated from there had his father not breathed heavily over a few shoulders."

Tragic or not, KokoGul would not leave out a single detail of this savory story. This was her first time telling it, a rehearsal of sorts as she would certainly be repeating it again and again.

"He was on his way home with his friends when they stopped to get some *nakhod* from one of the vendors in the bazaar. Boys like that cannot go five meters without a snack! They each got a pocketful of roasted chickpeas and went along their way when he started to scratch at some red bumps on his arms. By the time they'd turned the corner, he was in worse shape, coughing and straggling behind the others. The boys had no idea what had happened to him and decided to take him back to his house. He could barely walk by then and they put him on the living room sofa.

"His poor mother was home. She came

into the room, took one look at her son, and realized what had happened. When he was young, he would get the same red bumps when he'd eaten walnuts. She yelled for his friends to help her get him to the doctor, but the boys had already taken off. Fatana thinks they were up to something and got scared that they'd be in trouble. By the time she called her servant to help and managed to get him to the doctor he'd stopped breathing. He was finished!"

KokoGul covered her face in her hands, took a deep breath, and put her palms flat against the table. Her voice was mournful.

"They are just beside themselves with grief and shock. As we speak, they're making arrangements for the burial when they should have been making plans for his wedding."

Padar-*jan* leaned back, his mouth slightly open. My sisters looked pointedly at me. I kept my face as still as I could, unsure what I was feeling and not wanting my expression to betray my thoughts.

"Allah forgive his sins! To lose a son, a young man . . ." Padar-*jan* shook his head. He kept his eyes on KokoGul, glancing over just once to gauge my reaction.

"Such a shame. Such a shame. Just when we were getting to know their family better!

They seemed like such nice people, with good business sense and obviously better off than most in Kabul. They have another son but he's married already! Now we've lost our chance with them." KokoGul could not conceal her true disappointment.

Padar-*jan* looked at her and sighed. He had long ago accepted KokoGul for what she was, but that didn't stop him from hoping, day after day, that she wouldn't make every little event revolve around her. He cleared his throat. "I will find out more tomorrow about the *jenaaza* and the *fateha*. We'll pay our respects to the family. For now, let's have the meal that Fereiba's prepared for us. It shouldn't go to waste." He grew pensive. "We'll send some food for them."

"Send food? They already have a cook who prepares food for them. It's hard enough for us to feed the mouths we have here!"

"We will send food and pay our respects. We've marked happy days with them and shouldn't shy from their sorrow," Padar-*jan* said slowly and deliberately, his eyes narrowed at KokoGul. She sulked at his admonishment.

As a family grieved its son, I was ashamed to admit that I felt relieved, as if a yoke had been removed from my neck. But the weight of the misery I'd escaped was replaced by heavy thoughts.

I sat stone-faced while we ate. My jaw moved but I tasted nothing.

It could not have been coincidence.

I kept my face lowered, my thoughts so loud I feared my family would hear me and realize what I was. I was not invisible any longer.

In the orchard, I'd cupped my hands, raised my face to the sun, and prayed to God. When my neighbor finished his fateful prayer, I'd whispered *Ameen.* I'd pushed his words to Allah, as if I had any business praying with a stranger. His words, our words, echoed in my mind.

Please, Allah, bring a solution to my neighbor's situation. Please help her avoid the path that others are choosing for her and this suitor. She's not been able to take a peaceful breath in these weeks and surely things would only be worse with this suitor, as You know better than any.

A peaceful breath. A solution.

Please do not let anyone hold her back from her goals.

KokoGul was too distressed to eat. I hid behind her heavy sighs. My sisters gave one another curious looks, eager to get away

110

from the eerie silence of our meal and share their thoughts where my father wouldn't hear.

A quiet panic raced through me. It was entirely possible that I'd been complicit in this boy's demise. It was also possible that I was more than merely complicit. I might have been wholly responsible for God taking his life.

I chewed carefully, afraid I would choke. Allah was in a fickle mood.

I wondered if my neighbor had heard the news. The thought of him sent my mind reeling in a whole other direction. I questioned his intentions and the meaning of the words he'd sent into the heavens.

I fought the urge to run out of the house and into the orchard, to call on him to explain what had happened.

I would have to wait.

Apart from my mother's death, I was mostly certain that the world churned around me, unaffected by my existence. Maybe that was not so.

Two days later, our home had recovered its composure. My sisters accepted that I had nothing to say about the boy's death. KokoGul had resigned herself to continue on in her unexalted household. Padar-*jan* went to Agha Firooz to pay his respects, an exchange the two fathers had never anticipated. In my harried state, I started the laundry and realized I'd forgotten the soap. On my way to get the soap, I remembered the meat needed to be marinated. Hours later I found the forgotten laundry, sopping wet and still waiting.

My chest about to burst, I wandered into the orchard. Every step felt like a trespass. The branches that had once welcomed me like open arms now seemed to point at me with accusing fingers, witnesses to my crime.

I coughed lightly.

"Salaam," he called out cautiously.

"I wasn't sure if you'd be here."

"Good, it's you," he said brightly. "I wasn't sure either."

The cheer in his voice felt blasphemous.

"Did you not hear the news?" I whispered.

"News? What news?" His tone grew solemn.

"About the boy. You really don't know?"

"What is it? You sound distressed."

"He died."

"What? Is this some kind of joke, Fereiba?" he whispered back. There was a bite to his tone that surprised me.

"I would not joke about such a thing," I

said. In my next breath I blurted out what I'd been wanting to scream since KokoGul broke this news at dinner. "It's true. He's dead and it's almost as if we had prayed for it but we didn't, did we? What did we ask for? What sin have we committed?"

"Lower your voice," he cautioned. "You are serious then. Of course, we never prayed for such a thing. Don't be foolish. Tell me what happened to him."

I related everything I had heard from KokoGul. I'd gone over the events in my head so many times, it was almost as if I'd watched his last afternoon. I pictured him gasping, grabbing at his chest, his skin a fiery red, a storm raging from within and circling tight around his throat.

"Fereiba-*jan,* listen to me. This is shocking news and I know it might feel odd given our conversations but believe me, I had no intention of bringing him any harm. It was a prayer to God, not a curse. Whatever happened, it was never in our hands."

"But we prayed —"

"And that was all we did. We wished no evil upon anyone, I promise you. We only meant for you to be spared from misery. You must know that."

The orchard let out a soft breath, and the knot around my chest loosened. He was right. I did know that we'd meant nothing so fatal in our wishes. And I'd known from our first exchange that this voice in the orchard had a good heart. He had acted as a friend when I had no one to trust with my private thoughts. Even now, he was my only friend in a place and time where friendships between boys and girls did not exist. There were brothers and sisters, aunts and uncles, husbands and wives — but no friends.

I could not bring myself to look directly at him nor would I offer to shake his hand even though these would have been meaningless gestures in comparison to the intimacies we'd already shared. I felt my face warm to think how much I had relied on this stranger through the ugliest days.

"You're right. It was such a terrible feeling to think . . ."

"Don't think that way. You've been set free by strange and sad affairs. I won't speak badly of the dead, but you and I both know what type of person he was. This was not your doing. It wasn't my doing either, so don't put it on our shoulders."

I dared not interrupt when he was saying precisely what I needed him to say. In hindsight, I wonder if much of what he said was a bit too perfect. It was possible that, in my solitude, I'd created this friend out of a shadow of a person and brought him to life to fill a need, a dangerous trick of the mind.

"Fereiba-*jan*? Say something. Tell me you agree."

There was no room for doubt when I heard him utter my name. For the time being, he was as real and true and caring as I needed him to be. I couldn't leave, tied to him by an unseemly thread of my own creation.

CHAPTER 9
FEREIBA

"They blame you for his death. That's what I heard," KokoGul said flatly. The back of my neck grew hot. I stopped drying the dishes. The rag hung limply in my hand.

"Me? Why do they think it was me?"

"They say that he was a perfectly healthy young man and that he was taken from his family the day before they were to come for your *shirnee.* Of course, Agha Firooz's wife insists that you must be cursed. First your mother, then your grandfather, and now this suitor who was just hours away from becoming your fiancé."

My eyes grew moist. To name the people whose loss hurt me most was cruel.

"It's nothing to cry about," KokoGul admonished. "How could they not draw such conclusions? They're grieving and conflicted and they know your history. Maybe I should consider myself lucky to be alive." KokoGul chuckled.

It was possible she had made the whole thing up. I had a hard time telling with her. Sometimes, she got so wrapped up in her own version of the truth that she couldn't put her finger on the real story. I went back to drying the plates, but she continued.

"I went to pay my respects to his mother. As soon as she saw my face, she burst into a rage of tears and told me my daughter was a curse. She said ever since they started courting you, things had gone very badly for their family. I think a few of the women sitting around her heard, not many."

Oh God. In the quiet of a *fateha*, I was certain that every woman in Kabul had heard her. I would be Kabul's black maiden with whispers and raised brows following me.

"What did you say to her?" I asked hesitantly.

"What could I say to a grieving mother? I told her that I prayed God would give them peace and rest his young soul in heaven."

"I mean about me. About me being cursed."

"Fereiba, a *fateha* is not the time or place to argue. I told her I hoped that wasn't true." KokoGul took a glass and poured herself some water. "Anyway, it's terrible to speak of him this way now that he's gone,

117

but I hear he was a troublemaker — disrespectful and thieving from his own family. Homaira-*jan* said he once beat her young son so badly, he couldn't see out of one eye for a week."

"When did you see Homaira-*jan*?" I asked casually, keeping my eyes on the dishes.

"Oh, a couple of weeks ago, in the bazaar. She's back from her trip to India, showing off her new gold bangles, of course."

And yet she'd been preparing my *shirnee*.

Mother. All my life I had called KokoGul by this radiant and hopeful name, wishing for the touch of lamb's wool on my cheek and too often getting nothing but a cool draft.

"The ladies were talking at the *fateha*. Agha Firooz thought marriage would settle the boy and knock the mischief out of him. They'd been trying to find a match for him for months. Who needs that? We aren't here to give our girls as second or third options."

I snapped the dishrag against the edge of the counter. "But you were ready to give them my *shirnee* anyway, weren't you? Why am I so different?"

My tone was sharp. The hurt, unfurled, lay between me and KokoGul in a rare moment of honesty.

KokoGul's eyes met mine.

"My dear, there is a difference between you and Najiba, and I'm surprised you're asking me about it at this point. Najiba is simple. She's a pretty girl . . . pretty enough that she'll get attention. She comes from a good family. She's bright and polite."

"And me?"

"And you," KokoGul said, her words jabbing me like a finger in my sternum. "I have to be more careful with you. Yes, you're well mannered and have nice enough features, but *everyone* knows that you lost your mother. And *that* makes you different. And before you look at me with those angry eyes, remember that it is not my fault you lost your mother and it's not my fault that people talk the way they do. But it is up to me to do the best I can for you. Think about it, Fereiba. If you wait to dance on the moon, you may never dance at all."

"You don't love me the way you love them."

"And you don't love me the way you love your father. Or your grandfather. Don't think I don't know that."

I was silent. She was right, of course.

KokoGul, unfazed, went right back to being personally offended by the would-be suitors.

"I'm sorry she lost her son but I'm even

119

sorrier I wasted my time serving them tea and biscuits."

Padar-*jan* said nothing about the matter. He came in and out of the house, speaking to us gently about our classes but not a word about Agha Firooz or his son. I wanted my father to be different, but it wasn't something he could do. Though I was free of the suitor and his family, I was left to wonder how readily my family would have given me away. And when it might happen again.

My neighbor was my retreat. He recited poetry and complained about losing points on his last engineering exam. He spoke passionately of the work he wanted to do when he graduated. He wanted to go abroad and train with a foreign company. He wanted to explore the world. I loved to hear him talk about the university and its layout. He described the buildings and professors in such detail, I could close my eyes and imagine walking through its halls.

One day, he said something he'd never said before.

"It would be nice to get to know you and your family without a wall between us."

My cheeks grew warm. I smiled and wiggled my toes in the grass.

"But that would be . . . I mean, that's not . . ."

"I don't mean to be disrespectful. But I wanted to let you know that I was thinking our families should begin a conversation . . ."

"Do you know what you're saying?" I asked, half embarrassed. "Don't say things you don't mean."

"I wouldn't, Fereiba. Believe me, *qandem*." *My sweet.* My skin prickled to hear him say my name, the delicate but daring *"qandem"* settling in my ear like a soft kiss. "Do you know what I think about doing every day?"

I fell back into the grass and stared up into the branches, green teardrop-shaped leaves backlit by a defiant sun. Its white, red, and black fruits glimmered in various stages of ripeness. The light tickled my eyes.

"What do you think about?"

"Every day that I sit here and talk to you over this wall has made me think of climbing over it so I could look at you, walk through your father's orchard with you, and talk while we listen to songs on the radio."

I held my breath. The feeling in the pit of my stomach — the trembling feeling of falling off a cliff — this was new. I found it odd that I could recognize so easily something I

121

had never before seen or felt. This was love the poets described — I was sure.

"But the more I've thought about it, the more I've realized that I don't want to trespass into your father's orchard. I want to be welcomed through his front gate. I want to walk with you, hand in hand, without a wall between us, without having to hide our voices from the rest of the world."

Tears slid from the corners of my eyes, past my temples, and fell to the earth. For so many years, I'd received nothing but the watered-down love of my siblings, the resentful tolerance of KokoGul, and the guarded affection of my father. These words, ripe and whole, fed the emptiness I'd lived with my entire life.

"Fereiba."

"Yes?"

"You haven't said anything."

"I don't know what to say."

"You could say what you want."

I sat up and covered my face with my hands. I couldn't say the words with God's sun on my face.

"I want the same," I whispered, just loud enough for him to hear.

Two days later, there was a knock at our

front gate. Thankfully, I was elbow deep in a basin with clothes, socks, and soapy water so KokoGul went to answer it herself. A few moments later, KokoGul stood over me, watching me rub the ring from my father's shirt collars.

"After darkness always comes light. Wash my burgundy dress too. Looks like we'll be having guests this Thursday afternoon."

"Who is coming on Thursday?"

"Agha Walid's wife, Bibi Shireen, is coming," she said with a meaningful wink. "Seems our neighbors have something to talk about. You should wash Najiba's olive dress as well. No, on second thought, make it the yellow one. The green one makes her hips too wide."

I said nothing but nodded. KokoGul would be in for a surprise when she realized the conversation was not about Najiba. Just two years younger than me, my half sister had blossomed into a tall young woman, with straight black hair that curled girlishly at the ends. Her skin was milky white and her mouth a pouty rose. KokoGul claimed Najiba had taken after herself but it was hard to see much resemblance.

The home and orchard adjacent to ours belonged to Agha Walid, a respected thinker and engineer. KokoGul thought highly of him, not because she thought he was a brilliant engineer but because others did. Respect and rumors self-propagated in that way in Kabul. It was good and bad.

KokoGul was again wetting her lips. Another courtship, another round of choreographed flattery and boasting.

I stayed clear of the orchard and helped KokoGul ready the sitting room for Thursday afternoon. KokoGul picked out Najiba's dress, a flattering cap-sleeved, A-line cut that showed off her figure but maintained modesty. Just before they were to arrive, I changed into a shift dress with an embroidered neckline. KokoGul raised an eyebrow to see me wearing something I usually saved for special occasions.

"Don't spill anything on yourself," she warned. "Najiba might need that dress in the next few months."

I didn't know how KokoGul or Najiba would react when they found out the suitor was here for me. Najiba had been nervously excited when she heard of the Walids' visit. My first courtship had given her a taste of the process, and she was eager to feel the spotlight herself.

I opened the gate for Bibi Shireen, mother of my orchard friend. She'd brought her sister along with her. I greeted them quietly, afraid my tongue would tie if I said more than a few words. I led them into the sitting room just as KokoGul entered from the hallway. She beamed and opened her arms to welcome our neighbor. They kissed cheeks three times and smiled warmly. KokoGul signaled for me to bring some tea for our guests.

I stole glances at Bibi Shireen, wondering what her son might look like or if he even took after her. Her soft brown eyes smiled at me and settled the nerves in my stomach. Looking at her was like getting a message from my friend in the orchard.

Everything will be fine, he was telling me. *She's here to make things right.*

I prepared small dishes of yellow raisins, pine nuts, and pistachios. I walked back into the room just in time to hear Bibi Shireen telling KokoGul what an honor it was to have such a lovely family next door.

"Thank you, sweet girl," she said, as I placed a cup of tea before her and her sister. I hoped she hadn't noticed how much the cup had rattled in the saucer.

"With pleasure," I mumbled before making a quick exit back to the kitchen. I wondered how much her son had told her about me or our conversations.

Out of sight, I listened in. She continued to praise our family and then started to talk about her own. Her son, she said, was completing his engineering studies in a few months and was now of age to begin his own family.

"He will be standing on his two feet soon, what a mother dreams to see. We are very proud of all that he has done."

"As you should be. He takes after his father then. Agha Walid is much respected, of course."

"Indeed," his aunt added. "He's been a role model for his younger siblings and his cousins, my own dear son included."

"I see."

"KokoGul-*jan,* we come to you today on behalf of my beloved son, who is the jewel of our home and of our extended family. Praise Allah, I have been blessed with an intelligent, hardworking, and loving son, and I want to make sure that he will have a wife who will bring him happiness. It is time for him to start a family. As a mother, now that he is himself a man, this is one of the most important things I can do for him — to put the right woman at his side. Your family is a respectable family, a trustworthy family, and, praise Allah, a beautiful one."

"You are kind," KokoGul said, sitting

straight and tall with her hands folded neatly on her lap. She ate up Bibi Shireen's sweet talk.

"And so we have come to talk to you about your darling daughter," she continued.

"I see," KokoGul said, doing her best to appear at least a little surprised.

I held my breath in the hallway. Najiba was still in her room, wondering if KokoGul would signal her to join the guests.

"We believe that your eldest daughter would be a good match for my son."

"Well," KokoGul drew her hand to her chest. "My family is honored to hear this, but we had not yet considered marriage for our daughter. She is still young."

"Young, yes, but she is of perfect age to consider marriage. These are sweet days for young love to grow, wouldn't you agree?"

Her sister, Zeba, echoed her sentiments.

"Yes, this is a wonderful age for two young people to get to know each other and commit to each other."

"I think they would be a wonderful match. Our two families have respected each other for years as neighbors. Our children are grown and it is our responsibility, as their mothers, to think of their futures."

I could hear the clink of teacups on

saucers as the women planned what to say next.

"This is something we would have to consider carefully. I cannot even begin to think of giving my daughter's hand. We, too, have been honored to share a border with your family but . . . at this time, there is nothing more that I can say. As a mother, I'm sure you understand."

"Of course, dear KokoGul. We are here only to begin a conversation. I want you to know our interests are not superficial. I mean everything I have said. I know that your family must consider this and that you will take your time to think on it. But I'm also certain that you want to do what's best for your daughter, and it is my hope that you will see my son as the best match for your dear daughter, Najiba-*jan*."

Najiba?

I stifled the cry in my throat.

"Najiba is my dear daughter, a wonderful student and a giving sister. I've prayed for her, as I've prayed for all my children, that in her *naseeb* is a good person, a life partner who will honor her and our family."

"You are a loving mother, KokoGul. Your children are fortunate to have you and Agha-*sahib* as parents."

It was Najiba they wanted, not me.

CHAPTER 10
FEREIBA

KokoGul had been right. Our neighbors were courting my sister Najiba. When they'd left, I'd returned to my room. Najiba found me sitting on the floor wearing nothing but a slip. Scraps of fabric lay scattered on my lap, at my feet, behind me; I'd cut my shift dress into a thousand pieces. My sister wrenched the scissors from my hands and yelled for KokoGul. KokoGul suspiciously surveyed the scene from the doorway, conjuring her own theories as to what had caused my unraveling.

"Take the scissors and leave her be. I don't know what the meaning of this is, Fereiba, but we've no room for madness or destruction in this house."

Najiba looked concerned. I waited for them to leave. I could hear KokoGul whispering to Najiba in the hallway.

"She had a suitor and look what happened to him. Jealousy curdles the soul like a drop of vinegar in milk. Bibi Shireen knows Fereiba's story as well as the other neighbors do. People want their sons to marry respectable girls. Fereiba is your father's daughter and I mean no ill when I say this, but people see her as an orphan, as a girl without a family. She lost the only chance she had to marry into an esteemed family."

"But she has a family, Madar-*jan*," Najiba whispered in soft protest.

"It's not the same, my darling," KokoGul clucked. "I've tried to make her feel as much my daughter as you and your sisters, but she's kept herself apart. She's more comfortable doing the housework than being with us."

Throughout my life, KokoGul had given me just enough to believe this could be true. There were days she hugged me as she hugged my sisters, stroked my hair as if I were one of her own. There were days we sat together doing housework and laughing at something Mauriya had done. There were just enough of those moments to make me wonder if it was I who had kept myself at arm's length from the rest of the family.

I knew my beloved must have been devastated. I wondered if he even knew what his mother had done. It was not unheard of for mothers to make decisions on behalf of their reckless sons. Boys thought only of today. Mothers considered tomorrows. But my beloved was not most boys. He was an intellectual. He was my patient confidante, my keeper of secrets. He and I would have to fight to be together. I realized I should have expected nothing less.

Bibi Shireen had taken from us our budding affair. She'd denied the universe its chance to redeem itself for stripping me of a loving mother and father and of a childhood equal to that of my siblings. She had smiled demurely, allowed me to wait on her, and then pulled the world out from under my feet. Fueled by the flame of adolescent emotion, I fell deeper in love with the man yet unseen.

I sat under the mulberry tree for days, but he did not come. I stayed there for hours at a time, the coils of the bark imprinted on my back, proof of my devotion. Bibi Shireen returned to the house for a second and third visit. She was persistent and rushed, wanting KokoGul to agree to give Najiba's hand as if a clock were ticking. Her doggedness told me that my beloved knew nothing of her doings. Bibi Shireen had tasted the rumors about me and was hoping to save her son from marriage to Kabul's black maiden, the orphaned daughter-servant next door.

Najiba tiptoed around me. In my clearer moments, I pitied her. What should have been a joyful, exciting courtship had been spoiled by my rancorous behavior. I spoke few words and did not smile much. I was preoccupied with finding a way to communicate with my beloved without compromising our secret.

By the evening light, I wrote out Rabia Balkhi's blood-soaked poem on a piece of paper. I curled the paper into a ball and snuck out of my room at nightfall, winding my way past the cherry trees, under the grapevines, and into the nesting of mulberry trees against the wall. I paused and, hearing nothing but the distant croaking of a frog, I threw the balled paper over the wall where I hoped my secret love would find it and realize my devotion was unwavering despite those trying to keep us apart.

For days, I searched for scraps of paper on my side of the wall. I imagined the different ways he might send a message to me.

I kept dreaming even as KokoGul used the rolls of gold tulle and the silver tray she'd kept in her drawer to make Najiba's *shirnee*. I kept dreaming even on the day she placed the tray before an elated Bibi Shireen in our humble living room, my sisters looking on with quiet excitement as Najiba entered the room. She looked demure and kept her eyes to the ground as Bibi Shireen kissed her cheeks and embraced her tightly. She kissed her mother-in-law's hand.

I waited for him to protest but he said nothing. I realized that he would make no valiant motion to save us. This was not the love story I'd imagined.

How could I not stare at my sister's fiancé? After days of waiting alone in the orchard, how could I not gawk at the man I now believed had duped me into thinking I meant something? He was handsome, actually, which made everything worse. He had chestnut-colored hair and soft, poetic eyes. In his wide-lapel coffee-colored suit, he looked confident — but not overly so. His eyes moved around the room, lighting on guests and relatives just long enough to acknowledge their presence. Not once — I noticed because I'd made it my mission to — did his eyes fall on me or Najiba. I was quite creative in interpreting this observation.

Finally, there was no wall between us. This was what we'd wanted, wasn't it? He kissed my father's hands and KokoGul's hands.

My father welcomed him with a hearty embrace. Returning to his mother's side, he had looked up and given his bride a shy smile. I watched it all. I even went around the room offering colorful foiled chocolates to the few people who'd attended. Bibi Shireen's sister. Bibi Shireen's husband. My aunts and uncles.

KokoGul, wary of my erratic behavior, had asked Sultana to serve tea to the guests. She might have been right not to trust me with boiling water.

"Najiba," Bibi Shireen rejoiced tearfully. "From this day on, you are my daughter. You have two mothers, my beautiful girl. You have brought great happiness to our family!"

My beloved. My face reddened to think of our secret conversations. I felt small and stupid. He'd probably seen my love poem and shaken his head at my foolishness. He'd probably laughed that he'd let things go so far between us or maybe he was embarrassed that he'd ever considered me, the motherless stepsister, for a wife.

I wanted to run out of the room. I wanted to tear at the tulle and create such a scene that I would finally be heard. I wanted to spill my pain on the walls.

I stared on blankly, the slow realization

that KokoGul had been right settling in my heart. Jealousy had curdled the love I had for my sister. It was her moment of happiness, a union between her and a handsome young man from a loving family and I could not share in her celebration because of the dark thoughts thundering in my mind.

One thought echoed louder than all the others: Najiba now had two mothers and I had none.

CHAPTER 11
FEREIBA

His name was Hameed. Since he was no longer mine, I could say it without blushing. In a way, I was glad I'd never spoken his name. To me, it was nothing but a hollow string of sounds. Nor did his face affect me. I had no memory of his eyes and had never seen his hands. In so many ways, Hameed was a stranger to me.

The scent of the orchard, the sound of his voice, his approaching footsteps — those were the triggers for both my heartache and my rage.

I would never be so blind again.

The newly engaged couple spent time together, walking through the neighborhood in full view of others with their shy smiles and quiet conversations. Najiba blushed when she returned home. I knew why. I could have told her about our private conversations and the empty promises her fiancé had made to me, but I bit my tongue.

It was the noble thing to do, I told myself.

For weeks, I watched the couple come and go. KokoGul beamed and busied herself with the wedding arrangements. There were many busy afternoons spent with Bibi Shireen. They were just as taken with each other as the new bride and groom were. I kept my feelings to myself after that day. KokoGul excused my behavior after the *shirnee,* uninterested in exploring the matter further. She said nothing to my father about the dress I'd shredded.

I ran into Hameed in the courtyard once. He was waiting for Najiba, who'd run into the house to get a scarf. It was fall and the chill of the night air carried into the early morning. The house door slammed behind me. Hameed turned, his boyish smile evaporating at the sight of me. I could see the tension in his legs and arms. Every fiber of his body wanted to escape, our courtyard suddenly feeling like a small cage. He might as well have been inches from my face.

He muttered a faint greeting and turned to the side, his hands disappearing deep into his pockets.

I hesitated, wanting to retreat with the basket of wet clothes and return to the house, but the look on his face gave me strength. His eyes looked away in shame and his shoulders were pulled together, as if he were trying to fold himself in half.

"*Salaam,*" I said loudly and clearly. My voice surprised me. Hameed winced.

I walked past him slowly, aware of each breath and counting the steps between us. I made my way to the side of the house, still visible to him, where I began to hang the damp laundry from a clothesline. I snapped the moisture from each piece before draping it over the rope. It would be hours before anything would dry in the brisk air.

I could see Hameed fidget from the corner of my eye.

I wanted to hate him.

"Fereiba . . ." His voice was nothing more than a whisper.

My back was turned to him. I closed my eyes. Two drops of water fell from my father's damp shirt and landed on my toes.

"These things are family matters. Nothing was ever really in my hands."

I listened.

"And now I just want you to be happy. For the sake of the families, let's put it behind us."

His tone was dismissive. My shame boiled into indignation.

"Put what behind us?" I snapped.

"Do you really want to be this way? You

know I didn't mean to cause you any trouble."

"I don't know anything about you. Najiba knows even less."

He huffed in frustration. I turned around and met his narrowed eyes.

"You know if you say anything, it would look very bad for you," he seethed.

"If I say anything? Is that what worries you? I have no interest in spoiling my sister's life," I said, though it was a half-truth. "I pity her for winding up with a boy who pretends to hang his heart from a tree."

"You've no idea what you're saying."

"Don't I?"

He cast a quick glance over his shoulder and took two steps toward me.

"I told my mother to ask for the hand of the eldest daughter next door. Don't think I wasn't surprised when she came back having engaged me to Najiba. Anything I said after that would have brought shame on both our families."

I stared at him blankly. There are truths and lies and there are things in between, murky waters where light gets bent and broken. I did not know his face well enough to decide if he meant those words. I could not read the movements of his lips or the shadows behind his eyes. Did he want me to understand or did he want me to believe? And if I believed, would that be enough to change the rest of our story?

Najiba emerged with one of Sultana's scarves knotted at her neck. Her face broke out in a smile. She was no longer the bashful girl with eyes glued to the floor. She'd grown comfortable around Hameed and could walk at his side without feeling indecent. I could see the thrill on her face.

Hameed and I never spoke of our brief past again. I would never know if he truly felt anything more than a playful interest in me or if he'd been baited into a marriage he never wanted. The impropriety of our days in the orchard lingered and we rarely let our eyes meet. Najiba never sensed the shadow between us. If she did, she said nothing about it. I might have done the same if I were in her place.

In the days after my sister's wedding, KokoGul was again visited by Bibi Shireen and her sister. This time it was Bibi Shireen's sister, Khanum Zeba, who came in search of a bride.

Khanum Zeba came for me.

KokoGul had laughed. I knew my stepmother well enough that it did not bother me. I was not ready for marriage, not because I was too young or immature but because my heart was hardened. I'd seen the illusion of love but never the real thing. I had no reason to believe in love's existence.

But Khanum Zeba was the kindest woman I'd ever met. I imagined my mother would have loved her. As I stared at the intricate pattern of our living room rug, I heard her say things about me that had never before been said.

She is everything I want for my son.

The first time I saw her, I knew she was meant for our family.

I had to look at her. Her words emboldened me to raise my eyes and meet hers. The skin around her clear, brown eyes crinkled as she serenely explained to a very curious KokoGul why she chose me.

I dreamed once . . . years ago . . . of my son's wedding day. When I woke, I remembered every detail of it as if I'd attended the celebration the night before, including the face of the bride when we lifted the green veil for the nikkah. When I came to your home and met Fereiba, I recognized her.

Good for your son, KokoGul quipped, that you didn't dream of the baker's daughter — her skin's as dark as the bread he burns.

While others hid their smirks with a hand

141

over their mouths, KokoGul's comments fell flat on my future mother-in-law.

Your daughter is a special girl. She deserves a life full of roshanee, *light as warm as she is.*

Khanum Zeba's words were a bright, glowing moon hanging low in the night sky. KokoGul was aghast and ordered me out of the room, but Khanum Zeba walked over and placed her hand over mine, steadying my nerves.

I wanted to believe.

Chapter 12
Fereiba

In my years in Afghanistan, I survived many regime changes, starting with my mother's death and my father's remarriage. Some changes had been harder to swallow than others.

Khanum Zeba became Khala Zeba to me, once KokoGul placed my *shirnee* before her and agreed to give my hand in marriage. I'd never before seen her son, Mahmood. In a way, it was Khanum Zeba I had fallen for. Her son was merely her outstretched hand. But going through the motions of life together, Mahmood and I slowly became husband and wife.

When I told Khanum Zeba that I wanted to be a teacher, she insisted I pursue it. She'd been a teacher as well. I enrolled in a teaching program and worked my way through the courses with the support of a family I was barely a part of. My father and

KokoGul were content to see me attend the classes.

"School, school, school. Your husband is going to buy you chalk and notebooks for gifts if you don't make it clear you like things besides a classroom," KokoGul teased.

Mahmood and I were married in 1979, a year after our engagement and just as the Soviet Union's first baby-faced soldiers landed their heavy boots on Afghan soil. Having proudly earned a teaching degree in two years, I woke with fresh energy every day and took my place at the head of an elementary school classroom. The students were as eager as flightless, freshly hatched birds in a nest. It was for me to nurture their open minds, to teach them the words and numbers and ideas that would spread their wings.

Just two months after our wedding, Mahmood received word that his uncle's family, including four children, had been killed by Soviet rockets in the Panjshir Valley. We spent the next few months as newlyweds in mourning. I could hear Mahmood's aunts and cousins cluck their tongues at the incongruous sight of a new bride in a somber *fateha,* where the visitors came to

144

pay their respects to the family of the deceased.

It's just as they warned, came the whispers. *She carries the curse of bad fortune with her . . . and now she's among us. Her own family cautioned . . .*

Word of the rumors got back to us. My mother-in-law, Khala Zeba, scoffed at them. She said nothing when Mahmood made the painful decision to distance himself from the gossips in the family. He sheltered me from relatives with suspicious eyes and those who kept their children away out of fear.

Idle women are dangerous. Better you stick with your colleagues, women who busy themselves with home and work, like yourself. Don't mind the noise from the henhouse, Mahmood would caution.

I was relieved and surprised to have my husband reject such slander. My shoulders straightened to hear him defend me, especially to his own family. Mahmood and Khala Zeba reminded me of my grandfather, whose moral strength and unrelenting love often deflected KokoGul's hurtful words. Mahmood made the ground beneath me stop quaking. He gave me room and reason to love him.

I busied myself as he suggested. I spent an

occasional afternoon with another teacher I'd befriended and immersed myself in teaching. I expected a lot from my students and they worked hard. I knew I wasn't as stern as the other teachers, but I vied for their affection as much as they did for mine.

I cared about what I wore then and did my best to dress smartly. In my father's home, I'd dressed more like a girl — jeans, calf-length skirts, and collared T-shirts. In my new home, I dressed more like a woman — pencil skirts, ruffled blouses, buckled pumps, and always a shoulder bag. With Mahmood, I had my own household and was free to decide how my salary would be spent. I wasn't extravagant, just stylish enough to make my husband beam when we left the house for a gathering or to visit relatives. He looked at me as if I, too, gave him room and reason to love.

He believed in romance. He went on a trip once across the country. He was gone for two weeks and returned with fourteen letters he'd written me, a thick stack of his thoughts on our first meeting, the future of his job, and his favorite Hindi movie.

Your poor ears, Ferei. If I had this much to write to you, imagine how much I must talk!

At least we had each other to smile about in those days. The country suffered immeasurable losses in the tug of war between the Soviet Union and the mujahideen, Afghanistan's freedom fighters. More mothers buried their sons. More children limped to school, their limbs amputated by explosives disguised as dolls or toy cars. Mahmood and I listened to the news together on our sofa — his arm around my shoulder or my back leaned against his chest. He would shake his head in sadness as Afghans fled the bloodied countryside and sought refuge in the capital.

We lived contentedly for six years as husband and wife, but were quietly dismayed that my belly never swelled with child. We didn't speak of it directly but when I suggested that I wanted to be a mother, Mahmood agreed I should see a doctor. I went to see Kabul's most lauded women's doctors and took whatever pills they confidently prescribed. I swallowed the vilest concoctions of herbs blended by the elderly woman down the road. Month after month, my bleeding returned, until I finally crumpled as I dressed for school one morning and sobbed to Mahmood that he should not be deprived of fatherhood because of my barren womb. He held me as tightly and gently as I imagine only my mother could have and whispered in my ear that I should not speak such words again. I learned something very important that day.

Love grows wildest in the gardens of hardship.

Not long after, Saleem came along — a happy surprise that reignited the gossips. *See what they've married into,* they'd said in the years we were without a child. This quickly turned into whispers that I'd enlisted some black magic to lift my curse. My fellow teachers, on the other hand, rejoiced with me, and though most families were struggling in Kabul at that turbulent time, they scraped together what they could to bring gifts for the new baby. Hand-knitted, impossibly small sweaters, plush blankets, and a plate of sweet rosewater biscuits. Khala Zeba celebrated with us, bringing her best cooking and caring for her grandchild as I recovered from a difficult childbirth.

When we went to visit my family, I noticed a change in KokoGul. She treated me like one might treat a cousin who's come from out of town. She did not know what to do with me now that I was not hers to tease with her sharp tongue. Najiba was out of the house as was my brother, Asad, and my father had withdrawn from the world even more since I'd left our home. KokoGul was lonely without her audience. While outwardly it may have seemed that she'd warmed to me at last, I felt as if she had cooled. I went home often to see my younger sisters, but KokoGul kept her distance.

When Saleem turned four years old, the last of the Soviet troops retreated. It was 1989. We prayed for tranquility.

It was not to be. Things worsened in Kabul while Mahmood and I were stunned when a second miracle visited our home. We named her Samira. With a son and a daughter, we were even more desperate for peace to return to Afghanistan.

Rockets showered our city as rival factions tried to lay claim to the capital.

Saleem was anxious to have a normal boy's life. He asked me once to spend an afternoon at his friend's home across town. I refused to allow it.

But why not, Madar-jan? he whined. *Qasim is my best friend. I will be back before dinner-time.*

No, Saleem-jan. *Your father and I have already talked to you about this. That neighborhood is a magnet for rockets.*

I made my voice as serious as possible to

leave no room for discussion. I did not enjoy keeping Saleem from playing the way I'd seen boys play when I was his age, but we were living in a different time. He sulked for the remainder of the afternoon and went to bed without eating dinner, a punishment on both of us.

In the morning, our neighbor, Rahim, came by to chat with Mahmood. Rocket storms overnight had destroyed several homes and at least two children had been killed. I listened as I prepared bread and tea for breakfast. When we'd finished, I'd read from the Qur'an. How else could I protect us?

Saleem learned at school what I later heard from one of my friends. His friend Qasim had survived the rocket attack, but his three-year-old sister had been killed, suffocated under a pile of debris as her family tried to claw her free. Saleem said nothing to me and I had no words for him. This was a mistake. I should not have believed silence could protect us from the horrible truth.

The new rising regime, the Taliban, insisted that women dress more modestly and men grow beards in accordance with Islamic tradition. Every day, they issued a new set of decrees and meted out swift punishment for those who disobeyed. As a woman, I wasn't allowed to teach. Girls were not permitted in school.

This frightened and hurt me. The painful years when I was held back from school became the narrative of all girls. What would happen if one were to stomp and stab at an old wound? I was sick at the thought of so many empty classrooms.

These were razor-edged religious brutes. We could see them from our windows and heard their speeches. Though they were harsh and ignorant, some of our neighbors supported their rise and an end to the fighting.

We were all desperate for peace and that's what they promised.

Although Saleem was still in grade school, I sat in a living room with a group of teachers expelled from schools, huddled over glasses of diluted tea. Mahmood and I stayed up nights talking. We hoped our children wouldn't hear our hushed, anxious voices. Aunts and uncles came by with tearful hugs and kisses as they made their way out of Afghanistan. Saleem would ask us where they were going and looked puzzled to hear the list of countries: Pakistan, Hungary, Germany.

Khala Zeba collapsed while shopping in the market one day. When Mahmood and I got word, we rushed to her side. She'd lost consciousness. At the hospital, a doctor told us she'd had a stroke and there was nothing they could do to help her. If she were going to recover, it would be on her own. We brought her home, and for three days I sat at her side, touching cool, wet rags to her forehead and dripping broth into her mouth. Mahmood and I prayed over her and thumbed her worry beads. I talked to her even when she didn't respond. I wiped the thin stream of drool from the corner of her mouth as I'd done for my babies. My husband paced the room and kissed her hands, anguished with the feeling that he should be doing more. But there was nothing more to do. My mother-in-law left this life with as much grace as she'd lived it.

I should have been numbed by then, but I wasn't. I felt robbed of a mother I'd just found, the first woman to treat me like a true daughter. I missed talking to her. She'd taught me how to swaddle Saleem and how to soothe his colic. She'd watched after him when I was at my heaviest with Samira and cooked him rice with mung beans. It was hard to look at my children without thinking of her. I looked for a way to distract myself.

For a few months, I taught several of the neighbors' daughters in a makeshift classroom in our home. But when the Taliban executed three people in one week for running a secret school, even our neighbors kept their daughters home. Our once bright and cheerful home felt stifling and dark. Mahmood was becoming bitter and taciturn as well, reluctantly growing the beard required of him. At least the explosive skies had quieted with this new regime.

Saleem and Samira found ways to play and laugh at home. I could almost believe life was normal, listening to them from the next room.

Saleem entered the sixth grade in 1997. The Taliban, now in control in Kabul, had arrested a handful of Europeans for taking pictures at a women's hospital in Kabul. Mahmood and I stayed tight-lipped about the affair when Saleem asked us questions.

The Taliban feel that it is un-Islamic to take photographs of people, was all Mahmood told him. We couldn't risk him repeating anything more damning to his classmates.

If I were a European, I never would have left my home to come to Kabul. Not in those days. I would have stayed in Poland or England or Italy where there were no whistling rockets above, where meat and vegetables were abundant and women weren't afraid to step outside their homes. Why leave such a paradise to come to Kabul?

All television sets and video players were banned. Music was outlawed. Mahmood was wrathful, but it was only with me or within his closest circle of friends that he dared rant about the destruction of our society. He continued to work at the Ministry of Water and Electricity as a mechanical engineer. His original work had focused on bringing reliable fresh water and electric power to the outskirts of Kabul, but the focus changed under the new edicts. Every day there were new restrictions and warnings from the Taliban about what could or could not be built in Kabul.

"How many decades can we go on without progress or construction? This country is going back in time." His shoulders slumped as if they carried the weight of the world. He was the bearded shell of his former self. I wondered if I would ever again see the tall, proud man who would spin his children in the air until they dizzied with laughter.

Samira should have been excitedly gathering pencils and reciting the alphabet to prepare for school. We could not make Samira understand why she could not attend school like her brother. I told her it did not matter and put all my energy into teaching her formal lessons at home. It felt good to teach again and to defy the edict in my own way.

In 1999, despite the odds, my belly began to round again. We should have been joyous, but I felt like I was suffocating. I fought back tears every time I talked to Mahmood about our future.

"And now we are to bring another child into this Kabul? A Kabul that neither you nor I can recognize? For what? If he is a boy, he will grow up and know nothing but beards and fear. And God forbid this child has the sorry fortune to be born a girl! I just don't think I could bear it. Already, I am ashamed to let Samira see what has become of me. I have had to cower under the stick of those turbaned tyrants while they stripped me of my career, my friends, my freedom to walk about! What future can there be for my daughter?"

Mahmood felt just as defeated as I did.

"You're right, Ferei. It's time for us to go. Whatever hopes I had for this country are dead. Every day is worse. I'll find a way out for us, and I pray it'll be before this child is born. God, I wish I had followed everyone else. Now we could be in England, just like your sister and my cousin. I never imagined I wouldn't be able to send my daughter to school."

I was relieved to be planning our escape and fearful of leaving home. Without Khala Zeba, I felt no obligation to stay. Mahmood met with Rahim, who knew a government official, a title that meant less with every passing day. In exchange for nearly half our meager savings, we were promised stamped Afghan passports. Rahim acted as liaison in exchange for his own envelope of bills.

Crossing the border would be a hazardous venture even with passports. Rahim cautioned us to secure foreign passports as well since our Afghan documents would not get us very far. Rahim also knew a counterfeiter called the "Embassy." He was a crafty man who had once worked as a supervisor in Kabul's printing press. When the Taliban silenced the whirring of the press, the Embassy had quietly carted home a cloaked typewriter, stuffed bottles of ink into his coat pockets, and planned for his own family's future. He, like Mahmood and me, was a professional stripped of his profession.

There was a difference between us though. While the Embassy was too scared to leave Kabul, we were too scared to stay. It was still unclear who had made the wiser choice.

Chapter 13
Fereiba

Three months before I would bring my third child into the world, I sent Saleem to the market to pick up salt. My back ached and Mahmood would be home soon, eager for dinner. Without a grain of salt in our cupboards, the rice and stew would be a wasted effort.

Time often escaped my adventurous boy. I watched the clock and reassured myself that he had run into friends. The sun dipped below the mountain peaks. Saleem had been gone for two hours when he should have been back after twenty minutes.

I sat on a chair and tried to rub a knot out of the small of my back. My nerves were on edge. I hurried to the living room when I heard the front gate open, ready to lay into Saleem for dallying and anxious to have him back at home. But it was Mahmood, home a bit earlier than usual. He took one look at my face and rested his briefcase on the sofa. I saw his eyes scout the living room for a clue.

"What's wrong, Fereiba? Where's Saleem?"

I burst into tears. I hadn't been sleeping well in the last week, and I was feeling exceptionally run-down. My legs and back ached, and worrying about Saleem had put me past my tipping point. But I was home alone with Samira and she was sensitive to my moods, so I had tried to put on a happy face.

With his arms around me, Mahmood reminded me that Saleem had to pass by the street where his friends typically played and that rarely had our son taken the direct route home when he'd been sent for an errand. Mahmood and I were very different in that regard. I worried prematurely. He worried too late.

At my husband's suggestion, we sat down for dinner. I spread the vinyl tablecloth on the living room floor. Samira, more eager to please when her brother caused trouble, set out the bowls and spoons. It was a tasteless meal, with or without the salt. My heart leaped when I heard the gate clang shut. I was about to stand when Mahmood put his hand on mine.

"Let him come to us, *janem*," he said

softly. I nodded, moving the rice on my plate aimlessly. I looked over at Samira. Her dark eyes twinkled at the sound of her brother's footsteps.

Saleem entered the living room sheepishly. *"Salaam,"* he mumbled.

Mahmood looked over, his face calm and composed.

"Saleem, go and wash up. You are covered in dirt. I hope your soccer game was worth making your mother worry."

Saleem bowed his head. He put the bag of salt on the counter and muttered something close to an apology. By the time he returned, we'd cleared the dishes of everything but a small bowl of rice. Embarrassed but hungry, Saleem sat cross-legged at the tablecloth. Samira and I had cleared the other dishes. Mahmood sat in the armchair to read as was his nightly routine.

I peeked in and saw that Saleem had devoured his food in a breath. He stared blankly at the carpet. I felt his dread. The anticipation of a reprimanding was always worse than the reprimanding itself.

"Saleem, isn't there something you'd like to say?" I blurted, drying my hands on a dishrag. Saleem's head hung low, his body apologetic though he couldn't bring his mouth to form the words.

Mahmood lowered his reading glasses and put his book on the nesting table to his right. He was reading the poetry of Ibrahim Khalil, the prolific Kabul poet who was beloved by many in the Waziri family. As university students, Mahmood and Hameed had taken a course taught by Khalil. While I loved his verses, I couldn't help but think of Najiba's husband when I heard them. That I'd once allowed my husband's cousin to recite Khalil's poems to me made me wildly embarrassed. He tried, from time to time, to engage me with a quatrain or two, but it was not something I could share with Mahmood. It felt dishonest.

"Look up, *bachem,*" Mahmood said.

Saleem sat cross-legged before his father and slowly lifted his head. Mahmood paused, reconsidering whatever it was he was about to say.

"Let me read something to you," he said and picked Khalil's book up from the table.

Know that your fortune is not polluted
As infant you nursed of milk undiluted
The labyrinth of woe behind which you are
    gated
From your own fancy, was borne and
    created
For punishment is not the Almighty's intent

Nor does He disrupt, mislead or torment
Upon our shoulders, all malaise and grief
Are naught but the harvest we have chosen
    to reap

"Do you understand what these words mean?"

"Yes, Padar-*jan.*"

"Then tell me, Saleem-*jan,* what do they mean to you?"

"That I should not act like a child."

"Saleem-*jan,* I'm sorry that when you wake up every morning, this is the world that you see around you. I'm sorry that this is the Kabul, the Afghanistan that you are seeing. I wish you could have learned to take your first steps without rockets firing over your head. This is no place for a child, but because of that, it's all the more important for you to step up. You must find a way to make good of this situation — to reap a noble harvest."

I could see the resentment on Saleem's face. All he was ever told was no. This much he'd shared with me on more than one occasion. The things he *could* do were few; the things he *couldn't* do were endless. But Saleem bit his tongue and did not protest the injustice that even Mahmood admitted.

"Saleem-*jan,* my son, now is the time to

learn to look after your own actions. Your mother and I watch over you, but every day you are less and less of a boy."

Sometimes I argued with Mahmood that he needed to be firmer with the children. Why they feared his punishments, I could not understand. He did little more than lecture them and give them disappointed looks. But the children respected him, as did I. So many nights the children and I nestled around him, vying for space to listen to his stories. His arms wrapped around us all, tying us together in one package.

I lost myself in those moments, loving my husband more than I'd ever imagined I could. I often missed Khala Zeba and wished I could have thanked her for putting me in his arms.

In the night, with the children breathing softly beside us, Mahmood rubbed the knot in my back.

"Saleem will be a great man — he has a lion's spirit in his young eyes," he whispered. "Before we know it, the day will come when he'll be man of a house with little ones of his own. Do you know what I pray for, *janem*? I pray that day comes neither too early nor too late."

I took Mahmood's hands from my back and wrapped them around my waist.

"And I pray that it's in my *naseeb* to see that day."

"God willing, we'll both see that day," I managed to get out before the lump in my throat swelled.

CHAPTER 14
FEREIBA

A month later, we marked the holiday of Eid. Distant relatives and friends had been dropping by to pay their customary visits despite the city's somber mood. When we heard the knock at the gate, we thought nothing of it. Mahmood went to answer it, and I instinctively put a pot of water to boil for tea.

But the people at the door were neither friends nor family.

Gruff-looking men had barged into our courtyard and sauntered into the foyer.

"So this is the home of the engineer," one sneered, his words thick with distaste.

I gasped at the sound of men's voices booming from within our home. The teakettle fell with a clang, water pooling on the floor.

Saleem and Samira were at my feet drawing pictures on scraps of paper. I shot them a look and pointed upstairs. Frightened, they scurried up the steps without the slightest protest.

I threw on my *burqa* and looked into the living room.

Three men had entered our living room and were eyeing our belongings contemptuously. They wore loose-hanging caftans and pantaloons in khaki and gray, drab colors that made their pitch-black beards and machine guns stand out. Their guns were slung casually over their shoulders. The tallest of the three was twirling Mahmood's *tasbeh,* his worry beads, around his finger. When they caught sight of me, an azure apparition, in the doorway, they ordered me back into the kitchen.

Mahmood looked alarmed but composed. He had stepped in front of me instinctively and gave me a quiet, pleading look to follow their command.

I was terrified to leave my husband alone with these men who'd forced their way into our home, but I also had my mind on my two children hidden upstairs and the one I carried under my *burqa.* I lowered my head and backed into the kitchen, still within earshot but out of sight.

"You are an engineer."

"Yes." Mahmood's voice was controlled.

"And you work for the Ministry of Water

166

and Electricity," he said. From the soft clinks, I knew one of the men had turned his attention to the porcelain tea set in our glass curio. It had been a wedding gift from Khala Zeba. The cups were delicate, with gold leaf on the handles and dainty pastel painted flowers. We had no photographs, no television, and no radio, thank God. I hoped once they realized our home was free of contraband, they would leave.

"Yes, I do. Is there something that I can help you with?"

"We're looking for Mahmood Waziri, the engineer who works for the Ministry of Water and Electricity — the man who is known to be in defiance of our Islamic laws."

My heart raced. I glanced up the stairs and saw the shadow of two small heads peeking around the corner. I motioned them to back away.

"Defiance? But I have not defied any . . ."

"You'd better come with us so we can tell you exactly the sins you've been charged with committing."

"Sins? My brothers, there must be a misunderstanding." I detected a slight tremble in Mahmood's voice, but nothing compared to the way I was shaking.

"There is no misunderstanding."

"But, please, hear me out for one moment. I've done my best to comply with all the decrees that have been handed down —"

"We will not speak here, unless you wish to bring your wife and two children into the living room to watch us *charge you* with your crimes." Mahmood let out a deep sigh.

"No, no, no. That's not necessary. I'll come with you."

"Mahmood! Please do not take him! He is an innocent man!" I cried out, my voice shrill and unnerved. I was in the doorway, on my knees.

One of the men walked toward me, but Mahmood intervened.

"Please!" he said sharply, before turning to me. His fingers were on my shoulders, holding me up, as he looked through the mesh of my *burqa*. "Fereiba-*jan,* I beg you, let me speak with these men. I'm sure we can clear up this misunderstanding. You are needed *here.*"

When we were first married, I knew nothing about my husband. Time taught me that he was patient, nurturing, and principled. I was too bashful to look directly at him in the first month or so but in the warmth of his friendship, my guard melted. He undid all that this world had done to me. I realized, not long after our wedding, when I caught myself laughing at a joke he'd already told me twice, that I loved this man.

Fereiba, do you know what the most beautiful word for spouse is in our language?

What is it?

Hamsar. *Think of it. "Of the same mind." That's what we are, isn't it?*

That's what Mahmood did. He took rusted, tired words — things people could say to one another without feeling a thing — and turned them over in the palm of his hand. He would blow the dust off and make them shine with meaning so moving you were ashamed to have overlooked it.

He asked me questions and listened for my answers. He had his mother's generous heart and his father's wit. He did not live in fear of God because, he reasoned, a merciful God would not create us only to punish us for trivial earthly matters. Mahmood was logical and determined. He loved his children. He would discipline them and later chuckle at their mischief. He would stroke my forehead before we went to sleep, a touch light enough to make my eyes heavy but ardent enough to make me want to be awake. He wanted his work to be his footprint in Afghanistan, something his children would be proud of.

With no children to distract us in the early years of our marriage, I learned my husband well. I could hear Mahmood's thoughts when I looked into his eyes.

He was my *hamsar*.

With the men barking at him to follow, I turned to Mahmood's face — the blue grid of my *burqa* invading the most precious, private moment of our married lives. There was so much to say. His eyes whispered to me in a way only a *hamsar* could.

Take care of our children, janem. *I will do what I can to make this right. I'm sorry I've brought this upon us. I would give anything to stay at your side.*

My husband was escorted out of our home and into the blackest night of our lives. The men slammed the door behind them. Two porcelain teacups rattled off the shelf and smashed to the floor, leaving shards of white and pastel in their wake.

I heard frantic footsteps upstairs and knew Saleem had run over to the window. I never asked him what he saw. If I know my husband, he was conscious of his children watching him being led away. He would do nothing to make that night any uglier than it forever would be in their minds.

CHAPTER 15
FEREIBA

Saleem tiptoed to me. I had slipped the *burqa* off my head and slumped to the floor. I'd heard the car's engine hum into the distance. They'd taken Mahmood with them. My son sat beside me, and Samira watched from a safe distance. When Saleem could bear the quiet no longer, he broke the silence.

"Madar-*jan* . . ." he whispered.

I stopped him before he could say anything else. I had no answers.

"My son, go on back upstairs with your sister and sleep. I'll wait for your father."

I knew he was scared. I knew he wanted to be useful. He wanted to do things that would make Mahmood proud.

Samira was just nine years old on that night. She was an extension of me. Her moods ebbed and flowed in response to my own, just as the tides respond to the moon. If I brooded, Samira quieted, blowing her dark bangs away from her crinkled forehead. If I was happy, my daughter walked with a skip in her step. On that night, Samira became silent and trembled. With her hands drawn into tight, little fists, tears darkened her pillowcase.

Saleem woke at dawn and found me on the living room couch. I sat with my head against the wall. I cannot imagine what I must have looked like to him.

"Madar-*jan*?"

He had to call out to me twice.

"Yes, Saleem," I said. My throat was dry and raw.

Saleem hadn't known what to say. He simply felt obligated to break the silence and gauge the situation.

"Did you sleep, Madar-*jan*?"

I sat with my hands wrapped around the round of my belly; my swollen feet barely reached the floor.

"Yes, my son."

He looked doubtful and offered to bring me tea. I looked at Saleem, his hands wringing behind his back, his face knotted with fear. It was time for me to be a mother again.

"It is early still," I'd said. "It would be good to pray for your father."

We didn't bother to heat the water for the ablutions.

"In the name of God . . ." I whispered and began to wash my hands, mouth, and nose. I steeled myself against the icy touch of the water. I would not show weakness. I washed my face, behind my ears, my hands and feet.

With a rehearsed rhythm, Saleem and I stood, kneeled, and bowed as we mouthed the phrases we'd both memorized very early in our lives. I could feel my eyes glaze as I thought of the previous night.

I didn't know if my husband would ever be returned.

Our home froze in time, waiting for a sign.

Saleem helped with some chores and, though he was young, with going to the market for our basic needs. I was isolated. My siblings had fled Afghanistan along with KokoGul. My father stayed behind to look after his orchard, an hour from where Mahmood and I had settled. Mahmood's family was similarly dispersed, his sisters living in Australia. All we had left were distant cousins who were struggling, as we were, to feed their families and survive Kabul's new order. I sent word to our families. They were distraught, but not in any position to help. Mahmood's sisters begged me to keep them informed if I heard from their brother.

Raisa, Abdul Rahim's wife, came by frequently after hearing the news of Mahmood's disappearance. Some days, she sent a plate of butter or a small pot of rice. Raisa had always been a dear friend, but I dreaded her visits after his disappearance. Her eyes, moist with pity, were brutal reminders of everything that was wrong.

She had a matronly softness, a bosom that offered to pull you in and rock you to sleep as if you were one of her many children. On those bleak days, Raisa would stop by for short visits. Without a pause in conversation, she would tidy the kitchen and make a quick dish with whatever she could find in our cupboards.

"Fereiba-*jan,* any word?" she would ask vaguely.

"Not yet, but I'm sure any day now," I would say and I believed it. Mahmood was a marvel. I had no reason to expect anything less from him.

"Well, if there's anything that you and the children need . . ."

I steeled myself. I tried to keep the house in order, to give my children a way to sleep easy in the night. Samira mirrored my composure during the day but at night, her dark bangs clung to the cold sweat of her forehead. She whimpered and wailed in her sleep, a language I understood but refused to speak.

I found Saleem's notebook. There were hash marks on the back cover. He was counting the days since that night. There were forty-seven marks.

We were a home without a patriarch, the type of creature Kabul's beasts devoured on sight. On the day I was struck with sharp pains, I realized just how isolated we were without a man in the home. For hours, I'd turned my face to the wall when the pressure overwhelmed me. The children said nothing. We each played our part in the charade of normalcy.

But the fear of losing my unborn, of having Mahmood return to find me without his child, was enough to drive me out of the house without a proper escort. I slipped on my *burqa* and took Saleem by the hand. I left Samira with Raisa-*jan,* who pulled my daughter against her chest and nodded. She could offer nothing else.

"Saleem-*jan,* forgive me if I squeeze your hand too hard, *bachem.*" The pain was sharp and came with such force, I nearly doubled over.

"Are you very sick, Madar-*jan*?" Saleem asked quietly once we'd turned off our street.

"No, *bachem*. I'm sure it's fine. Everything will be better once your father comes home."

The look of doubt on Saleem's face did not go unnoticed. My confidence was beginning to stutter and stumble. Samira had sensed it too. Every day, she retreated further into herself.

"Is the baby coming now?" Saleem's questions were practical. He was so much like his father. I hadn't realized just how much he'd grown in the last year.

"God forbid, *bachem*. It's still too soon. Babies need nine months and nine days. Nine months and nine days," I repeated, hearing my mother-in-law's voice. There was much she'd shared with me before she'd left us, squeezing a lifetime of mothering into a few short years. She'd been the one to hurry the midwife to our home when my labor pains began with Saleem and Samira. She'd held my hand as I'd brought her grandchildren into the world. As the time grew near for this child, I felt her absence more and more.

With one hand on my belly and my eyes to the ground, I did not notice the three men round the corner. We were just a hundred meters from the hospital entrance.

"Have you no self-respect, woman? Where is your *mahram*?" A glob of saliva landed at my feet. I took a step back. My son's grip tightened on my fingers. I tried to position myself in front of him.

"This is my son. He is escorting me to the hospital. I am in severe pain and am in a . . . condition."

Were these the men who had come for Mahmood? Would they know anything about his whereabouts? Before I dared to ask, a stick cracked on my shoulder. I doubled over, my hands covering my belly.

"Please don't!" Saleem cried as he threw himself over my crouched form.

"Only loose women speak of such matters so openly! Have you no shame in front of your son? Where is his father? Or maybe he does not have one."

My body quaked with rage, but I said nothing. I had to be practical too.

"We ask your forgiveness. Please let us be on our way," I said through gritted teeth.

"Get back to your home. Go home with your boy and try to carry yourself as a respectful Muslim woman. You have no need for the hospital. Keep your woman troubles to yourself and spare your son the shame of being seen with you."

Sharp pains pierced my pelvis and shoulder, but I got back on my feet. I pulled my bewildered son by the hand and turned around. After just one step, I felt a snap against my back. They'd lashed out twice more, for good measure. I squeezed Saleem's hand, anticipating his reaction.

"Madar!" He was angry.

"Say nothing, *bachem,*" I whispered. "Let's be on our way, my love. I am fine."

Saleem's face burned with fury. It hurt him to do nothing, even if it was what I asked. In bringing him as my escort, I'd asked him to be the man of our home. In telling him to do nothing, I'd struck him back down to a boy. He supported me as I hobbled back home. For an Afghan, pride is harder to swallow than a bag of nails.

We stopped several times so I could catch my breath and rest against a wall. The way home was much longer than I remembered.

I lay in bed for three days, praying for God to watch over me and my child. The pains waxed and waned. Raisa stayed at the house until nightfall and made simple meals for the children. She put wet cloths on my forehead and made me drink water from a copper bowl engraved with a *sura* from the

Qur'an. Saleem and Samira were somber and inseparable. They clung to each other like two lost travelers trying to keep warm on a bitterly cold night.

On the third day, Raisa burst into our home with fresh determination. She pulled a small pouch from her pocket and dropped a handful of small, dark seeds into a bowl. As she trickled boiling water into the bowl, she whispered prayers into the musky steam. Raisa sat behind me with her back to the wall, propped me up in her lap like an infant, and brought the bowl to my parched lips. I hadn't the strength to ask what she had brewed and let the warmth make its way down my throat.

Raisa made a meal of stale bread and added more water to the meat broth we'd been drinking for four days. We had money, but there was no food to be found in the markets. Two days of rocket fire had sent all the street vendors and shop owners into hiding and left the city's stomachs grumbling behind blackened windows.

I woke in the night, a sliver of moonlight catching my face. I took a deep breath and felt the baby stir. The pain in my back and flank had subsided. As I pushed myself to sit, my head spun just slightly, then steadied itself.

I thanked God.

Saleem looked at me with cautious optimism. He didn't trust this world, and I couldn't find the words to restore his faith. Maybe it was more than words I was lacking.

I sent Saleem next door to thank Raisa-*jan* for her help and to let her know she could tend to her own family without worry. Saleem returned with news that Abdul Rahim and Raisa would be coming over shortly.

I boiled water for tea and searched the cupboards for something to serve them. We would not have survived the week without their kindness.

They knocked on our front gate quietly. I met them in the courtyard and led them into the living room, eager to show Raisa that I was very much back on my feet.

"You should be resting still, Ferei-*jan*," she chided.

"Allah bless your family with many happy years." I hugged her tightly and kissed her cheeks. "I don't know how to thank you for everything you've done. You've put me back on my feet and kept my children fed when you have a household of your own. Mahmood and I will never forget this."

Raisa looked as if she had just taken a bite

of something horrid and was waiting for the right moment to spit it out.

"Fereiba-*jan,* let us sit and talk," Abdul Rahim said. "Saleem-*jan,* look after your sister for a bit, *bachem.*"

When Abdul Rahim, the gentle giant who lived next door, called Saleem *my boy,* I knew. Everything I needed to know was in that seemingly trivial endearment, the word he'd slipped in instinctively wanting to fill a sorry void. Abdul Rahim, a loving father, knew the needs of a young man. A young man needs someone to tousle his hair, to put a hand on his shoulder, to watch him fiddle with a broken watch.

A young man needs to be someone's boy. *Bachem.*

No wonder Mahmood had respected our neighbors the way he did. He'd seen the goodness in them long before they'd needed to show it.

My son was without a father. My children were without their father.

Saleem, my obedient boy, headed off to sit with Samira. I knew he would listen in and I did nothing about it. I couldn't protect any of us from our reality. I sat down and let Abdul Rahim tell me what he needed to tell me.

"My brother works for the . . . two weeks

ago . . . taken by Taliban . . . disagreed with their actions . . . man of ideals . . . brave . . . workers found a body . . . note in the pocket . . . forgive me for sharing this with you . . ."

Raisa wrapped her arms around me. She sobbed, her heavy bosom heaving. I'd known for weeks, but some truths need to be said out loud before they can be believed.

Mahmood would never come back. We'd had our final moment together just a few feet from where I sat. He'd told me everything he needed to in that last moment, his fate written on his face. He had known from the moment the men entered our home.

Saleem slipped back into the living room and walked over to Abdul Rahim who sat with shoulders slumped, his hands folded between his knees.

"Kaka-*jan*?" he said.

Abdul Rahim met his gaze.

"My father — he is not coming back?"

It was not a boy's question. It was the question of a young man who needed to know what to expect of tomorrow and what tomorrow would expect of him.

CHAPTER 16
FEREIBA

I had to get my family out of Kabul.

With Mahmood gone, there was nothing left for us. We would almost certainly starve once the money ran out. The imminent arrival of our third child complicated matters.

Samira had not spoken since the afternoon of Raisa and Abdul Rahim's visit. She gave her answers in nods and gestures. I spoke softly with her, trying to coax the words from her lips, but Samira remained silent.

I found Saleem in our bedroom, staring at his father's belongings. Unaware of my presence, he touched the pants, brought a shirt to his cheek, and laid the pieces out on the floor as if trying to imagine his father in it. He picked up Mahmood's watch from the nightstand and turned it over in his hand. He slipped it on his wrist and pulled his sleeve over it. It was a private moment between father and son, so I snuck back down the hall before he realized I'd been watching.

My son thought I was too wrapped up in my own grief to know what he suffered, but I observed it all. I saw him kick the tree behind our house until he fell into a tearful heap, his toes so bruised and swollen that he winced with each step for a week. I held him when he allowed me, but if I started to speak, he would slip away. It was too soon.

If I thought of my last exchange with Mahmood, so did Saleem. I could see the remorse on his face as clearly as I felt it in my heart. We would have done things differently, Saleem and I. We would have had much more to say.

From what Abdul Rahim was able to gather, the local Taliban had decided to make an example of Mahmood Waziri. The rest of the family would not be targeted, he believed, but no one could say with any certainty. Even in the light of day, there was little certainty in Kabul. The cloak of night made all things possible.

I couldn't bear to have my children out of my sight. I sent Saleem on errands to the marketplace only when I was truly desperate. Just one month after the news of Mahmood's assassination, my belly began to ache. At first, I thought it might be the balmy winter air bringing a cramp, but as I walked from room to room, the familiar pains became clearer.

I paced the room, my lips pursed and my steps slow.

"Nine months, nine days . . . nine months, nine days . . ." I repeated softly.

Just a few hours later, Raisa coaxed my third child into the world. I named him Aziz.

"Saleem and Samira," I managed to get out. "Meet your father's son."

Aziz would need to gain some weight before we could venture out of Kabul. As I nursed him, his face started to take on his father's features: the squint of his eyes, the dip in his chin, the curl of his ears.

Abdul Rahim kept a watchful eye on the widowed Waziri family. He invited Saleem to sit with him when he returned from school. I don't know what they talked about, but Saleem always came home pensive. I was grateful my son had Abdul Rahim to turn to.

Abdul Rahim and Raisa agreed that it was best for us to leave. We had no family to help us. I feared my son would be swallowed by the Taliban, and as a woman, there was little I could do to help us survive.

"We're going to leave," I told my neighbors. "I have no choice but to get my children out of Kabul. Their stomachs are empty, their lips parched. There's nothing for us here."

Raisa nodded in agreement.

"There's no telling if things will get better. They could get worse. As much as I hate to see you go, I can't bear to watch you stay with things like this. If Mahmood-*jan*, God give him peace, were with you, it would be different. But like this, Kabul is worse than a prison for you."

"I'm going to need your help."

Abdul Rahim had nodded. He'd been anticipating this conversation.

Three months after Aziz was born, I gathered my children and packed two small bags with what I thought we would need most: clothing, a parchment envelope with a dozen family pictures, and whatever food we had left. I'd said nothing to the children until two days before we were to leave. Saleem looked resentful that he'd been kept in the dark. We lived in the same space, with the same dismal thoughts, and yet, for the better part of our days, we were confounded by each other. We were a family beheaded and floundered around as such.

"What if they find out we're leaving?" Saleem's voice was quiet with fear.

"They won't find out," I promised. I had no other way of answering. His expression flat, Saleem held my gaze for a few seconds too long. He had seen through me.

I told myself things would be better once we escaped Kabul's toxic air.

I sent word to my father that we would be traveling to Herat. I wanted to see him once more before we set off. But Padar-*jan* was a man who preferred to live in the comforts of yesterday. The letter I got back was nothing more than I had come to expect from my father. The orchard was in such bad shape I would hardly recognize it, he said. Armies of beetles had tunneled through the wood. He had taken to sleeping some nights in the grove, hoping his presence would scare them away but they were quite brazen. The past winter had been especially harsh and he would need to do much coaxing if he wanted to see even a single basket of apricots this year. They were more delicate than children, he believed. It saddened him that he could not do more for us now, but he looked forward to seeing us on our return.

People have different ways of saying goodbye, especially when it is forever.

A few weeks earlier, Abdul Rahim had

knocked on our door and handed me a large envelope. Raisa was with him. Her moist eyes belied the encouraging smile on her face.

The passports Mahmood had purchased were enclosed, even his own. I had touched his photograph, the size of my thumb, and hurt anew that he was not here to make this journey with us. I made the painful decision to ask Abdul Rahim to sell it back to the Embassy for whatever he would give. There was no room for sentimentality. Now the time had come to leave.

"Wear your sturdiest shoes. Today is the day we begin our travels. And remember, if anyone asks you, we are going to visit your aunt in Herat. Say a prayer. We will need God to watch over us."

When Saleem reached into the closet for his winter hat, I caught a glimpse of Mahmood's watch on his wrist. I opened my mouth to say something but decided against it. It was best to leave the matter between father and son.

There was much we could not take with us: Saleem's soccer ball, Samira's set of plastic dolls, the fractured china set my mother-in-law had gifted us. I looked at my pots and pans, blackened with fire. The handwoven carpet in the living room had watched us grow from bride and groom to a full family, and then bore witness to the night we were undone. Tears of joy, tears of heartbreak had melted into its pattern. I left it all, the pieces of our broken life, for Raisa. I knew our home would not remain vacant long. Once Mahmood's cousins learned of our escape, one of them was sure to claim it. Kabul had become a game of musical chairs with squatters, militants, and relatives plopping into an empty house before someone else could claim it.

Abdul Rahim checked his watch nervously. We were on a timeline. Our neighbors had offered to escort us to the bus terminal. If we were stopped, Abdul Rahim would say he was my brother.

I carried a bag in one hand and had Aziz tucked under my *burqa*. Saleem had a knapsack strapped to his back and held Samira's hand, following behind Abdul Rahim but walking ahead of me. He and Samira both looked back frequently, as if they thought I might wander off.

The terminal was a widened road with buses parked in haphazard rows. At the front door of each bus, a man stood calling out the bus's destination. We found our bus and saw that it was filling quickly.

"How long is the ride, Madar-*jan*?" Saleem whispered.

"Very long. Try to sleep — the time will pass more quickly."

The children and I filed on. I went to the women's section in the back with Samira and Aziz while Saleem took an empty seat in the men's section up closer to the driver. I kept Aziz on my lap, and Samira sat beside me. Seats were limited, and more than a few of the younger women were forced to stand.

The bus rumbled onto the main road. *Burqas* lifted like theater curtains as conversations picked up.

In the second hour, Samira fell asleep, despite the bumps and jumps the bus took on the rough road. Even Aziz and I dozed for a few minutes, waking only when the chatter grew in intensity. Then I realized we were no longer moving.

My right leg burned with pins and needles. After three hours of tinkering and cursing, the bus driver was able to restart the engine. We were back on the road but moving at a snail's pace. Twice more the bus driver had to disembark and curse the engine back into working order.

Three days later, we finally reached our

destination, the cantankerous driver yelling for everyone to gather their belongings and exit.

We were in Herat.

"Your father used to come here a few times each year, on behalf of the ministry," I told my children. "He was leading one of the projects in this area."

Saleem kicked at the dirt as he followed the blue shadows off the bus.

"Why didn't he ever tell me about it?"

"It was long ago," I said, taking note of the resentment in his question.

We waited, as Abdul Rahim had instructed us, and an hour after our arrival, we were approached by a couple. A short man in his fifties whispered my name as a question.

"Khanum Fereiba?" he asked.

"Yes," I confirmed with relief.

"Abdul Rahim and Raisa-*jan* have told me to expect you." He motioned for his *burqa*-clad wife to join him.

I ushered my children ahead of me, and we followed Asim and Shabnam to their home. Shabnam was Raisa's sister, their voices and matronly figures remarkably similar. We would stay with them for just a night. By the following evening we would be on a bus headed for the Afghan-Iran border. Saleem and Samira were disappointed, especially once they'd met the couple's young children. Samira played with the girls while Saleem held Aziz and listened in on Asim's warnings for the treacherous road ahead.

"You must be wary of the people you will meet," he cautioned sternly. He swirled the tea leaves in his glass prophetically and continued. "Herat is the doorway to Iran, so we hear and see much of the traffic that passes. The Taliban are present here and look for any opportunity to make an example out of someone. You know, of course, their rules on *mahram* escorts. And they know that many people are trying to make their way into Iran, so keep your eyes open and try not to attract attention."

Asim and Shabnam lived in a three-room home that had not gone unscathed in the rocket attacks. Parts of the roof had been patched, and the windows were boarded up. With her *burqa* off, Shabnam's resemblance to Raisa was even more apparent. Saleem and Samira smiled to see her familiar face. I listened intently as Asim went on.

"You'll be traveling in a small van. Usually, they are very full and there's hardly room to breathe, so keep your little ones at your side. They'll be nervous. The driver should take you across the border and into

Iran. The price for the passage has already been settled, but they will try to wheedle more from you. Keep all your monies and valuables well hidden. Look very reluctant and give him a little token piece. Make the driver believe that's the very last thing you have."

I looked at Saleem, wanting to tell him to run off and play so he could be spared this conversation. On the other hand, maybe he deserved to know what he was about to be involved in.

"Bear in mind that the van will only take you to the border. You'll have to walk across on foot. The smugglers make the crossing under cover of night. Once you get to the Iranian side, there will be another van waiting for you. This van will take you to Mashhad. I believe Abdul Rahim has given you the address for your contact there. There are many Afghans in Mashhad and, *inshallah,* they will help you to find your way. I understand that you'll be going on to Europe. The road ahead of you is difficult, but many have traveled it."

I sighed heavily. Saleem took notice.

"I pray God will make us among the many who successfully pass through it. This is the only way I see for my children. I hope I'm making the right decision."

Shabnam nodded sympathetically.

"You are a mother and a mother's heart never guides her children down the wrong path," Shabnam reassured, her plump hand squeezing mine.

The children, exhausted from the bus ride, slept well while I nodded off, waking periodically to find myself still in Herat, unable to believe that I'd actually set off on a journey so dangerous with three small children. In the dark room, amid the hush of night breathing, I still wondered if I'd made the right choice.

What was it that my orchard angel had promised me so many years ago?

In the darkness, when you cannot see the ground under your feet and when your fingers touch nothing but night, you are not alone. I will stay with you as moonlight stays on water.

I closed my eyes and prayed he hadn't forgotten me.

CHAPTER 17
FEREIBA

There wasn't much time for me to reconsider. If I'd had just one more day, I might have lost my nerve. The desert before us made me dizzy with fear.

Aziz was not nursing well. He was sleeping more and fussy when awake. The journey to Herat had not been an easy one and we were all exhausted.

In the afternoon, I leaned over my sleeping children and kissed their foreheads gently, whispering to them to coax their eyes open. Night, the time when the border was most vulnerable to trespass, was approaching. Holes opened up and scared, desperate people crawled through. While war had turned some Afghans into lions, it had turned a good number of us into mice as well.

Shabnam gave us bread for our journey. Asim led us to the meeting point. Saleem and Samira followed his footsteps. They held hands as dusk settled in, a half-moon luminous in the cloudless sky. We stood at the storefront of a mechanic's shop and waited. It could be minutes or hours, Asim had said with a shrug, but the van would come.

Forty minutes later, with Aziz twisting and grunting uncomfortably, a van rounded the corner. I pushed the children behind me, pressing them against the shop's façade. The van came to a stop just a few feet from us.

"Get in," whispered the driver. *"Quickly."*

This was Mahmood's plan for us, I reminded myself, as I ushered my children into the van. *Trust him that this is the right thing to do.*

Two other families were packed into the van, each with four or five children. I whispered a greeting and led my family into a corner of the hollowed-out vehicle.

There was no room for idle chatter. Too much weighed on our minds. Thick silence was cut by Aziz's noisy breathing as it harmonized with the rusted engine.

Just outside Herat, the driver stopped the van and leaned over the back of his seat.

"From here, we cross the desert and then the border. You will all pay now or be left here." His tone was dry.

The driver got out of the van and opened

the back door. He pointed at the man sitting across from me who crept out to settle his family's fare. His wife and children watched on anxiously, nervous to be even a few feet apart from their father.

Next went the father of the second family. I looked at my children, watched them stare unabashedly at the fathers.

I must be everything to them, I told myself.

I stepped down to meet the driver, leaving Aziz on Saleem's lap. I handed over a small envelope and waited while the driver nimbly thumbed through the bills I'd already counted and recounted.

"You and your children are traveling alone."

I nodded.

"That's a problem. I don't think we can take you."

I tried to steady my voice.

"What's the problem? The money is all there."

"You know how it is. I'm taking a risk by bringing people across. But you, an unescorted woman . . . you understand? This is a much bigger risk for me and not one I can do for this price. It's not fair to me."

Though Asim had predicted this, I seethed to hear the driver's reasoning. If we were stopped, no one would pay a bigger price than I. But I was prepared. I would play his game.

"Please. Have mercy on me and my children. We have nothing left. What are we to do for food?"

"Sister, what is anyone to do for food? I have children too. Do I look like a king? Who will have mercy on me?"

The border was so close I could taste it.

"This is all I have left," I said and reluctantly slipped a gold ring with a turquoise stone off my finger. "This was a wedding gift from my late mother-in-law, God give her peace. Now I pray I'll find a way to feed my children."

"God is great, my sister," he said as he stole a quick glance at the stone before stuffing it in his jacket pocket. "Your children will be provided for."

The road roughened as we left Herat's limits. When the van came to a stop, we all held our breath. I put my hand on Saleem's.

"This is the border," the driver announced. "The guarded passage is ten kilometers that way. There's a trail that cuts through the mountains. I'll lead you across. It's not easy, but many have crossed it before you. Keep your children close and keep them quiet. Watch your feet. There are loose stones, scorpions, and snakes to worry about. Watch for my flashlight."

Saleem and Samira pressed themselves against me, terrified by the driver's warnings. Under my *burqa*, Aziz's breaths felt moist and rapid on my neck, as if even he felt nervous.

We trod carefully, following the distant yellow glow of our guide's flashlight. When I heard a hiss, I nudged the children along without breathing a word. They were frightened enough without naming the shadows. For hours, we stumbled through the dark, falling and scraping knees, bending ankles. I'd flipped my *burqa* back and let it drape behind me, like the other women. I'd swaddled Aziz with a long muslin cloth and tied him around my torso. I held my children's hands as we did our best to tread carefully.

Samira's hand pulled out of mine and I heard a yelp.

"Samira! What happened? Where are you?" I strained my eyes to make out her shape.

"She fell, Madar," Saleem said calmly. "I'm holding her hand." Even as Samira's ankle had turned in under her, he had held on.

Samira whimpered softly in the dark.

"Can you stand, my love?" I watched the

distance between us and the others widen.

"Get her up and walking," the driver hissed at us. "We cannot fall behind."

I felt around for her ankle. My hand touched something wet and warm, and I realized she must have cut it against a rock. I prayed it was not too bad. I took a scarf from our bag of clothing and tied it around her ankle.

The driver's light grew dimmer. My heart fluttered with alarm.

My daughter pressed on, though I could tell she was limping. Saleem did his best to support her weight, but he too needed to be careful with his footing.

God forgive me for putting them through this.

An hour later, the mother of the family ahead of us slipped, with her two-year-old in her arms. Their cries rang out in the night.

The flashlight turned on them. The mother's face looked horrified.

"What have I done?" Her husband was at her side, helping her up. The baby's arm had twisted grotesquely, bent between the elbow and wrist in an obvious break.

They were distraught. I wanted to help but didn't know how.

The baby howled when his father tried to touch his arm. The driver stood over them, sighed heavily, and spit into the darkness.

"Look, there's nothing you can do for him here. If you have something with sugar, give it to him. It might quiet him down. We must keep moving. He'll fall asleep soon enough."

The baby's moans carried on into the day. His mother held him gingerly and did her best to keep his arm from jostling.

It was easier to walk in the day but harder to look at the children. Their eyes were heavy, their feet blistered and bleeding, and their lips parched.

We stopped only for a thirty-minute break — daylight would be upon us soon. I rationed out our food and gave the children a few bites of Raisa's biscuits. I dripped water into Aziz's mouth, but he was listless. I nursed him under my *burqa*. He suckled, but weakly.

Saleem and Samira curled up next to each other and fell asleep in seconds. Samira's ankle was swollen and purple. Her small gash had started to scab. I ached to think how she'd kept up with us.

At dawn, Iran came into view. Waiting for us, at the foot of the trail and at the side of a small road, was a dark van. The driver motioned for us to follow as he jogged to the vehicle. He slid the door open and we piled in, the smell of stale sweat and acrid breath concentrating in the small space. I could see my hesitant relief mirrored in the faces around me. We'd made it this far but were still very close to the border. If the van were stopped, we might be sent back to the checkpoint and returned to Afghanistan.

Our guide sat by the van's driver. The two spoke in low tones, pointing at the road ahead of them.

I watched the dusty landscape through the window. Though Iran had the same colors and smells of Afghanistan, it felt foreign and strange. We were far from home.

The little boy's groans synchronized with Aziz's. His crooked arm lay across his chest, swollen, contorted, and purple. His mother stared at it helplessly and wiped away tears. Her husband called out to the driver.

"Excuse me, friends, but we need to take my son to a doctor. His arm is in terrible condition and he's in much pain."

"The contacts at your destination will help you find a doctor."

"But, please, it's been broken for so long. It's getting worse every minute."

"I don't know where the doctors are and you are in this country illegally, in case you have forgotten. If you want to be safe, you will wait until your contacts can take him somewhere."

Luckily, Samira's ankle had not gotten much worse. It was still swollen, but the gash was healing. Aziz was a bigger concern, lacking the energy to fuss.

The open landscape gave way to buildings and a grid of roads. The smugglers dropped us off at an apartment building in Tayyebat, a border town. It was a four-story building with cloudy windows that overlooked the street.

"Take off those *burqas*. Wear these." The driver tossed two black cloaks into the back of the van so we could better blend in with the Iranian women.

We were sent to an apartment on the second floor. The other family headed up to the third floor.

"May God be with you," I said as we parted ways. "I'll pray for your little boy's arm to heal quickly."

"And may God be with you too, my brave sister," came the mother's broken voice. "Allah keep you all healthy and safe in this journey."

The trip from Afghanistan to Iran had been a largely silent one. It was not a time for making friends. I did not have enough for my own children and could not afford to befriend a stranger who might take any little bit of what we had.

The door opened and a woman ushered us into the two-room apartment. I was grateful for shelter. This was one way for sympathetic Iranians to house Afghan refugees and earn some money in the meantime. I was much more at ease around this strange woman than the shifty men who'd gotten us here. She fed us a simple feast of bread and yogurt. We slept soundly for the first time in days.

After one night, we were put on a local bus and sent to a similar apartment in Mashhad, a bigger city where we would be staying until we were ready for the next leg of our journey. Our time in Mashhad was relatively easy. We were hosted by another Afghan family who had fled Kabul a few months earlier. They had crossed the same treacherous desert trail and narrowly escaped capture once they entered Iran. They were living as refugees now with modest means but generous spirits.

In exchange for a small sum, we were given a room and a place to take a warm bath. The children were fed and Samira's ankle returned to a proper size and color. Aziz cooed contentedly — a most inspirational sound. We were restored.

Iran had opened its doors and accepted

hordes of Afghans as refugees. Countless others lived there illegally. But Iran was never in the plan Mahmood and I had devised. Many Afghans complained of being treated poorly, and opportunities were scarce. If I wanted to give my children a real chance, we needed to continue. The longer we waited, the heavier our feet would become.

Within a month, I'd planned our route to Turkey. I booked bus tickets to Tehran, the country's capital. In my flowing black *burqa,* my tired children in tow, we blended in with Iran's peasant class, migrating across the country in search of a better life.

From Tehran, we caught another bus and traveled across the border into Turkey, this time using the passports Abdul Rahim had secured for us. The customs officer stared at me and my passport picture, stamped it, and handed it back with an uninvited caress on my wrist that I ignored in light of our falsified visas.

We'd put one more border behind us — one more buffer between us and the life we'd left behind. Turkey looked less like Afghanistan than Iran had. The language, the earth, the food — everything was one degree more foreign. On reconsideration, it was we who were foreign. We were drifting into lands where we were not welcome and scared every step of the way that we would be sent home, a fate I could not bear to consider.

I was leading my children into an unknown world, and whatever happened to us, to them, was my responsibility. It would have been easier to close my eyes and disappear, to not be responsible for their next meal or keeping them safe while we trespassed borders. But these lives depended on me, even Saleem who could brood like a grown man and questioned the choices I made. The shadow of hair on his upper lip, the way he shouldered our bags, the wristwatch he coveted — Saleem believed he was a man. As much as I needed him to be just that, I was also afraid for him. The person most likely to drown in the river is the one who believes he can swim.

In a pouch I'd sewn into my dress was all the money I'd managed to gather by selling off our household belongings. Gone were our dishes, a silver plated tray, a chiming clock. I kept my jewelry in the pouch as well. It was all we had to finance our trip to England. Mahmood had chosen England because we had family there. I wasn't sure it was the best decision but he insisted.

I did not want to impose on our relatives in England, especially when I didn't have Mahmood by my side. But to change our destination would be letting a time in my past matter more than it should. I could not afford to be sentimental about material belongings, but I could be as emotional as I wanted about my husband. I wouldn't change our destination now. I wouldn't change a thing Mahmood had decided for us. In some way, it made me feel my fingers were still intertwined with his, following his lead.

Besides, I had no better plan in mind. We would go to London.

CHAPTER 18
FEREIBA

We landed in the small Turkish town of Intikal, a cozy village skirted by large plots of farmland. The air was clean, and the green landscape reminded me of my father's orchard. On our first afternoon, we set out to secure shelter. Thankfully, Mahmood had taught Saleem enough English that he was able to communicate with at least some locals. My son's English was undeniably better than mine.

"Come, Saleem. Let's go and talk with the men there," I said, pointing to a group of men coming out of a *masjid.* I fixed my head scarf. I'd put away the black Iranian *burqa* to better blend with the dress of this new country. It felt good to wear a simple head scarf. It was like slipping into my past.

"Madar-*jan,* why don't you wait here with the little ones. It's better if I talk to them alone. You don't speak much English anyway."

I wanted to disagree.

"I can do this, Madar," Saleem said, looking straight at me.

I nodded.

I watched on as Saleem walked from one man to the next, each waving him off with a head shake, a scowl, a shrug. Saleem looked around. I saw him toy with the watch on his wrist, glance at it briefly, and survey a group standing near the mosque's side entrance.

An older man emerged, dressed in a suit that showed the fades and frays of frequent use. Saleem's eyes were drawn to him as were mine. His stature, his salt-and-pepper hair, and the gentle smile on his face — if my husband had lived another twenty years, he would have looked like this man. Whether Saleem had the same thought or if there was something else about the man that drew him in, I dared not ask. He approached cautiously. The man cocked his ear as Saleem spoke then looked over in our direction, squinting.

The man's name was Hakan Yilmaz. He and his wife, Hayal, lived in a modest home just a few blocks from the main part of the village. He'd worked for years as a professor of politics while Hayal had been an elementary school teacher. They'd raised two boys, now grown men with families of their own.

When the couple retired, they moved back to Intikal to be near Hakan's sisters and brothers. They were warm and unassuming people — more worldly than their modest village home would indicate. They were the kind of people who saw an Afghan mother traveling with three children and could guess the story behind such a sight.

Saleem had explained to Hakan that we were looking for simple shelter and that we would gladly pay for a brief stay. Hakan put a hand on Saleem's shoulder and led us to his home where we met his wife, Hayal. Hayal, a petite woman with soft eyes, was delighted to have a babbling baby in their home. Long retired, she still had the presence of a schoolteacher. Her brown hair was tied back into a neat bun and she wore a simple navy blue cotton dress with a small tan sash around her waist. Samira took to her immediately.

They showed us to a small, vacant bedroom with its own door to the outside. We were welcome to use the kitchen, they said, and made no mention of how long we could stay.

My heart found an ally in Hayal, though we did not share a language. In words and gestures she likely did not understand, I explained that I'd been a teacher in Afghanistan before the Taliban and that the children had fallen behind despite my home-schooling efforts.

I nearly sang out with joy when we laid our heads on soft pillows, our full bellies and the kindness of strangers keeping us warm.

The next morning Hayal brought out a crate of elementary math books and stories in English. Samira's eyes widened with an excitement that thrilled and hurt me. I explained to Hayal that Samira was bright but hadn't spoken since we'd left home. Hayal seemed to understand, connecting the missing father with my daughter's mutism. She looked over at Samira and patted the empty chair next to her. Samira sat down as Hayal turned to the first page.

I could hear Saleem in the next room, and though I knew only a handful of English words, I caught that he was talking to Hakan about finding a job. He would work hard, he promised.

I hadn't spoken to Saleem about working. I stepped away from Hayal and Samira and walked over to the window. Hakan spoke of nearby farms where migrant workers found employment. I wanted to interrupt, but I didn't.

My thoughts drifted.

I'd had no idea when Mahmood's hand was first placed in mine what he would come to mean to me. Among the few photographs I'd brought was one from our wedding, a simple ceremony. I'd worn an emerald green dress, pleated from the waist down and with lacy shoulders. My face had been made up by one of KokoGul's friends. My lips and eyelids were heavy with colors that I would never again wear. Mahmood wore a black suit, the collar of his dress shirt flaring out past the lapels, and a red rose tucked into his breast pocket. Mahmood had looked steadily into the camera, but I stared blankly at the floor.

When I looked at that picture, I wanted to go back in time and tell myself to look at him, my husband. I wanted to tell that bride that she, like the guests eager for a lavish celebration, should rejoice in this union.

He was much more than a husband. It took time for our love to grow but it did, in patches and spurts, fed by the good and bad of the world around us. Every promise we kept, every squeeze of the hand, every secretive smile we exchanged, each crying child we comforted — every one of those moments narrowed the distance between us. By that night, that horrible night when

Mahmood was ripped from our lives, the space between us had vanished. We were pressed against each other, a husband and wife bound together not by marriage, but by the harmony of our hearts.

Death could not undo us, I'd learned. My *hamsar* was with me still. He would watch over us, my beloved husband, as we made our way into tomorrow.

Fate will make things right in the end, though only after the work has been done, the tears have been shed and the sleepless nights have been endured.

I wanted to believe him.

For my family to reach a new life, I would need to rely on Saleem. I would need to admit he was not a child. Mahmood had been better at giving Saleem the space to stretch his wings. I coddled my children, ever afraid of being an inadequate mother. I wanted to do all the things for them that hadn't been done for me. I wanted them to feel taken care of, loved, and secure. I was failing.

Saleem looked at me differently now. Gone was the boyish sparkle, that trusting gaze that made me feel like I could do no wrong. He stood by my side, not trailing behind. It was time for me to give him the space he needed.

I had brought us this far — from Kabul, through Iran and into Turkey. This had been my journey. My story.

But what would happen to us from this moment on would be as much Saleem's tale as it would be mine. I could not continue telling his story for him. It would not make me less of a mother if I let go of his hand and let him stand on his own feet. If only Mahmood were around to tell me I was doing the right thing and that I was no less of a mother for mothering him less.

I could hear my husband's hushed voice. I could feel his hands resting on my shoulders. If I closed my eyes, I could almost feel his kiss on my forehead.

Let him speak, Ferei. You've told our story. Now let Saleem tell his.

CHAPTER 19
SALEEM

The following morning, Hakan took Saleem to the village limits where leather-faced people huddled in groups. There were men and women of all shapes and sizes, and a handful of children clinging to their mothers' skirts. Hakan explained that trucks would pick up the workers and deliver them to the farmlands where work was plentiful.

Hakan felt uncomfortable leaving Saleem, but his presence was not helpful. He turned the corner and went to pay his sister a visit. It was spring and temperatures were rising, even this early in the morning. Saleem touched his fingers to his face, feeling the row of fine hairs on his upper lip. This day marked a new Saleem. He was determined and ready to be treated like a man. Even his mother had looked at him differently this morning — as if she could sense the change in him.

Aziz, a nomad baby, now was starting to

grab at things they dangled in front of him and cooing. He would likely be crawling soon, Madar-*jan* predicted. Saleem watched his baby brother growing and wished his own metamorphosis into manhood would come with the same speed. He wanted hair on his face, chest, and everywhere else he knew it was supposed to be. He looked himself over carefully in the privacy of his baths, noting the changes that no one saw but him. He wanted his arms to thicken with the road map of veins he'd traced on his father's forearms. His voice cracked and wobbled, so his words were sparse. Soon, he hoped, his voice would catch up to him.

The responsibility he felt for his family and the respect Hakan showed him made him feel like a man even if his body didn't. Saleem moved about in the crowd, looking for friendly faces. Hakan knew none of the farmers and was not able to offer much beyond leading him to this gathering place. Saleem was unsure what would happen once he arrived at the farm and looked for someone who might help.

Most of the people in the group were older. They smoked cigarettes and squinted under the bright, morning sun. There were about thirty people in all. The women kept to themselves and formed a loose mass off to the side. Some wore colorful triangles of cloth as head scarves, tied primly under the chin, with modest long-sleeved shirts and calf-length skirts. Taken together, they were an eclectic bunch, with a mosaic of patterns that dizzied the eye.

Saleem wanted to approach the women but refrained. If he wanted to be treated as a man, he would have to act like one. He took a deep breath and sat on the curb beside a man who looked to be in his forties. Saleem rubbed his palms on his thighs, trying to think of how to strike up a conversation. The man cleared his throat roughly and spat a thick, yellow glob onto the sidewalk. A slammed door would have been more inviting.

Saleem's stomach turned. He stood and looked at his watch, touched its face, and ran his fingers over the worn leather band. Toward the back of the crowd stood three men in their late thirties, chatting casually. Saleem took a chance. He walked over, but just as he neared, they stopped speaking.

"Hello. You are working on farm?" he asked, his voice crossing an octave. Saleem felt his face warm with embarrassment.

The men watched him inquisitively. One nodded, a man dressed in a lime green shirt and loose navy slacks, who looked to be the eldest of the three. Saleem was surprised to hear him speak in Pashto.

"Are you Afghan?"

The Waziri family spoke Dari, but Saleem was able to recognize and understand basic conversation in Pashto as well. He nodded emphatically.

"Yes, yes I am!" he affirmed in Dari.

"You have come to work?" one of them asked in amusement.

"Yes, we've been here only a few days." Saleem combined Dari with Pashto. The men seemed to understand.

"So you are traveling with people?"

"Yes, with my family. My mother, my sister, and my brother." One of the men took out a half-smoked cigarette and relit it. His brows perked at the family inventory.

"Where did you come from?"

"From Kabul. We went to Herat and then to Iran. From Iran we came to Turkey, but we are trying to get to England." Saleem was relieved to have found Afghans, as if he'd come upon a street sign confirming his route.

"England, huh?" They all chuckled. "With a mother, and two more kids? Hard enough to travel alone. If you're smart, you'll stay here and find a way to make money without getting arrested. That's all you can hope for."

Saleem did not appreciate their pessimism. He decided to shift the conversation.

"How do you find work at the farms?"

"You'll see, and you'll wish you never asked. Trucks come and take you to farms bigger than you've ever seen. You go to the farmhouses and see which farmer will pay for a day's work. They'll offer you pay that will stink worse than the animal dung you'll clean."

"How much will they pay?"

"Does it matter? You're not in any position to negotiate. If you can get something to eat from them, do it. It's the next best thing to money."

The man with the cigarette finally spoke. He'd been wanting to ask something.

"Where is the rest of your family now? Are they here?"

"Yes, we're staying with a Turkish family — a husband and wife. They've given us a small room, but I don't know for how long."

"And you have a brother and a sister?"

"Yes, and my mother."

"My friend, what is your dear sister's name?" he said with a wink.

Saleem clenched his teeth. "Thanks for

the information," he muttered. He gave a nod to the man in green and ignored the other two. Saleem walked away and fumed at the way his own people would treat him, as if he was incapable of defending his family's honor. He cursed his stupidity for being so loose lipped with strangers.

Saleem turned the corner and found himself staring through the window of a ceramics store, the glass so smudged it felt as if he were gazing into a different time. Inside, a man in his forties swept the floor slowly.

Everywhere he turned, Saleem saw his father.

He'd even seen him in Hakan. Something about the way he'd stepped out of the *masjid,* the look of peace on his face, fresh from prayers, had been reminiscent of Padar-*jan.* He was everywhere and nowhere.

The sound of engines brought Saleem back. He returned to the crowd and piled into the back of the three trucks idling on the corner. He made sure to stay clear of the Afghans he'd met.

The farms were just as they'd described. Each house sat on its own plot, separated from its neighbor by acres upon acres of green rows. When the trucks stopped, the medley of passengers disembarked with their small satchels and scattered toward their respective farms. Saleem stood in the dirt road, unsure. He watched the able-bodied workers disperse, going left and right. One older woman plodded down the road, the tap of a cane setting her pace. She seemed to be headed toward a run-down yellow home. Saleem followed.

In the front of the house, a boy no more than eight or nine years old brushed the flank of a dusty-brown donkey. The sprawling house was in worse shape than its neighbors but surrounded by gridded acres of ample crops. Surely this house, whose only field help seemed to be an older woman, could use a helping hand.

Saleem let her lead the way.

About halfway to the house, she shot a look over her shoulder without pausing her step. She was round and scowled. Saleem quickened his pace until he was near enough to make out the lines of her weathered face. He cleared his throat and said hello. She did not look Afghan. She had choppy, black hair cut like a man's and wore a floral print dress, the material so stiff it seemed to hover around her legs without touching them.

She looked at Saleem and mumbled something in response. Saleem pointed at the yellow farmhouse ahead of them and asked her if they needed more people to work. She frowned and shook her head. Saleem, unsure if she'd understood his question, continued on.

In his best English, Saleem offered his services to Mr. Polat, the lanky landowner. Mr. Polat looked him up and down, shrugged his shoulders, and introduced him to farm labor.

At the end of the first day, Saleem lingered, thinking the farmer would pay him for his labor. But Mr. Polat shook his head, refusing to pay for a day of learning. He told Saleem to return tomorrow and earn his money. Saleem bit his tongue until he was back on the dirt path at sunset. He kicked and spat at the ground. The woman who'd worked alongside him watched without comment. As they waited for the trucks to take them back to the village, Saleem reached into his pocket and strapped the watch back on to his wrist. How would he explain to Madar-*jan* that he had worked from morning to evening without receiving any wages?

Saleem begrudgingly worked four full days with his only compensation being a piece of grilled chicken between two slices of bread.

He picked tomatoes until his back ached and his fingers had numbed. The woman he'd followed to this house was Armenian, he learned later in the week. Though she spoke no English, she managed to communicate two important things to Saleem: first, how to distinguish the ripe tomatoes from the unripe by the flesh and weight; and, second, that Polat would pay him eventually. Saleem tolerated the unpaid week because he had few options and feared going through another probationary period if he tried another farmhouse.

At the end of the week, Polat handed Saleem a few crumpled bills. There was no discussion or negotiation. Saleem stared at the money in his palm, nothing much to speak of, and nodded. It wasn't even enough to buy his family a meal.

From that day on, Saleem was paid at the end of the day, but the amount was inconsistent and unrelated to how many buckets of tomatoes he was able to fill from the fields. When the Armenian woman saw Saleem fingering his bills in dismay, she griped alongside him in her own tongue.

Soon Saleem's nails became ragged and rimmed with dirt. He developed calluses on his palms and on the pads of his fingers.

His face was salty with perspiration, but he felt good. He worked like a man. Like his father might have. The money wasn't much, but he turned it over to his mother with pride.

Hakan didn't ask Saleem about his wages. Hayal accepted the few bills that Madar-*jan* quietly tucked into her hand every week, but soon after she would spend it on food they shared with the Waziri family. They seemed happy to have children in the home and Madar-*jan* did what she could to look after the house. She swept the floors, washed dishes, and did laundry while Hayal tutored a silent but inquisitive Samira. She would tap her pencil and look to Hayal when she filled in the answers to the arithmetic problems.

They were comfortable in Intikal, but Saleem still worried.

"Madar-*jan,* it will be forever before we are able to save up enough money to get us to Greece. Maybe we can ask some family for money? Maybe we should call England?"

Madar-*jan* dried her hands on her apron and sighed.

"My son, I've been thinking the same thing. I'll try to phone them, but I don't think they have much to send. Last time I called, your uncle said they were barely able to pay for their daughter's school supplies. Maybe things are better now. I don't see what options we have." Fereiba began to think out loud. "Maybe we shouldn't go to London. Maybe we should start elsewhere."

But there was nowhere else to go. The rest of the family had dispersed to India, Canada, and Australia. India offered little opportunity for a better life while Canada and Australia were simply unreachable without a visa.

Madar-*jan* leaned against the counter and stared at the ceiling tiles. Yesterday, she had started cleaning some of the neighbors' houses, thanks to Hayal's referrals, but it was not enough to keep Saleem home. She looked at her son.

"It's very bad there, isn't it? On the farm?"

He had started to tell her about the farm after his second day there, but the look on her face made him stop short. He smiled and shook his head. Her face relaxed. They would survive in this way, telling each other that things were better than they were.

Chapter 20
Saleem

Mr. Polat made Saleem's fourteen-hour days long and hard. It was August and the height of tomato season. Work was plentiful, even on the ramshackle Polat farm, with its soil rockier than all the neighbors.

Saleem learned to tell the hour by the sun's position overhead. From morning, he willed his shadow to grow longer and longer so that his workday would come to an end. He got a fifteen-minute break when Polat's wife would bring out sandwiches. Every day, a thin sandwich with a glass of lukewarm water. As monotonous as it was, the food soothed his growling stomach, and the water put out the burning of his dry throat.

Mr. Polat and his wife had four children. The young boy who had watched Saleem in the front yard that first day was the middle child, Ahmet. Behind him were twin girls, around three years old. The oldest child was a girl, Ekin. Her name meant harvest in

Turkish.

Ekin was around Saleem's age, lanky like her father and with similarly drawn features. She was unattractive, even to a sheltered adolescent boy. Her skin was freckled and her hair a stringy mop of curls.

Ekin watched Saleem from a distance as she helped her mother hang laundry on the clothesline behind the farmhouse. By the end of August, she was free of her studies and lingered around the farm. Bored, she spent more time around Saleem and the Armenian woman. She especially liked to saunter about when Saleem cleaned out the barn.

This was a new chore that Mr. Polat had assigned to Saleem as it required more effort than the woman could have mustered. The barn sheltered two donkeys, three goats, and a few chickens. The air was heavy and rank with the smell of dung and wet fleece. Saleem had never tended to animals before, and the odors seared his nostrils. He dreaded those days when Mr. Polat tapped him on the shoulder and pointed to the barn, a rake in his hand. Polat took a few moments to point out what needed to be done and walked out.

Saleem raked the moist hay and soil into the wheelbarrow and carted it off to a corner of the farm where the manure would eventually compost. The stench clung to his clothing and skin. Saleem kept to himself on the bus in the evening, knowing he turned noses on his way home.

While Saleem breathed through his mouth, Ekin would wander idly past the open barn doors, again and again. She began to clear her throat as she passed by. Soon, she began to sit on a crate in the corner, a casual observer to his work. How or why she stomached the smell baffled Saleem. One day, she began to speak to him in broken, elementary-level English.

"Not good," she observed. "Still dirty."

"I am not finished," Saleem answered, keeping his eyes on the ground. He doubted a Turkish father would be much different from an Afghan one when it came to his daughters. He wanted no problems with Polat. Ekin had a tall tumbler of water in her hand. She gulped loudly.

The barn's dust had dried his tongue and airways. The sound of her drinking made him furious but he said nothing.

"What is your name?" When she did not get a response, Ekin repeated her question, louder and annoyed. "I said, what is your name?"

"Saleem," he mumbled.

"Saleem?" Ekin played with her stringy hair. She picked through the ends, her fingers getting locked in the knots. "This is name for old man. Why you have old man name?"

Saleem's lips tightened.

"Why you not clean there? It will still smell if you do not clean this. The animals will be sick. My father will not be happy."

Saleem remained tight-lipped, finished as quickly as he could, and returned to the fields where the Armenian woman raised an eyebrow and nodded in the direction of the barn. When he shook his head in frustration, she smiled. They were beginning to understand each other.

A week later, Ekin saw Saleem make his way into the barn. She followed after, turned the crate over, and sat on it, stretching her legs out before her.

"The summer is too hot. I am in the house all day. It is too long! School is better. Better to see my friends."

Saleem's silence was not a deterrent.

"Here, there is nothing. I cannot talk to my friends. I am alone." She paused. "You do not go to school so you do not know. Have you been to a school?"

Saleem raked harder.

"I know the work people do not go to school. But my father and mother say I must learn so I will not be a worker. They say I must be a schoolgirl and be clean, have a nice life. Why you do not talk? It is good you are not in school. In school the teachers say you must talk!" She laughed, tapping her heels on the straw-covered floor.

Mrs. Polat's voice rang out. Ekin stood with a heavy sigh. She brushed the straw off the seat of her pants and left the barn, throwing Saleem a curious look on her way out. Saleem was thankful for the reprieve. A few moments with Ekin was more exhausting than a fourteen-hour workday. But before he could fully enjoy the silence, she returned with his lunch sandwich in her hand.

"Here," Ekin called out from the barn door. She paused and looked down at the sandwich in her hands. She brought it to her face, so close that Saleem could see her nose brush against the meat. "It is good. We can eat together?"

Ekin sat on the crate and just as Saleem walked over to claim his sandwich, she carefully pulled it into two pieces and handed him half. Saleem watched angrily as the bread and chicken disappeared between her teeth.

"This food is for me," he objected.

"But we eat together," Ekin replied, confused. "Like friends, okay?"

"No. No. No. Not okay!" Saleem's back ached. His fingertips burned, and his stomach growled angrily.

Ekin seemed surprised by his reaction. After a moment she stood, reached into her dress pocket, and pulled out a packet of two small sugar cookies. She tossed the packet onto the crate and walked out of the barn without saying a word.

Saleem, furious, could think only that he would be hungry for the rest of the day. The half sandwich she'd left him was not much sustenance, and there was no use complaining to Polat or his wife. He threw the rake to the ground and shoved the half sandwich into his mouth. He looked the sugar cookies over and wondered what they meant as he scarfed them down.

Ekin did not venture out into the fields, but Saleem could feel her eyes on him from a distance, watching him pick tomatoes as she pretended to read a book. The Armenian woman noticed Ekin's presence too and clucked her tongue disapprovingly. She put two fingers to her lips and shook her head. She pointed to the six rows of tomato plants left to harvest and patted her pocket.

Say nothing, she was telling him. *Get back to work and earn your money.*

Saleem knew it was sound advice. As a young child, he'd seldom worried about money. If he did think about money, it was to wonder if he had enough to pay for a piece of candy or a soda in the market. They were far from wealthy, but Padar-*jan* made sure they had plenty. After his death, Madar-*jan* rationed their savings and meted out small allowances for groceries and the absolute essentials. Saleem knew they had little, but it never occurred to him that their funds would dry up entirely. Now that he was passing his wages over to his mother, he understood that they were financially in a very precarious position.

There are too many of us, Saleem thought on the truck ride home. He recalled the thick envelope of cash his mother had traded Abdul Rahim for the documents. The price of documents, food, and smuggling fees multiplied by four left the Waziri family with little reserve. Samira was too young to realize how hard Saleem worked every day. She stayed home and helped Madar-*jan* with chores but only when Hayal wasn't catching her up on school lessons. Aziz was even needier.

Saleem regretted his thoughts. He loved

232

his sister and brother very much, but the frustration and fatigue was beginning to wear him thin.

Every day, his mother needed more of him. Saleem ignored his desire to curl up against her. There was no room for him to be a child. Saleem still ached for his father, but he often thought it was Padar-*jan*'s decisions that had put their lives in danger. On other sleepless nights, Saleem lamented his childhood mischief and the disappointment he'd caused his father. He was a kaleidoscope of feelings when it came to his parents.

And now Saleem was the breadwinner. The more he thought about it, the more he felt like the head of their family and the less he felt like taking orders from others. Mr. Polat kept his burgeoning adolescent ego in check but when it came to his mother, Saleem's tongue was loosening. He said things he would not have dared to say a year ago. He shot her looks he knew were out of line, but he gave himself latitude to do so. He worked long hours, kept the family fed, and wanted his opinions respected.

He returned to the Yilmaz home to find his mother cleaning the kitchen. Samira and the baby were already asleep.

"Are they all right?" he asked, slumping

into the chair.

"They're fine. Aziz's eyes look for you, though," she offered with a weak smile. She slid a plate of food in front of him and sat with him while he ate. Things were not fine, he knew, but she wasn't going to burden her young son with her worries. He was doing enough.

It was good to be cared for, Saleem thought, as he fell onto the floor cushion and closed his eyes.

CHAPTER 21
FEREIBA

"Why is he always sick?" Saleem asked. He'd walked in to find me sponge-bathing his baby brother. Aziz was pale and whimpering. He'd vomited twice already.

I wrapped a towel around Aziz and laid him on the floor gently. I didn't have a real answer for Saleem.

"I think it's the changes. The air, the food — everything is different here. And he's so little. His body must be having a hard time adjusting." I drizzled olive oil onto my palm and rubbed my hands to warm them. Even as I gently massaged Aziz's chest and belly he seemed to be uncomfortable. "Maybe Aziz needs some vitamins to make him stronger."

Aziz hadn't gained much weight since we'd arrived in Turkey. I was trying everything I could. I used the few Turkish words I'd learned in the market to purchase fruits and vegetables. *Havuc, bezelye, muz.* When my vocabulary failed me, I resorted to pointing and rudimentary sign language. I picked through the herb bundles and found those I knew had healing properties. I boiled them and spooned the tea into Aziz's mouth. I fed him the greenest spinach, the juiciest pears, and ground-up chunks of meat with an extra bit of fat on them. None of it seemed to make an ounce of difference.

Saleem walked into the kitchen. I heard his heavy sigh and the wooden chair legs sliding against the linoleum tiles. My explanation hadn't satisfied either of us.

"We will take him to the doctor tomorrow, Saleem," I heard Hayal say. "Eat your dinner. An empty stomach will only make you more upset."

Samira was in the kitchen as well. She'd set out to prepare supper for her brother as soon as she heard him come through the door. Everything she'd felt for her father had been redirected to Saleem, a deep adoration that came with expectations and needs. She was that bulky winter coat that kept him warm but slowed his step.

Samira did what she could to help. She helped mash fruits and vegetables to feed Aziz. She watched him while I went to the neighbors' homes to clean or do small jobs.

She always looked drained when I returned.

"Aziz is not easy, *janem.* He's scarcely any better when he's with me."

Samira was unconvinced.

Hayal and I traveled down the long village road to see Doctor Ozdemir who had, years ago, cared for her sons. The doctor was still practicing and had been joined by his son. Their home was at the far end of town. Father and son saw patients in a small room adjacent to the house. The setting was simple but cozy, with the doctor's wife stopping in with a small plate of cookies.

I was nervous, too nervous to eat anything. Mrs. Ozdemir read the apprehension on my face and I could see she wanted to say something but we did not speak the same language. She exchanged a few words with Hayal and placed a comforting hand on my shoulder.

I looked at my son and, for a second, saw him through Mrs. Ozdemir's eyes. Wisps of hair clung to his moist forehead. His head was starting to look too big for his body. He did not look well, I had to admit, and it had been so long since I'd seen him smile or say a single word. I couldn't imagine what our situation would have been like without the inordinate kindness Hakan and Hayal showed us. I wondered how I could ever repay these total strangers for all they had done.

Aziz twisted and writhed in my lap to get into a more comfortable position. He hated to lie down. I knew him well, but I could not say what was wrong with him, just that he was nothing like my other children and it frightened me.

Doctor Ozdemir entered the room, his warm smile fading when our eyes met. I realized how distressed I must have looked and stood to greet him. The doctor had a mop of gray hair, a solid paunch above his belt. I trusted him and his silver hair immediately and knew something good would come from today's visit. He nodded his head in greeting and motioned for me to take my seat again. He pulled another chair from under the counter and sat across from me.

Through a unique medley of Turkish, English, and Dari, we were able to communicate. Where words failed, we gestured and mimed. At the doctor's request, I placed Aziz on the examination table and undid his shirt and pants. Doctor Ozdemir pursed his lips in consternation even before he laid a hand on the baby. Aziz had fallen asleep but as he started to wake, his chest rose and fell dramatically. He wriggled left and right, unable to pull himself up to sitting.

Doctor Ozdemir pulled at the skin on Aziz's belly and listened intently to Aziz's chest for what seemed like an eternity. Using a light and a wooden stick, he peered into Aziz's mouth and then pressed his fingers against Aziz's round belly, again and again, inching his way across his body. My heart raced.

"Doctor-*sahib*," I interrupted as respectfully as I could. "Is there a problem?"

I looked nervously to Hayal, hoping the doctor understood.

Doctor Ozdemir sighed deeply. He removed his stethoscope from around his neck and wrapped Aziz in his blanket before placing him back in my arms. I propped him up in my lap and turned my attention back to the doctor who began to speak slowly, enunciating carefully and reading my expression. His words fell heavy on my ears as I strained to understand what he was saying. *Problem.* That was all that had been confirmed.

"What problem? Does he need antibiotics? Vitamins?"

Doctor Ozdemir shook his head no while he repeated "antibiotic" and "vitamin," words that needed no translation from Dari to Turkish.

Doctor Ozdemir pointed to Aziz's chest, to his heart and repeated the one word that he had been able to communicate. *"Problem. Kalp."*

"Kalp?" Another crossover word. *Kalp* meant heart. I felt my arms grow weak.

The doctor stood up and pulled a book from the countertop. It was a soft cover book, its binding taped together more than a few times. He began to flip through the pages to find a picture that would help him demonstrate his point, but he quickly lost patience and tossed it back onto the counter. He pulled a pencil and paper from his desk drawer and began to sketch.

I pulled my chair closer to his. He drew a heart and started to open and close his fist rhythmically. Then he drew two shapes and began exaggeratedly breathing in and out. *Lungs,* I thought. The heart and the lungs. I nodded, and the doctor returned to his rudimentary drawing. He pointed to the heart and again opened and closed his fist, but slower this time. Then he pointed to the pictures of lungs and began to shade in the bottom parts. Something was blocking up Aziz's lungs. Doctor Ozdemir again started his exaggerated breathing, but this time he did so with difficulty, breathing faster and harder, his face drawn in fatigue.

I thought a baby, my baby, was too young to have problems with his heart. I felt a sense of overwhelming hopelessness. How could we possibly fix something that was wrong with his heart?

Doctor Ozdemir knew his message had gotten across. He tapped his pencil on the sketch he held in his lap. Intikal was a small town, and there was nowhere to do the things he felt were necessary. There would be no X-rays or blood test. Aziz needed a hospital and even if we were able to reach the plentiful resources of a city, I had no money to finance all that this baby would need. Doctor Ozdemir shook his head.

The doctor had reduced my world to a graphite sketch on a scrap of paper. I needed to hear Doctor Ozdemir's grand conclusion. He rubbed at his forehead, pulled a paper pad from the pocket of his white coat, and scribbled something on it. He handed the prescription to Hayal, and between the two of them, they informed me that these medications would help keep Aziz comfortable temporarily, but that his condition would only worsen with time.

Hayal's eyes watered. She had trouble getting the words out.

It was not language that got in the way of our communications that day. Had he spoken Dari fluently, I still would not have understood my son's prognosis. The doctor looked at me, and in his eyes, I could see he was not surprised by my reaction. I would refuse to accept, he knew, just as so many mothers did up until the very end and sometimes long after.

I pushed aside everything I was being told and held on to what I could do. I needed something tangible to keep me afloat.

"I will give him this medicine," I said. "How many times a day? For how long?"

They understood me. Doctor Ozdemir made loops in the air with his pointer finger, continuously. *Hafta* meant week in both Turkish and Dari. *Every week*, he motioned with his hand that the medicine should go on. I nodded.

"Return in two weeks' time," the doctor said. Hayal nodded, thanked the doctor, and asked him something I did not catch. Doctor Ozdemir shook his head and gently waved her off. He touched my elbow and stroked Aziz's forehead before he walked out.

I was numb. Hayal started to usher me out the door with only that small square of paper in her hand.

I didn't know how much the medicine would cost. We retraced our path back to the house, a quiet between Hayal and myself. At the pharmacy, I pulled bills from my change purse to pay for the bottle of liquid the pharmacist prepared. Not wanting to wait, I pulled the blanket back from Aziz's face and pointed to his mouth. Hayal relayed my urgency and the mustached man nodded. He opened the bottle and poured a small amount into a plastic spoon. I brought the dark liquid to Aziz's thin lips.

My child's heart was more broken than mine. I buried the rage I felt toward my husband, for his decisions that had brought me here. So much was not his fault and I knew that when I had the strength to be rational. But other times, when my shoulders started to give under the pressure of it all, thoughts of my husband were clouded with resentment. I saw pigheadedness instead of perseverance, pride instead of principle, and denial instead of determination. The light of our marriage dimmed. I prayed for a way to love my husband in death as wholly as I'd loved him in life.

In the name of God, the merciful and compassionate, cried my heavy heart.

CHAPTER 22
SALEEM

Saleem had listened quietly as Madar-*jan* relayed the doctor's thoughts. She maintained her composure with clipped phrases and the reassurance that the medication had already made a difference. But the truth was in the space between her words, the hollows that Saleem and Samira had grown to recognize and fear. Samira met her brother's gaze, her face drawn under the weight of all she left unsaid.

Saleem had kept his eyes on his baby brother. Aziz was sleeping comfortably, his breathing quieter. Hakan, having heard the news from Hayal, had sighed, shaking his head. To Saleem, it was a look of pity and he resented it. He sweated in Polat's field every day so that he would not have to be pitied. The expression on Hakan's well-meaning face, the hand on his shoulder — Saleem wanted to run from it all.

Saleem sat on the edge of the school soc-

244

cer field, plucking blades of grass. Judging by the sun's position in the sky, the children should be coming out soon. He could feel them stirring in their seats, watching the minutes pass and anxiously waiting for their teachers to dismiss them. A lifetime ago, in a far-off land, Saleem had been the same — eager for the moment when he could stuff his papers and pencils into his knapsack and scurry out the door.

But that was a different time, a different Saleem. This Saleem longed for a school with classmates, with friends. He longed for a normal life. More painful than Kabul, the normal life was now touchably close and yet unreachable. The longing brought him here, to the shaded, grassy field of the schoolyard. He passed the school every day on his way to the truck stop. It was a constant reminder of how things could have been different.

Saleem had arrived at the farm earlier in the day and let Polat know he would need to leave early. He mumbled a half-truth about his brother. The farm owner had grumbled, and Saleem knew to expect a cut in his wages. But Polat had few options for labor, and Saleem knew he would be welcomed back tomorrow.

If he couldn't live a normal life, he would

watch it. He wanted just a few hours with his feet cooled by the grass. He wanted an afternoon just for himself, away from the backbreaking work.

Saleem tried to picture Aziz's heart. He could feel his own beating, pounding sometimes, in his chest. Saleem had seen an animal heart once. He had gone with his father to the butcher shop for chicken, a rare treat to mark the Eid holiday and the culmination of a long month of fasting. Their household budget had tightened when Padar-*jan*'s wages became inconsistent.

Saleem had watched as the butcher wiped his bloodied hands on a cloth and came over to speak with his father. They exchanged pleasantries before Padar-*jan* asked to see what chickens the butcher had. The butcher raised an eyebrow, and Saleem, the young son, felt his chest swell with pride. The Waziris were not the average customers asking for the cheapest cut of meat. They were here for the best.

While his father and the butcher haggled over the price, Saleem looked to see what the butcher had laid out on display. A skinned lamb was strung up on a hook. Chunks of meat and shiny organs were lined up in short rows. They fascinated and nauseated Saleem. He remembered tugging on his father's sleeve.

"Padar-*jan,* what are those?" he had whispered, not wanting to draw the butcher's attention but unable to stifle his curiosity.

"Those are chicken hearts."

Padar-*jan* and the butcher chuckled to see Saleem with one hand to his chest, trying to feel his own heart beating, his eyes glued to the apricot-sized hearts on the block.

The school doors opened and the students squeezed out in a boisterous flood. Saleem envied their schoolbags, their notebooks, their lack of responsibility.

Boys his age headed onto the field, a group of about eight or nine. Saleem looked down at his watch as they neared. He did not want to be caught gawking. The watch hands had stopped turning last night. Saleem tried winding it again though he did not expect it to help. It was an engineer's watch, an uninterpretable dial within the dial. Padar-*jan* probably would have been able to repair it. Saleem kept it on, hoping it would spring back to life spontaneously.

One of the boys on the field, the lankiest in the group, pulled a soccer ball out of a satchel. Saleem felt his feet fidget for the feel of the leather. He couldn't bring himself to get up and walk away.

They probably won't even notice me, he reasoned. He turned so that he was only half facing the boys who had begun to pass the ball around, their feet tapping as they crisscrossed the field. Their voices rang out, undoubtedly shouting obnoxious comments to one another in Turkish slang that Saleem did not understand.

They came together in a loose huddle for a moment, two boys shooting glances in Saleem's direction. Feeling like a trespasser, Saleem brought himself to standing, brushing his backside. He was about to walk away when he heard a yell in his direction. He turned reluctantly. The lanky ringleader repeated himself loudly. Saleem did not know how to respond and simply shrugged his shoulders.

"No Turkish."

"No Turkish?" The boy laughed and switched into English. "You like to play football or you like to sleep in grass?"

Saleem felt a rush. He followed the boy over to the others who had already broken into two teams. One team was short a player.

"You play with them," the lanky boy

declared. He paused and looked Saleem up and down. "You have a name?"

Saleem paused, wanting to be sure he was not being mocked.

"Saleem," he finally answered, taking his watch off and placing it in his pocket.

"Saleem? You talk slow. I hope you move fast."

Kabul had been full of boys like this. Saleem sauntered over to his designated team and greeted the guys with a quick nod. They looked him over in turn and began to assume their field positions.

As the ball tumbled from boy to boy, Saleem was transported. He was in Kabul, catching a quick street game with neighborhood friends before light fell. He ran after the ball, kicked it away from boys whose names he did not care to know. He tapped it, passing it to his new teammates, boys who otherwise in the marketplace might shun him as a foreign migrant worker. He was not an outsider here. The ball came his way again. Saleem dribbled to the goalpost, watching for defenders and trying to stay ahead of the others.

His team lost by a point but he'd played well enough to have won the respect of the group. The lanky boy gave Saleem a sidelong glance, panting and sweaty.

"Where are you from?" he asked, wiping his forehead with the back of his hand.

"Afghanistan," Saleem answered hesitantly. The boy seemed unfazed.

"My name is Kamal."

Kamal and Saleem became friends, as much as a native and an immigrant could in Intikal. From that day on, Saleem joined the boys once a week for a soccer game, returning from the Polat farm to play for an hour or two and sometimes going back to the farm to resume work. He was exhausted and ravenous on those days, but it was worth it to feel the grass under his feet, the pats on the shoulder, and the wind on his face. Polat grimaced but tolerated Saleem's absences since he made up for the work he missed.

At home, Saleem kept his new activities to himself. He could not bring himself to tell his mother that for an hour a week he felt free. He saw his mother's anxious face when he came home. She spent every moment fussing over Aziz and scrounging for any work to pad their pockets. Samira continued to pitch in, either watching Aziz while Madar-*jan* worked or helping out around the house for Hakan and Hayal. Though it felt dishonest, Saleem kept his sport to himself.

On the field, Saleem was too tongue-tied to make smart replies when the boys tossed around the usual jeers. He hoped his silence came off as cool indifference. Kamal continued to poke at Saleem and didn't seem too disappointed that he didn't get much response.

In the evenings, the boys sometimes gathered in town to have a soft drink and ogle the scantily clad women in magazine ads. Saleem only met up with them on occasion, self-conscious about his sweaty work clothes and vine-chafed hands. Unable to keep everything from his mother, he told her he'd met some nice local boys and would join them for a soda. She was encouraging, which only made him feel worse that he'd kept so much from her.

Kamal, having walked Saleem home once, knew where they lived. Still, Saleem was surprised to come home from the farm one evening and find his friend sitting in the kitchen with Hakan. On that night, Saleem learned that Kamal was as adaptive as a chameleon. It was a quality he admired for its usefulness.

"Saleem, good timing. You have a visitor," Hakan announced with a smile.

"Hello, Saleem," Kamal said jovially, rising from his chair.

"We were just chatting. I'm happy you are getting to know the neighborhood boys. And as it turns out, I know Kamal's father."

"Hello . . ." Saleem was caught off-guard. He was not thrilled to see Kamal at home. "You . . . you know his father?"

"Yes, isn't that interesting, Saleem? I had no idea that this was dear Mr. Hakan's home!"

"It is Intikal. We are bound to know each other. But I haven't seen Kamal here since he was a young boy, just barely the height of this table," Hakan said with a chuckle. Kamal grinned, looking remarkably wholesome.

"Yes, it turns out that my father and Mr. Hakan taught at the same university," he explained.

"Indeed, but Kamal's father is much younger than me. He was new — a very bright professor. The students loved him then and now. Although I'm sure his son misses having his father around during the semester."

Saleem's surprise must have been obvious in his face. He had a lot to learn about Kamal. Hakan stood up and took his teacup to the sink. He tousled Kamal's hair on the way. Saleem could understand most of their conversation but had to focus. Kamal's Turkish was a cleaned-up version of what Saleem usually heard him speaking.

"Well, you boys enjoy yourselves. Kamal, give your father my regards when you speak to him. Tell him I'll be waiting for a visit when he returns. It would be nice to catch up with him at the end of the semester."

"Of course, Mr. Hakan. I'll tell him. I'm sure he'll be most pleased to hear from you. Just a few more weeks and he'll be home."

Hakan walked out of the kitchen, and Kamal punched Saleem in the shoulder playfully.

"Hey, come on, man. Get that look off your face! And some of that sweat, too, while you're at it."

Saleem smiled sheepishly and went to wash the hard day's work from his face, neck, and arms. Madar-*jan,* Samira, and Aziz were in the back bedroom. Aziz was already asleep and Madar-*jan* was braiding Samira's hair. Saleem greeted them and leaned over to kiss his mother's cheek. She had met Kamal, she told him, and was happy that Hakan seemed to know his family. He seemed like a nice young man.

"He is," Saleem said. "We're going to go for a little walk, all right? I'll be back soon."

"Okay, *bachem.* Be careful and don't stay too late. A mother should see her son's face too, you know." Saleem promised to return soon and walked back out to find Kamal waiting impatiently behind the house, a cigarette dangling from his bottom lip.

"Ah, much better! Now maybe you won't scare the girls away," he said, laughing.

Saleem and the professor's son went out into the market in search of some mischief that would entertain them for about an hour. It was a taste of a life so deliciously normal that Saleem wanted to fall to his knees and pray for it to last.

Chapter 23
Saleem

Kamal, Hakan, and Hayal made Saleem feel settled in Intikal, thousands of miles from "home." It was harder to think of Intikal as just a temporary stop on their way to England.

Aziz's condition had improved slightly. His weight and appetite still lagged, but he didn't look as uncomfortable. Madar-*jan* gave his doses religiously and was grateful for his improvement. In her second visit with the good Doctor Ozdemir, Madar-*jan* had prepared a special dish of *mantu* dumplings. She had felt compelled to show her gratitude somehow, but he again declined any fee for the visit.

But even as things seemed to be turning around, Saleem knew they would eventually have to plan their next move if they were to make it to England. Madar-*jan* had called their family in England several times but was unable to get through.

She seemed reluctant to call again even though Saleem knew they were the Waziri family's only hope. Aziz's medications were an additional draw on the family's meager monies. There was nothing to save him from the brutally long days at the Polat farm. If it weren't for the generosity of Hakan and Hayal, they would have been on the street for sure.

Kamal and Saleem spent more time together off the soccer field. With the connection between Kamal's father and Hakan, Madar-*jan* was even happier about Saleem's new friend. She wanted him to be social and enjoy his time away from work. When Kamal invited Saleem to join him at his second cousin's wedding in the village, Saleem was hesitant. He wasn't certain how the rest of Kamal's family would receive him, the migrant worker with manure under his fingernails. Madar-*jan* encouraged him to go.

Weddings in Kabul were major social events, dampened only in the last few years by the stringent restrictions of the Taliban. Madar-*jan* had always loved getting dressed up, the banquet halls, the music, and the sight of the bride and groom embarking on a new life together. Though she did not speak much about her own wedding, Saleem knew it was the first time she'd been the center of attention and that it had marked a break from the hardships of her childhood. More times than he could count, Saleem had heard the story of his parents' wedding — the car draped in flowers and ribbons, the drummer who led their celebratory procession down the street, the music that had gone on until four in the morning.

"What will you wear, Saleem? Let's see here . . ." she said as she rummaged through his duffel bag and pulled out a pair of pants. She continued digging. "Here's your button-down shirt. This should do. Why don't you try it on?"

"Madar-*jan,* the wedding is three days away."

"What if it doesn't fit? Better we know now than on that day."

The pants were undeniably short and the shirt hung loose on his shoulders. Madar-*jan* let out the one-inch hem and restitched it so that his ankles were not completely exposed. The pants and shirt would have to do.

On Friday night, Saleem walked the fifteen minutes to Kamal's house, his palms sweaty. On his ride back from the farm, he'd started to imagine what it would be like as a total stranger amid a Turkish family's private celebration. He had serious doubts about going. Afraid of disappointing Kamal, he chose to push his apprehensions aside.

Saleem would be joining Kamal and two of his cousins to drive to the wedding together. The rest of the family had already left. The celebration was being held at a farmhouse outside of town, and the boys were eager to get there before dinner was served.

Kamal's cousins were older, in their twenties, but cut of the same unruly cloth. They were chain-smoking young men who told lewd jokes and went home to mom's cooking every night. The cousins barely raised an eyebrow to see Saleem, reassuringly disinterested. They parked the car and headed into the house, hoping that they had timed their arrival well to miss the religious ceremonies and make it for the food and music that would follow.

They were right on time. The bride's and groom's families were shaking hands and congratulating one another. The smell of roasted meats and baked cheeses wafted through the air. Food was to be served shortly and this left time for the guests to wander around, for relatives to catch up on gossip, stories of the old days, and complaints about the unseasonably hot weather.

Saleem drank it all in. *This could be an Afghan wedding,* he thought to himself. It really was no different. A circle of men chatted in one corner. Women were laughing in another. Turks and Afghans were more alike than he had thought.

The food was delicious. Since Saleem had barely had time to eat anything when he came home from work, he arrived at the party ravenous. He kept his eyes on his plate. Quite a few girls in the room had caught his attention, but he did not want to be caught ogling them. Although they were dressed modestly, their calf-length dresses showed off the shapes of their youthful curves. One girl had chestnut hair that curled around her face and brushed against her cherry lips. Saleem made extra effort not to stare in her direction.

"Do you want some more food? I'm going for seconds. Or maybe you're worried you'll split your pants?" Kamal said, nudging Saleem with his elbow as he stood up.

"No, I'll come with you. I would gladly split my pants for this kebab." They walked over to the long tables where trays of food were laid out. Off in the corner, the bride and groom stood chatting with a few guests.

"The family's been waiting a long time

for this wedding," Kamal explained. "The bride is my cousin. The groom comes from a family that lives nearby, a neighboring farm. He's been in love with her for years. There's another family that wanted her to marry their son so that they'll inherit this land eventually, but she wasn't interested and her father doesn't like them anyway."

Just like Kabul, Saleem thought.

They filled their bellies, listened to music, and watched the men grow rowdy as the hour grew late. There was clapping, feet and elbows bouncing to the music blaring from a stereo system, the rhythm and the instruments reminiscent of the music of Kabul's past. Tea and syrup-soaked pastries were passed around. Saleem, more sated than he could ever recall being, still did not turn down the flaky baklava or the pistachio-coated nougats offered to him. If only he could have shared this feast with his family. He licked his sticky fingers and wondered if there was a way to slip something into his pockets without being noticed.

"Hey, let's get a smoke. It's too hot here, no?" Kamal suggested. Saleem agreed and followed his friend out to the back of the house. His eardrums buzzed. Saleem took a deep breath of fresh air, stretched his arms out, and smiled. Kamal looked amused.

"Having a good time, are you?" Kamal asked, taking out a cigarette and matches.

"It's been a long time since I've been to a party. A really long time."

"Yeah, well. This is life in Intikal. Every day is a party," he said sarcastically, the cigarette casting an orange glow in the night. The boys began to stroll around the shed behind the house when they stopped short.

Explosive sounds thundered through the night — followed by screams.

Saleem's instincts kicked in first. He grabbed Kamal by the shoulder and pulled him to the ground.

"Stay down!" he yelled. On their knees, the boys crawled around the side of the shed to get a look at the house. Kamal did as he was told. There were loud pops, more screaming, and the sound of breaking glass.

"What's happening?" Kamal screamed, panic in his voice. The screams were more familiar than the gunshots to Saleem. Those were the screams of people under attack.

"My parents!" Kamal yelled, his voice breaking.

"Quiet," Saleem warned, throwing his arms around his friend to keep him calm. "Quiet for a minute."

Three shadows ran out of the house,

leaped into a car, and roared off. Kamal and Saleem ran back into the house as the car lights faded down the road. The screams had melted into wails.

Blood. Saleem's stomach reeled at the smell of gunpowder and metal. People were huddled in two corners of the room, groans echoing over the sound of festive music made for a macabre cacophony. Two women snatched curtains from the windows to make bandages. Kamal's mother was one of them, shouting her son's name even as she tore at the fabric.

"Mother!" Kamal ran over to her. She dropped the fabric and grabbed him by his shoulders.

"You're not hurt? You're all right? Oh, thank God!" she cried.

"I'm fine, I'm fine. Where's Father?"

"Helping your cousins over there." She picked up the curtain and ran over to a mass of people crouched over one woman.

Saleem stood locked in place.

People were yelling, walking around him as if unaware of his presence. He saw their mouths move and heard a noise, the sound of frightened, hurt people. He saw people running. Arms and legs moved around him, sometimes pushing him out of the way. He couldn't move.

Saleem was back in Kabul. He heard rockets, saw people burying young children and families crying after disappeared fathers. His breathing slowed, and his eyes grew blurry.

There was no escape. The bloodshed had tracked him down to Intikal. How naïve he was to think he had left it all behind. It danced around him, taunting him and poking at his sides. It had followed him all along, waiting for him to grow complacent. Saleem had buried his head under a pillow as a young boy to muffle the sounds of the rockets. Now he put his hands over his ears to deaden the cries.

Saleem caught a glimpse of one of the victims, the bride's father, his white shirt turned crimson. The color drained from his face as his daughter lay over him shrieking.

Everywhere he turned, Saleem saw his father.

Chapter 24
Saleem

His mother barely stirred as Saleem crept into the bedroom, his heart still pounding. He could hear Samira's soft breathing. His eyes tried to adjust to the dark as he felt for his mattress on the floor.

"Thank God you're home," Madar-*jan* whispered. "It must be so late. Get some sleep, Saleem-*jan.*"

"Yes." That was all Saleem could get out without his voice breaking.

He walked into the washroom and let out a trickle of water from the faucet. He let it run over his hands and between his fingers. He brought his palms to his face and held them there.

Get some sleep, Madar-*jan* had said. *Get some sleep.*

Saleem slipped out of his pants and shirt and slid under his bedsheet. He stared at the ceiling, traced its cracks in the dark, and tried to block out all he'd seen. But it all came back. The bride, her dress stained with her father's blood. Her brother, shot in the leg but alive and yelling as they'd shoved him into a car to be taken to the hospital. Two others had been lucky, bullets just grazing their arms.

Lucky, Saleem thought, *was relative.*

It was forty-five minutes of chaos. A few cool heads had taken control and shouted out orders. Someone took the inconsolable bride into a back room. Her new husband, paralyzed with fear during the mayhem, felt his own body for bullet wounds that were not there. One of the shooters had aimed directly at him and fired, but the gun had jammed.

Lucky.

Saleem found himself whispering his prayers, as if his father's hands were on his shoulders, turning him away from the windows and bringing him to the ground. He touched the lifeless watch on his wrist, absent of the soft ticking that once lulled him to sleep.

Kamal's father had driven them home, filling them in on what had happened. Three men had burst into the house. They'd been recognized immediately as sons of the neighboring farm family — boys who had wanted this bride for their own clan.

Slighted and incensed, they'd decided to exact their revenge on the young couple's wedding night.

They directed their aim at the bride's father, the groom, and then the bride's brothers. Guests ran for cover, hiding under tables full of celebratory sweets and escaping into adjacent rooms.

They'd spared the bride, a punishment in itself.

Kamal had never seen more than a bloodied nose in a street fight.

Things are different outside the town's limits. People take their own revenge when they feel they've been dishonored.

It was forever before the police officers arrived. They shook their heads and went from person to person, assessing the damage. They took notes, but it was unclear what they would do about the attackers. Kamal's father decided to take the boys home. His mother was in another car with his aunts and cousins.

Saleem had fallen asleep thinking of what Kamal's father had said.

Grudges don't die — people do.

Saleem woke abruptly to the sound of Madar-*jan* shrieking. She ripped the bedsheet off him. He bolted upright, his eyes bloodshot. Her hands were on him, touching his chest and face.

"What happened? Why is there blood on your clothes? Where are you hurt?"

The night came rushing back. Saleem cocked his head back and put his hands over his eyes.

"It wasn't me. I'm not hurt," he said. Samira was wide awake, staring nervously. "They were shooting, Madar-*jan*. It was terrible."

"Shooting guns? What in God's name are you talking about?"

Madar-*jan* was not fully convinced that her son was whole and searched his body for hidden wounds.

Saleem pulled her hands away and stood up to shake the slumber from his eyes. He had tossed his bloodstained clothing by the floor cushion, a gruesome sight in the early morning hour. He told her everything, keeping his voice low in hopes that Samira wouldn't be too frightened. He told his mother how he'd helped lift the bride's brother into the car so he could be taken to the hospital.

If he'd had a bit more sleep, he might have had the sense to filter some of the gore. By the end, he was crying. He'd been unable to move for so long, he lamented. She listened intently, a hand over her mouth in disbelief. Samira had moved closer, sidling next to her mother, and listened with the intent of an adult. Madar-*jan* whispered words of gratitude to God for sparing her son.

Madar-*jan* pulled Saleem to her and rocked him as she did Aziz. He didn't resist, cherishing the smell of his mother, the comfort of her arms, and her kisses on his forehead. She asked Samira to put the water to boil and get breakfast started for Hakan and Hayal. Samira rose obediently.

"And your friend, Kamal . . . he was not hurt either?"

"No, Madar-*jan,* he was outside with me. He is all right."

"His mother and father?"

"They were not hurt."

When Hakan and Hayal came down for breakfast, Saleem repeated the entire story once more. His Turkish had improved immensely since he had started hanging out with Kamal and the boys. He searched for a few words here and there but relayed the night's events to them. Hakan and Hayal sat stone-faced. Hayal instinctively put a hand over Fereiba's. To Saleem, the violence at the wedding was starting to feel more like a story than an actual event.

Madar-*jan* searched their faces for an explanation. How could something like this happen in Intikal? Hakan rose and said he was going to Kamal's house to see his father. He was dressed and out the door within minutes.

"I'm late for work. I should already be at the farm, Madar-*jan*," Saleem said, instinctively looking at his watch. "I'll get hell for coming in at this time."

"Saleem, *bachem*, you are not going to the farm today. After everything that happened last night, it's out of the question. I want you with me."

Saleem looked down at his hands and realized he was trembling slightly. He knew he must have looked like death and had the sudden urge to bathe, to scrub the night's events from his skin with hot water.

Hayal made him a cup of tea with honey and brought him a plate of bread and cheese. Saleem ate silently. Samira stayed close by but quiet. She warmed a bottle of milk for Aziz and propped him up on her lap so that he could take his breakfast. For the first time in a long time, it looked like the Waziri baby with the broken heart was in better shape than the rest of the family.

Saleem went to the washroom and turned the water as hot as it would go. He let the water cascade over his head, his face, his shoulders. He closed his eyes and saw the bride's face, blood streaked across her cheek. He heard her brother's moans. Saleem opened his eyes to try to see something else, but the visions were burned into his retinas. He scrubbed at his skin until it was red and raw. His temples throbbed. He turned the water off, his skin stinging at the towel's rough touch.

Madar-*jan* sat in the bedroom, on the edge of her bed. She looked mournful.

"Madar-*jan*?" Saleem said, hesitantly.

"I thought we were okay here," she whispered. "This was not supposed to be like home."

Saleem sat beside her.

"I brought us here because we thought it would be safer. We thought this would be better for you. What have I done?"

Without Padar-*jan* around, there was no one to share the blame for the plan that had landed them in Intikal. Saleem pressed his forehead against her shoulder.

"We could not stay in Kabul, Madar-*jan*. We had nothing left. We were going to starve there — or worse."

"Aziz was okay there. He was fine until we left home." Her eyes were glossy, filled with thoughts of a rosy yesterday that existed only in her mind. "Samira wasn't washing strangers' dirty dishes and folding their laundry. You weren't working your hands to a bloody mess from dusk till dawn. We were okay in Kabul, but I brought us here."

Fereiba had wanted to keep her children healthy, fed, safe, and free from working as indentured servants. She'd failed on all accounts.

"Madar-*jan,* we were not okay there." Saleem crouched in front of her, jarred by the way his mother seemed to be speaking about him and not to him. "Don't you remember? We were scared. We had no money and couldn't leave the house. There was barely air to breathe."

"I wanted my children to be children. I wanted them to laugh, to play . . . to learn. I wanted them to do the things that I should have done as a girl. How far must we go? How fast must we run?"

Saleem could not find the words, much less arrange them in a way that would bring any relief. It broke him to hear his mother talk this way and to know the thoughts she was likely hiding from her children on most days. Her smiles, her cheerfulness — had it all been to make them feel reassured? Her eyes were tearless. She was not speaking out of emotion. These were thoughts that came from the most honest part of her spirit. This was the result of her careful analysis and her astute observations. This was very real.

"We'll be okay, Madar-*jan,* you'll see. This was the worst of it. We'll get to England before you know it and we'll be okay." Saleem's voice wavered. He was nowhere near as confident as his mother.

But Madar-*jan*'s expression changed, as if a switch turned on. Her lips tightened and her eyes focused with a glint of resolution. She pulled her shoulders back and met Saleem's hopeful gaze.

"Yes, my son. That's exactly it. We will go to England." Saleem felt relieved that his mother had shaken her trancelike state. He nodded in eager agreement.

"Yes, Madar-*jan,* we just need to set aside a little more —"

"No, we must leave. We are leaving In-tikal. We are leaving Turkey."

"Leaving Turkey? But, Madar-*jan,* we haven't —"

"God could not have sent a clearer sign. The time has come for us to continue our journey. We will thank Hakan and Hayal for their hospitality, pay whatever debts we owe, and pack our belongings. Every day that we stay here is digging ourselves into a deeper hole. If we don't leave now, we may never go."

Madar-*jan* believed in moving forward. She always had.

CHAPTER 25
SALEEM

Hakan and Hayal were almost tearful when the Waziri family left. Fereiba tried to pay Hayal for the final month of rent, but Hayal gently refused. With her heart in her throat, she told Fereiba to use the money to take care of the children. She handed Madar-*jan* a bag of foods she had prepared — enough to last a few days without spoiling. The mothers hugged tightly. In the months they had lived together, they'd become good friends. Hayal was the whisper in Fereiba's ear telling her God sent miracles in unrecognizable forms. Fereiba, distracted by her circumstances, did not always recognize the voice in her ear and sometimes took it for her own. But Hayal was a true friend, lifting Fereiba without needing to be named or thanked.

Samira clung to Hayal. She did not want to let go of her teacher and her friend, her source of security.

Hakan watched with leaden shoulders. He'd kept a respectable distance from Fereiba and the children. They were orphaned and vulnerable, and he did not want to transgress their privacy as he knew the rest of the world would. What they had been subject to and what they would be subject to were beyond his control. All he could do was give them a respite under his roof, which he did because he believed it to be right.

Hakan had taken on a father's pride when he looked at Saleem. The boy was strong-willed and determined. He was teetering between boyhood and manhood, a dangerous time. He saw the way Saleem looked at his mother, the look of a boy who refuses to believe what he has not learned for himself. Fereiba would struggle with him, Hakan predicted, but Saleem was too devoted to stray far. He wrapped an arm around Saleem's shoulders and squeezed.

Saleem was taller than he had been when he first met Hakan coming out of prayers so many months ago. He bit his lip, feeling as if he was betraying his father by leaning into Hakan's paternal gesture. These small moments gave him resilience, though.

"Saleem, your family has a long and difficult journey ahead. God sees all that you've done for them and for yourself. I'm sure your father is quite proud of you and the man you are becoming. We will pray for you. Trust with caution and don't get discouraged."

Saleem nodded solemnly. Hakan's words surprised him and made him feel small. He had snuck to the soccer fields when he said he was at the farm. He had smoked cigarettes and pocketed snacks from the street kiosk when the shop owner's back was turned. He'd resented his baby brother's needs and even Padar-*jan* for being so stubborn that he'd kept his family in Afghanistan until it was too late. No one knew these pieces of Saleem. He was cagey, a boy with secrets. He wanted so much to be the person Hakan described.

He looked at Hakan's face, still discomfited by the inexplicable resemblance to his father's. He felt the memory of his father fading with each passing day. Some nights, Saleem lay awake, trying to recall Padar-*jan*'s image, his voice, his smell. With each day, yesterday was pushed into a darker cranny of his mind. With each night, Saleem had to reach deeper into those recesses to find his father. Saleem clung to the images he had, fearful they would fade into a blinding whiteness. This, too, he was ashamed to admit.

Saleem hadn't bothered to go back to the Polat farm even though he was owed five days' worth of wages. He knew Polat would refuse to pay him if he wasn't going to be returning. Ekin, who'd returned to haunt him as if nothing had happened, would find another way to busy her afternoons. With Kamal, Saleem's farewell was awkward. Their friendship had been based on the lightness of childhood, boyish activities of little consequence. The bloodied wedding and Saleem's departure brought a weight to their bond that neither boy expected or wanted. Kamal, not bothering to brush the hair from his eyes, quietly wished Saleem a safe journey. Saleem turned his back on his first friend outside of Afghanistan, knowing they would never speak again.

The Waziri family left Intikal on a bus headed toward Turkey's west coast, where ports and ships provided easy passage to Greece. They had the Belgian passports Abdul Rahim had secured for them and would not have to rely on smugglers. If these passports got them through customs, they would be well worth the high price Madar-*jan* had paid for them.

The bus ride was long, bumpy, and quiet. The Waziri family watched Turkey's verdant landscape go by in silence. They were leaving behind a life they'd come to enjoy, days that passed with the comforting rhythm of a drumbeat. Again, Madar-*jan* was leading them into an unknown.

It was a day's journey to Izmir, on Turkey's western shore. When they neared Izmir's port, Saleem's senses were hit with the briny air, a smell unfamiliar to his landlocked nose. He looked at the others. Their eyes shimmered, reflecting the glimmering turquoise waters. The sea, a place where sunlight bounced from here to there, from water to the hull of a ship to the wings of a seagull. Samira smiled, the sun warming her face. Fereiba stroked her daughter's hair. It was a brief moment of joy, but one that gave them reason to press on.

Saleem found a ticket booth and purchased one-way rides for the entire family. The ticket agent, busy chatting with the agent in the adjacent booth, barely looked at their passports. He waved Saleem off when he inquired about a ticket for Aziz.

Tickets in hand, they turned again to the cerulean expanse and marveled at the enormous ships docked there. Never before had they seen waters bigger than a river.

"Water is *roshanee,* it is light. To be surrounded by so much of it . . ." Fereiba let the sea air fill her lungs. "This must mean something good for us."

Her family needed the light of good fortune.

The ticket agent had pointed out a navy blue ferry, a building afloat. Saleem's stomach leaped with boyish excitement. He led his mother and siblings to the pier to claim their seats. The wind cast a microshower of cool droplets on their cheeks. Samira's hair flew into her face and she giggled trying to brush it away. Saleem and his mother paused. It had been a lifetime since they'd heard that laughter.

Choppy waves lapped at the boat, and Saleem and Samira leaned over the rails to get that much closer to the ocean. The ride was too short and well before they'd had their fill, the crew announced their arrival in Chios, a Greek island where the Waziri family was to catch yet another ferry to Athens.

Surrounded by tourists in shorts and backpacks and commuting Greeks, Saleem and his family hoisted their bags over their shoulders and tried their best to look inconspicuous. Each leg of their journey had a checkpoint, a place where their pounding heartbeats and falsified documents could give them away.

But entering Greece turned out to be much easier than they'd anticipated, and they were soon on the next ferry. Chios to Athens was a longer journey, more opportunity for Fereiba to soak in the vast waters and pray they would herald brighter days. Eight hours later, they reached the port of Piraeus, and nerves began to kick in again. Samira had fallen asleep, her head resting on Saleem's shoulder. Madar-*jan* bit her lip nervously as they neared the dock.

The men in uniforms standing at the pier ratcheted up the family's anxiety. Saleem and his mother kept their faces steeled. Saleem's stomach quivered as if he carried under his shirt a balloon stretched so taut that the slightest movement might cause it to burst, alerting the world to his transgression. They were ushered forward with the crowd. Saleem felt eyes boring into his back, but nothing happened. Soon they were standing amid the flurry of taxis in the port city of Athens.

Turkey has one foot in Europe and the other in Asia. Things will be different in Greece, Hakan had cautioned them. *You will be outside the Muslim world, for better or worse.*

Saleem and his mother knew Pakistan,

Iran, and India had grown increasingly fatigued by the burden of Afghan refugees. This was not the case with Europe or America. People who fled to Europe never spoke of returning. Word of their happy, new lives traveled like the scent of ripe peaches in the summer breeze. Europe had sympathy for the war-ravaged people of Afghanistan and offered an outstretched hand.

Hakan had been concerned by Saleem's rosy view of what life would be like in England. Saleem had talked of attending school and having his mother return to teaching. Hakan knew immigrants, including thousands of Turks, faced misery in Europe, but he cautioned only gently. Some would hate the Waziris for trespassing, for sucking at their nation's teats, for looking different. But there was no better alternative for the Afghan refugees, and he felt it useless to disappoint them so early in their journey.

Saleem had pushed aside Hakan's warnings. Now the family walked about the port city, wondering if it might be possible to pass for Greeks. Since they'd left Intikal Madar-*jan* had folded up and put away the head scarf that had been forced upon her by the Taliban. She was happy to leave it behind. Here in Greece, she could dress as she did in the Kabul of her youth. Fereiba ran her fingers through her loose hair, feeling renewed.

They stopped in three hotels looking for lodging but were discouraged by prices too steep for their shallow pockets. One front desk clerk took pity on Saleem and directed him to a smaller, cheaper hotel a half kilometer away. She drew him directions on a paper napkin before returning her attention to the small television under the desk.

Attica Dream turned out to be the best they could do. Saleem negotiated the rate from forty euro to twenty, promising to be very clean and quiet. The clerk, a woman in her fifties, saw Madar-*jan* with three children and four bags in tow and then turned to a leather-bound ledger on the desk, tapping her pencil on the grid of numbers and dates. Attica Dream had survived decades without renovations, and the owners did not seem to mind the lack of interest in their lodgings. They'd long been overshadowed by newer hotels in the area and the owners didn't seem to care much. Their advancing age would drive them out of business, if the lack of guests didn't.

The clerk sighed heavily and nodded in agreement, trying to appear as if it were a huge sacrifice to rent the room for so little.

Saleem pulled out the bills he had changed in Chios and paid the woman for one night while she extracted a key from a wooden box. Saleem led his family up the creaking steps and into the room with two beds. The mattresses were old and lumpy, but they were happy to get off their feet, stretch their legs, and rest their shoulders.

Saleem's legs throbbed as his head hit the pillow. He closed his eyes and thought of how far they'd come. Maybe it had been the right time to leave Intikal. Or maybe they should have left long ago. This was the next phase of their travels, Madar-*jan* had told them.

So here we are in Greece, Saleem thought as he tried to get to sleep. *But now what?*

CHAPTER 26
SALEEM

The hours crept by with Saleem awake, listening to the remote sounds of conversation and footsteps on the street below. Athens was alive at all hours. Eventually sunlight began to filter through the gauzy curtains. Samira stretched her arms and arched her back with her eyes still shut. Aziz flipped onto his belly, and Fereiba's legs slid to the floor. She rubbed her eyes and stood. Saleem felt very adult watching them wake, as if not being able to sleep indicated some sort of maturity.

They splashed cool water on their faces in the bathroom so small Saleem could touch all four walls with outstretched arms. The last of the food Hayal had packed for them was spread out on a newspaper and divided.

Saleem took a shower and headed out to find food and ways to get to Italy. Athens was far more expensive than Intikal, and even this run-down hotel would exhaust their funds quickly. Saleem tucked his passport deep into the pocket of his jeans along with a few euros.

The hotel clerk, as disinterested this morning as the previous night, advised Saleem to take the subway to Omonia if he wanted to find food. The silver snaking train roared into the station and then slithered back into the tunnel with new passengers aboard. Saleem watched what others did and followed, boarding the train in nervous exhilaration. He checked the scrap of paper in his pocket, matching the stop the clerk had written out for him against the map on the subway wall. He twirled the watchband around his wrist, feeling surprisingly unnoticed by the people around him. He, on the other hand, was absorbed with the hum of the train, the bitter smell of coffee, the snap of newspapers being opened.

Hakan had told Saleem he would see many immigrants in Greece. He wanted to find them and ask how best to travel to Italy or find cheap food. After getting off the train, he kept his eyes on the street map he'd picked up and buried himself in the crowd when he saw uniformed officers walking by. He wound through the city's plazas, a maze of wide buildings and paved streets. The men dressed the same as they had in Turkey, but the women looked much different. Women walked about in tight shirts with necklines low enough to draw his adolescent eyes. Bare arms and legs moved around him, oblivious to his gawking. There were people of all shapes and colors wandering through the streets, many with cameras and small books, pausing occasionally to snap a photo.

Saleem carried his empty knapsack on his shoulder and hoped to fill it before returning to the hotel. He reached a roundabout, a much grander version of the one in Kabul with curbs, lights, and more cars. Extending out from the roundabout like an outstretched hand were smaller streets lined with shops.

Men with skin as black as night crouched on sidewalks with burlap sacks full of purses. Their eyes drifted left and right, scouting the scene. They mumbled to passersby, trying to hawk their wares. These men looked even more foreign than him, Saleem thought, and he grew nervous to approach them.

Farther into the market, he came upon two men peddling stick figures that danced to the sounds of the radio, sidewalk marvels. Saleem reminded himself of his purpose and looked at the men. Not as dark as the ones he'd seen a few meters back, they looked to be from India. A blond-haired woman pulled her toddler away from the toys, her hair reflecting the sun. The man reinforced the child's resistance, making the figure dance toward his stocky legs. The woman shook her head, picked up her protesting child, and hurried down the street.

The street vendor sat cross-legged on the concrete, utterly bored. He barely looked at Saleem.

"Speak English?" Saleem asked cautiously.

The man gave an almost imperceptible nod of the head. Saleem continued.

"Where are you from?"

The man paused, wondering the same thing about Saleem.

"Bangladesh," he said finally, his eyebrows lifted and a finger pointed at Saleem.

"Me? Afghanistan."

The man nodded as if to say he had guessed as much. He'd been in Greece for a year, he told Saleem. He tried to catch the attention of pedestrians, but none looked his way. Saleem pushed on.

"I am here with my family. We want to go to Italy . . ."

"Many, many Afghanistan people," the

vendor commented absently.

Saleem paused.

"Here? Afghan people are working?" Saleem's interaction with Afghans in Turkey had left a bad taste in his mouth, but there was still comfort in finding people who came from the same corner of the earth.

"Where? I want to find Afghan people. Please help?"

"Afghani people . . ." the Bangladeshi man began, cocking his head to the side. With a flick of his left hand, he pointed into the distance. "Afghani people not here. Far. Eat, sleep together."

"Where? Tell me please, mister?"

"Far, far," the man shooed with both hands and a shake of his head for emphasis. "Metro. No walk."

Attiki Square, the Bangladeshi man finally said. It was distant enough that Saleem could not find it on his metro map. With prices as steep as he'd seen, he was not surprised other Afghans had taken refuge outside the city center. The man raised an eyebrow and looked at Saleem expectantly. He pointed to his dancing stick figures, untouched, and waved Saleem away.

Saleem decided to look for food first. He fingered the bills and coins in his pocket. It wasn't much. He walked by a kiosk selling newspapers and bottles of water. The sun had moved higher in the sky. Samira would be hungry soon, though she wouldn't say so.

He touched the face of his watch nervously. From a large gray building to his right, people emerged carrying heavy plastic bags. He saw loaves of bread sticking out from some of the satchels. Saleem followed the crowd through the glass double doors.

The building was shaped like a hangar, deep enough that he could not see the end and had to tilt his head back to get a glimpse of the ceiling. Three long lines of stalls split the room into rows. Saleem's nostrils flared. He smelled brine, fish, and onions. He turned to the left and walked ahead. The concentrated smell of sugar made his mouth pucker. Saleem dove in.

He walked up and down the rows. His eyes bulged to see the fruits, vegetables, cheeses, pastries, and olives. Stickers told him he had little hope of affording most of what he was seeing.

Saleem's heart pounded as part of him began to plot.

No one is watching you. Just like Intikal. Choose carefully and quietly and look for an exit.

Saleem sauntered to a stand in the first

row. The man behind the table laughed, explaining something passionately to two customers considering his dried fruits carefully. Saleem picked up two packets of dried apricots and turned them over slowly. He had dropped his knapsack from his shoulder to his elbow, where its unzipped mouth begged for loot. Saleem's downcast eyes surreptitiously moved left and right.

No one is watching you.

Quietly he dropped one bag of apricots into the knapsack while he leaned over to place the other back on the stand. The owner looked over momentarily, saw Saleem replacing the apricots, and turned his attention back to the Greek couple.

Saleem walked away slowly and tensely, ready to bolt at any hint his actions had been noted. Nothing. He looked around some more. There were loaves of flatbreads, round breads, and cheese wedges on a corner stand, not ten yards from the door. Saleem's stomach grumbled in encouragement, his mind calculating the shared portions. From where he stood, he could read the price on the toothpick flag sticking out of one of the cheese wedges. Far too many euros. Saleem moved in closer. The thick braid of dough was topped with a heavy sprinkle of sesame seeds.

Saleem took one more look at the distance between the stand and the door. Once outside those glass doors, he would make a quick left and head back in the direction of the hotel.

Six or seven people crowded around the bread table, but mostly on the adjacent side with the cakes and pastries. Saleem casually picked up one of the fat, braided loaves and considered it. Next, he picked up a large, round flatbread and peered at it, covering the braided loaf that hung directly over the open mouth of his knapsack. Holding the two loaves in his left hand, he reached over with his right and picked up a large cheese wedge.

Suddenly, the vendor's voice boomed out over the crowd and customers pushed closer to the table. Saleem felt a rush in his cheeks. He looked up and saw that the man, an older gentleman with gray hair and a white apron, had sliced up one of his pastries, a long syrup-drenched doughnut. He offered the bite-size samples to the customers, none of whom had noticed Saleem's sleight of hand.

"Ela, ela!" Saleem had just turned his back to the stand. He froze in place and debated whether to turn or simply run, his mouth as dry as sawdust.

The aproned man barked something in Greek as he pushed the metal tray of dough-nut samples in Saleem's direction.

Is this a test?

The baker gave an eager nod. Saleem positioned himself in front of his knapsack, afraid its bulkiness would give him away.

"Dokimase!" The baker winked. Saleem took a sticky piece of doughnut from the tray and the man nodded in approval, turning his attention to a middle-aged woman and her husband who had smudged the glass display case to point out their order. Saleem picked up the knapsack and walked as evenly as he could to the exit, his weighted bag bouncing against his back with every step.

A breeze chilled the perspiration on the nape of his neck.

Chew, he told himself. The syrup made his tongue stick to the roof of his mouth. He swallowed without tasting anything. He moved absently through the winding streets, accusing eyes all around him. He made several turns to put the market and its customers behind him. Within minutes, he'd lost track of his lefts and rights. He was panting and lost.

With his back against a stucco wall, he looked across the street and saw a sign for the metro. The bread vendor's eager smile toyed with his conscience.

I'm sorry, he thought. He truly was.

But he felt something else too — something he didn't intend to feel. He lifted his bag and felt its bulk, pounds of success. He would feed his family for a couple days without costing them precious euros. Every bite they ate, everything they did was measured in days of tomato picking or housecleaning.

Something — fate, the universe, God — something owed the Waziri family a break, Saleem rationalized. Abdul Rahim's hand was on one shoulder. Hakan before him. Padar-*jan*'s voice rang through his head.

Saleem-jan, *my son, reap a noble harvest.*

In the hotel room, Saleem spread the bounty on newspapers.

"If your father were with us, he would be so proud," Madar-*jan* said, sighing as she broke the bread and cheese into pieces. "God bless you for what you do to keep this family alive. So much food! How much did all this cost?"

Saleem replied with a number so unreasonable, it made him angry that his mother did not question it.

They ate in the silence that filled most of

their days. It was easier not to say the things they were thinking. Samira chewed slowly, sesame seeds crunching between her teeth. She tucked a wisp of hair behind her ear and looked at her brother. Saleem turned away quickly. She had spent enough nights sleeping within arm's reach of her brother to know when he was hiding something.

"There's a part of town where all the Afghans live," he announced. "I'll go there tomorrow morning and talk to people. Maybe they'll have something useful to say."

"A whole Afghan neighborhood so far from home! God bless them . . ."

While she prayed for others, Saleem doubted anyone prayed for them.

"I'll try to find out how people travel out of Greece and into Europe. Maybe they can tell me how people earn some money here." He told her about the Bangladeshi man selling dancing stick figures. He told her about the metro and how he'd paid for his ride. He described the market and the streets, the roundabout that reminded him of Kabul. Samira and Aziz listened in. He exaggerated his story, made the buildings taller, the train faster, and the people friendlier. He created a caricature of his day, mostly for Samira's benefit. It was more interesting, he thought.

As their stomachs filled, their confidence grew. They could make plans for tomorrow and the days after.

"You will have to be persistent and determined. And I believe you will. *Inshallah, bachem.*" Madar-*jan* sighed again, chewing the stolen food gratefully. *God willing.*

CHAPTER 27
SALEEM

The following morning, Saleem headed out with a confidence spurred by the previous day's success. The hotel owner had agreed to let the family stay on through the week at a lower rate in exchange for Madar-*jan* helping out with cleaning and kitchen work. Samira stayed in the room and watched over Aziz while Madar-*jan* did chores downstairs.

Saleem had directions for Attiki Square, which was much closer than the Bangladeshi man had implied. He wound his way through streets and shops. Today was quieter than yesterday but it was early yet.

He approached a kiosk. The woman inside the booth was busy stocking shelves with packages of cigarettes. Saleem looked at the newspapers, thumbing the first pages as if any of it was decipherable.

Bottles of soda sat next to the rack of newspapers. With no one else on the cobble-stoned street, Saleem slipped a bottle into his knapsack, his eyes on the woman's back. When she turned, he picked up a package of chewing gum and placed it on the counter. He pulled a handful of coins from his pocket and she took what was due. He nodded in thanks, slung his bag over his shoulder, and continued on down the sidewalk.

Once he had made a few turns, he took the soda out and took a big gulp. The sweet syrup fizzed on his tongue. It did not taste as good as he thought it would, nor did he feel the thrill he'd felt the day before. He drank it as quickly as he could, eager to be rid of it.

Saleem walked under clear skies, admiring the tall buildings around him, scrollings and curls carved into their façades and a rainbow of rooftop colors. This city was vibrant and nothing like the monochromatic Mashhad or even Intikal. Bare-legged women laughed, flirted, and smiled in the streets. Some had painted eyelids or lips and looked like the women Saleem and the boys had ogled in the magazines of Intikal's newsstands. Here they were, close enough to talk to. Young men and young women walked together unabashedly. Saleem found himself staring outright. Few people noticed. Some quickened their step to put distance between them. Most were too wrapped up in their own conversations.

Farther down the road, Saleem saw three men, probably in their early twenties, leaning against a sculpture and chatting amicably. They had dark eyes and thick brows with thin features. Refugees were much like their clothing — tired, frayed versions of their former selves. Saleem had learned to spot them from a distance.

"Hello," Saleem called out hesitantly. He was certain they were Afghan.

The men looked over, brows raised in curiosity. They were equally trained in recognizing people on the run. They waited to hear from him.

"You're Afghans, aren't you?" he asked.

The three men broke into wide grins.

"What gave us away, huh? Our empty stomachs or our shamelessly handsome faces?" Belly laughs. Saleem felt himself relax. He had a good feeling about these guys.

"It is nice to be able to speak to a fellow countryman. I feel as if my tongue has been tied for months," Saleem admitted.

"Really? Well, release the beast, my friend. Set your tongue free!"

"We have not seen you around," said one of the men, the shortest of the group. "My name is Abdullah. Where have you come from?"

"From Turkey."

"Oh, good for you! You survived those waters! We heard a few people weren't so lucky last week. They drowned on their way here. God must have saved you," Abdullah said.

"Lucky you, for sure. I nearly drowned when I came over," his friend added. This man was taller, with a round face and scant mustache. "The one I came on . . ."

His friends groaned good-naturedly. They prepared themselves to hear his story again.

"The one I came on looked like cardboard boxes and plywood stitched together. There were supposed to be only eight of us on that boat but these bastards . . . you know how they are. And the waves were horrible that night. In the daylight those waters look beautiful. But in the night, those waters eat people alive."

Saleem felt a wave of gratitude.

Thank you, God, for the passports that spared us such a nightmare.

"How long have you been here?" Abdullah asked. "And this is Jamal, by the way, and his friend over here is Hassan. What is your name?"

"Saleem. I've been here only two days. A

Bangladeshi man told me that the Afghans were in this area."

"Oh, you're new to town! Let's welcome you to Greece, since no one else will." His friends let out a chuckle.

"Yeah, you're going to love it here as much as we do, right?" Hassan had a long, raised scar that snaked down his forearm. Saleem tried not to stare.

"How long have you been here?" he asked the trio.

"I've been here for two years," Hassan answered first. "These boys came about six months after me. You've been here two days? Where are you sleeping?"

"By the port. We can't stay here. I have an aunt and uncle in England and we're trying to get there."

"We? You're not alone?" Jamal asked.

"Er, no," Saleem hesitated. He reminded himself not to share everything. "I have my family with me."

"Oh, you lucky boy! You made it through from Afghanistan with your family! How many are you?" Jamal's eyes widened. He looked impressed.

"There are four of us," he said simply. He didn't want to attract the same unwanted attention his family had gotten in Turkey.

"Really lucky!" Abdullah agreed. "Most of

the Afghans you will find here in Attiki Square are like us — here on their own. There are many boys your age here. Everyone is hoping to apply for asylum and be accepted, but this country does not accept any refugees. We're all here but we aren't supposed to be."

"We're harder to get rid of than the lice in Hassan's hair!" Jamal jested. Hassan punched him in the arm playfully. Saleem was reminded of Kamal and the boys back in Intikal. But it felt good to understand every word that was spoken for a change. It was a conversation without the work. "But you say you want to see Afghans. We'll show you where you can find the Afghans." They led Saleem down the street a few blocks and then made a left behind a large graffiti-painted building. The area looked remarkably different from the neighborhoods Saleem had been exploring yesterday. There were no shops. There were no tourists.

In a large patch of weeds behind the building, the group of three Saleem had just met multiplied. There were men and boys everywhere, milling about outside makeshift tents or sitting on overturned pails. There were two small fires burning, with people sitting or lying around them, drinking palmfuls of water from five-gallon buckets.

The squalor rivaled that of Kabul's worst-hit areas. This was the dark side of Athens, the secret world of people who did not exist. They were neither immigrant nor refugee. They were undocumented and untraceable, shadows that disappeared in the sun.

Hassan and Jamal went off in search of food. They would scrounge near restaurants for discarded food. Abdullah told them they were wasting time and took Saleem around to meet some people.

"Even here among your own people, you need to be careful who you talk to. Especially you, since you have a family and all. For instance, you see that guy in the corner with the yellow shirt?"

There was a man sitting on the ground, his back against a tree. Saleem realized that everywhere, people were clustered. This man was alone.

"Yes, I see him."

"Well, that's Saboor. Leave him alone."

"Why should I leave him alone?"

Abdullah lowered his voice and began to retell what was probably the camp's most-oft-told story by now.

"He's a snake. He steals from his own people, people who are no better off than he is. In a place like this, there are no locks, no gates, just pockets and plastic bags. Usually, the most valuable thing you have is food. Anyway, people would wake in the middle of the night to find him sneaking around like a rat and rifling through their things. Small things were going missing here and there. And when you have nothing, that's more than everything.

"Anyway, two weeks ago, one of the guys, Kareem — he's a nice enough guy from Mazar — he had gotten a potato from somewhere and ate half. He was saving the other half. He wakes up in the morning and realizes the other half of his potato is gone. And then, what do we see? Plain as day, there goes Saboor, with a half-eaten potato in the far end of the park. Kareem was furious. He marched straight up to Saboor, something no one had done until that point, and accused him of taking his potato. Saboor, straight-faced, told him that he had gotten the potato from a church handout. But there hadn't been a church handout that week.

"Kareem kept on him. Accused him of lying, telling him to give the potato back, to apologize to everyone for all the things he had taken since he came. Saboor looked Kareem dead in the eye and said, 'If anyone else wants to cause trouble like this bastard here, let me warn you. You all have families

303

in Afghanistan and I know your names. My friends back home would not mind paying a visit to people you've left behind. Try me and see what happens.' Since that day, we all just avoid him."

"If he's got such powerful friends, why would he have left?" Saleem asked, his body turning away from the man instinctively.

Abdullah shrugged his shoulders. "It's probably a lie, but no one wants to find out. Just stay away."

Abdullah next took Saleem to a group of six boys playing cards. Some of the boys were young, just barely older than Samira. As a newcomer, Saleem was welcomed and everyone was willing to share with him bits of refugee wisdom.

They had arrived together, a group of about fifteen young men. They'd been directed to go to "the ministry." The ministry bounced them to another place, an office called the Greek Council of Refugees. The council was largely uninterested in the boys. They were told that they could apply for asylum if they got a job, but, they were warned, no one would hire refugee boys. And there would be no food or shelter provided.

The young men, along with a few families, had come from a place called Pagani, a name they spat out with a shake of the head. Pagani was a detention center for immigrants on one of Greece's many idyllic islands. The building was a cage, as the boys described it, the biggest cage any of them had ever seen. It teemed with refugees who'd struggled to leave their countries, only to be trapped in Greece. Men, women, and children overwhelmed the building's capacity three times over. The modest courtyard could hardly accommodate a fraction of the residents. People went for days without stepping outside. There were at least a hundred people to each toilet.

No one knew how bad it was here until it was too late. For a few, Pagani had been so damaging that, even in the open air of Attiki Square, their breath turned into a nervous wheeze at the mention of the detention center.

As unaccompanied minors, Pagani awaited them, but the boys refused to go back to the cage. Jamal, Hassan, and Abdullah had decided to live together in an apartment they shared with nine others. They had dreamed of going to Germany where they'd heard refugees were granted asylum, given housing, and fed. But in Greece, police officers stopped them and asked for "papers."

"The papers do not mean anything," Jamal explained. "They gave us 'papers' in Pagani and told us to keep them on us at all times. Be careful with the police here. Even with those papers, we are targets for them, like dogs in the street. Even at some of the churches that give out food, the police may be there. There is no asylum here."

Saleem spent the day listening, disheartened. Outwardly charming and beautiful, Greece was a hostile place, and many of the young Afghans Saleem met regretted the money they'd spent to reach her shores.

In the following days, Saleem returned to Attiki. The boys told him the places to avoid and brought him along to the churches where food and water were distributed.

Once he learned about Pagani, Saleem became very reluctant to let Madar-*jan* wander off on her own with his sister and brother. Though they had passports, they were false ones and would likely be detected. He could not risk the family being deported to Turkey or, even worse, Afghanistan.

Saleem continued to steal food and staples like soap, but he loathed doing it and was growing more and more paranoid every day. It was a calculated risk he had to take if they were to have enough money to get them to England.

Periodically, a local Greek humanitarian organization came by Attiki Square. Volunteers would talk to the refugees, attempt to assist with document issues, and hand out food and water. A nurse came along with them and placed a Band-Aid here or there or offered a course of antibiotics. The group's resources were limited too. They were young idealists, mostly, indignant that their government could subject refugees to such degrading conditions. They wanted to set things right and they were, oftentimes, the only reliable source of information and food.

Some of the young men in the square were reluctant to trust even the aid workers. Saleem was one of those people. He avoided making eye contact with the young people who walked through the park with their purple T-shirts, their organization's name and logo printed in large type to identify them from afar. They asked many questions and even wanted to take pictures.

Saleem felt safer questioning their motives. He felt his chest puff to think he had outsmarted the aid workers, as if he had more street sense than those boys who let their stories be scribbled into tiny notepads or voice recorders. He did his best to steer clear of every one of them.

Until he saw Roksana.

Chapter 28
Saleem

"We cannot go on this way, Saleem-*jan*," Madar-*jan* whispered to him. Samira and Aziz had fallen asleep.

"What do you mean?"

"In a matter of days, we will have no more money and we still have a long road ahead. We cannot wait for a miracle."

"I know."

"Thank goodness you have at least found a way to work for food."

Saleem bit his lip, thankful for the darkness. He'd told his mother that he'd been hired by a café in town to sweep floors and unload boxes in exchange for food. It was a plausible explanation, especially to willing ears. In reality, no one would hire him. Saleem had returned several times to the market and snuck through other shops, taking what he needed to feed his family. It was a sin imposed upon him, he felt. To make himself feel better about it, he ate just enough food to keep his hunger at bay. It was not easy.

"This job may not last. We need to get to England before the money runs out," Saleem agreed.

"Yes, we do. We'll also soon need more medicine for your brother. I cannot take him to any doctors or get him medicines here. It will cost more than we have and someone might turn us in to the police."

"You're right, Madar-*jan,*" Saleem admitted.

Deciding when to embark on the next leg of their journey was a difficult decision. It was a gamble either way.

"We need to find a way to get to England. I think the train would be best, as Hakan had told us. Airports are full of checkpoints. Perhaps if we stay on the ground, our chances at slipping through will be better."

"I'll go tomorrow to find the train station and I'll see if the Afghans know anything about the trains."

"There's something else, Saleem. We've got to make some hard choices now, and I've been thinking about this a lot. We cannot stay here in this room any longer. Even the price they have given us is more than we can afford. Our money is running out faster than I had imagined it would."

This simple room with its exposed wires and badly cracked plaster, the decrepit sink from which water trickled — all this was a palace to Saleem. When he left Attiki and walked into this space, when he lay on the bed and felt the coils dig into his back, when he looked over at the second bed and saw his mother and sister sleeping two feet off the floor instead of outside, he was a king. This room let him rise in the morning without the hopelessness the boys in Attiki felt. It gave him reason to believe that fate had something more in store for his family than a rickety ship that would capsize in open waters. To give up this room was to give up so much. But to stay — to stay was to choose to bleed slowly and have no strength left to reach the tomorrow they hoped for.

"It will not be easy. We will need a safe place, especially for the nights." Saleem knew some of the boys in Attiki slept only a few hours a day, afraid to close their eyes after sunset when a new world of dangers emerged.

"You look like you could use some water. Here," she said in what sounded like perfect English. Roksana, a volunteer with the aid group, held out a plastic bottle. Saleem fol-

lowed the hand up to a slim wrist, a grace-
ful arm. It only got better from there.

She wore a purple T-shirt tucked loosely
into a slim pair of jeans. Her dramatically
straight, black hair, fell loosely to the side as
she tilted her head. She looked about his
age, maybe sixteen. Her eyes, rimmed in
black pencil, caught his attention with a
flutter of lashes. She did not smile nor did
she look at him with sympathy.

"Thank you." Saleem took the bottle from
her.

"Of course. What is your name?" she
asked. Though she had a face that would
inspire an overly romantic Dari love ballad,
her tone was all business. She was the kind
of girl so striking that she'd hardened her
demeanor out of necessity, especially in a
place like Attiki.

"Saleem," he answered. *And that's all you'll
tell her,* he reminded himself. But Saleem
felt his defenses coming down as he looked
into her eyes.

"Okay, Saleem. I haven't seen you here
before. How long have you been here?" He
wished her to say his name once more.

"A few weeks . . . but I am not staying
here," he said, suddenly feeling embarrassed
that she might think he slept in the park.
He took a casual swig of water.

"Oh? Where do you stay then?"

Another swig as his mind raced. *Good question,* he thought, and turned the conversation around.

"What is your name?" he asked gently. She paused and looked at her clipboard before responding. It was clear she was not happy with his question.

"Roksana."

"Rokshaana?"

"No. It's Rok-sa-na," she repeated, emphasizing the pronunciation.

"But this is an Afghan name . . . Rokshaana!" he repeated with a smile.

"It is my name, my Greek name," she said, her lips pulled together tightly.

"But you know Iskandar, er . . . Alexander. He married an Afghan woman. She was Rokshaana. It is the same name," Saleem explained. It felt good to show her he knew a bit of history. She looked like she might have regretted approaching him but exercised patience.

"I am not her. My name is Roksana. And that is enough about my name," she said. "Tell me, Saleem. Do you want to stay in Greece or do you want to leave?"

"Nobody wants to stay in Greece," Saleem said quietly.

Roksana, less naïve than most girls her

age, was not surprised to hear Saleem say this.

"Where are you trying to go?"

"England." Saleem sighed. Saying it out loud, it seemed like an impossibly far destination. "My aunt is there."

"Ah, England," Roksana nodded as she looked out at the other refugees. "Yes, England is very popular."

"Greece is beautiful, but Greece does not want us here."

"It is a small country. The government does not have the money to help everyone."

"But you . . . you give food and help."

"We are just people, not the government." Roksana did not go into ideology or motives. She was not here to sing about the cause. It was her quiet presence that spoke to her beliefs. Saleem felt ineloquent around her.

"You do not agree with the government?" Saleem felt a little apprehensive for her. Where he came from, it was more than dangerous to blatantly oppose the thinking of those in power. Roksana was young and bold. His father would have liked her.

"We believe that people should be treated decently. We know what happens when people come to Greece, and we don't think it should be this way."

"People cannot apply for asylum here. Why is it so different?" Saleem had initially been frightened by the stories he'd heard about Greece from the boys in Attiki. He worried that the rest of Europe would be similar, a dead zone where his family would be adrift forever and in fear of being sent back to Afghanistan. The life of transience was exhausting both physically and mentally. But the Afghans he'd met also told him tales about the better worlds. Places deeper into Europe, countries like Germany, the Netherlands, and Sweden, did not turn up their noses the way Greece or Turkey did. Afghans there had been given second chances at having a normal life.

"Most people do not understand our system. How did you get here?"

Saleem did not want to answer. He twisted the cap back on the bottle of water and shrugged his shoulders cheerfully. His playful elusiveness made Roksana laugh.

"Tell me what happens here," Saleem said instead.

"Yes, yes. Okay, forget the question. This is what happens to most people who come here. They are arrested and the police take them to detention centers. They should be clean and safe places for people to stay, but there are too many people. There is no room. People say it is like a prison, even for children. They say it is worse than the place they came from. Sometimes they stay there for months.

"One day, the doors open and they get some papers. The papers say you have one month to leave Greece. Some people even get a ticket to Athens so they can leave from there."

"But asylum? There is no asylum?" Saleem was once again grateful for the false passports and the good fortune they'd had not to be stopped in Piraeus. They'd breezed through checkpoints without a second glance. According to what Roksana was telling him, their story was an exception.

"There is no real asylum. You must have work to get asylum. How can people find work?" She waved in the direction of the park. "First, you need a work permit. And for a work permit, you must apply for asylum. You see the problem?"

"Why are your friends here talking to refugees and writing these papers?"

"We volunteer. We want to be here. No one is giving us money to come. We come because we want to help."

Saleem looked at Roksana and wondered what kind of person he would be if he were in her shoes. He tried to picture himself as a high school student in a peaceful Kabul, coming home to his mother and father. Would he take up the cause of strangers? Would he care enough about how people were being treated that he would spend his time handing out food and filling out applications on their behalf?

He hoped he would. But it was very possible he wouldn't.

Just picturing himself in that utopian snapshot was painful, though. It was possible he would never be restored to the person he once was, the person who'd been able to laugh and dream and call a place home. It was possible that person, like his father, lay in an unmarked grave somewhere in Afghanistan.

On their second encounter, a day after Saleem's family left their room in the Attica Dream, Roksana was more direct.

"*Ela,* you want to apply for asylum or no?" Roksana was in no mood to mince words today. They sat on the concrete steps leading to the park. He wanted to ask her if she knew of a place his family could stay. Tonight would be their first night on the streets.

"Roksana, you ask me this again? I do not want to stay in Greece. I want to take my family to England. And you tell me Greece does not give asylum. These papers are for what?" Saleem felt terribly clumsy speaking in English, but he was thankful he could have even this much of a conversation. There was much he would have said had he been able to speak in Dari. She would have looked at him differently, he thought.

"But they do grant asylum *sometimes*. It depends on the story of the person or the family. Everyone is different." She looked off in the direction of the square pensively. "I think you have a story."

"A story? What do you mean?"

"A story. The reason why you and your family left Afghanistan. Some people left because there was no work or because they were tired of war. But I think you have something a little different. Maybe you do not want to say it, but maybe it can help you to apply for asylum."

"We left for many reasons."

Roksana looked at him patiently. After a long pause, Saleem started talking, his voice subdued.

"It is true, there was no work and the war was terrible. People were waiting . . . for peace or to die." Saleem looked off toward the street, the buildings. He had not talked to anyone about his life in Kabul, the things he saw. He hadn't wanted to rehash those dark times any more than he already did. In his mind, they were like the sound of a dripping faucet, a relentless sound that amplified in the quiet. And yet, he continued.

"My sister could not go to school. My mother could not teach. My aunts, uncles, and cousins — everyone left. My family stayed. We listen to rockets in the sky and pray the rockets do not fall on our beds. There was no music. There was only life the Taliban way. Sometimes we think maybe the Taliban is better than fighting. Maybe the Taliban make the fighting stop but they bring more problems.

"My mother cannot go outside without a man. There was only me. I go to the market and find food but we have only little money. There was no job. We understand that soon there will be no food and no money and no life."

Roksana listened intently. Her eyes stayed on the ground.

There was silence. Saleem wandered through his broken memories. He had been only thirteen or fourteen at the time. Looking back now, he appreciated much more just how desperate their situation had become — especially now that the burden of feeding his family fell on his shoulders.

"Saleem," Roksana started, her voice barely above a whisper. "What about your father?"

Saleem twirled the watch around his wrist.

"My father . . ." he began slowly, feeling his chest tighten as he spoke. "My father was an engineer. He worked for the Ministry of Water and Electricity. His work was with water."

What an injustice to his father's work to not be able to relay it in more detail. Saleem felt inadequate.

"My father, he believed . . . he believed some things are important for the country but some people . . . One night, three men come to our house. I hear them talk with my father. I never see my father after that night."

Saleem pressed his fingers against his eyes to plug the tears. He kept his head down.

"I am sorry," she whispered with a hand on his shoulder. "I did not mean to . . ."

"No, no," Saleem said. He resented her hand on him and the pity in her voice. Resentment hardened him, and the knot in his throat released. He took a deep breath and continued, his composure regained. "We left Kabul. We were afraid these men, maybe they will come back. Or we will die hungry in our house."

"Saleem, let me help you with the application for asylum. Your family deserves to have this story heard. You have a good case."

"But there is no help here. We have nothing. In England, we have family. Other countries, they will give us something. My mother, my sister, my brother — they need food and a home."

Roksana's eyes softened. She did not disagree with him.

"What will you do in England?"

"What will I do?" Saleem laughed. His shoulders relaxed. "I will drive a red car and eat in restaurants and watch movies!"

Roksana said nothing. Saleem's smile faded as he thought about what he really wanted to do in England. He wanted to go to school with his sister. He wanted to take Aziz to a doctor. He wanted to see his mother working as a teacher again.

Saleem turned to Roksana, a twinge of resentment at the privileges she enjoyed.

"What do you want here? You go to school, yes?"

Roksana attended an international school in Greece with instruction in English. Her parents wanted her to be around people of different nationalities, she had explained.

"Roksana, why do you come here? You have a nice school. You can go with your friends, your family. Why do you want to be with Afghans in a dirty park? You are Greek. For us, it is different. We are Afghans, lost from Afghanistan."

She turned away, avoiding his pressing gaze.

"We are not so different, Saleem."

Chapter 29
Saleem

Saleem woke to the feeling of pins and needles in his leg. It took more than a moment for him to realize what he was feeling. He'd only been asleep an hour or two. He'd been too anxious to close his eyes for most of the night.

Roksana had told him about this playground, nestled in among the apartment buildings that housed the middle class of Athens. In the evenings, the area was serene. It was off the busy street and had no pedestrian traffic after the nearby shops closed. The Waziris tucked their bags out of sight behind the corner of a building, and Saleem pushed Samira on the swing until it was dark enough. The entire family climbed into a small wooden playhouse and huddled tightly. His mother had taken a wool blanket from the hotel before they'd left and used that to cover them as best she could.

Madar-*jan* sat with her head against the

side of the playhouse. Her eyes were closed, but by her breathing Saleem could tell she was awake. She opened her eyes when she felt his leg brush against hers.

"Sorry, Madar-*jan*," he whispered. "I did not mean to wake you."

"Good morning, *bachem*," she said. Indeed it was. The sky was just starting to lift from black to a midnight blue. "I hope you got some sleep."

"I think I did." A jarring pain shot through his neck as he turned his head. He rubbed the knotted muscle. Samira lay with her head on Madar-*jan*'s side. The bundle of layers that was Aziz lay in Madar-*jan*'s arms. It looked as if she had not moved since last night.

But she will not complain, Saleem thought. She leaned in closer to Saleem.

"*Bachem,* I'm going to step out before people start to rise and walk about. I'll sit on one of the benches by the swings and leave you and Samira to sleep for a bit longer. Once I start to see people walking around, I'll wake you as well."

Saleem nodded. "I'll come with you, Madar-*jan.*"

"No, stay. Samira will feel better if she wakes up to see her brother with her. You didn't really sleep much. Stretch your legs a bit and see if you can get a bit more rest."

Saleem was too exhausted to argue. His heavy eyes closed again. It felt like only minutes later that he heard his mother whisper into the playhouse to wake them. People were walking their children to school. The family had survived their first night on the street. Saleem wondered how many more nights would pass before they had a real roof over them again.

Saleem could not do much in the early morning. He needed the cover of crowds to run his unlawful errands. Roksana was in school. She promised to meet him in Attiki in the afternoon. She was his only hope at this point, but when they met, he could tell from her expression that she did not have promising news for him.

"No one knows of a room. I have one possibility that I am working on, but I don't know yet. How was the night?"

"It was all right — quiet and not too cold. It was much better than any place I would have found." As long as they were not dragged off in handcuffs, Saleem could not ask for more.

"Saleem-*jan,* how are you? Enjoying a visit with your girlfriend, eh?" Jamal said in Dari. Roksana instantly shot him an icy look, her eyes narrowed. Saleem looked from her to Jamal and saw that he had noticed the same reaction.

"She's kind to waste her time trying to help guys like us. We should show her a little respect." Saleem had not intended to sound like he was admonishing Jamal, but he did not want to hear them talk about her in that way — even if they meant no harm by it.

"Saleem, the great defender of honor!" Jamal smiled. "Hallo, Roksana. How you are today?" he said in overenunciated English.

"Good. Get some sandwiches from Niko before they are all finished." Her tone was flat and unamused.

Jamal, distracted by his empty stomach, did not bother to wonder if Roksana had picked up on him talking about her. He made a dash to where Niko stood with a large cardboard box. There was silence before Roksana resumed the conversation where they had left off.

"The train is the best way for you to go. Really, in Europe they do not check for passports since you will be traveling between EU countries. The borders are open now. I can go with you to the train station to buy the tickets if you want."

"Please. It will help me very much."

"When do you want to go?" The smudged black liner gave an edginess to her look. When she wanted, though, her eyes warmed with a smoky softness.

He had not brought enough money with him, nor did he have the passport the ticket agent would want to see. He asked Roksana to meet him the following day at the train station. In the meantime, she would continue to look for better shelter for them.

Hang on, she told him, *things will get better.*

It rained that night. It started light at first, but then the drops grew heavier and slipped through the slats and into the playhouse. Saleem woke to find Madar-*jan* covering Aziz and Samira with what she could find, trying her best to keep their heads dry. Ten unrelenting minutes went by. Samira was wide awake, wiping rain tears from her cheeks, her bangs plastered against her head. Only Aziz remained dry, a plastic bag held over him by Madar-*jan.*

"Saleem-*jan,* take my place with Aziz. I'm going to find something better to cover us. We need to stay dry," she said.

"I'll go, Madar-*jan.* Let me do it," he offered.

"No, *bachem,*" she said carefully unfolding her legs to extricate herself from the miniature house. "I need you to stay here with them. I won't be long."

It was torture for her to be gone. Saleem looked at his siblings. He was wholly responsible for them now. The feeling overwhelmed him. Was this how Madar-*jan* felt or was it different for her as their mother? If she did feel overwhelmed, she hadn't really let on.

What if Aziz has trouble? What if Samira starts to cry? What if someone comes and takes us away?

All the resentment he had for being the one running the family's errands while Madar-*jan* tended to the younger ones, all of it melted and was replaced with a yearning for Madar-*jan* to come back. It was late, the hour when the underworld trolled the streets. If she was spotted by the police, she would have no way of returning to them.

He strained his eyes to make out her shape from the plastic window of the playhouse, but it was dark and the rain made it nearly impossible to see. Minutes ticked away.

When she did appear, her hair was drenched, her sopping clothes clung to her. She'd gathered rocks from the playground and used them to weigh down the layer of plastic bags she'd pieced together to block the seeping rain. It worked.

Their clothes and bread were soaked, though the rain let up in just an hour. Well before sunrise, Madar-*jan* folded up the plastic bags and returned the rocks to the flower beds. She was saving the bags, Saleem could see, for when the rain returned.

They changed into drier clothes in a public restroom. Saleem used a few precious euros to buy fresh bread and juice from a local shop. They ate quietly, exhausted from a restless night.

Saleem and Madar-*jan* counted their remaining money and set aside what Roksana had estimated they would need to purchase the train tickets. Saleem stuffed the money and his Belgian passport as deep into his front pocket as he could and set out. By afternoon, he was anxious to have their tickets purchased already. It was a huge relief that Roksana would be meeting him at the station.

He wished he could be more like Roksana. She was cool and confident. While he knew her parents traveled quite a bit, he did not know what they did. She was an only child, and her mother and father gave her quite a bit of autonomy for her age. Anytime he tried to learn more about her, she deflected his questions and turned the conversation back to his situation.

She stirred feelings in him. Feelings he knew he should squelch but couldn't. It was hard not to watch her. He could only hope she did not notice. He buried the urge to wrap his hands around her waist or bury his face in her neck. She did not seem uncomfortable around him, so he doubted she knew how he felt. Or maybe she knew but did not mind. Saleem could entertain that possibility for hours on end.

Saleem waited outside the train station, trying to look as casual as possible. He had used his reflection in a store window to finger-comb his unkempt hair into place. He spotted her across the street, a backpack slung over her shoulder as an afterthought. Saleem straightened his posture. She had on a black fitted button-down shirt with sleeves rolled up to her elbows. Her jeans tapered to a delicate ankle.

"Hey. How was the night?" she asked.

"It was okay," he shrugged with a weak smile.

"But the rain. Did you stay dry? I did not even know it had rained until this morning. I was thinking about your little brother all day today." There it was. Another clue that she saw him as more than just another refugee. He tucked her comment away with others he'd collected in their conversations. He would think more about it later.

"We were all right. It was wet but we . . . we covered. He is okay today."

"I am glad to hear that. The newspaper says there is no more rain for the rest of the week so it should not be a problem again."

"That is good."

"All right, let's go and find you some tickets, huh?" Roksana led the way. Together, they looked at the overhead board that listed the train schedule. "Did you plan where you want to go?"

"Yes, we will go to Patras and take the ferry to Italy."

Roksana nodded in agreement.

"Yes, I suppose that is the best way. You brought some money?"

Saleem pulled out his passport and the folded-up bills. Roksana told him to hold on to it. She looked for an open counter and indicated for Saleem to follow. She stepped up to the clerk and put on an especially cheerful voice. Saleem watched as she chatted amicably. The clerk, a middle-aged woman that Saleem would not have thought to approach, laughed and shook her head. Roksana half turned to Saleem and held out her hand. He gave her the money and passport without the clerk noticing.

They walked away with train tickets to Patras. Roksana was so at ease. Saleem could not recall the last time he'd been so comfortable. It seemed like all his life, his movements had been shadowed by fear. The monster may have changed shape and color over the years, but it was steps behind him, always.

Today was Wednesday. Their tickets were for Friday morning. Weekend travel was busier and they would stand a better chance of getting lost in the crowd. Madar-*jan* had decided it was time to sell off some of her jewelry. Saleem would need a day to find a way to turn her bangles into cash they could use for food and transportation.

"I do have some good news," Roksana said as they reached the street. "I wish it could have come sooner. I found a place for you and your family to stay. I know you'll be leaving soon, but at least you won't be on the street. One room. It is an older hotel run by a couple — my friend's grandparents. They are selling the hotel in two or three weeks to retire and it is in bad shape, but they have a room. They'll ask you to help them with a few things around the hotel, since they are old, but they are kind people. I explained your situation and they said if you help them enough with their move, they will not ask any money of you."

"Yes," Saleem agreed excitedly. He could hardly believe their good luck. Maybe Madar-*jan* had been right. Maybe last night's rain had brought *roshanee* after all. Roksana handed him a scrap of paper with the hotel's address on it.

"Don't thank me. You can thank them. Good luck, Saleem. I know it's not easy, especially with the entire family. I really hope the rest of Europe treats you well." She looked at her watch. "I need to get back home, but I'll be here Friday morning before you leave. I want to make sure you all get on the train. And I'll write for you which ferry you'll need to take from Patras. You know, in Patras there is a large camp of refugees. More Afghans are there than in Attiki and the situation is not good. Do not end up there, Saleem. From what I hear, it is a dead end."

He nodded, then watched her slide her backpack over her shoulder and cross the street. He would have one more chance to see her. He hadn't been ready to say good-bye to her today.

Their looming departure made him more anxious. He did not know what would be available to them once they got on the train or even in Patras. He stopped by a few markets on his way back and snuck away with what he could. He pushed aside thoughts of Roksana and reminded himself of the dwindling funds he'd counted out with Madar-*jan*. It was almost dark by the time he got back to his family. Madar-*jan* looked relieved to see him.

He understood a little better how she felt every time he left but only slightly. He could not possibly know everything that ran through her mind any more than she could his. There were things they said out loud to each other, things they whispered with a twitch of the face, and things that were stoically hidden. Mother and son were divided by age and role and by the desire to protect each other. But, though they could never admit it, their secrets were also designed to protect themselves and their relationship. Some things neither would want to know about the other even if they could. Some secrets saved them.

Saleem unloaded his bag and Madar-*jan* carefully rationed out what they could eat that night and what they needed to conserve for the journey. He gave her the tickets and passport, which she tucked into the draw-string pouch that hung around her neck, under her blouse.

"Aziz had another episode today," she told

him quietly.

Indeed, Aziz's color was more sallow than yesterday. He lay on the bed, a pillow propped behind him. He'd gained a bit of weight since he'd started the medication they'd purchased in Turkey. He'd started walking, speaking a few words, and even giggling from time to time. Saleem did not see him much, and when he did, he kept a distance. Things were different with Samira. He liked having her near, her head against his shoulder as he talked about his day. But Aziz was a child who stared at him expectantly and needed so much. Saleem could not manage it. He turned away, ashamed of his own resentment.

"We need to get him to a doctor in England. The medicine is not doing what it used to. His color is not good, and again he is looking so tired." Madar-*jan* looked defeated. Saleem wondered how his brother would fare on the journey ahead. "I'll call your aunt tomorrow and tell her of our plans. Maybe things are better for them now." She paused, choosing her next words carefully. "Saleem-*jan,* we cannot depend on them. It's important to remember that."

"Why? She's been telling us to come to London. Didn't she promise to help once we got there?"

"It's just that sometimes people want to help . . . but something gets in the way. I want us to be ready to rely on ourselves alone since it may come to that even once we get there."

"Never mind with that, Madar-*jan*. We've got a room for tonight. The girl from the aid organization found it for us. Let's go now before it gets late. All that rain last night, maybe it was *roshanee*, just like you always say."

Madar-*jan*'s face twinkled like embers stoked by a breeze.

She quickly gathered their few belongings and they set off to find the Hotel Kitrino, the Yellow Hotel. The owners were a gray-haired couple, kind enough to touch Aziz's cheek softly and to show them to a room. When Madar-*jan* tried to ask what they needed done so she could begin right away, they gestured for her to sleep the night and begin tomorrow.

On Thursday, Madar-*jan* removed the gold bangles her father had given her before her wedding and gave them to Saleem with a heavy heart. They had been placed on her mother's wrists when her parents wed. Her father had hidden them away until it was Fereiba's time to marry. It was all she had of her mother. She'd loved to hear them clink together softly every time she reached into a drawer, while she washed the dishes, and as she turned the page of a book. She would look at her wrist, coils of gold dancing with her every movement, five perfectly round embraces from the mother she'd never seen. Her father had undone the velvet drawstring pouch and put the bangles in the palm of her hand, closing his fingers over hers in a single, quiet moment. Had his eyes grown moist or had she imagined it? He was with his bride again, the woman who would never be replaced and whose absence had fractured their lives. Fereiba understood in that moment that while her father mourned his wife still, he'd never understood how his daughter mourned her mother. It was his loss and his alone. She did not hate him for this flaw, but she was able to see him more clearly. KokoGul had been right about him all along. Her father was content to contain himself in his orchard; his myopic love failed them all, not just Fereiba. No wonder KokoGul had picked up and moved on with her daughters.

And though it had been her father to put the bangles in her hand, it had felt as if her mother had drifted in while Fereiba slept, slipped them over her daughter's fingers, and slid them onto her arm. It was the gentle touch of a mother, a touch Fereiba had never known until she'd held Saleem in her arms for the first time, pressed her lips to his forehead, and realized she had much to give him, much that she'd never received.

Saleem knew none of this when he took the bangles from his mother. He could see only that she looked uneasy.

"My mind is restless today. I wish you would leave the pawnshop for tomorrow. We can stop by on the way to the train station. We could all go together."

"It's not far and we don't have much cash left, Madar-*jan*. Who knows what will happen in Patras. We'll need money for food and the ferry or else we'll be stranded."

"But today . . ."

"I'm going, Madar-*jan*. If we hide in a room every time we are nervous, we will never make it to England."

Fereiba bit her tongue. She began to dress Aziz and asked Samira to wash some of their clothes. She was going to see to what needs the hotel owners had. She turned away as Saleem put the bangles into his pocket and buttoned it to make sure they would not fall out.

Fereiba did not see the hesitation on her son's face — that second where he considered his mother's warning and chose to ignore it because he wanted to be braver than her.

"I'm going to the pawnshop now and then I'll be back in two hours," Saleem promised.

It was a promise he would not keep.

PART TWO

CHAPTER 30
SALEEM

An entire lifetime can change in one afternoon. The rest of the world can continue on, unaware of a quiet, solitary cataclysm occurring a few feet away. A police officer stood to Saleem's left, twirling a set of keys on his finger. A second officer rested his outstretched palm on the concrete wall above Saleem's right shoulder. He could feel the officer's breath on his cheek.

"Where do you stay?" The smell of garlic on his breath made Saleem's stomach turn. He dared not look away. He stared at the caricature of himself in the officer's sunglasses — his eyes wide and fearful. His adolescent face hadn't taken on the angles of manhood yet. A shadow lined his upper lip but nothing more.

"Again, please?" Saleem felt his voice quaver. In the few weeks he'd been in Greece, Saleem had picked up a few phrases but not enough to sound convincing. He tensed his shoulders, hoping to steady his words.

"Where do you sleep? Where is your home?"

The officers huffed and shook their heads at his blank stare. They were lighter in complexion than Saleem's deep olive skin, his color deepened by the months he'd spent working under the sun. The officer with the keys gave in and spoke in English.

"Where do you stay here?" he said, angrily.

Saleem's mind raced to come up with a plausible story. He couldn't lead these officers back to his family.

"I not stay. I am visitor. I come for shops," he explained meekly, pointing in the direction of the stores down the street. The officers both snickered.

"Shops? What did you buy?"

"Ehh, nothing. Today, nothing." Saleem willed them to lose interest.

"Nothing? Okay. Where is your passport? Papers?"

Saleem's stomach reeled. He tasted bile. "Passport? I do not have my passport." The owner of the pawnshop opened the door, saw the two officers on either side of his last customer, and quickly retreated into his shop.

"No passport?" The officers exchanged a

glance that Saleem could not interpret.

"My friend . . . he has my passport."

"What is your name?"

"Saleem."

"Where are you from?"

Saleem felt his heart pounding in his ears. Could he make a run for it? Unlikely. He was pinned against the wall in a busy market. Tourists walked in and out of shops, door chimes dancing in their wake. A dark-skinned street peddler kept his eyes averted as he packed his dancing stick figures into a sack. People walking by looked over with vague interest barely enough to slow their steps. Only the gray-haired man grilling corncobs seemed sympathetic. He wiped his hands on his half apron and nudged the fallen husks into a pile with the toe of his shoe.

It was hot enough to sweat even in the shade. Saleem was thirsty and hadn't eaten since last night. If he ran, they would overtake him quickly. The officers wore blue uniforms, felt berets, and button-down shirts tucked crisply into navy slacks. He stared at their thick belts weighed down with radios, handcuffs . . . pistols. Running was not an option. Neither was refusing to answer their questions.

"I am . . . I am from Turkey." Saleem had

rehearsed this part with his mother at least a hundred times and even more on his own. Other refugees had warned him about the chain of questions. He hoped they'd advised him wisely.

"Turkey?" The officer seemed repulsed. He shot the key jangler a knowing glance. "And how did you come here?"

Saleem nodded. "Airplane."

"Who came with you?"

Saleem shook his head. "I came alone." He prayed nothing in his voice or his eyes gave him away. He kept his hands glued to his sides.

"Alone? You are how old?"

"I am fifteen."

"Fifteen? And where is Mama? Papa?"

Saleem shrugged his shoulders.

"They are not here?" The older officer was losing patience, his thumbs hooked on his ominous belt. Saleem shook his head. They exchanged a few words in Greek, their angry expressions needing no translation. Saleem knew international law entitled minors to asylum, but he'd also learned that on the streets, those laws offered as much protection as a broken umbrella in a hurricane.

The officers looked him over, head to toe. Saleem shifted his weight, feeling their eyes on his black polo shirt, the collar and shoulders outlined in a white stripe. His jeans were frayed and faded, washed repeatedly in a sink with cheap soap. His clothes had fit him snugly back home but now, months later, they hung on his frame. The thinned rubber soles and blackened laces of his sneakers attested to his brutal journey. The English-speaking officer looped his keys onto a ring on his belt and nudged Saleem's shoulder to spin him around. He patted Saleem's waist briefly before mumbling something to his partner.

"Turn around." Saleem did as he was instructed, his eyes glued to the ground. "No passport? No papers?"

Saleem shook his head again. His three-hundred-dollar Belgian passport was in his rucksack, back at the hotel. He'd left it there, fearful he would lose it before the next leg of their journey.

"Come." The instruction was simple. Saleem thought his chest might burst. He could not go with them! What about his mother? Saleem looked at the officers and stole a quick glance at the cobblestoned path busy with souvenir hunters and locals. Was there something he could say to dissuade them? Could he buy his way out? If he followed, he'd surely be whisked away to jail, probably even shipped back home.

He was fast. He had always been fast, but in the last few months he had probably become even faster. He was unmistakably lighter on his feet and felt stronger, having carried his siblings and their modest baggage. The more he thought about it, the more convinced Saleem became. He could do it. He *should* do it. If he went with the officers, there would be no one to take care of his mother, sister, and brother.

Saleem's feet sprang to life, almost without his consent. He ducked under the officer's arm and ran furiously. He raced past the pawnshop, past the corn seller, his shoulders bumping against startled tourists. He heard yelling behind him. Off the main pedestrian way was a hopeful maze of side streets. Saleem ran down an alley on his left with smaller shops and fewer people. Just a few meters and it ended. He could go right or left. With nothing promising in either direction, he went left. He needed to put distance between himself and the officers, but he couldn't head back to his hotel.

Saleem turned another corner. A resting stray dog lifted his head curiously as Saleem panted and surveyed his options. Which way? This part of Athens was disorienting; there were no guiding landmarks but Saleem knew a main road was just a few blocks away. He rounded a corner and ran directly into a couple, their arms encircling each other's waists. They stumbled, cursing as Saleem steadied himself and raised an apologetic hand. The alley opened into a plaza with an old church in the center, a relic surrounded by posh modern shops. His eyes scouted the intersection, looking for the next twist in this labyrinth. He felt conspicuous, wild eyed and exposed.

The metro, Saleem thought.

But where was it from here? Saleem pressed his back against a wall as he searched for a clue. The street sloped downward and, from what he remembered, the metro station was lower than the rest of the market. He hadn't been on it since that first day, not wanting to squander their funds while his own feet carried him fine. He took a deep breath and set off running again, his eyes scanning the scene in search of blue uniforms. He didn't see any. He kept his head low and wove through people, hoping for human cover. His mother's voice echoed through his thoughts, just long enough to propel his shaking legs.

My mind is restless today. I wish you would leave the pawnshop for tomorrow. We can stop by on the way to the train station. We could all go together.

*It's not far and we don't have much cash left, Madar-*jan. *Who knows what will happen in Patras. We'll need money for food and the ferry or else we'll be stranded.*

But today . . .

*I'm going, Madar-*jan. *If we hide in a room every time we are nervous, we will never make it to England.*

Saleem would later regret being short with her, but he could not think of that now. The metro sign loomed in the distance. His pace quickened. He stopped short at the arched entrance, a bridged staircase that led to the open tracks. His calves burning as he listened for the rumble of the approaching train. He could see nothing in the distance yet. Saleem did his best to appear calm, wishing he could better conceal himself, but he needed to stay close.

The vibrations passed through his thinned soles. He stole a nervous glance at the booth just inside the entrance and rehearsed his plan. Jump the turnstile just as the train pulled in, board it before anyone could stop him, and take it as far as he could possibly go. Even better, he'd switch at a connecting station and stay on the system until he was sure he had lost the officers. Saleem could not help but break into a smile as he saw the steel giant turn the corner. He would not tell his mother about the police officers.

Just as he lunged for the turnstile swearing he would listen to his mother's intuition every time going forward, angry fingers clawed into his shoulder and pulled him back. He spiraled around. His arms flew outward, but there was nothing to catch.

The train was loud enough to muffle Saleem's cries as it pulled in and out of the station.

CHAPTER 31
FEREIBA

Maybe this is how it is meant to be. A wife without a husband. Children without a father. Perhaps incomplete is the very definition of a normal family. Where did my lofty expectations come from anyway? Afghanistan is a land of widows and widowers, orphans and the missing. Missing a right leg, a left hand, a child, or a mother. Everyone was missing something, as if a black hole had opened in the center of the country, sucking in bits and pieces of everyone into its hard belly. Somewhere under our khaki earth is everything we've ever lost. I've heard the gray-haired Afghans living in foreign lands say, "Bury me in Afghanistan when I die. Return me to the land I came from." They say it's for love of country, but maybe it's because they think they'll be reunited with all they've lost there. Others stubbornly refuse to leave Afghanistan, no matter what is happening in our streets.

Maybe because they think the earth will open up and return to them all that has been stolen.

I believe in no such thing.

What is gone is gone and will not come back. When the earth swallows, it swallows forever and we are left to stumble along feeling the absences. These are our burdens.

My son is hardened. He is becoming a man without the guidance of a father. I let him run with boys because he cannot be around women only. I can only teach him what I know. He needs to learn the ways of men and I pray that he will be safe while he does so and that I will be able to pull him back if he strays too far. He will resent me more if I do not give him this space. Already his words and accusing eyes are those of a man while his face and body remain that of a boy. He's not the boy he was a year ago.

I miss the boy Saleem once was, mischievous and coy. I miss his laughter. I miss having his arms around my neck. All these were lost back home, in the land of the missing. Even if we reach England and settle into a new life, I know Saleem will never be that boy again. What is gone is gone.

My children inherited from me the misfortune of a missing childhood, as if the time they spent in my womb stained them with a *naseeb* of hardship.

Now I wait for Saleem to return from the pawnshop. My gold bangles, the only piece of my mother I had, are gone now and can be counted among the missing. I hated to part with them, but how could I keep them while my children are put to work or hungry? What Saleem brings back will be my mother's gift to my children. It will not glitter or sing like wind chimes, but it will be her soft kiss on their cheeks.

KokoGul had never known about the bracelets. Unlikely they ever would have graced my wrists if she had.

"So what else have you hidden from me, dear husband?" she'd asked in a half tease. "Maybe these walls are full of treasures gathering dust. Why did you not let me keep those bangles in a safe place?"

"What place could be safer than somewhere unknown to you?" my father had retorted.

"Well, let me see them at least before they leave this house for good." KokoGul had beckoned me to her. I'd stuck out my wrist, not wanting to slip them off for even a second. "Hmph. From a distance they looked thicker. Actually, they are very thin and flimsy. More like gold plate."

Every hallway creak brings a tightening in

my chest. I hope Saleem returns soon. He had said two hours, but it has been much longer. I should not worry. When he returns, he'll tell me he got caught up playing soccer with friends, that he lost track of time because he was with boys, the afternoon sun bright on his face. I will shake my head at him, but I will be happy for him, too. If only his father could see him now, our wayward boy, carrying his family on his back. My husband would put his arm around me and grin as he did when one-year-old Saleem took his first triumphant steps.

Things will be better once we get to England. Despite what her husband says, I know Najiba will help us. We will have them to lean on until we find our way, but it will not be long, God willing. If we have gotten this far, we can make a life for ourselves in any country. We need only a chance. Somewhere in the world, there must be a place where we will be welcomed as a long-lost sister, not stoned away like an unwanted snake in the garden.

Please hurry back, Saleem. The hour is late and my faith too shallow to reassure me much longer. Please come back soon.

CHAPTER 32
SALEEM

The ride to the prison seemed an eternity. Saleem could feel the sweat trickle down his back. His window was open about an inch — just enough to make him wish he could roll it down more.

"Please, sir, I must go. I will leave Greece tomorrow. I will not be a problem. I do not need help."

"You will leave tomorrow? Very easy, yes?"

Sarcasm was never lost in translation.

They reached the outskirts where tourists dared not venture, and Saleem's cheeks were hot with tears. They passed by the narrow road that led to the Yellow Hotel, an unimaginatively named lemon-colored building. He fixed his eyes on the street but saw no one. In an hour the sun would start to set and Madar-*jan* would begin to worry.

At the prison, Saleem was led past desks and officers, most barely looking up as he passed. He was taken toward the austere back of the building where two African men and one Greek man sat in a cell. Saleem felt the urge to run for the nearest exit, but with every passing minute, his chances at valiance grew slimmer. The older officer motioned to another policeman to open the cell for Saleem.

"Get in."

Think, Saleem told himself. *Think of something to say that will make them pity you. Something that will make them let you go.*

"Please, I will go home. Please let me go, sir," Saleem said, making one more ineloquent plea for mercy.

"You will go. You will go here."

With a quick shove to his back, Saleem stumbled into the cell. His shoulders hunched in defeat. The other prisoners glanced over with the kind of vague interest that idleness breeds. The men had no desire to make eye contact, much less conversation. Saleem shuffled to the back corner of the cell, about twelve feet by twelve feet in size, and sulked like a caged animal. He leaned his back against the cold wall and slowly slid to the ground, his knees bent against his chest.

Madar-*jan* would leave Samira to look after Aziz while she searched for him, Saleem knew. She might try to find the pawnshop. Perhaps the store owner would tell her that the police had stopped Saleem. Maybe she would faint or become hysterical right there. Saleem reviewed the afternoon's events and kicked himself for being so careless. The man of the family sitting, useless, in a jail cell. His adolescent muscles burned at the thought of his mother and siblings left on their own, the money from his mother's gold bangles tucked into his left sock where it did them absolutely no good.

Saleem spent the night in prison.

In the solitude of the crowded cell, he had time to reflect. Saleem had spent months looking over his shoulder and worrying about this very scene, winding up in a cell. He no longer had to worry about it. The sense of dread was gone, though replaced with new fears.

As his mind settled, he took stock of the men around him. Two African men sat side by side, mumbling to each other without the effort of eye contact. The Greek man would look at the others and grunt, his face twisted in annoyance. His cell-mates ignored him mostly. Saleem's mind wandered.

Life would be different if my father were alive.

It wasn't a new thought, but it felt especially loud and true as he wondered what would become of his family. When he needed to break his train of thought, he stood and walked the length of the cell, keeping close to the wall, but it was of little use. His mind was just as much a prisoner as he was.

Saleem nodded off intermittently over the course of the night, waking up with his neck stiff and pins and needles in his legs. He changed position frequently and grew to hate the smell of the concrete floor.

Should I tell them the truth? Wouldn't they pity me? If they knew what happened, they couldn't possibly send me back to Afghanistan. But what if they did?

In the morning, his stomach grumbling, Saleem was taken into yet another room for questioning. He was seated across a bare table from a new officer, who had introduced himself with a name that sounded like it started with the letter G. It was too foreign and cumbersome for Saleem's tongue. The officer blew a dense cloud of cigarette smoke across the table. Saleem held his breath and exhaled slowly, hating to let this man's smoke waft through his lungs as if it had every right to.

This officer was very different from the two who had brought him here yesterday evening. He was older, middle aged, and smaller framed. He wore a gray shirt, but paired with the same navy blue slacks and burdened belt of the two who had arrested him. His breast pocket bulged with a pack of cigarettes. Salt-and-pepper hair framed his weathered face, cut so short it stood on end. His eyebrows and mustache curved downward in a way that made his entire face droop.

Officer G spoke English well and did not seem to be in any kind of rush. He looked thoughtful before he started to pose his questions to Saleem. Saleem wondered, briefly, if this man might have pity on him and allow him to go free.

"How old are you?" G's eyes squinted as he sucked on the filtered end of his cigarette, his teeth yellowed with years of nicotine and coffee.

"Fifteen," Saleem answered, determined to stay consistent with the answers he had given yesterday.

"Fifteen. Hmm. Fifteen." There was a pause. "And where do you come from?"

Saleem had spent a good deal of the night preparing for this question. Yesterday, he had told the officers he was from Turkey.

But if he told them where he was really from, they might send him back there. He didn't think he would survive if he was sent back to Afghanistan alone.

"Turkey." Saleem braced himself.

"Turkey?"

Saleem nodded.

"You are Turkish. Hmm. Why have you come here?"

"I want to study," he said honestly.

"Study? You cannot study in Turkey?"

Saleem did not respond.

Officer G pulled a sheet of paper from under his notebook. He slid it across the table. "Read this."

Saleem looked at the paper. He recognized the writing as Turkish. The characters were the same as the English alphabet but with dots and curved accents that reminded him of Dari. He had learned conversational phrases but knew he would stumble horribly if he tried to read. He was cornered. He wet his lips and reminded himself that this officer was not Turkish. He probably couldn't read the text either.

"Please, mister, water?"

The officer cocked his head to the side and stood. "Water? Of course." He exited the room and returned with a small paper cup that held no more than one sip, barely enough to wet his mouth. Saleem accepted it and felt his hopes for mercy wane. He looked back down at the page before him and started to sound out the words with as much confidence as he could muster. He looked up at the officer.

"Translate, please," Officer G said casually, taking the cigarette pack out of his pocket. He used his last cigarette to light a new one.

Saleem's whole body tensed. Was he being toyed with? His breathing quickened, and he felt his throat tighten. He wanted to be back on the cold, gray ground of the cell. The officer waited for his response.

"You are not from Turkey," he declared simply when he saw Saleem squirm in his chair. "I ask you again. Where are you from?" His words were carefully enunciated so that there would be no mistaking the question or its importance.

Saleem recognized defeat.

"Afghanistan."

"Ahh, Afghanistan. How did you come here?"

"I came from Turkey."

"Boat?"

Saleem shook his head. "Airplane."

"Without passport?"

"I have passport but my friend . . . he take it."

"How long are you here?"

"One week," Saleem lied insecurely. As best as he could figure, the longer the time he had illegally been in Greece, the angrier this man would become.

"You want to stay in Greece?"

Saleem shook his head.

"Where do you want to go?"

"I want to go England."

"England." He chewed on Saleem's answer before asking his next question.

"How old are you?"

"Fifteen," Saleem said.

"Fifteen?" Officer G doubted this as much as his other answers.

"Yes."

Thinking of the darkness they'd left behind in Kabul, Saleem convinced himself even the most stone-hearted officer would take pity on a lone adolescent. Officer G stepped out of the room and returned with a can of orange-flavored soda, the sort that universally appealed to children. He popped the tab and slid it across the table, then lit himself a cigarette.

"Your situation is bad," he said simply. Saleem watched his face. There was no arguing that fact. "And if you do not tell us the truth, it will only get worse for you."

Away from his family, Saleem had nothing to lose. Exhausted and desperate, Saleem heard a softening in the officer's voice, the tone of a father chastising his son. He took a long sip from the orange can. The warm fizz tingled in his mouth and coated his throat with a reassuring sweetness. He felt his shoulders untense like the freshly popped soda can with its quiet hiss.

"I will tell you now," Saleem said limply. "I will tell you my story."

The officer leaned back in his chair, inhaled deeply on his cigarette, and nodded as Saleem returned to the night that was blacker than sin.

Chapter 33
Saleem

"Stay here. Doctor come now." Saleem watched blankly as Officer G exited the room. A doctor? His mind felt fogged from his sleepless night. It was difficult to focus.

An hour later, a man in a collared shirt and slacks entered the room. He had a white doctor's coat slung over his arm and a tawny leather bag in his hand. He was heavyset, the buttons of his shirt looking ready to give way. His face was round with jowls that sagged despondently. He looked like a Russian cartoon character Saleem had once seen on a black market video.

The doctor muttered something as he entered the room. He dropped his bag and white coat on the table. From the leather case, he pulled out a stethoscope, a small penlight, and a pair of latex gloves. He sat in the chair that Officer G had occupied and motioned for Saleem to come over to him. Saleem slowly rose and walked over.

The doctor gave him a general once-over and then stood to begin his inspection. He shined his light into Saleem's bloodshot eyes and dry mouth. He motioned for Saleem to remove his shirt. Saleem could smell his own staleness as he lifted his arms. The doctor didn't seem fazed. He brought his stethoscope to Saleem's chest and listened while he stared blankly at the ground. He peered closely at Saleem's underarms before slumping back into the chair. He tapped Saleem's waistband.

"Take this off," he said simply. Saleem felt blood rush to his face.

"No!" he blurted. He took a few steps back, putting the table between him and the doctor.

The doctor let out a tired sigh.

"Take off. I must check," he said. He checked his watch and looked at Saleem expectantly. Saleem crossed his arms, his skin prickled with anger. The doctor waited a moment, his fingers tapping on the table. Quickly, his face grew serious and his eyes zeroed in on Saleem.

"Take . . . OFF."

In his voice was the clear message that there would be no way out of this. Saleem felt incredibly alone and small. He took a few deep breaths before doing as instructed, his fingers fumbling nervously with the button and zipper before he slowly brought his pants down to his ankles. His briefs hung loosely on his hips. Saleem stared at the ceiling.

"Take off." The doctor touched the waistband of his underwear as he snapped the gloves over his thick hands. Saleem felt a heat rush over him. What was this doctor looking for?

Saleem's breath was a slow and bitter exhalation, an effort to expel his humiliation in a whistle of air. He pulled his briefs down to his knees. The doctor adjusted his lenses and peered interestedly at the area between Saleem's legs. From his bag, he pulled out a paper tape measure and used it to assess whether Saleem's body had a different answer to the age question.

Saleem hadn't been naked in front of anyone since he was a small child. Part of him wanted to drive his fist through the doctor's curious glasses while another part of him wanted to curl up into a ball and wail. The exam concluded before Saleem could act.

"Okay, finished." He motioned for Saleem to pull up his underpants and jeans, as he jotted something into a notepad that fit in his palm. "Any health problems?" he asked as Saleem hurried to pull up his briefs and jeans.

"No. No problems."

"How old?" The question resurfaced. It dawned on Saleem this was the reason for the doctor's visit, explaining his focus between Saleem's thighs, the part of him that had changed most in the last few years.

"Fifteen," Saleem answered meekly.

"Hmph." The doctor paused briefly to look at Saleem's face and scribbled a few more notes. He packed up his tools, retrieved his white coat, and exited the room without any further conversation.

Alone, Saleem began to pace the room, his anger fanned by exhaustion. He let out a short yell that bounced from wall to wall. He yelled again — longer and louder.

Saleem put his palms and forehead against the wall. It felt cold and real, realer than the rest of his situation. He brought his right palm against the wall a second time, harder.

Again and again, harder and harder, Saleem slapped his palm against the cold wall as the past twenty-four hours spun through his head: the policeman grabbing his elbow as he exited the pawnshop, the cigarette smoke blown in his face, the doctor examining his genitals with more attention than the customs officer had paid to their travel documents, his mother frantic in the hotel or searching the streets, Samira frightened and silent, his father watching and shaking his head in disappointment, Aziz's tiny chest heaving with discomfort. They exploded above him like a shower of rockets, raining down on his head and shoulders when there was nowhere to run and nothing that could be done.

Saleem was pounding the wall with two hands now, enraged and crying. He didn't notice the door open behind him.

"Hey! Hey!" Saleem felt a hand pull his shoulder. It was Officer G, a cigarette dangling precariously from his bottom lip. "You crazy?"

Saleem turned around and slumped to the floor, weakened by his outburst. He hadn't eaten since yesterday afternoon. Almost as if the officer and Saleem realized this at the same time, he left the room and returned with a plate. There were a few pieces of chicken kebab and pita bread. He put the plate on the table unceremoniously.

"Eat something."

Saleem's breathing slowed. His palms stung, pulsing. He returned to the table in defeat. He took the food and chewed bite after bite, tasting nothing. He stared at the plate, letting his eyes gloss over and his muscles relax. The officer watched Saleem, a specimen in a jar. Captivating to his captors.

Saleem ate without looking up or saying a word. Maybe if his belly stopped growling, he could come up with a way to get out of this mess. Maybe he could figure a way to get back to his mother.

CHAPTER 34
SALEEM

Two Turkish police officers stared down at Saleem and the other refugees. Herded onto a boat like cattle, Saleem and a dozen similarly thwarted migrants had been returned to Izmir. The Turkish officials were not pleased to have to reclaim these refugees but those were the rules. Refugees were to be returned to the first country they entered and the burden was on that country to deal with them. It was a cause of persistent resentment between the Turks and the Greeks. The handoff had been terse.

Saleem watched the Greek officers smirk as they handed over a stack of papers and unloaded their cargo onto Turkish soil. Few words were exchanged between the two sides but their sentiments were clear.

Not our problem anymore, the expressions on the Greek officers read.

Thanks for nothing, the sarcastic reply on the faces of their Turkish counterparts.

They took their frustration out on the refugees, grabbing people by the arm and shoving them into a van waiting at the port. Thighs overlapping, shoulders pressed together. One small window in the back did little to ventilate a van full of refugees who had been languishing in a Greek detainment cell for days, weeks, months.

Every step of the way, Saleem had promised that if released, he would leave Greece immediately. His pleas drowned in the sea of similar pleas authorities had heard before from so many others facing deportation.

Saleem wanted to be the one, the exception to the rule. He wanted to be able to look back at the moment and recall how close he had come to being deported, how close he had come to being separated completely from his family. But everything — the seat beneath him, the smells around him, the people standing over him — told him he was not in the least bit different from any other ragtag passenger in the van.

There were Africans, a few eastern Europeans (Saleem guessed by their appearance and their unfamiliar language), and even a few Turks. There were no other Afghans, which made Saleem feel both more alone and relieved at the same time. He was not in the mood to talk when he felt it would not help.

*Where does Madar-*jan *think I am? Could she have found the pawnshop? Maybe they've gone to the train station to wait for me there. Maybe they even got on the train, thinking I would show up. They could be anywhere now. Madar-*jan, *how frantic you must be! How will I find you again? What can I do by myself?*

Saleem's mind was a thunderstorm, moments of peace interrupted by electrical flashes of dread and a flood of remorse.

So much for roshanee.

His fingers toyed with his watch. It had been two days since his arrest.

I wish you would leave the pawnshop for tomorrow. We can stop by on the way to the train station. We could all go together.

*If we hide in a room every time we are nervous, we will never make it to England, Madar-*jan.

Saleem's head hung down. A thousand times the conversation had replayed itself in his mind.

Why did I have to snap at her? Please, God, do not let that be the last time I talk to her.

He thought of his last night with Padar-jan. Memories of the things he regretted saying collected like beads on a *tasbeh.*

The drive was long, jostling. It was a relief to be herded off the vehicles and into another grim-appearing building. Here they were led into a large room, and each immigrant tried to find a square of cement floor to claim as his own.

Saleem filed in with the others and slid up against a cinder-block wall. He touched his ankle, hoping no one was watching him. The wad of bills was still there, right where he had left it. He prayed he would not be searched. If they confiscated his money, he would have absolutely nothing.

Hours passed. A latrine in the corner collected their waste. The air burned with the sharp smell of ammonia. Two men sobbed, not bothering to hide their faces. Dignity had been lost long ago.

Saleem closed his eyes. One or two at a time, the refugees were taken out of the holding room and led into an interview room. Some people came back and others did not. Saleem was not sure which to hope for. When a guard pointed at Saleem, he stood and followed him down the hall. He was instructed to take a seat at a small table. The police officer in front of him looked from Saleem to the document on the table.

Keep your answers the same. Remember what you told them in Greece.

The questions started. Saleem was now familiar with the process.

Where did you come from? Why did you leave Turkey? What were you doing in Greece? Who was traveling with you? How old are you? The truth — what is your age?

I am from Afghanistan. I do not want to be refugee in Turkey or Greece. I am alone. I am fifteen.

For the most part he was able to respond to their questions in Turkish, the rest he filled in with English. This seemed to entertain the officer.

Fifteen? Hmph. The same suspicious sneer. *Why did you leave your country?*

Saleem decided to be forthright with them, selectively.

I want to go to England. My country, there are Taliban. They are dangerous. We had no money, no school, no work. They are killing people.

Were they thinking of sending him back? He could not go back. He would not survive there on his own.

Are you a soldier?

Soldier? No! I was a student. My father was engineer. They took my father and . . . they kill him.

Saleem's heart broke to say the words. They looked dubious. He'd been herded and poked at like livestock and still they wanted more.

You do not want to be in Turkey?

Saleem shook his head.

But you speak some Turkish.

Saleem nodded, unsure if this would help or hurt him.

Do you know anyone here in Turkey? Did you live here?

These questions were trickier. Saleem told the officer he had met some boys, but he did not know where they were. He had lived in a small town and worked on a farm but he did not remember where that town was. He did not want to go back there, he assured the police.

The officer left and then returned with another man. They stood outside the door to the room and spoke quietly. Saleem could not hear what they were saying nor could he read the enigmatic expressions on their faces. Had he made a mistake in his answers? Did they think he was lying? What were they deliberating?

His head ached. The combination of human odors, hunger, and cigarette smoke had brought on a throbbing headache. He was tired and felt the chair pushing against his bones.

They entered together.

You must leave Turkey.

Saleem nodded.

You must not return to Turkey. And if you are arrested somewhere else, you must tell them you have never been to Turkey. Do not speak Turkish. You speak some English. That is enough for you.

Saleem was uncertain what their warnings meant. It almost sounded as if they were going to blindfold him, spin him around a few times, and push him off into the unknown. Were they sending him back to Greece? Iran? The officer was not pleased with Saleem's reticence. He may have mistaken it for something else.

He took one broad step in and slapped Saleem against his temple.

Saleem suddenly became very afraid.

If you are found again in Turkey, it will be a very unpleasant experience for you.

Slap. Saleem's ear throbbed. He kept his head bent.

Do you understand what I am telling you? You speak Turkish, no? Why do you not want to speak now?

I understand, Saleem managed to get out.

An officer grabbed him again by the elbow and led him quickly and brusquely through the hallways and out a door. Saleem stumbled, staggering to keep his footing.

The sunlight burned his eyes. His hand went up reflexively.

He felt one firm blow to his backside and he was on the ground. Another boot hit his left rib cage and dirt flew into his open mouth.

Maybe you really are fifteen years old. You fall like a boy, not a man.

One officer laughed.

You must not be found again in Turkey. Find a way out and don't come back.

Saleem stood up cautiously and nodded. He'd been freed. The officer slammed the door shut. Saleem was outside. He paused, unsure if this was some kind of trap or test. A moment passed and the door did not reopen. No one came around the corner.

Saleem took a few small steps away from the building. Still nothing happened. With a rush of adrenaline, he broke into a run. He could escape. Saleem ran down the quiet streets and ducked behind some buildings. He did not know where he was or where he was going, but he knew he wanted to get away from the police station before they changed their minds.

Saleem panted heavily with his hands on his knees. His mouth was dry and gritty as he tried to spit out the dust that coated his tongue. His stomach reeled and he spewed bile against the wall. A pain shot through his left side. He breathed deeply and waited for it to pass.

There were no footsteps behind him, no sound of running officers in pursuit. They were not looking for him, but they'd been clear that they should not find him. Saleem needed to leave this town as soon as possible. He had some money. Could he get back to Greece without a passport or any travel documents?

*What should I do? Madar-*jan, *please tell me what I should do!*

He tried to calm himself. He could feel his thoughts spinning wider and wider away from him.

Focus. Think. You can do this.

Saleem quieted his own thoughts. As the chaos in his mind relented, he heard his mother's voice.

Find a safe place. Find food. Get back to Greece.

Saleem looked around him. There were no shops or stands. No people to approach. He was like one of the boys in Attiki now. He had stepped out of his story and into theirs, away from the privilege of a passport and family. He had no jewelry to sell and only the bills he'd kept hidden to help him get through. The journeys he'd heard of in Attiki, the survivors he'd met, haunted him.

His head began to uncloud. He wiped his

mouth with the back of his hand.

I must look like hell.

Saleem wound his way through the streets, looking for a busier area and the things he would need: food, shelter, and a way to get back to Intikal.

Intikal was the only place he could think to go. In Intikal, he could turn to Hakan and Hayal for help finding his mother. The thought of being in their home again brought him comfort.

Food was easy enough to find since he was desperate and tired enough to pay for it. He would need strength to continue. The shop owner frowned in disgust but accepted the sweaty euros he had pulled from his sock.

Toasted sesame bread, the cheapest food he could find, calmed his angry stomach. It was afternoon. Saleem could feel eyes boring into him and imagined fingers pointing his way. A thousand tiny drums in his head begged him to sleep.

Saleem found a public restroom and did his best to wash the filth off his face. He rinsed his body with water he cupped in both hands. He moved his left arm slowly, his side aching.

The boys in Attiki had talked about their journey into Greece. Some had taken small boats run by smugglers. Other had snuck onto trucks that were loaded onto ferries. Both ways were dangerous. Everyone had stories of people perishing in the waters or dying in the undercarriages of freight trucks. Saleem did not know where he would even find a smuggler now. It was best to make the long trip back to Intikal, regroup, and come up with a solid plan.

It was a painful choice but Saleem walked out of the restroom with halfhearted resolve. He asked around and found his way to the bus station. In six hours, a bus would leave for Intikal. He bought a ticket and waited.

Saleem fell asleep to the low rumble of the bus's engine. At least between here and Intikal there would be no more checkpoints, no police officers. And at least in this country Saleem could hold an intelligible conversation. His head bobbed against the stiff headrest with every dip in the road. He dreamed he was on the bus but with Madar-*jan,* Samira, and Aziz in the next seats. They were going to Intikal together, a bag of jewelry and personal belongings stored under their seats.

The trip was longer than he recalled, but Intikal looked unchanged and welcoming. Saleem saw the mosque where he had approached Hakan on that first day. It was a good feeling.

He passed the shop where he and Kamal had pilfered cigarettes and candies for sport. The shop owner's back was to the window as he stocked his shelves with boxes of cookies. Saleem stuffed his hands deep in his pockets and kept walking.

It was early evening. From a distance, Saleem could see a light on at Hakan and Hayal's house. He could have run to their door and collapsed on their front porch, but he was wary of alarming them. He took slow deliberate steps, thinking of what he was going to say. His breathing quickened. His fingers trembled as he knocked on the door.

Hakan answered. His eyes bulged to see a boy he barely recognized.

"Saleem!"

"Mr. Yilmaz . . ." Saleem began. "I have nowhere else to go . . ."

"Come in, come in!" Hakan craned his neck into the street. "What about . . . ?"

"They are not with me," Saleem said plainly.

Hakan pursed his lips and led Saleem into the kitchen. He called out for Hayal, who looked even more startled to see Saleem. She threw her arms around him. Saleem's eyes closed. It felt good to be in their warmth but he felt so filthy, he nearly pulled away for her sake. She set off to make some hot tea and warm up some food. Hakan and Saleem sat at the kitchen table.

"Where is your dear mother? And your siblings? Are they all right?"

"I don't know. I think they are okay, but I do not know. Maybe they take the train or maybe they wait for me in Greece, but I don't know how to get back there."

His responses were choppy and puzzling. Saleem sounded as frayed as he felt. Hakan and Hayal exchanged looks of concern.

"Eat something, dear boy. You look like nothing has passed your lips in days!" Hayal mothered him while Hakan tried to understand what had happened after the family left Intikal.

"You took the ferry to Athens — all of you? Where did you stay?"

Saleem was too exhausted to filter how much he shared with them. He told them about the first hotel and then the Afghans he had met in Attiki Square. He told them about their decision to leave the hotel and save their euros for their travels and the brisk nights they'd spent in the playground.

Hayal cringed to hear him talk about Fereiba and the younger children sleeping in the cold rain. Saleem went on. He talked about the Yellow Hotel and the train tickets they had purchased. Then he got to the pawnshop and the police. His voice began to choke. Hayal put a hand over his. The police station in Greece. The police station in Turkey and then the only place he could think to come to, the Yilmaz home in Intikal. Odd how in this moment, Hakan and Hayal felt more like family than any of his aunts or uncles. If Madar-*jan* knew he was with them, it would bring her so much comfort.

Hakan leaned back in his chair. As parents, they'd had the same thought. The only possibility was to reach the Yellow Hotel, but Saleem did not have the phone number.

"Maybe we can find the number but we will need a computer," Hakan said.

"A computer? Kamal's family! They have a computer!"

"Saleem, Kamal's family moved away after that wedding. They are gone. But I have another friend nearby who may be able to help. I'll go to his house and see if he can help find something. But first, tell me everything you remember about this hotel."

Saleem wrote out the hotel's name and the cross streets as best as he could remember. While Hakan left to search out the number, Hayal prepared a much needed bath for Saleem.

Warm water relaxed his neck but not his mind. He could not stay here forever. He had to get back to Greece.

He put on the clothes Hayal had laid out for him, a pair of pants and a shirt her sons had outgrown and left behind. Hakan returned with good news. He'd been able to track down the phone number of the hotel on the Internet. Saleem, who'd been nodding off on their sofa, was suddenly awake and ecstatic.

"I must call! I must call now! Maybe they are there!"

"I know," Hakan smiled, but he seemed hesitant. "I have a calling card. We can try the number now but . . . but Saleem, you must remember it is possible that they have taken the train. They may not be there and that does not mean something bad."

Saleem nodded. He was glad he was not making this call by himself. Whether or not he was able to reach them, he would need someone to turn to when he hung up the phone.

Hakan read the instructions on the back of the card and dialed the string of numbers until they were finally connected. He handed the phone to Saleem, whose knuckles blanched as he listened to the trill of the phone ringing on the other end.

A click, a throat cleared, and some mumbling.

Saleem recognized the old man's voice.

"Please! I need to speak to my mother. Is my mother there?" His words were a jumble of English, Turkish, and Farsi, an emotional short circuit between his thoughts and his tongue.

"Who is this?" The voice on the line was confused, suspicious. Hakan put a hand on Saleem's elbow. Slow down, he motioned. Saleem took a deep breath and focused his English.

"Please, my name is Saleem. I was staying at the hotel with my mother. I need to speak to my mother. She is there with my brother and sister!"

"Ah, the boy! Your mother looks for you. She is in room. Maybe you call back later. Now I am busy."

"No, I cannot call later. Please, my mother. I must speak to her now!" The old man detected the desperation in his voice.

"Okay, okay." He muttered something in Greek that Saleem did not understand.

The silence was interminable. Hakan and Hayal watched Saleem's face anxiously.

Fereiba's voice crackled through the

receiver. Saleem leaped to his feet and, like a tethered animal, paced as far as the coiled line would allow.

"Saleem? Saleem, *bachem*? Is it you?" Her voice trembled.

"Yes, Madar-*jan*," he said. "It is me."

"*Bachem*, where are you? Oh, thank God! I've been so worried!"

"I'm in Intikal, Madar-*jan*, with Kaka Hakan and Khala-*jan*. The police caught me and sent me back to Turkey."

"The police? Oh God, you are in Turkey!" Madar-*jan*'s mind was racing as she processed the implications of this news. "Are you all right? Were you hurt?"

"I'm all right, Madar-*jan*. I'll find a way back to Greece, but I don't know how long it will take."

It was not so much that they needed to make a painful decision but rather that a painful decision had been made for them. Saleem spoke first.

"Madar-*jan*, you have the passports and the train tickets. Take Samira and Aziz and get yourselves to England as soon as possible. I have to find a way to get back and it may not be soon enough since I don't have my papers. But if you wait for me, Aziz might get worse."

"I can mail the passport to you. I can send

it to Hayal-*jan*'s house." Madar-*jan*'s voice was laden with guilt. "But, Saleem-*jan,* what about money? Did the police take everything from you?"

"No, I have the money from the pawn-shop. If you can send me the passport, then I can take the same route and before you know it, I'll meet you in England." Part of him wanted Madar-*jan* to say no, to tell him that she would wait for him in Greece and that they would all go together to England. Surely, she wished for the same but their plan had to take Aziz's broken heart into consideration.

"Oh, my son. God keep you safe from harm. Saleem-*jan,* give me their address. I'll mail the passport. Your friend, Rokshaana, she came to the train station. She saw us. She knew who we were. She's so kind and she said she'll come again here later today. She can help me mail this passport to you."

Madar-*jan* had met Roksana? Saleem slipped back into the chair and rested his forehead on his hand. His head hanging, he closed his eyes and let gratitude wash over him.

Thank you, Roksana. Thank you.

Hakan tapped on his watch. The calling card would soon run out of time.

"Madar-*jan,* I don't have much time left

on this card." He turned to Hakan and asked for their address. He relayed it to Madar-*jan* as quickly as Hakan could scribble it on a scrap of paper.

"Saleem-*jan, bachem,* I'll mail you the train ticket and the passport. Forgive me, we will take the train, maybe tomorrow. Aziz needs to see a doctor. But be very careful, please! Say a prayer with every step and keep your eyes open. Sweetheart, believe me, I wish I didn't have to —"

The line went dead. Saleem cradled the receiver. As his mother's voice vanished, Saleem's journey changed. He was on his own now. Tonight would be the last night that the Waziri family could sleep in relative peace, aware of each other's whereabouts and well-being. Saleem's family had met Roksana and she would guide them through the next few steps. Fereiba was comforted knowing Saleem was with Hakan and Hayal. Tonight, if they could just keep their minds off tomorrow, they would all get some rest.

Saleem crawled onto the familiar mattress and fell asleep in seconds.

He woke in the morning, his eyes opening to the same cracking plaster he'd watched for months. He returned to the fault lines, the places where the paint had chipped away and the ceiling peeked through, exposed for what it really was. Saleem ran his fingers through his hair and down his arms. He touched his side and winced when he reached his flank. He expected to feel the same fault lines on his own body, places where the weight of the load had started to break him open and expose him for what he was.

Early morning light drifted through the gauzy, cotton curtains. The fog was lifting. Saleem had slept more than half a day and woke with a renewed clarity.

He would wait for his passport. It could take two weeks for the passport to arrive. That would be two weeks without income. There was only one thing to do. Saleem got up and buttoned his shirt. He would go back to the farm.

Mr. Polat smirked and spat, but he needed the help. He told Saleem to go into the field and begin his work. The Armenian woman chuckled to see him as if she'd known all along he'd be back. She shook her head and resumed her work, muttering something under her breath that he would not have understood even if she'd yelled it out to the skies.

Saleem understood though.

What use was it? You packed your bags and sat on a boat and prayed and for what? Nothing has changed because nothing will. You tried to cut free of these vines, but they will only grow tighter around you.

Saleem said nothing to her but stood for a moment with his back to the sun, his shadow stocky and bold between the rows of tomato plants. She was wrong. Everything had changed since he'd last been on this farm. He was a true refugee now but one who had seen the ocean. He'd heard the sound of waves and smelled the salted ocean air. Every step of the journey had altered him, changed his very coding irreversibly. He had crossed the waters once and would cross them again — accompanied not by his family but by the tiny mutations in his being that gave him the strength to do it on his own.

Chapter 35
Fereiba

I wish for no mother to face the choice I had to make. Nothing could be harder.

I'm weighed by a guilt so heavy that it takes every ounce of strength I have to put one foot in front of the other and continue.

How Saleem found his way back to Intikal, I will not know until I see my son again. I never should have let him leave that hotel room. I should have been his mother and raised my voice and stood my ground. My skin prickled that day when he talked of going to the market. Can a mother commit a greater sin than ignoring her intuitions? I pushed it aside because I wanted to give him the space he wanted, the space his father believed he needed to become a man.

Mahmood was not always right. I can see that from here, clear as the brilliant blue sky. He made decisions with his mind. He stood for what he believed to be right and logical and good — all romantic notions that failed us. Kabul was no place for ideals. I knew that. I told him as much. Ideals and guardian angels are for children and times of peace. They have no place in this world. We should have left Kabul long ago, followed my siblings to safer places while we were still whole. I let him overturn my intuition, snubbing our noses at God's warnings.

To hate him, though, would be another shade of blasphemy.

He is not here, and I cannot alter the path we decided on together. I cannot change the conversations we had. I stood by him because I loved him and trusted him and wanted to honor the choice we made. His goodness, the nectar he offered the world, attracted one, then two, then a swarm of bees. They circled him, humming, until that moment when they released their venom. Even after he was gone, I could still hear the sound of them, circling my family. But this was my own doing. I let Saleem, my firstborn, walk out the door and into an unforgiving world and now I cry that he has not returned. I am the mother I swore I would never be.

I have reasons for my choice. Aziz looks terrible. He has not gained weight and I see the strain in his sallow face, the tiny blue vein running across his temple, the bones of his back looking like beads on a string. I need to get him to help if he's to live to see his brother again. He is so light in my arms. He is my last child, the one I will carry for as long as I can, because he makes me a mother for that much longer. When he is awake, I watch his movements. I see Saleem in him too. He is very much like his older brother, headstrong and resilient. Each struggles in his own way but Saleem can stand on his feet. His voice, coming from the safety of Hakan and Hayal's home, told me he could find his own way.

I made a choice. We took the train from Athens. Could I have done things differently? I could have. But my intuition told me that Aziz could not. Forgive me, Saleem, but we could not wait for you. For your brother, the brother I know you resent and adore, I had to move on.

There could be nothing worse than choosing between two children. Ask me to choose between my right arm and my left and I will give you one. But ask me to choose between two of my children and my heart shatters into a thousand pieces. Children are touched by heaven — their every breath, every laugh, every touch a sip of water to the desert wanderer. I could not have known this as a child, but I know it as a mother, a truth I learned as my own heart grew, bent, danced, and broke for each of my children.

Samira watches me in silence. She is no longer a girl, her body assuming the delicate curves of a young woman. Thank God, she looks to be much wiser than I was at her age. I was naïve. I think of how I believed people — the boy in the orchard, KokoGul. I imagine my daughter holds her tongue because she knows words mean nothing, accomplish nothing. She's shown the quiet strength of a woman since we left Kabul. She has done as much for her little brother as I have. She has rocked him through his sweaty fits, patiently fed him when he would push the food away, and shouldered our bags when I could not. All of this matters more than any words she could say, though I yearn to hear her voice again. More than anything, I want to hear her laughter.

She misses Saleem. She's incomplete without him and will not speak until he returns — until something is given back to her by a world that just keeps taking away. Her heart mirrors my own, and it is for her that I hold back my tears. I've had enough. I'm tired of being trapped. Each morning when I wake and find that nothing has changed, I think I am finished.

Were it not for my children, I would be. For them, I cannot be finished yet.

I may find Saleem again. I may put my arms around him and hear his voice and have him returned to his family. Even if I am so fortunate, I will not be the same. I will always be the mother who left a son behind. It is the hell I live in now and will live in forever.

The train has pulled out of the station. We are on our way. People look at us but our tickets are not questioned, nor are our documents. Some would call that lucky but lucky is relative.

Samira stares out the window; Aziz's head rests against her side. She is thinking of her brother, no doubt, and wondering if her mother has made the right choice. I cannot explain it to her. It is a thing that cannot be packaged into words.

CHAPTER 36
SALEEM

Saleem rushed home every day to see if the passport and train ticket had made it to Intikal. A week after he'd returned, he had sheepishly approached Hakan and produced a few bills to compensate for his room and board. Hakan shook his head and told Saleem not to speak of money again. Saleem bit his lip and nodded, an ineloquent but understood gesture of thanks.

Ten days went by and still no envelope from his mother. Saleem's mood was further fouled by Ekin's interest in his return. She stood behind the farmhouse pretending to read or tend to the herb garden Polat's wife kept behind their kitchen. She made an effort to stay visible, watching Saleem from the corner of her eye. She said things Saleem did not want or need to hear.

"Where did you go?" Ekin laughed. "My father cursed for two days when you didn't come back. You're lucky he let you work again."

Polat, from time to time, would shoo her back into the house, but he seemed oblivious to her fascination with Saleem. Their conversations were unbalanced. She talked and Saleem listened, afraid to say anything that could be taken the wrong way. He bit his tongue as she droned on about school and radio and things he could not possibly know.

Sixteen days and still no passport in the mail. Saleem was having trouble sleeping. Hakan had tried calling the hotel again, but the owner said the family had left long ago. Saleem could only hope that meant that they'd boarded the train successfully and possibly with Roksana's help. Maybe they'd even made it to England by now, though he wasn't sure Madar-*jan* had a plan for getting from Italy to England.

The passport was a whole other matter. Saleem had no way of knowing if the documents had been mailed or if they'd made an error with the address. Maybe they'd been confiscated by the postal system. He would wait. That precious booklet with his grim-faced photograph and invented birthday was the only way he could avoid the death traps the Attiki boys spoke of. He remembered the dark figures who had transported them across the border into Iran. He'd heard the man push his mother for more money, and he'd heard worse stories from others. The underground world was one without laws or codes or safety nets. Some people were transported successfully. Others never made it. No one knew what really happened in the shadowy world of smuggling beyond the few stories that bubbled to the surface.

On a Monday afternoon, Ekin sauntered behind the house where Saleem was tilling the soil for a new crop and wondering what he would do if the passport didn't arrive by the end of the week.

"I bet the water runs black when you bathe," she said with a grin.

Saleem kept his head down and dug the hoe heavily into the dirt. She wasn't sure why he hadn't laughed.

"You do not speak much. I don't know why you are so quiet. Did you work on a farm where you came from? I've lived on this farm all my life, but I bet you've picked more tomatoes in a day than I have in a lifetime."

Saleem, in a different state of mind, might have been able to realize that she meant some of what she said as flattery. To him, she was as soothing as sandpaper.

Ekin was wearing a calf-length pleated skirt and a blouse. She leaned against the rail of the fence and began to play with the cuff of her socks, pulling one up to her knee and then the other. Saleem thought of Roksana. The two girls were so different.

"Does your mother work too?"

"No."

"What about your father?" She was bullish. Saleem's fingers clutched at the handle of the hoe tightly enough that he made himself nervous. He shook his head.

"I have work." His words were stretched taut and ready to pounce. Ekin paid no attention.

"I know. You are a good worker and that's why Baba took you back. He said at least you're not like the others." Ekin pursed her lips. "I've heard some of the immigrants bring drugs with them. Baba says that's what makes so many people lazy and slow."

"Ekin, leave me alone! I am working!" he thundered. He could not bear a single sentence more from her. Ekin's jaw dropped.

"You yell at me?" She sounded stunned.

"You don't know anything about my family or why I have to work here on this farm.

I'm tired of listening to you!"

"I know more than you do!" she cried defensively. "You don't know how to talk to someone who's trying to be nice to you. You only know about tomatoes and animal shit! At least I go to school and don't stink everywhere I go! Maybe you should learn about a few things before you start screaming!"

"You know so much? You know nothing! I went to school too, but schools close when rockets fire on our homes. We leave and come to this country and here I work for almost no money. I work to be with my family . . . to have food for my family. You know how it is to be alone? No one to help you?" Saleem's voice faltered. He still had the hoe in his hand and was working it into the soil with a concentrated fury. He'd nearly forgotten Ekin was there, making her mostly unimportant.

"I do not know where my family is," Saleem said in a melancholy whisper. "Your baba thinks he gives too much money but I work many days for nothing. I work here again because I have *no* choice."

Ekin was quiet. Finally.

Saleem channeled his anger and focused on the work he had to do. He didn't bother to look up and see the expression on Ekin's face. He did not see her eyes water or the way she bit her lip or slipped away trembling. Dig, pull, lift. Dig, pull, lift. He swung the hoe because it was all he could do.

Saleem did not see Ekin for a week after that. His outburst had driven her away. He felt no remorse for it. Every day that passed he became testier. It was now nearly three weeks since he had spoken to his mother. He wasn't sure how much longer he could continue holding out hope that the passport would arrive.

And then Ekin came back. It was early in the morning, and Saleem headed into the barn after giving a quick nod to Polat, who was already on a plow and heading off into a distant field. Mr. Polat usually kept to himself, working long days but not in any proximity to Saleem or the Armenian woman.

Saleem went into the barn to check on the troughs. He looked for a pail to bring in fresh water.

"Saleem." Her voice was a sheepish whisper.

"Mm," he grunted. He didn't bother turning around and dug through a stack of equipment trying to find a pail.

"I . . . I am sorry." She was behind him now. Just inches away from his back. He felt her fingers touch his shoulder and he tensed. An apology? This, he had not anticipated.

"I didn't mean to say . . ."

He nodded with his head bent, a quiet acknowledgment of her gesture. She sounded sincere, and he was too exhausted to be angry. Her words meant more than he thought they would. Her words made him feel just a bit more human than he'd felt in a long time. His mood softened.

Ekin's fingers moved from his shoulder to the back of his neck, slowly and deliberately. Saleem was paralyzed, unsure what she was doing. He was afraid to move. Her touch was surprisingly gentle, much gentler than her words had ever been. She moved in closer. He could feel her warm breath on the nape of his neck.

What is she doing? I should move away. I should . . .

Her fingers tangled themselves in his inky hair, teased his scalp, and returned to his neck and shoulders. Her other hand touched his shoulder and lingered on his arm. She was tentative, but when he did not pull away, she leaned in and pressed her face into the space between his shoulders. Something in him stirred. Saleem's eyes closed.

Ekin pushed him gently into the barn's

recess and out of the sun's light. Hay crinkled under their feet. Saleem's feet moved at her guidance, but he did not turn to face her. He could not face her. The light was dim, darting through eyelet openings in the slat roof.

Why is she doing this?

"I only wanted to talk to you," she whispered to Saleem so quietly that he was not sure if he had heard her or imagined it.

He turned slowly, his curious body acting without thinking. They were face-to-face, but the darkness was forgiving. She touched his cheek. Saleem found it easy to disregard every terrible conversation they'd had. There was something tender and exciting and irresistible about the moment. His hands moved on their own accord, traveling to her narrow waist, tracing the outline of her hips and sliding upward. She brushed her lips against his cheek. He turned his face, and their mouths connected. Clumsy and wet. Saleem felt another part of him grow anxious. As long as his eyes stayed closed, he could ignore the world.

Their feet shuffled in the straw.

"Saleem . . ." she whispered. His eyes opened and he pulled back abruptly as if he'd touched a hot stove.

A thousand thoughts rushed into his

mind. What if Mr. Polat were to walk in? Why was he even touching her? He took a step back and hit a wall. Ekin recoiled, surprised by his sudden shift.

"I should . . . you should go," he said simply. She paused, and then she spun around and raced out of the barn. Saleem was left to wonder what aftermath to expect. If her father or mother found out . . . his heart pounded to even think of it.

Saleem paced the barn and wondered if he should leave before Polat came chasing after him. He waited and strained his ears for the sound of Mr. Polat raging toward the barn. Nothing. Saleem inched toward the barn door and peered out apprehensively. Off in the distance, he could see Mr. Polat still riding his plow. Mrs. Polat was at the back of the house, hanging sheets on a clothesline. There was no sign of Ekin.

He cautiously resumed his work, but it was hours before his pulse slowed to normal. His eyes darted back and forth as he worked, careful not to be caught off guard. Sunset came and Saleem left, tired and sweaty from an extraordinarily exhausting day.

Saleem found himself back on the truck the next morning, wondering if he was walking into a trap. He approached the farm tensely and on guard but, just as the day before, Polat barely acknowledged his appearance. Saleem stayed on alert all day and was thankful Ekin stayed out of sight. He'd thought about those moments in the barn, puzzled by her actions and unable to decipher her motives.

What girl touches a boy? How shameless.

But he also wondered why she'd approached him. Her condescending tone and spiteful comments . . . had that all been a front?

Saleem was even more puzzled by his reaction. He hadn't pulled away.

His body had responded to her with its own urges. He could still feel her skin under his fingertips, her half-ripe curves beneath his palms. Last night, he lay awake on the mattress and let his fingers move along the nape of his neck, the way Ekin's had. The feeling gave him a thrill.

He wondered if she kept away because she was angry or if it was because she was ashamed.

From time to time, Saleem thought he caught glimpses of Ekin watching from the back window or slipping through the side door. She remained elusive. Saleem was grateful. He had no words for her.

■ ■ ■ ■

As the days slipped by, Saleem became even more restless as he waited for the envelope his mother promised him. He had even checked in with the neighbors to see if the passport had been delivered to the wrong address. A month passed and there was still no sign. As optimistic as Hakan and Hayal tried to appear, Saleem could tell they too were beginning to think the envelope would never arrive.

Ekin finally broke her silence. The sun was setting and Saleem had just finished planting a bag of seeds that Polat had given him. It was time for winter crops and Polat wanted to grow sugar beets. Saleem had put the tools back into the barn, piled them into a corner, and stretched his back. He heard hay crackle and turned around to see Ekin's thin frame by the barn door. She did not approach him.

"You are finished?" she said softly. She looked away, one foot tucked behind the other in a bashful pose. Saleem could sense her discomfort and felt a wave of pity.

"Yes," he replied. He stayed where he was. The distance between them was protective.

"You don't like working here." It was a

statement, not a question. Whatever she was about to say, Ekin had rehearsed. He could almost imagine her, watching from a distance and thinking of what she would say to him.

"I thought maybe you would . . . I did not mean to make you angry or sad. I did not know. I want you to take this and do not come back here. It is better if you do not come back here." She held in her outstretched hand something folded up in a piece of notebook paper.

"What is it?"

"Just take this. And go. Please . . . please just go." Her voice sounded strained, like a child on the verge of a tantrum. She took a few steps toward him but kept a distance. Saleem was a fire that would burn her if she got too close.

The packet was within reach. Saleem took it. Ekin was unpredictable, but her demeanor was changed. Saleem could sense she was not toying with him and that whatever she was offering had not been an easy decision for her to make.

His fingers closed in on the paper. Ekin whipped around and ran out of the barn. Saleem watched her go before undoing the folded paper carefully. Packed within, he found a thick wad of bills. His eyes widened.

There was more money than he could estimate, bills of all different denominations.

Saleem panicked, folded up the bills, and stuffed them into his pocket. He listened for the sound of approaching footsteps and heard nothing. Where could Ekin have gotten this from? When he saw no one nearing the barn, he slipped out of view again and took the money out of his pocket. As he fingered through the bills, his heart quickened and he broke out in a sweat. He was left with one question.

Should I take this?

After months of laboring for every lira, selling off Madar-*jan*'s last pieces of jewelry for a few euros, and stealing bread to feed his family, Saleem could see no other possibility. He needed this money and believed he deserved it. He stuffed the wad into his pocket and smoothed his shirt over the lump. With a deep breath, he stepped out of the barn and walked across the yard toward the small road. He did not turn around or stop to see if the Armenian woman was behind him.

He sat in the back of the vehicle and pushed his pocket against the side of the truck. He kept his head low and did not meet anyone's eyes as they traveled the dusty road back to town.

In his pocket was a bundle of hope. He could afford to pay a smuggler to get him across the waters and back into Greece. In the last week, Saleem had come to the quiet realization that the passport he was waiting on was not coming. Every day he stayed in Intikal was a day lost. By now he could have been reunited with his family. The money in his pocket was nudging him to make the decision he knew he had to make.

He also knew that the money Ekin had given him had been stolen from her father. There was no way he could return to the Polat farm.

I need this. I put up with Mr. Polat's orders to do this or that, and then do it over again because it was not good enough. I could not argue when he refused to pay me. This money can get me out of here and back to my family. What does it matter why she did it?

He'd made his decision by the time he walked through the side door. He could hear Hayal in the kitchen. He would not tell them about the money. There was no way to explain it. He needed to leave for the port right away and make his way to a boat for Athens. This was the only way.

Once he was certain Hakan and Hayal had retired to bed, Saleem counted and re-counted the money until he was convinced

410

it was real and that it was enough to get him back on course. It was far more than what the pawnshop had paid for his mother's bangles.

Saleem had never seen his mother without those gold bracelets. He knew only that they had been his grandmother's, a gift to the daughter she never met. He felt for his father's watch on his wrist.

Madar-*jan* must have felt the same about her bangles. They were her only link to her mother.

Though he had no idea where she was, Saleem could now see and hear his mother more clearly than in all those months that they'd traveled side by side, jostling against each other on buses and ferries, sleeping in the same room, and doting over Samira and Aziz. The fog lifted and his mother crystallized before him as a real person. Saleem shut his eyes in the dark and wrapped himself in his mother's forgiving embrace. He prayed for another chance.

CHAPTER 37
SALEEM

It was harder to say good-bye to Hakan and Hayal this time. While Saleem had money and heart on his side, he also had no documents to facilitate his travel across borders.

His kind hosts were surprised by his sudden decision but did not try to dissuade him from leaving. Hayal busied herself getting together food, two pairs of wool socks, three shirts, and a windbreaker for Saleem. He rolled the clothing up and stuffed it into a small backpack that he slung over his shoulder. A brisk wind heralded the arrival of a colder season, and the extra layers could save him.

The wad of bills stayed close in his pocket where he could feel its reassuring bulk press against his hip. If he were caught, the money would be found, but he could not bring himself to hide it anywhere else.

Saleem retraced his steps and took the bus back to the coast. His skin prickled as the bus drew closer to the police station in Izmir where he'd been sent off with a rough farewell.

Saleem's palms grew sweaty. In his solitude there was not much he could do to steel himself. He fell back to the words he'd heard his parents whisper in unsteady moments, in moments of hope and moments when they wanted to feel comfort.

Bismillah al Rahman al Raheem . . .

In the name of Allah, the most Gracious, most Compassionate . . .

Saleem had considered the two ways he knew of to get to Greece. He knew he could look for a smuggler to get him across the waters. That would cost a lot of money, especially if he smelled the desperation on Saleem. If it used up all his funds, he would have nothing left to get him from Greece to Italy.

The boys in Attiki had talked about people crossing over on cargo ferries leaving from Turkey and going to Athens. Trucks were loaded onto ships for transport. Jamal had filled him in on what some people had done. He hadn't painted a pretty picture.

First, you sneak onto the undercarriage of a truck when no one is looking. The ports are busy so you have to do it when the truck driver and the guards are distracted. Then you have

413

to stay there, not moving, until the truck is loaded onto the ship. When it is on the ship, you have to be completely still and quiet, however long the ride is. The tricky part is then at the final port where you have to get off the boat without anyone noticing.

Somewhere between Intikal and the port city, Saleem had decided he would try to make his own way across. Smugglers were too risky, and he couldn't afford to lose all his money when he still had so much farther to go.

Saleem got off the bus and quickly ducked into a small side street to get his bearings. He discreetly scanned his surroundings for any signs of uniforms. He needed to get to the port. It was already afternoon and unlikely that he could sneak onto a truck today, but it would be best if he could find a secure place nearby to spend the night.

He asked a shop owner for directions to the port, and he was directed to yet another bus. The local bus, much smaller, took him to where the town met the ocean. He saw the same massive ships docked and smaller ones floating by piers with groups of people walking on and off. With guards, crews, and passengers milling about, making a mad dash for the ramp was not a feasible plan.

Be smart. Be very careful.

The port was bustling. Saleem stood opposite a major road that ran like a divider between the town and the docks. Beyond the gates, he could see a huge lot of containers, large rectangular freight boxes of different colors with writing on the sides. He watched a couple being loaded onto a ship.

But how would you know when the container was set to be shipped or where it was going?

He spent the evening watching the ships, studying their procedures and their patterns, and making note of the piers. He needed to find the gaps, the places where he had a good chance of getting by without being noticed.

Farther along, there was a dock where people moved in and out of passenger ferries. The Waziri family had boarded here to get to Athens. How different that boat ride was! They'd been petrified of being caught but they'd been together. They'd rejoiced in the sight and sound of the sea.

We had no idea how easy we had it then. If only it could be that simple again.

Saleem kept walking until he reached a secluded grassy area on the port side of the highway. It was just behind a construction site, and he could see the workers were packing up their tools and heading toward the road. He had a good view of the docks.

He used his backpack as a pillow, leaned it against a tree and studied the scene. It was later now and harder to make out what was happening in the distance but he paid close attention anyway, straining to see what he could. Within an hour, a magnificent sunset glazed the sky in oranges and purples. Moments later, it was dark and Saleem was completely alone.

He picked up his backpack and walked cautiously to the small building nearby. It was still under construction. He peered into its dusty windows and saw no one within. There were exposed pipes, bricks, and tools everywhere. The doors were locked. He snuck around to the back of the building and tried the windows. He was lucky. He crawled through an unlocked window and landed, with a thump, inside a skeleton of a room with only its framework and no walls. Every creak and howl made his skin jump. He put on an extra shirt and zipped his jacket up and stretched his legs on a folded gray tarp.

Saleem woke to the sound of men's voices in the distance. His eyes opened slowly.

The construction workers! It was morning and they'd returned to start a new day. Saleem grabbed his bag and climbed back out of the window before they could make it into the back room. He heard voices shouting behind him but did not stop or turn around. He ran, darting between cars to cross the highway, and dodged behind an apartment building. He was panting, his tongue thick and dry as if it were coated with the white dust he'd brushed off his clothes and hair. Confident no one was chasing after him, he walked toward a corner store to buy a bottle of juice and then got back to work.

Cargo vessels were loaded onto trucks and, from there, onto ships. Saleem got a bit closer to the shipping yard, but the containers were all locked and impenetrable as far as he could tell. They would not be easy to break into. There were freight trucks, eighteen-wheelers backing into the ship slowly while passengers walked single file up the ramp and onto the deck level. Saleem's plan was beginning to take shape.

Saleem went to the ticket booth and asked for a ferry schedule. The woman at the desk gave him a pamphlet, which he took back to the outer limits of the dock to read.

By midmorning, Saleem had watched three ships dock and take off again with fresh loads of passengers and freight. He was starting to get hungry when something caught his eye. A dark-skinned man, who looked to be a few years older than Saleem, strolled casually by the fence surrounding the cargo container lot. As inconspicuous as he was trying to be, he was nearly six feet tall and his head turned left and right every few moments. Saleem recognized the nervous walk right away.

Saleem watched the man make a quick, agile climb over the metal fence and into the yard. Saleem craned his neck for a better look. The African man wound his way past the cargo vessels and stood at the edge of the lot where trucks backed onto the ships. Crouched behind a red container, he waited a few moments before making a break for a truck waiting to be loaded onto the ship. He dashed toward the gap between the cab and the trailer, trying to find a space to crawl under. Saleem held his breath.

Two men ran over in his direction. He had been spotted.

Saleem moved a few steps closer, anxious to see what would happen. The man heard yelling and scrambled onto his feet. He charged into the maze of containers, weaving his way in and out of vessels.

Saleem bit his tongue.

That could be me. That easily could be me.

The man made a nimble climb back over

the fence and ran across the highway, just a few meters from where Saleem stood. As he neared, Saleem could see a streak of blood from his hand. He did not appear to notice his own injury.

"Hey!" Saleem called out. "Hello!" The man looked over as he slowed down to catch his breath. He looked at Saleem with suspicion.

"Your hand!" The man was about twenty feet away now. His forehead glistened. The man looked startled but quickly recognized Saleem for what he was too.

"Your hand!" Saleem repeated, pointing to his own left palm.

The man looked down, unfazed. He nodded at Saleem and walked down the street, careful to keep his hand out of view.

Saleem's trepidation increased. It was one thing to hear stories from the boys in Attiki but quite another to stand at the port and watch people being chased. He could imagine what might have happened if the African man had been caught.

Two nights more, Saleem slept in the nearby construction site and left before the work crews returned in the morning. He used as little money as he could for food, just enough to keep his energy up. He spent his days studying the port. Once, he'd even seen the African man return to survey the possibilities, his hand wrapped in a cloth bandage and held close to his body. He made no daring attempts and did not seem interested in talking to Saleem.

By the third day, Saleem decided to make his way onto the docks. A ferry for Athens was coming in at noon. Thirty minutes before the ship's arrival time, three trucks pulled in and backed up toward the ramp in preparation. The drivers got out, chatted with others, and got some food.

Saleem began his dangerous flirtation. He tossed his backpack over his shoulder and walked casually toward the trucks. Passengers were just starting to file in, wheeling compact suitcases behind them or carrying duffel bags over their shoulders. Saleem hoped he was blending in.

Saleem broke away from the group and wandered over to the side where the trucks idled, thick plumes of smoke rising from their exhaust pipes. He moved in closer when he saw no one paying attention. Two drivers had their backs turned to him, standing just in front of a truck. Saleem was about thirty feet away. If he could get to the back of the cab, there was a chance he could slip into that gap and then get under the carriage of the truck. But he would have to be quick about it.

One driver pointed at something off in the distance. Saleem acted before he could give it a second thought. He made a dash for the truck, trying to keep his footsteps as light as possible. The drivers were on the opposite side, still engaged in conversation. Saleem looked for something to grab onto behind the cab. There were pipes and coiled wires but no place for him to slip under and clutch. He crouched down and grabbed at something so hot that his hand jerked back reflexively.

He found a rod that ran from behind the front wheels down the length of the chassis. It was thin but it might support him. Saleem had flipped his backpack so that it rested on his belly. As he grabbed at the rod, part of it dislodged and clanged against the ground. The drivers, alerted by the sound of metal on pavement, came around to the back of the truck just as Saleem was scrambling to his feet.

Run. Just run.

They were behind him, hollering and cursing.

Run.

The boys back home would have bet on Saleem. They would have bet that he could outrun the truck drivers and make it away without them ever getting close to laying a hand on him. He'd been that fast on the soccer field, so quick on his feet that he would have time to turn his head back and smile at the boy chasing behind him, panting and reaching with an outstretched hand.

But that was a different Saleem. That was a boy who had a mother and father to go home to. That was a boy whose belly was full of his mother's cooking and new sneakers on his feet. That boy wasn't here.

The boy who ran from the truckers was hungry and alone and had only the strength required to hunch over tomato vines or rake animal shit with someone standing over his shoulder.

This Saleem was much easier to catch.

They grabbed him by the collar and pulled him back. His feet, still trying to propel forward, flew into the air as he was thrown to the ground. His face hit blacktop, and searing pain ripped through his jaw.

The rest Saleem would remember only in bits and pieces, in souvenirs left on his body by those men who were tired of being used by refugees and tired of having their trucks checked and rechecked by customs agents. Brown boots and angry words.

He had tried to get back on his feet. He

staggered.

One burst of adrenaline.

Run.

They yelled behind him.

Their voices faded as Saleem managed to put some distance between them.

His backpack slapped against his chest violently. He leaned against a brick building, out of sight. The adrenaline gone, he began to feel again. His ribs throbbed, and his legs felt as if they might buckle. His shirt was torn and pants covered in dirt. His pulse pounded in his ears, not loud enough to drown the sound of their shouts.

His lip was bleeding. Saleem wandered in and out of narrow side streets, staying away from pedestrians. He wanted to be invisible.

Saleem stumbled into a vacant warehouse and waited for his eyes to adjust to the dark. He crouched against the wall. He closed his eyes and tried to ignore the hurt.

Please, God, let me rest here.

He was broken and did not know how much more he could take.

Chapter 38
Saleem

For two days, Saleem mostly slept. He'd lost track of day and night. Every time he started to wake, his mind coaxed him back, unable to muster the strength to face a new day and ignoring his hunger.

On the third day, his stomach argued for food, unsatisfied by the half bottle of juice he'd dug out of his backpack. He touched his lip and knew the swelling had improved. He could move about, not as sore as he had been. He changed his clothes and stood. His head spun.

He'd miscalculated. He didn't know enough about trucks or their bodies and his ignorance had set him back. He felt like a failure.

Saleem wandered outside, shielding his eyes from the bright sun. He walked down into the market and bought a twist of bread and a bottle of milk from one of the corner shops. The owner watched with a raised eyebrow, but Saleem kept his head down and paid quietly for his purchase, eager to get out of sight.

His stomach cramped as he ate, but Saleem could feel himself recovering, his head clearing. As the sun sank into the horizon, he made his way back to the construction sites, purchased some more food along the way, and found a dusty, familiar shelter.

There were no options. Saleem would either persist or rot in this country, away from his family. His bruises would heal. He needed to learn from his mistakes.

He went back to watching the docks from enough distance that he was out of sight from the truckers. He stared at the ferries and tried to find an opening. There were blue-and-white-uniformed crew members guiding passengers onto the ship. There was no getting past them and onto the main deck.

He could try the trucks again. Maybe go around the back this time, though he remembered one of the boys in Attiki telling him about a friend who had died from inhaling the exhaust fumes for too long.

He turned his attention back to the containers, but they were daunting. Saleem's hopes dwindled. He was beginning to think that he would have to seek out a smuggler, though he had no idea where to find one. Tomorrow, he promised himself, he would stroll through the town and look for refugees. Someone had to know of a smuggler. Saleem returned to the docks to make one more scouting expedition before nightfall.

The last ferry for Athens was scheduled to leave in fifteen minutes. As he neared the ships, Saleem saw a driver step out of his truck and make his way to the loading area where two young women in blue-and-white uniforms stood chatting.

When he was sure no one was looking, he went around the back of the truck and crouched down to get a look at the undercarriage. He saw nothing he could latch onto without repeating last week's mistake. He stood again and stared at the padlock on the bottom of the truck's back door. There was no way in. Saleem studied the bottom of the door and realized something else.

There was a platform. And more than that — there was a small latch on the side of the door.

He stepped up onto the platform and grabbed onto the side of the truck. He managed to perch himself and get his right foot onto the small latch. He dug his fingers onto the edge of the truck, his breaths quick and nervous. He pushed himself up against the latch, his foot nearly slipping from the small hold. He reached as far as he could to grab onto the truck's roof but couldn't get his fingers onto the ledge. Voices neared. The drivers were coming back. Down or up, he needed to go somewhere.

With one last determined effort, Saleem leveraged all his weight on his right foot and swung his left leg upward. The metal ledges dug into his hands. His left foot landed on the lip of the roof with a thud. Saleem strained to pull the rest of his body up.

His biceps burned from the effort but he'd made it. He lay flat and still on his belly with his head turned to the side, hoping his backpack was not visible from the ground. The voices were within a few feet but by their easy tone, he knew they'd not seen him in the twilight.

Moments later, the truck jerked with the start of the engine. He was moving in the direction of the ship. There was another bump as the truck backed onto the ramp. Saleem's cheek slapped against the cold metal.

The driver maneuvered the truck into a spot alongside several other trucks. More came in after them and the air became warm and thick with fumes. Saleem pulled his shirt over his mouth and nose. He heard a door slam and heard footsteps walking away. Within the space the trucks were parked, voices echoed and it was difficult to tell which direction they were coming from. He raised his head just slightly and saw two figures walking off the ramp, exiting the ship. There was the second ramp. Saleem could make out the line of travelers climbing the steps and boarding the boat, their luggage in tow. Not too long ago, he and his family had boarded a ferry in the same civilized manner.

He could hardly believe how far he'd come.

Within minutes, the horn sounded, ramps were raised, and doors were closed. Saleem clung to the roof of the truck in the ship's underbelly, afraid to celebrate this small success. When he was certain no one was walking about in the space, he slowly sat up and tried to look around. It was dark and he couldn't make out much, but that gave him peace that he, too, would be hidden from view.

The next stop would be Chios and from what Saleem remembered, this was a short leg of the journey, an hour at most. From Chios they would travel to Athens, a much longer journey. Maybe nine hours? The question was how Saleem would get off the ship once it docked in Athens. He'd watched them unload incoming ships in Izmir again and again. All he could hope for was to stay on the truck unnoticed until a time when he could slide back down and make a run for it.

When he heard a shift in the ship's machinery, he guessed they were nearing Chios. He slid back onto his belly and stared at his watch.

I've gotten this far, Padar-jan.

Minutes later, the baritone horn sounded again and they were back on the seas. By now it was late into the night and the passengers were probably nodding off in their padded seats. Saleem opened his backpack, grateful he'd bought a bag of chips and a bottle of juice earlier in the day. He would need the energy in Piraeus.

His mind drifted to his family and where they might be. On a train. In a detention center. Sleeping in a park. Their documents were well made and would get them through, Saleem told himself.

Saleem felt for the wad of bills in his pocket. Ekin. He remembered the way she stirred feelings in him — feelings of shame and curiosity at the same time. Maybe he should have let it go on . . . just to know. He had not understood her or what was happening.

And Roksana. He would find her when he got to Athens. She would know what had happened to his mother and siblings. Saleem closed his eyes and pictured her face. He missed her. He missed having someone to talk to. He floated into a light sleep, his mind twisting the real into the surreal. It was Roksana, not Ekin, nuzzled against his cheek. His hands were on her waist and slipped around to the small of her back. Their lips met, an electrifying sensation that made Saleem wake with a strange tingle.

The ship was silent except for the hum of the engine. His dream lingered. He tried to close his mind around that feeling, the closeness he'd felt to Roksana. He tried to keep it from evaporating into his awakeness as pleasant dreams did too often.

Saleem had lost all sense of time in the dark. He had no idea how much longer till they reached Piraeus. He closed his eyes again and tried to sleep.

Saleem's eyes snapped open to the sound of voices in the cargo area. He immediately flipped onto his stomach and flattened himself. The voices were close.

Piraeus. The drivers were returning to their trucks and preparing to disembark. Passengers were starting to make their way to the door where they would pick up their stored luggage. Saleem's head ached from the traces of black fumes that had settled into the air he had breathed. He ignored the throbbing and tried to stay focused.

The ship dropped anchor and dragged to a stop at the port. Trucks were parked facing the ramp. When the gates had lowered fully and the hopeful light of a crescent moon crept in, Saleem heard the cab door open and close. Engines rumbled to life. Saleem felt the gears shift beneath him as the truck disembarked.

It was just before daybreak. The truck rolled onto the dock and pulled to a stop.

Saleem lifted his head a few inches. Bleary-eyed passengers walked about, making their way to the main road or the taxi stand a few meters away. He stayed alert for anyone in a uniform, anyone who would try to spot him. It was too close to the piers he decided, and he lowered his head again, hoping the truck would stop somewhere before heading down any major road.

A quarter mile down the road, the truck paused. It was a red light and Saleem's best chance. He grabbed his backpack, slipped it over his shoulders quickly, and slid down the back of the truck, his foot feeling for the latch to help him step down. He found it just as the truck started to move again.

His left foot hit the platform. His hands skated down the sides of the truck, metal grating against his skin. Headlights glared on his back, horns honked. He leaped to the ground, his ankles screaming. The truck driver, oblivious to the chaos behind him, headed down the road as Saleem darted into an alley before anyone could chase him down.

The sun was up before he stopped moving. He passed by familiar places, the first hotel they had stayed in, the café where they had purchased some food on the day they arrived, and the metro stop that Saleem had taken to venture into Athens.

Roksana. He needed to find her. She was the only person who could tell him where his family might be and what may have happened to his passport. But he didn't want to face her looking the way he did. He hadn't had a proper bath in a week. His hair was matted to his head and his clothes were dusty and tattered. The construction sites and the docks had not been easy on him.

Saleem used the morning to find a public restroom. He washed as best he could and changed into a fresh pair of clothes.

He took the metro into Athens. It was a weekday and there was a chance that Roksana would drop by Attiki after school. Saleem had no other way of contacting her.

Back at Attiki Square, he told Jamal and Abdullah about being sent back to Turkey and being separated from his family. They shook their heads in disappointment, but not surprise. When he was last here, he'd felt different from these men. He'd felt above them. All that was gone. Alone, he was one of them now. He saw himself in their faces now, in their ragged clothes and in the plastic bags that held all their worldly possessions.

He slept in Attiki that night, but remembering that he would be within yards of the infamous Saboor, he stuffed his cash into his underwear and wound the strap of his backpack around his wrist. After the many lonely days and nights in Izmir, it felt good to be around people he knew and to hear the boys teasing and joking with one another.

It was his second day back. Saleem wanted to search for food but was afraid he would miss Roksana. He sat with his back against a tree and listened to Abdullah tell stories of his childhood — spitting watermelon seeds into the stream behind his home, scaring his younger cousins with stories of djinns. Abdullah painted a picture of an Afghanistan no one would ever leave. He was only reliving the good but Saleem knew better. They all did.

And then she came. Saleem leaped to his feet at the sight of the familiar purple shirts. Abdullah burst out laughing and slapped his calves.

"Ah, the real reason you've come back! You think she'll take you in and give you asylum, eh?"

"Abdullah, don't say that. It's nothing like that."

Saleem was nervous. Four figures approached and Saleem held his breath. He spied Roksana, carrying a large box. Saleem walked over, when he wanted to run. He did not want to bring any more attention to Roksana for both their sakes.

He called her name softly.

Roksana's eyes widened in surprise.

"Saleem?"

She put the box down on a bench and put a hand on his arm.

"Saleem, where have you been? What happened to you?" She looked him over. He had lost weight in the last week alone. "Are you all right?"

"Yes, I'm fine," Saleem said, conscious of her touch. His body tensed and she pulled back. Roksana's edge had softened. He resisted the urge to wrap his arms around her.

"Tell me," Roksana said as she sat on a cement step. She looked up at Saleem and he took a seat beside her. His questions came first.

"Roksana — my mother. Where did she go? Did they take the train?"

They'd left the day after Saleem had spoken with his mother. Roksana had gone to the train station and recognized them, though she'd never seen them and though Saleem was not there. She'd guessed, she'd said, by the look on their faces. They looked like they were missing something . . . someone. She didn't tell him much about his mother, hiding how Madar-*jan* had really looked behind simple words. Roksana had helped them get onto the train to Patras, though she didn't know anything about their journey after that. They'd left over a month ago.

"You have not heard from them?" Roksana asked.

"No. I hope they're in England with my aunt." He sighed.

"Can you call your aunt?"

Saleem did not have her phone number. There hadn't been enough time or level-headed thinking in their brief conversation for Saleem to ask his mother for the number. He had no way of contacting them, nor did he have a way of finding his family once he got to London.

Roksana wanted to know everything that had happened. Madar-*jan* had told her something about the police, but she hadn't shared much more beyond that.

Saleem recounted the whole story for her while she listened intently. She bit her lip and shook her head as he described the way the police had kicked him around before letting him loose in Turkey. It felt good to finally be able to talk about it with someone like her, someone who listened and didn't think he'd had it coming.

"Saleem, this is bad. You have to do something. You can't get stuck here like all these other guys," Roksana warned, her eyes on the rest of the Afghans shifting aimlessly through the park. "You need to find a better way. I wish you at least had that passport I mailed to you. I'm sure it was stolen. You can't even trust a damn envelope to get from here to there without someone going through it."

"It's gone. I must go to Italy with no passport. It will not be easy."

"No, and it's very dangerous." Roksana thought it over. "Maybe you can get another passport. But . . . it's a little risky."

"A passport? From where?" Saleem looked at her curiously.

"They are costly, I think. For a European passport — maybe hundreds of euros," she said, though she sounded unsure. "I don't really know but some of the guys here might."

Saleem had money and told Roksana as much.

"Keep your money hidden away, Saleem. Maybe it's better if you don't say anything to the boys here," she warned, nodding in the direction of the others. "Fake papers don't always work anyway."

It struck Saleem that a girl like Roksana should have nothing to do with Attiki Square, a jungle of cement and weeds, framed by buildings and deceptively serene trees. Men lazed on sheets of cardboard. It looked more like a corner of war-ravaged Afghanistan than a peaceful European nation. Roksana should have run in the opposite direction but she didn't. It was a curious thing.

"Why do you do this, Roksana?" he asked pensively. She said nothing, letting his question melt into the silence between them.

Saleem looked up at her. What did she see? Did she see his clothes or his stringy hair? Did she see a friend or a refugee case? Saleem hadn't known what to expect from Europe, but it surely wasn't this. He hadn't expected to be tossed about and under threat every step of the way. If Roksana was trying to undo what had been done to him and his family thus far, there was a long way to go.

Before she could answer his question, one of the other volunteers waved her over. They needed her help.

"Where are you going to stay tonight?" The edge in her tone returned. She was back to business. "Do you want to go back to the hotel?"

Saleem shook his head. Maybe Roksana was here because he was that person who could make her feel selfless and giving. Maybe it had nothing to do with him and everything to do with her. Something bitter took root within him though he didn't know why and he wasn't proud of it.

"No, I will stay here."

Roksana nodded, then stood up and

brushed her backside with her hands. Saleem had no way of knowing how many times she'd asked herself the same question. Why bother to come here? Why bother doing anything for one refugee when a thousand more were on their way in?

She could have walked away from him for good. She could have lumped him in with the others. But she didn't see him the way she saw the others.

Roksana regretted that she couldn't tell him more about his family's whereabouts. She'd watched the train pull out of the station, but beyond that moment, anything could have happened to Fereiba and the two younger children. Anything.

CHAPTER 39
FEREIBA

I've dragged my two children along with me from rail to rail, from country to country. At each checkpoint, each customs control, I wait for the moment when we will be found out. My worst fear is the same as my biggest hope — separation from my children. I wonder if I'll be apart from Saleem forever or if he'll be the only one of us to make it through. Samira is a young girl, a dangerous time to be alone. Aziz is frail, a flower that will quickly wilt if plucked from the bush. I pray at some checkpoints that my children be granted asylum even if I am sent back. At other checkpoints, I pray we are sent back together. Cornered mothers pray for strange things.

When the bombardments back home were at their worst, a teacher I considered a friend made crazed decisions each night. One night, she made the children sleep with her and her husband, all in the same room.

Another night, she put each child alone in a different room. Every night was a gamble. They could all endure or perish together. Or they could gamble that perhaps one or two of them would survive. Each night, without fail, she prayed most fervently that God not spare her if her children were taken. These were pleas she could only make to God in her quiet thoughts because to speak them aloud would have blackened her tongue.

In the last year, as I've tried to give my children a safe life, I've felt more like a criminal than anything else. Even righteousness is an ambiguous thing.

From Greece to Italy, from Italy to France. It is now the last leg of our journey, from Paris to London on a silver-and-yellow train that looks like a rocket blazing through an underground path. It is on this last voyage that I leave Aziz in Samira's care and gather our Belgian passports. I slip them into my black leather handbag and take them with me to the restroom in our car, a narrow square of stainless steel. One by one, I rip each page of the passports into tiny shreds and let them fall into the toilet like the snowflakes that will meet us in London. I tear them apart and undo our false identities. I am again Fereiba. My children are again Samira and Aziz.

I've been cautioned by the people who had gotten me this far.

They must not see your passports. Do not tell them how you got there. Tell them only that you want asylum. Tell them why you had to run. Tell them how they came for Mahmood — what happened to him might be the only thing that saves you.

The customs check in London will go very differently than all the others. This time we will be honest and put ourselves in our most vulnerable position yet. Thus far, we've cowered and ducked and lied every time we passed an official. In less than an hour, that will change.

My hands shake as I stand over the toilet and watch to be sure every last flake vanishes into the swirl of water. I lean against the wall and steady myself with a hand on the steel sink. It is refreshingly cool to the touch.

Metal. It is everywhere. The trains, the rails, the stations. Each train stop is a beast of permanence. Soundly constructed with the glint of modernity. This sink, the tracks, the roof over the station — they are the difference between the Afghan world and this world. This world stands strong and shiny and capable. From our homes to our fami-

442

lies, Afghanistan is made of clay and dust, so impermanent it can be sneezed away. And it has been, over and over again.

I want a life that won't crumble between my fingers. I'll be returned to dust one day, but until then let me and my children endure.

I think of my father, alone in his browned orchard, sleeping in a grove of organic rubble. I don't know if he is alive or dead. It's been so long since I last heard his voice. I know why he refused to leave. He learned to love the transience of everything, an acceptance that can only come when we near the end of the road. Whether the end comes today or tomorrow does not matter to him. He is ready to be returned to the earth. In and out, he will breathe the dust of the crumbling orchard walls and the soil of the gardens every day until, like an hourglass, his lungs fill. Time will stop then.

It is easier to love my father from a distance. From here, I do not see his weaknesses or his failures. From here, I see only those glimmering moments when he looked at me as his best and most precious child, those moments when he talked about my mother and made me feel whole. The rest of my childhood . . . well, maybe it's best if it crumbles to nothing.

I meet my reflection in the mirror. I look much older than I remember. I touch the skin of my face. It feels rough. I'm almost glad. I never was a very delicate creature. Every day, my skin thickens and I find myself doing things I never imagined doing, not even with the help of my husband. The stronger I am, the better our chances of survival.

I've left them too long. I need these moments though, moments when I can step away, collect the pieces of myself and return to them as a mother.

But the seconds tick on and I must return to my two children. The moment we've been preparing for is almost here.

CHAPTER 40
SALEEM

A half week later, Roksana returned. Saleem scrambled for what he would say to her. He hadn't felt good about the way their last conversation ended. He hoped she hadn't detected the ugly twinge in him. She did the usual distributions with her colleagues before making her way over to Saleem.

"Can you meet me in the playground where you stayed with your mother? Later tonight — around eight o'clock?" Saleem agreed, ready to apologize, but she moved on quickly. Before he could attempt any further conversation, she and the other volunteers had left.

Saleem did not want to miss his meeting with her. He spent the afternoon listening to Abdullah and Hassan tell the same tired mullah jokes they'd told a thousand times before. The one about the mullah and the pumpkin. The one about the mullah and the one-eyed donkey. Afghans loved to poke fun at their clergymen.

"The guy walking along the riverbank sees the mullah on the other side and calls out to him: 'Hey, how do I get across?' and the mullah says: 'Are you a fool? You are across!' "

Hassan chuckled. To laugh at a joke he'd laughed at as a boy in Afghanistan was to call to mind better times. There was a sweet nostalgia to these droll vignettes. Had Saleem been less anxious about the hour, he might have appreciated them more.

He spun his watch around his wrist. Judging by the sky, it was probably nearing seven o'clock.

"My friends," Saleem yawned. He rose to his feet slowly, hands on his knees for support. He arched his back and let out a soft grunt for good measure. "My back is so stiff . . . I think I need to walk around a bit."

"You sure you want to walk? If you'd like, I can have my chauffeur take you for a drive."

Saleem forced a smile.

"Maybe next time."

At the park, three young girls propelled themselves upward on the swings, pushing their legs out and bringing them back in as they swooped back down. Two school-age boys climbed a wooden ladder and crossed a play bridge. Their parents watched on, stealing sidelong glances at Saleem.

He made them uneasy. It might have interested them to know that they terrified him.

He consciously stayed back, sitting on one of the farthest benches and keeping his gaze off into the distance. He considered walking away and coming back when they had taken their children home. But he did not want to risk missing Roksana. She made him feel human again, and he was not willing to pass that up. There was a newspaper on a nearby bench. Saleem picked it up and returned to his seat, pretending the Greek characters on the page made sense to him.

Roksana finally came, standing behind him without saying a word. The children had gone by then, led away by their parents who shot one final look over in Saleem's direction. She was probably late. Maybe she knew Saleem would have waited all night for her.

"Saleem."

He spun around at the sound of her voice. Why did it feel wrong for them to meet like this? Why did he feel so awkward about it? There was something clandestine about the hour and the setting.

"Here, try this," she said, handing him something wrapped in a folded sheet of wax paper. She took a seat next to him on the bench.

"What is this?" he asked, undoing the paper.

"Kebab. My mother makes great kebab. Thought you should try some yourself." She slid onto the bench, moving the newspaper and taking a seat beside him. The kebab was still warm — the ground meat and spices made Saleem's mouth water. "So you've learned how to read Greek, eh?"

Saleem grinned even as he bit into the meat. The first morsel melted under his teeth and tasted better than anything he could remember.

"You like it?"

"Mmm, it tastes like . . . it tastes like home." Saleem licked his lips and closed his eyes. "Thank you!"

Roksana laughed.

"You are welcome. Thought you would enjoy that," she said. "I wanted to talk to you and see if you have any ideas. To get to your family, you know?"

Saleem sighed.

"I don't know." Parts of him still felt battered and bruised from his trip over from Izmir.

"I asked the people I know, but no one knows anything about getting documents made. I think it's because they're afraid to tell me. I'm so sorry, Saleem. I wish I could help more."

Saleem was disappointed, but it was a feeling he was getting used to.

"I know you try. It's okay. I must find another way."

The farm work, the street life, the hunger, and the beatings had taken their toll. His body was not maturing so much as it was aging under the stress. He was certain that was what Roksana saw when she looked at him.

"*Ela,* I had an idea. I was thinking about your aunt and uncle. When you get to England, where are you going to go? It is a big country and you'll be lost without an address. If you give me their names, maybe I can help you to find them? I can search on the Internet. I cannot promise anything, but it would be good to check at least."

"You will try?" Saleem used the wax paper to wipe the grease from his lips. "My aunt is in London. They live in apartment."

Roksana took a pen and scrap of paper out of her shoulder bag.

"Write down their names for me. Your aunt, her husband, your cousins. Write it all down, and I will see what I can find."

"My aunt, her name is Najiba. She is my mother's sister. Her husband is Hameed Waziri. He is my father's cousin. These are the names I saw on the letters they sent to us in Afghanistan."

"Good," Roksana said, stuffing the scrap of paper back into her small bag. "And another thing, Saleem."

Anything, he thought. *Just sit here with me and keep talking.*

Saleem was content to listen to her, to watch her lips move, to watch the way she pushed her bangs away, and the way her lashes fluttered.

"I know it is not easy to be in Attiki." Attiki was a nice way of saying homeless. "And I thought . . . I just wanted to say that if you want, you can come to my house this weekend for a proper bath. I thought it might make you feel better."

Saleem's face lit up. He turned to look at her directly. Under the glow of the streetlamp, Saleem could see Roksana's face blush.

"My mother and father will be away from home for some time this weekend. If you want, you can come for an hour."

He wondered if he should accept her offer. Her parents would not know of his visit.
What if they came home unexpectedly? Was
this worth the risk? He looked at Roksana
again. That perfect curve of her lips, the
quiet rebellion in her eyes. Yes, it was
definitely worth it.

"That is very nice. Please, yes."

Roksana nodded and pointed to a building down the street. She told him to make
note of the green awning out front. He was
to come by on Saturday afternoon. She
wrote the apartment number down on
another piece of paper and gave it to Saleem. She got up to leave.

"It is late." She turned around again, as
an afterthought. "Saleem, you won't say
anything to the others in Attiki, will you?
We are not . . . I mean the people from the
organization . . . we're not supposed to have
contact with . . . our work is supposed to
stay only in Attiki. You understand?"

Saleem nodded. He had no intention of
sharing any of this with the guys in the park.
The evil eye always lurked in shallow waters,
and this was just the thing to draw it to the
surface.

He watched her adjust the strap of her
messenger bag and walk away. He could not
turn his gaze from the synchronized sway of

her hair and hips, a gentle femininity.

Saturday was three days away. Saleem rested his head that night, picturing himself walking into Roksana's home. He closed his eyes and dreamed.

In his dream, he was in their bathroom. Warm water cascaded down his head and shoulders. His skin felt light. He caught a palmful of water in his cupped hands and brought it to his lips. Swathed in a towel, he stepped into a large, vacuous room, dark enough that he could not make out the walls. Roksana approached him in jeans that celebrated every adolescent curve. She smiled, touched his wet shoulders, and wiped beads of water from his chest. She pulled him closer.

Saleem woke up abruptly. He bolted upright. It was pitch-dark.

He remembered he was in the square, on the steps of an old building with Abdullah snoring a few feet away. He'd been dreaming. He felt the familiar but still uncomfortable feeling of being aroused and leaned his head back, waiting for it to disappear.

But then he sensed something else.

As his eyes adjusted, he could make out the bulky shape of a man crouched over his feet. Saleem recognized the silhouette. It was Saboor.

"What do you want?" Saleem blurted.

"You must have been having a good dream," Saboor whispered. Saleem could hear the smirk in his voice.

Saleem positioned himself. His hand flew to his side to confirm his monies were untouched. He'd wrapped his bills in a rag and pinned the bundle to his underpants, the most secure place he could think to keep it. He felt the lump nudge against his groin.

"What do you want?" Saleem asked again.

Abdullah's snoring went on uninterrupted.

Saboor smelled of stale sweat. Saleem could feel his meaty hand on his shin, then sliding up to his knee. His touch made Saleem jump. They were standing, staring eye to eye.

"Just wanted to make sure you are sleeping well, my dear boy." He chuckled. "Now you can go back to your dreams and I will go back to mine." Saleem watched his figure slip away quietly in the darkness, through a maze of bodies, as he made his way back to his own makeshift tent.

It was impossible to sleep after that. Saleem stared into the dark and listened for the sound of footsteps. He cursed Abdullah for sleeping through the whole thing. But how long had Saboor been there? Had he put his hands on Saleem as he slept?

The last thought made Saleem wild with fright. He had heard from the others about Saboor pilfering from others but nothing more than that. It was so freakish he almost believed he'd imagined the whole thing. But even under the cloak of night, it was real, fresh, and made his skin crawl.

At dawn, Saleem's eyelids grew heavy. Even in the relative safety of daylight, it was hard to resist closing them.

Abdullah woke up and found Saleem blinking slowly.

"Eh, you are awake already? Good morning, my friend! Welcome to another day in Attiki. Wish I could offer you a proper breakfast, but if I could, then you would not get the true Attiki experience," he quipped.

Saleem, grim faced, was suddenly alert — the slumber quickly vanished with the need to share his overnight encounter.

"Abdullah, something strange happened last night," Saleem began, his voice tight and tense. He was not sure how his friend would react. Maybe the whole thing would sound made up.

"Not that strange, actually. Happens to all

guys. Welcome to manhood, little boy." Abdullah sat up and stretched his arms over his head.

"Listen to me for a minute, will you? I woke up in the middle of the night and Saboor was sitting right there, just over my feet." Saleem pointed to the spot where he'd seen Saboor's crouching figure.

"That bastard — he was trying to steal our things!" Abdullah turned around and checked for his plastic bag of belongings. He relaxed when he saw everything still in its rightful place.

"I do not know why he was here. I don't think he was stealing anything. He was acting . . . he was acting strange."

"Strange? What do you mean strange?"

"I mean, he . . . well, when I woke up he was . . . he was just sitting there watching me." Saleem rubbed the fog from his eyes. It was difficult to form the words. "And then he touched my leg."

Abdullah sat up straight. His face tightened with alarm.

"He touched your leg? Why didn't you wake me up?"

Saleem shook his head. He didn't know why.

"I asked him twice what he wanted and I thought that might wake you up, but then he stood up and I didn't know what he'd done." Saleem felt exceptionally filthy this morning. He hated that Saboor was just a few yards away.

Abdullah paused, rubbed his eyes roughly, and lowered his voice.

"There was a young boy here last month. Do you remember him? Just a little school-age kid. He was here with his older brother. Anyway, one day the kid woke up like the djinns had come for him in the night. We woke up in the morning and he was vomiting. When his brother tried to talk to him, the kid started screaming his head off. We had no idea what had happened to him but I happened to notice the boy look over twice in Saboor's direction. Saboor gave him the iciest look I've ever seen. Scared me, really. Two days later, the boy ran into a busy street and got hit by a car. He died right there in the road."

Abdullah shook his head at the memory.

"It was terrible. His brother was a complete mess after that. The police came and took him away and none of us said much of anything. He wouldn't have survived long the way he was carrying on." Abdullah let out a heavy sigh. The memory troubled him. "I don't know what happened, but since then I've wondered if Saboor didn't have something to do with it. There was something really strange about the way that boy looked at him. And Saboor, it was like he'd silenced the kid from across the square with just a look."

Saleem felt his throat knot.

Abdullah sat with his bent knees drawn to his chest. His right foot tapped out the urgency of his story.

"It is bad enough to be trapped here, but to be trapped here with him . . . God have mercy on us. I'll warn Hassan and Jamal at least. If you start telling everyone, you never know what that animal will do. We've got to watch out for ourselves, Saleem, and for each other. That's the only way to survive in a place like this."

Saleem nodded. He needed a way to protect himself. Now, he realized, he was truly on his own and defenseless. In the months before he'd disappeared, Padar-*jan* had taken to sleeping with a knife under his mattress. He thought the children didn't know, but Saleem had seen it and wondered what Padar-*jan* was afraid of so he could fear it too. But, with the privilege of childhood, Saleem could close his eyes and feel reassured that his father would defend them from whatever it might be. Maybe that was the moment a child became an adult, he thought — the moment your welfare was no longer someone else's responsibility.

He had to watch out for himself now, as Abdullah said.

He would get a knife, just like Padar-*jan*. He would find something heavy and deadly, not a trinket.

He could have slept, but he walked instead. He worked his way through the market shops, browsing from windows and wandering into a few stores that looked promising. He found a few kitchen knives, an antique dagger with a decorated metal sheath, and a pocketknife bearing the Greek flag. None of these would do.

In a tiny shop set off in an alley, he found precisely what he was looking for. The shop window was a dense display of goods, heralding the mess inside: a sewing machine, a stool, a stack of books, kitchen utensils, children's clothing, a pair of work boots, and an old globe. Saleem walked in, a door chime signaling his entrance. Somewhere in this pile of items had to be a reasonable blade. He was right. The shop owner was an older man with wire-framed glasses. He had a miniature screwdriver in his hand and was probing the insides of an antique clock whose pieces had been dissected out and spread on the glass countertop. A row of antique clocks sat behind him in various stages of disrepair. Saleem gave him a nod and began to weave his way through the three narrow aisles.

Bowls on top of pillows, a thermos surrounded by old cassettes, used reading glasses next to a box of lightbulbs — there was no rhyme or reason to this store. Saleem's eyes scanned until they landed on the bottom shelf. Buried beneath a stack of table runners was a bronze handle. Saleem pulled it out and saw that the handle inserted into a decorated, bronze sheath. He slid the nicked cover off and found a six-inch blade singed with rust. It was old but more beautiful than any knife Saleem had ever before seen.

This was exactly what he wanted. Saleem touched the blade lightly. It felt bold and intimidating against his palm. The tip was still sharp enough to prick the pad of his finger when he pushed against it. He slid the knife back into the sheath and held it up to his waist. It would fit inside his jeans, heavy but he could secure it. Saleem walked it back up to the front, where the man was still fiddling with the clock's gears.

"I want to buy please. How much?"

The old man looked up, his lenses nearly falling off the tip of his nose. He looked at the dagger and then at Saleem.

"Twenty euro," he said and returned to his tinkering. Saleem shifted his weight and considered how much he was willing to pay.

"Mister, I give you ten euro. No problem."

"Twenty euro."

"Mister, please. Ten euro." The man looked up again to get a better look at Saleem. He took his glasses off and laid them on the table.

"Eighteen."

Saleem paused. He thought back to last night and the hand on his knee.

"Fifteen euro, please," he offered. The man nodded. He held out his palm as Saleem counted out bills. He tucked the handle into the waist of his pants. Just as he was walking out the door, he paused.

"Mister, you fix the clocks?"

"Mm-hmm." The shop owner had already gone back to work and didn't bother to look up.

"You . . . you can check my watch?"

At the mention of a watch, the old man's head lifted. He held out his hand expectantly. Saleem quickly unfastened the band, then slipped the watch off his wrist and into the man's open palm.

The shop owner turned it over, shaking it gently while he held it up to his ear. He mumbled something and dug through a plastic bin until he found the right tool. He pried open the back of the watch and pulled out a set of fine tweezers. He touched the cogs gently and nudged and tapped. The parts were so small, Saleem could not see what he was doing. After a few moments, he snapped the back on again, turned it over, and wound the dial.

He handed the ticking watch back to Saleem unceremoniously.

"Is okay now. You fix the time."

Saleem took the watch, his heart leaping to see the small hand tick away the seconds. His father's watch worked again!

"Mister, thank you! Thank you very much! Thank you!" Saleem leaned across the counter and wrapped his arms around the startled shopkeeper.

"Yes, yes." The man slid out of his arms and waved him off. His spirits lifted, Saleem set out again and found a strip of fabric outside a clothing store. He looped the material around the knife's handle and tied the band around his waist, knotting it by his belt buckle to keep it in place.

Saleem looked to his left and saw a road that led to the hotel. He looked to his right and saw signs for the area of the food market where he'd stolen their first meals.

He bit his lip in shame to think of all he'd taken. It was not something he would do again, he vowed. *A man,* he thought, *would find a more noble way to feed his family.* It became important to Saleem not to feel desperate and criminal.

And there was one more thing Saleem would do to restore the Waziri family. Madar-*jan* would have warned him against being so rash, but Saleem decided, in one impulsive flash, to walk eastward. This was not something he would have discussed with her anyway. Maybe having survived this long with empty pockets gave Saleem the audacity to act impractically.

A bold plan in his head and purpose in his step, Saleem listened to the reassuring tick of his watch and grinned.

CHAPTER 41
SALEEM

"Hurry." Roksana tugged at his elbow. "We have nosy neighbors."

Saleem took a nervous step into Roksana's home. He could not begin to imagine what might happen if her father came home to find an Afghan refugee sitting in his living room.

"Maybe I should . . ." he mumbled.

"It's all right. Just come in."

She closed the door behind them, stealing one last peek into the hallway to be sure none of the other apartment doors were open. Satisfied, she led him from the foyer into the living room.

Saleem's eyes swept across the room, taking it all in. Neat beige sofas huddled around a low, espresso-stained coffee table atop which sat a few books. Old, sepia-toned photographs hung on the walls. Backlit linen shades gave the room a soothing feel. Their apartment was probably the same size as the Waziri home in Kabul but looked much more modern and spacious to Saleem.

"My parents have just gone out for the afternoon so we should be quick. I just wanted you to get a proper bath to use."

Her voice was different. She was not her usual cool self. She fidgeted and averted her eyes. Saleem was not sure if Roksana was uncomfortable to be alone with him or worried that her parents might return earlier than expected.

"Roksana, maybe I go . . ."

"No," she said, understanding how un-welcoming she'd sounded. She took a deep breath and started over. "Everything's fine." She smiled, her composure restored. Saleem was impressed and quietly envious. His anxieties had full rein over him, he thought.

From the living room, Roksana led Saleem down a narrow hallway and pointed at a door. "This is the washroom and here's a towel. Shampoo and soap are there. I'll wait for you in the other room, okay?"

It was more than okay. It was wonderful. The washroom was unlike any he had seen. Lemon yellow walls made the space bright and cheerful. The sink was a glass bowl anchored into the wall. A row of mint green miniature ceramic urns sat on a floating shelf, a wisp of baby's breath propped in each. A frosted glass door slid open for the shower.

Saleem felt awkward and out of place in the most beautiful washroom he'd ever seen. He fumbled with the faucet. He took off his clothes and folded his knife and money sack into his jeans. He stepped into the shower and let hot water run over him, a murky swirl disappearing down the drain. Saleem scrubbed his body until the water ran clear, washed his hair three times, and then reluctantly turned the water off. He stood for a moment, the room steamy and warm.

Water, he thought with a new appreciation, *is most certainly* roshanee.

Saleem towel-dried, re-dressed, and stepped into the hallway. To his left, half-open French doors led to an office. In the center of the room was a heavily carved wooden desk. Three sides of the room were bookshelves made of the same cherry-colored wood. So many books! It reminded Saleem of the time his father had taken him to his office in the Ministry of Water and Electricity. They'd visited the ministry's library and its stacks thick with texts, feathered pages, and dusty bindings. Saleem was keenly aware at the time that no other five-year-old would be allowed to wander through the rows, a fact that was more interesting than any of the books in the enormous room.

For years after, Saleem's father would chuckle and remind him of the most memorable part of that day.

*And then the chief engineer came in and asked if you would like to work in the same building one day and you said, "No, sir. My mother gets angry sometimes because she says Padar-*jan *gets lost in his books. I don't want her angry with me too."*

Saleem wondered how Padar-*jan* had never tired of repeating such a simple childish comment. At the same time, part of him had never tired of hearing it either. With a sigh, he returned to the present.

This must be her father's office, Saleem realized.

Saleem took three steps into the office to get a closer look at the shelves with books perfectly arranged by the height of their spines. He touched the glossy book jackets. Many of the books were in English, some in Greek. There were books about medicine and philosophy, from what Saleem could gather. He turned to the shelf behind the desk. On the bottom row, something caught his eye — Farsi lettering along the spines of one entire row of books.

Saleem hunched over to get a better look. Sure enough, the titles read, *Afghanistan: A Nation's History; Afghanistan: The Fallen Empire;* and *Collection of Afghan Poetry.* Why would they have so many books on Afghanistan? Did Roksana's father speak Dari?

Saleem thought back to days in Attiki when the guys would make snide and often lewd comments about her, the cold glares she would shoot their way, almost as if she understood. Saleem looked around the office, confused. On another shelf across the room sat a small statue, no taller than five inches. It was an eagle carved out of a brilliant chunk of lapis lazuli, a blue stone as unmistakably Afghan as the similarly colored *burqas.*

"You are finished?" Roksana was in the doorway.

Saleem turned around abruptly, ashamed to have overstepped his welcome.

"Sorry. I saw the books and I wanted to see . . . there are so many but . . . Roksana, your father, does he speak Dari?"

"What?" She stiffened visibly.

"There are many books on Afghanistan. And they are in Dari. And this bird, this stone is from Afghanistan. Why . . ." Saleem's half-formed thoughts stumbled out as he tried to make sense of it all. "My mother. You talked to my mother? Do *you* speak Dari? Your father . . . did he work in Afghanistan?"

Roksana shook her head, sighed, and smiled coyly.

"*Ela,* Saleem, my father . . . my father did not *work* in Afghanistan." She spoke in a hushed tease.

"But then why —"

"He *lived* there. He was born there. My father is Afghan."

Saleem's jaw dropped. He looked at Roksana through narrowed eyes, as if seeing her for the first time. If Roksana's father was Afghan, then Roksana was . . .

"Half Afghan and half Greek," Roksana explained, with a hand on her chest. "My mother is Greek. My father came here as a young man to study medicine but ended up doing something different. He married my mother and has lived here ever since. I learned to speak some Dari from him. Not very much but enough that I can have a conversation."

Saleem clapped his hands and broke into a grin.

"You are Afghan!" he cried in Dari, the words sliding effortlessly off his tongue. "I knew there was something about you! I just did not know what it was! Is that why you do what you do? But your father, he probably would not like to know that you are around Afghan boys, especially boys that . . . boys like . . ."

Roksana rescued him from having to say it.

"My father doesn't know where I spend my time. He wouldn't like it, but not exactly for the reasons that you think. It is more complicated than that. I don't tell anyone because I know that it will cause problems. I want to help, but you can imagine how difficult it would be for me if those boys knew that my father is Afghan."

Saleem understood this perfectly. As long as Roksana was Greek, she would be held only to Greek standards. The men in Attiki would not judge her clothing or her behaviors by Afghan standards. But if they knew she was Afghan, they may not be so forgiving. Or they might pursue her. She would have men approaching her for all the wrong reasons. Just imagining it made Saleem want to keep her away from Attiki.

"You are right. I will say nothing."

"Thank you. Let's eat something and then we should leave."

Saleem followed her to the kitchen where she had warmed up a flaky spinach pie, roasted chicken, and something green and leafy. Saleem ate until he thought his belly might burst. Roksana laughed to see him lean back and groan in discomfort.

"How was it? Looks like you enjoyed it."

"Oh yes, I like it very much! I had food for three days." Saleem laughed, patting his flat stomach.

"Good. Now let me clean up and we can go. You can wait in the other room if you want," she offered.

"No, I want to . . . I will stay with you. I can help," he offered sheepishly. Roksana's eyes brightened, and together they cleared away all evidence of their clandestine lunch. Roksana grabbed her sweater and they headed out the door.

"Today we will go to the Acropolis. Have you ever been there?"

"Acro— what did you say?"

"Acropolis," she said slowly. "Follow me. I'll show you."

For this one day, Saleem was a tourist, one infatuated with his personal guide. They wandered through the bustling streets of Athens and its differently flavored neighborhoods and landed at the foot of the steps that led to the Acropolis, ancient ruins atop a hill with a majestic view of Athens. Saleem had seen the structures from a distance but had never ventured close. Today, Roksana told him about the temple dedicated to Athena, how it had changed hands many times over the course of history and was controlled by the Ottomans at one point. She showed him the amphitheater and explained how this was once a center for the community.

Saleem was fascinated. They sat down to rest along a low wall that formed a perimeter for the buildings. He kicked at a stone sullenly.

"What are you thinking, Saleem?"

"Hmm? Oh. I was thinking these buildings — they are so old, so many years. But they look better than the newest buildings in Kabul."

What he wanted to say was that two thousand years of peace could be undone in a month of war. Roksana understood.

"Yes, well, people are very good at destroying things, good things."

"Things look really bad in Kabul. Everyone is leaving. Even in Kabul, Afghans are living like refugees." He looked at Roksana quickly and then turned his eyes back to the ground. "That's all people will see when they look at Afghans."

"Saleem," she said gently. "I don't see a refugee when I look at you. I see someone who should be in my class, sharing books and playing sports, sitting in cafés. I see you."

Her fingers touched his hand and squeezed briefly before letting go.

"Does your father miss Afghanistan? He is away from home so long. I do not know. Maybe I go back one day. Sometimes I miss my home."

"No, my father doesn't miss it. He loves his country, but he says Afghanistan is like a woman too beautiful for her own good. She will never be safe, even from her own people. He left the country when life was still normal, but he is different, I think. After the wars, he said it was not the same country. He listens to the news and talks to his family there, but it only makes him more upset."

"But to live for so long in a different country . . . no one here speaks Dari, the food is different, there is no *masjid* to go for praying —"

"*Masjid?* My father is not a man of religion. He believes that people have destroyed religion and religion has destroyed people. He says he believes in God, but he doesn't believe in people."

Maybe he was right, but Saleem had never before heard an Afghan who did not consider himself a Muslim.

Saleem asked her how she'd learned to speak Dari.

"From my father. And my grandmother. She lived with us for a few years before she died. My father loves the language, the poetry. It's the rest that breaks his heart. I think he is happy here in Greece but sometimes . . . sometimes I find him reading his books or looking at old photographs. I think there is a piece of Afghanistan still in his heart and it makes him sad."

She stood up and dusted off the seat of her jeans. She felt uncomfortable discussing her father's thoughts with Saleem. "It is late," she said, changing the subject. "I should go home."

Saleem had dreaded this, the moment when she would leave him.

"Roksana, thank you . . . for everything. Today was a nice day." He stood up and slung his knapsack over his shoulder.

"You are welcome." They headed back down the steps, trying not to lose each other amid the hordes of guided tours each speaking a different language. At the foot of the hill, Roksana turned quickly.

"Oh, one more thing . . . I almost forgot! Good news for you," she said as she reached into her bag for a scrap of paper. "I think I found your uncle's address in London!"

Saleem's eyes widened.

"I found his name on the Internet. I think this is the address. I could not find the telephone number, but at least when you get there, you will know where to go."

Saleem took the scrap of paper and stared incredulously at the numbers and street name scribbled on it. He felt infinitely closer to reuniting with his family. Roksana had given him a real destination.

"Roksana, you helped me. You helped my mother. I really . . . thank you."

Saleem looked close to tears. Roksana shifted her weight and looked away, uncomfortable.

"I'll see you around." She gave his arm a light squeeze. "Be careful, Saleem."

Saleem returned to the square exhausted from his day as a tourist. Abdullah had teased him when he returned. Despite having put on the same worn clothing, Saleem did look much refreshed from his shower.

"Well, well, well, is this Saleem or some movie star? Is it your wedding day? How did you manage to get your hair so clean?" He ruffled Saleem's hair for good measure. Saleem ducked and grinned.

"I found a bottle of shampoo. Took it to

one of the public restrooms and stuck my head in the sink. You should have seen the way people looked at me," he fibbed.

"I bet they did!"

It was night. Most of the guys had tucked themselves into a corner to get some rest. Saleem, Abdullah, Hassan, and Jamal were in the same corner, having lined up their cardboard sheets. The need for security was balanced against the need for personal space. It was the unspoken code of the park. Saboor had been away from the park all day and seemed to have returned worn out. He was one of the first to retire to his spot under a tree.

Good, Saleem thought. *Just sleep and leave us alone.*

He dreamed of Roksana again. She was walking in a park with Madar-*jan,* Samira, and Aziz. Aziz was walking, his cheeks fat and pink, his bowlegs barely keeping up with the others. They were laughing, chatting. Samira bubbled with excitement, her hand in Roksana's. Then Roksana turned to him, her eyes twinkling flirtatiously.

And suddenly he was awake. It was pitch-black. Everything was invisible. His senses were on edge. He could smell something . . . was it sweat? Saleem concentrated on being perfectly still. He heard nothing and saw nothing.

You're imagining things, he told himself. *Go back to sleep.*

Saleem closed his eyes again and willed himself to return to his dream. He had just started to drift off when he felt it. A hand on his thigh. Saleem jerked in fright. Another hand slapped against his mouth. Saleem grabbed the wrist with both hands, but the grip was firm and callused. Hot breath in his ear.

"Be still, dear boy. Be still. Just relax and we can be good friends." Saboor was fumbling for Saleem's buckle. Saleem tried to wriggle out from under his grasp, but Saboor's massive weight held him down. He could barely breathe.

"Quiet or you'll regret it."

No, no, no! Saleem tried to get the hand off his mouth and nose. His legs kicked but hit nothing. He clawed at the hand, but it was heavy and unmoving. *No, no, no!* His stomach turned to feel the hand reach into his waistband.

Saleem reached behind him and fumbled for the handle that lay against the small of his back. He twisted left and right and finally felt it come out between his fingers. He could barely make out the silhouette above him, but he could feel the rancid breath on his face.

He had the handle. In one swoop, he pulled out the knife and thrust it into the dark space above him. He heard a gasp and something push back against him. The hand on his mouth released, the one on his crotch retracted.

"Let me go! Let me go! Let me go!" Saleem yelled out.

Saleem could see the shadow move, stumble, and fall backward. The others had woken.

"What's happening?"

"Who's yelling? Everybody all right?"

"What's going on?"

Saleem was on his feet. His eyes adjusted, and he could make out Saboor's outline as he limped away, holding his left side. Saleem felt someone grab his arm and jumped back.

"Hey, hey, Saleem! It's me, Abdullah! What happened?"

What happened? Saleem was not sure. Was this real? What had he just done? He felt numb, dazed. He looked down and could now make out the blade, still in his tight grip.

"Oh God. Oh my God. Oh God." Saleem was crazed. "He was here! He was on me!"

"Hey, it's Saboor! Saboor has been hurt!" Voices called out in the darkness.

"He's bleeding!"

"What happened to him? Who did this?"

Abdullah was at Saleem's side. He pulled a lighter out of his pocket and flicked on a flame. The rusted blade glinted in Saleem's hand. A drop fell from its tip.

"Did you stab him?" he whispered in disbelief.

"I . . . I . . . he was on me! His hands were . . ."

The distant voices continued to call out. People were confused and panicked.

"He's hurt. Someone should do something!"

Saleem's fingers felt moist, sticky. He looked at his right hand.

"Saleem, stop! Where are you going, Saleem! Wait!"

Saleem's feet pounded against the ground as he wove through small side streets and in and out of alleys. He stumbled and fell in the dark, tripping on loose stones. There was no mistaking the blood, now dried by the breeze, on his right hand. He could feel it. He could smell it, the metallic smell of life. Saleem remembered Intikal. He saw the bride's brother, his clothes bloodied, his face twisted with pain.

Saleem wished he could run into his mother's arms, bury his face in her shoulder, and listen to her soothing voice tell him that he had done the right thing. He wished his father had been sleeping beside him, so that Saboor never would have dared to come near him. But Saleem was also thankful that neither of his parents was here at this moment, to see their son, a fugitive in the night, blood on his hands.

Chapter 42
Saleem

Saleem held the aluminum pot over the makeshift stove, with its bricks laid out in a square, kindling burning within. The handle was hot and getting hotter. Flames licked the blackened bottom. Saleem wiggled his way closer to the fire. A chill in the air made his jacket feel especially thin.

The water was starting to boil.

"Is it ready yet?" Ali called out from inside.

"Yes, just now." Ali came outside and looked inside the pot. He opened a tea bag and carefully let half its contents tumble into the pot.

"Take it off the flame now. I'll get the bread so we can have our breakfast. It looks like it might rain later today. What do you think?"

Saleem slipped his sleeve over his hand and used the cuff to grip the handle. He ignored Ali's last comment. Ali had said the same thing every day for the last two weeks, no matter what the appearance of the sky. Saleem hadn't noticed on the first day, but on the second, when they were inside listening to raindrops pelt against the plastic tarp overhead, Ali again predicted that it would rain later in the day. Saleem thought he was joking but turned to see Ali's face looking grim and pensive.

Ali had to be close to Saleem's age, but he was much shorter. Saleem had spotted him when he found the Afghan camps in Patras and was drawn to him specifically because he seemed young and unthreatening. He was Hazara, a different ethnicity than Saleem. Had they been in Kabul, this would have mattered a great deal. In the refugee camp of Patras, where the men all ate and slept in the same squalor, it mattered very little.

The refugee camp in Patras was very different from Attiki Square. Attiki was a forsaken corner of a city, bordered by buildings and within meters of a normalcy. Patras was a shantytown — better in some ways and worse in others. Instead of cardboard sheets, thin blankets and shopping carts there were actual walls and roofs. One man had even opened a barbershop of sorts, having found a stool and some scissors.

Thick tarps functioned as roofs for those who had not found sturdier materials. And the hundreds of people who lived here, mostly Afghans but some wandering Roma and Africans as well, made small stoves from stones and bricks to cook simple meals. The housing was better, but it was bigger and attracted more attention from the surrounding neighborhood. It was a blemish in their city, a place where vagrants huddled in desperate filth. Greeks didn't know what to do with Patras — raze it to the ground or make it better because it was inevitable that the refugees would just come back.

Patras was supposed to be a transit point. Even before the Afghans, other refugees had come there en route to Italy and the rest of Europe. There was a long tradition of finding ways of sneaking across to Italy, either on trucks or cargo ships. Saleem had become one more person in that shared history.

He was a more seasoned traveler by the time he arrived in Patras. He'd been there for months now, probably having passed a birthday at some point but it was hard to know and even harder to care. The days and weeks had blurred in his travels.

I need to get out of Patras, Saleem thought as he watched the tea steep, the amber leaching from the leaves and into the hot water.

His mind shifted back to Attiki, as it often did during the day and even more inescapably in the nights. He thought of his last night there, Saboor's heavy hand over his mouth, Abdullah's astonishment to see the blade, and the way he'd run through the night to get as far away as possible. Saleem had washed the blood off his trembling hands and cowered in an alley until daylight. He had not said good-bye to anyone, not even Roksana. He hadn't bothered to go back for his knapsack, since it held nothing more than a few extra clothes. He had boarded the first bus he could find to Patras, where it had not been difficult to locate the refugee settlement.

He wondered if Saboor was alive. It was not that he would have regretted killing him, but it mattered because it changed the definition of Saleem. Flesh wound or fatal wound — it would remain a mystery. Though he was far from Afghanistan, the war and bloodshed followed him still. Refugees didn't just escape a place. They had to escape a thousand memories until they'd put enough time and distance between them and their misery to wake to a better day.

Saleem's nights were tortured. He woke often and saw figures in the shadows. He was returned to his childhood, that time when the brain has matured enough to shape creatures and dangers from the dark. He was increasingly restless and felt his personality changing. People irritated him or scared him. There was little else they could do.

"Did you see Wahid's leg?" Ali asked. "They stitched him up like a rice sack! He's been limping around telling everyone it didn't hurt, but I heard he cried like a baby when they did it."

"Yes, I saw it."

Wahid had been chased away from one of the trucks headed into Italy, and the metal fence he had scaled had torn into his shin. He'd been cared for by a paramedic from a humanitarian organization that had set up post near the camp. Wahid's injury was not unique.

"Do you not know what today is?" Ali asked. "It is *Da-Muharram.* I've been keeping this sugar and rice for today. I'll make *sheerbrinj* tonight and we'll pray."

Da-Muharram was the anniversary of the day that the Prophet Mohammad's grandson was martyred in battle. Ali's family followed Afghan tradition and marked the day with *sheerbrinj,* or rice pudding, distributing food to the poor, and prayers.

"Today? Really?" More interesting than the holiday was the promise of *sheerbrinj.* Saleem's mouth watered, recalling how the creamy sweetness of Madar-*jan*'s rice pudding, topped with ground pistachios, would melt in his mouth. "You know how to make it?"

Indeed, Ali knew very well how to make rice pudding. They shared the *sheerbrinj* that night with three other young men who lived in the adjacent shelter. Huddled inside, they laughed and teased one another, taking a few moments to bow their heads in prayer. No one got more than a few spoonfuls but it was enough to sweeten their mouths.

"You know what they say," Ali joked. "Even the oldest sandals are a blessing in the desert."

Other than that holiday, Saleem kept to himself. He had little interest in making friends here. He kept quiet and listened. Everyone in the camp had a story, but Saleem was in no mood to share his. Nomads had no business forging relationships, he told himself.

Patras reminded Saleem of Izmir. It was on the shores of Greece, an exit point, and offered the same treacherous passages to the next body of land. Saleem had made a few attempts at sneaking onto trucks but failed miserably and only narrowly escaped getting caught. He watched the other stragglers and tried to learn from their failures.

All the while, he kept his two safeguards on his body — his money and his dagger. He was careful not to let anyone see a shadow of either and kept them within reach even while he bathed in the makeshift shower area. He eyed everyone with suspicion. He needed the shelter that this camp provided, and unassuming Ali was the best roommate for him under the circumstances. Ali liked to talk and seldom asked questions. It was a fitting arrangement.

Saleem was eager to leave before anything happened. Even the Greek medical staff had been targeted in the growing conflict for being vocal in their criticisms of the government. The refugees were on edge. Police were increasingly present and stopped them more often to ask for documentation.

Each day was a repeat of the one before. Saleem woke and felt for his money and knife. He would scout the transit points and try to find an opening to get to Italy.

It was morning again. Saleem heard Ali

walk outside and relieve himself behind their room. He came back in grinning.

"You're awake! Good morning to you. I had such a good dream last night. We were walking, me and you, in these streets with big buildings, like the ones in the movies. There were people all around dressed in such fancy clothes and driving such fancy cars. We asked someone what country it was and guess what they said — America! Can you imagine that? I guess if you walk far enough, you will eventually hit America, eh?" Ali chuckled.

"Forget about America," Saleem grumbled, his eyes still heavy with sleep. "We're having a hard enough time getting to Italy."

"That is true," Ali laughed. "Today does not look like a good day for a long walk anyway. It looks like it is going to rain today." He opened the door again, stuck his head out, and looked at a brilliant, blue sky.

Saleem had no interest in being contrary this early in the morning. He hurriedly washed up with the water that had chilled in the brisk night air. The camp was a dilapidated neighborhood of single-room homes, one up against another. Clotheslines were strung from home to home like cobwebs. There was no real supply of water or electricity, but a few refugees had snaked a pipeline from the nearby apartment buildings. One water pump served the entire settlement with an inconsistency the refugees cheerfully accepted.

Saleem returned to the port and the familiar dance of trucks, ships, and passengers. He watched a few men make a run for it, scaling black metal fences and nearing the trucks cautiously. They inspected undercarriages and looked for footholds, jostling handles to see if they could climb into trailers.

Saleem looked around, watching the activity from a few meters away. There were three trucks lined up and not a driver in sight. His feet itched to give it a try.

He scanned the area again while the potential of the moment made his heart quicken and his tongue dry. He darted across the street and climbed onto the fence, swinging his leg over and jumping to the ground on the other side. He jogged to the unattended trucks. A few of the guys from the camp were there, pondering the best way to get on a truck.

One boy tried to pry at the lock on one trailer. Two others had already slipped under to check out the chassis. Saleem watched their feet dangle on the ground as they readied themselves for the short drive onto the cargo ship.

He ducked his head down to see what they were grabbing. He saw a boy close to his own age, judging by his facial hair. The boy's face was red as he strained to keep his entire body off the ground. He caught Saleem peering.

"Go, brother! There is only room for one person here!"

Saleem nodded in understanding. He looked around for another truck, another mousehole to crawl through, but saw none. Disappointed, he and four others jogged back to the fence to regroup.

"Police! Police! Run, boys!" a panicked voice yelled out.

Saleem turned around. A police car was coming down the road. They picked up their pace and climbed over the fence as quickly as they could. The car pulled up a few yards away and the doors swung open. Two officers sauntered out.

Saleem jumped over with the others, his ankle stinging from the impact. He scrambled to his feet and ran, breaking off in a different direction from the others. Everyone scattered. The police picked two of the boys to halfheartedly chase for a few meters, enough to make a point. Saleem cut a sharp turn to duck behind some trash bins alongside an apartment building. He panted, his chest burning.

When ten minutes had passed, he walked back to the camp. Ali was sitting outside the room with four other men. They had overturned buckets and plywood crates for chairs.

"Where've you been, Saleem?" Ali called out.

"Went to the port," Saleem replied, taking a seat with the others. They were not surprised. There was nowhere else for them to go in Patras, especially with the rising hostilities.

"No luck, eh?" Saleem had met these guys before but he could not remember their names. Was this Fareed? Or Faizal?

"No. The police came and chased us away."

Haris shook his head. He was in his thirties, a veritable elder in this community of juveniles. His perspective was a little different from that of the others.

"Can you blame them? Have you looked at this camp? People don't want to look out their windows and see this."

There was silence. Haris was right, but it felt better to be angry. Resentment was a unifying sentiment among the refugees. It felt good to sit around and agree, to have a common enemy and a shared struggle. It felt good to be understood. Haris's rationality would not give them the charge they needed to keep going.

Ali looked at the sky. "It does look like it is going to rain today."

"For God's sake, what is it with you and the rain!" Saleem exploded with the force of an agitated bottle of cola. The talk about the camps and running from the port this morning had riled him and he unleashed it all on Ali in that moment. "Always, every single day!"

There was a pause. Saleem's outburst had surprised the others. Ali's face froze, then turned red and splotchy. Saleem regretted his words immediately, but it was too late. He looked down, ashamed and unable to face Ali.

Ali stood up and went inside.

"You don't know anything about him, do you?" Hakeem asked in a castigating tone.

Saleem looked up.

"Do you have any respect for a guy who shared his space with you?"

"I didn't —"

"You want to know what happened to him? Ali lived on my street in Kabul. He was outside his house when his mother called for him and his brother to come back in. She told them it looked like it was going to rain and that they should get back inside. His brother listened. Ali didn't. He said he would find other people to play with and went down the street. And that was when the rockets flew right into his house. Killed his entire family. Ali came running back to find his brother stumbling into the street, falling to the ground in flames. Ali tried to put them out, but it was too late.

"It broke him. All he remembers is his mother warning him to come into the house because it looked like it was going to rain. All he hears is her voice and it repeats in his head over and over again. I think he wishes he had gone back into the house and been crushed by those rockets instead of living with the memory of watching them die."

Saleem stared at the earth. His face burned with remorse.

"So leave him and his crazy talk alone."

"I didn't know —"

"Of course you didn't. But do you think *anyone* here has a happy story?"

Saleem kept his mouth shut. Hakeem stood up and sighed in frustration. The others stood up too but for a different reason. A crowd was starting to gather nearby. A few men were jogging over and calling out to the others.

Saleem felt very much like an outsider at the moment.

"What's going on?" Hakeem called out.

"Get Akbar!" yelled one of the men. "It's Naeem! He was killed at the port today! They are bringing his body back."

Chapter 43
Saleem

Akbar was not a real Mullah. He had never been formally trained in religion, but he was one of the oldest in the camp and had a decent repertoire of *suras* committed to memory. More important, he had a soothing, convincing tone that filled the gaps in his qualifications.

Only when the body was brought back to the camp did Saleem realize Naeem was the one under the truck, the boy who urged Saleem to find a different truck.

Naeem had nearly made it onto the ship before he lost his grip and slipped from the truck's undercarriage. The exhaust fumes had likely dizzied him. As the truck rumbled toward the ship, the driver felt a grotesque thump under his tires and the hollering of voices in the distance. He had let out a bloodcurdling screech to find Naeem's mangled body under his bloody tires.

The few Afghans who lingered watched

from a distance and saw the boy fall, roll, and twist under the tires. They were too far to do anything but fall to their knees and cry out. By the time they reached the truck, there was nothing left to do but gather his body.

Naeem hung limply, carried by two men. As they neared, the gruesome details came into focus. His face and body were purple with massive bruising. His left forearm dangled absurdly from the elbow.

Saleem looked away. He felt his stomach reel and closed his eyes. He walked slowly, then quickly, then ran to the latrines on the outer corner of the camp. His stomach emptied once, twice, three times. He breathed deeply and remembered the determined look on Naeem's face. He had nearly made it. Nearly.

Akbar gave out the instructions. He would be buried that very evening. Haste was dictated both by Islamic guidelines and by the hushed concern that the local authorities would step in. They washed Naeem's still form and wrapped him in a white sheet, as was done back home. They chose to bury him in a wooded area near the camp, thick with trees.

There was a hum through the community that the police might come into the settlement but they never did. They had no interest in walking through the tarp-covered shacks. They cared only when the chaos spilled out into the rest of Patras.

Akbar instructed the men to stand side by side. They faced the direction of Mecca, Naeem's body laid out before them. Saleem joined the others, though he wished he could be anywhere else. Ali stood at his side, tears running down his face. Solemnly and in unison, they followed Akbar's lead. They formed three rows, about fifty men total, heads lowered and hands folded just below their navels, their elbows tucked at their sides. Akbar led the incantations. They whispered the verses together. Fingertips moved to their ears and back in synchronized motions.

Saleem had not prayed since his father's death, but the *dua* rolled off his tongue naturally. It was a whisper he'd said a thousand times as a child, sounds that spoke of a shared experience, a common path to healing. He felt supported by the strangers standing around him. Prayer was a journey in itself, taking him home in a quiet verse. He moved with the others and he understood. There was nothing but a single breath between them and Naeem. A single devastating moment could return any of them to the dust from which they came. Naeem was close enough to touch and yet irrevocably unreachable.

Saleem prayed over the young man's body out of respect. Out of guilt. Out of fear. It could have been him under that truck. It could have been his body lying here before strangers.

He had lost his place. He strained his ears to hear his neighbor's whisper over Ali's sniffles.

My father did not get even this much of a funeral. God alone knows how his body was treated. Not a soul to wash him, pray over him, carry him to a resting place and bury him with a bit of ceremony. I should have carried him. I would have done these things for him if I'd known. I should have looked for his body. I'll never pray over his grave.

Saleem could not focus. His mind ran off in desperate directions, thinking about the war, his father, his family, and how long he could live with his feet flailing in the air. At some point, he would come crashing down.

Ali began to wail. He called out Naeem's name and covered his face with his hands. He spoke in sobs. The sound of him made Saleem's whole body tense. He shifted his weight and tried to block Ali's voice, tried to hear himself pray.

Hakeem and his cousin stepped out of the line of men and took Ali by the elbows. They quietly led him away so the *jenaaza* prayers could continue without distraction. His voice faded as they walked off. Saleem understood this now. Sometimes the storm in a person's mind raged too strongly.

They carried Naeem's body as one. All the men wanted to help shoulder his weight. Akbar noticed Saleem standing back and called him to join in.

"It is our duty to carry our brother, *bachem.* Come and take part."

Bachem, Saleem heard. *My son.* His shoulders relaxed. He had not been called *bachem* in months. His soul must have been hungry for it.

"There is *sawaab* in these deeds."

Saleem stepped forward. Maybe the blessings of a good deed would be useful to him. He did as Akbar said. Naeem's body was hoisted up by two rows of men. Saleem squeezed in and reached up with his right hand. He was touching Naeem's knee. His hand trembled, and he focused his eyes on the feet of the man in front of him.

Don't think. Just follow.

But it was hard not to think. Saleem felt suffocated as the men jammed together to carry the body. Saleem's chest grew tight, as if the men had squeezed all the air from the small space. One breath. One breath separated him from Naeem.

Others stepped in to take their turns. Saleem was eager to let them take his place. He stood at the edge of the crowd. Akbar looked over and gave him an approving nod.

They lowered Naeem's body into the trench they'd dug out with hands, scraps of metal, and a sense of brotherhood. There was no coffin, just two pieces of cardboard. It was the best they could do and the best any of them could hope for should they end up in Naeem's place, a makeshift grave to mark the end of a makeshift life.

CHAPTER 44
SALEEM

Though it took longer than he cared to admit, Saleem worked up the nerve to go back to the port. The others were equally apprehensive to try again. They'd learned, through the paramedics and aid workers in Patras, that no one at the port knew what had happened to Naeem. Some said the boy had walked away from the accident, and others claimed he'd been carried off by friends. It had not prompted many questions.

Saleem was demoralized but had no choice. He loitered about and watched the trucks and passengers from a distance. When he closed his eyes, he saw Naeem's face. He was tempted to return to the camp but with only three hundred euros, Saleem needed to accept the risk if he was ever going to make it to Italy and have hope for the rest of his passage.

He watched and studied and tried to

understand the schedule and pattern of the ferries and trucks. Opportunities could come at any time, he reminded himself. He kept his eyes open and replayed what he'd done in Izmir. It was possible.

When the opportunity came, it was a moment as ordinary as any other.

Saleem scaled the fence and crept closer and closer to the trucks. He was behind some cargo containers when he heard a truck pull up, brake, and release a thick plume of black smoke skyward. The burly driver, his forearms thick with hair, got out and rolled open the back door. Saleem crouched to the ground and watched intently.

The series of events that followed occurred in a matter of seconds, one privately cataclysmic moment. The driver's cell phone rang, a high-pitched chime. He answered it with a lighthearted greeting, the pleasant conversation relaxing his step and leading him away. Saleem was no more than eight feet from the platform. He watched the driver, the phone to his ear and a can of soda to his lips, saunter around toward the truck's cab.

Saleem did not stop to think. If he had, he never would have made it out of Patras. He pushed the truck door open wide enough to slip his slim frame through.

He was inside. It was dark, and he was tightly jammed against what felt like stacks of crates. He guided himself with his hands, waiting for his eyes to acclimate. No commotion outside. Not yet, anyway. Saleem slipped between two towers of crates and ducked low, pushing the crates in front of him to make a wall. Motionless and tense, he waited.

A trickle of sweat slid down his back.

He did not think about his mother or Samira or Aziz in these moments. If it occurred to him just how badly he wanted to be with them again, to have their arms around his neck and their eyes brighten at the sight of him, his nerves would have gotten the best of him. He focused on taking small, silent breaths.

The driver's voice neared. He was back at the truck's door, still on the phone. Saleem put his chin to his chest and crouched as low as he could.

The door opened wider. Light poured in and Saleem held his breath. The driver opened one of the crates, rifled through its contents, and then slapped it closed again. Glass bottles jangled against each other. The driver laughed, his fortuitously cheerful conversation continuing. The door came down hard and locked shut with a steely click.

Pitch-black.

He was alone.

He breathed.

Chapter 45
Fereiba

I left Afghanistan with three children clinging to me. Right now, I hold my daughter's hand. Samira and I cannot bear to look at each other, nor can we bear to let go. There is a cup of black tea on the table in front of me, along with some magazines and a box of tissues. The tea has gone from hot to cold without me taking a sip. The dog-eared magazines have pictures of smiling people who look nothing like me and know nothing of my life. That leaves only the box of tissues. One tissue has half freed itself from the box and dangles toward me as an offering.

But I refuse.

The walls are painted a light blue, the color of a *burqa* left out in the sun. I wonder if I'll ever see this color and think of birds' eggs or light-washed waters. For now, it still takes me back, and not forward.

Samira's hands are warm. The sweater

she's wearing is one Najiba's daughter has outgrown. My daughter looks like a new girl in it. Her face has already started to fill in. What a difference it makes to see her bangs drawn back with a new tortoiseshell barrette that her aunt brought for her. It is a luxury to think about hair and clothes. I remember the clothing I used to wear in my first years with Mahmood. Now, I think of just how unimportant clothes are . . . and yet how life changing they can be.

Truths can be wholly contradictory, the blackest black and the whitest white all at once.

It's now been two hours. The faces around us have been kind and unjudging. Their words slow and patient. The nurses smiled at Samira and she smiled back. It made it easier for me to see my youngest child led away. He watched me as he was rolled away, his fingers writhing, pulling at my heart-strings. The nurse put a hand on my arm and squeezed gently, saying wordlessly that she, too, was a mother and they would take good care of my son.

If they can mend his heart, there is hope for me.

In the few weeks since our arrival, much has happened. The hardest part was the first step — approaching the customs officer with nothing but the bare truth of why we were there, a white flag begging for mercy. The customs officer scowled and huffed and led us away as others watched, thankful not to be in our shoes and craning their necks to hear what was being said. We were a curiosity. I kept my eyes on the officer, unable to meet the onlookers' stares.

We spent hours in one room before being shuttled off to another. At some point, they brought in an Iranian man. He translated my words into English, dryly and mechanically. Not once did he smile or offer a word other than what he was asked to say. He was not there to be our friend or advocate and made certain that point would not be misunderstood.

The process had begun. We were sent to a shelter, a building with small rooms and shared bathrooms. There were other refugees there, all in the same process. People of all different colors and tongues. Unable to communicate, we eyed one another with cautious distrust, as if we were vying against one another for a single opportunity, as if there could be only one winner among us. We wondered who had the most compelling story. Who among us was most worthy of this country's sympathy? It was a disturbing, silent rivalry.

We were interviewed again. I gave every detail. I told them about my husband and the work he did and the enemies he'd somehow made. I told them of the night the men came to our home and took him away. Samira stared at the floor and listened. We'd not spoken of that night since it happened. The interpreter relayed our story to a woman who made notes, nodded her head, and moved on to the next page of questions. I told them about Saleem and how he disappeared along the way. I told them so they would have a record of my son for when he appears. They confirmed names and dates of birth and names of family members and addresses and all kinds of details. I was asked again and again for the same information, so many times that I thought I might trip over my answers, even though they were truths.

My sister Najiba was permitted to visit us. I fell into her arms. To be around family is to feel the possibility of growing roots again. When they asked about Saleem, my heart dropped. I'd been hoping he'd somehow made it to England ahead of me and was already in his aunt's home, waiting for us to make our way there. My sister held me tightly. Her family came with her, Hameed and the children. The reunion was bittersweet, clouded by Mahmood's absence. Hameed wiped away tears to see me without my husband, his cousin. For the moment, everything else between us, the twisted way he'd married into our family, was pushed aside. I had other, more pressing worries. Saleem was still missing. My sister did her best to keep my spirits up.

He will come soon enough, Fereiba-jan. *He's always been a clever boy. He is his father's son.*

Yes, he is.

We live in a small apartment now with a single bedroom and a small kitchen. It is modest and glorious all at once. While they consider our pleas, we have been granted identification cards and a few pounds per week for food. More than anything, I am grateful that they have evaluated Aziz. The dear doctor from Turkey was right. Aziz had a hole in his heart and needed surgery urgently, the doctors here told me. They would treat him while we waited for our case to be reviewed. With or without an interpreter, there was no way to express how grateful I was to hear that.

If only I could share this news with Saleem. I look for him everywhere we go. I see boys of his height or with his hair color and pray that one of them will come running toward me. I hear his voice in crowds and turn frequently and abruptly, wondering if I'm walking past him without knowing it. What if he is here but cannot find us? Samira knows and is unsurprised by my behaviors. She does the same. Harder than anything is not knowing where he is.

I dare to imagine a perfect world. I dare to dream that the woman writing my story on those many pages will stop and remember that a boy by the name of Saleem Waziri is here and in search of his family. I dream that I will tell him his brother is well. I dream that we receive a letter declaring that we will not be sent away and that we will be allowed to work and go to school and stay in this country where the air is clear and life is more like metal than dust.

And while I'm thinking of these things, a woman in a green hospital uniform walks toward me. Her hair is covered in a blue puff, the same grating blue as the walls. She removes her mask as she approaches. I stare at her face, anxious to see what news she will bring of my son. I can tell nothing from her eyes. I dare not stand up because she may very well knock me down with what she is about to say. I have no choice but to wait and listen.

It shouldn't be much longer now.

CHAPTER 46
SALEEM

Again, a new language. Again, a new people.

But everything was the same. It was the familiar feeling of being lost. The same things made his skin clammy and his mouth dry: uniforms, refugees, checkpoints, trains, and the sight of food.

After what felt like an eternity, Saleem felt the ship stop moving and the trucks began disembarking. The truck had rolled off the ramp into the port in Bari, the eastern coast of Italy. Getting off the truck had been the tricky part. Saleem had waited for the truck driver to make his first stop and open the back door. When he did so, Saleem pitched his coiled body off the platform, nearly knocking the driver to the ground. Like a mouse discovered in a cubbyhole, he scrambled to his feet and took off running.

Run. Just run.

Sunlight stung his unaccustomed eyes. He ran toward the road. There was yelling behind him. He ran faster and turned left when he saw an opening between two buildings. It was a street corner. When he'd put enough distance behind him, he slumped down between two Dumpsters and waited.

It was dusk before Saleem started to walk again. He walked with purpose but without direction, a bewilderment in his step that he'd made it this far. Saleem's eyes drifted upward to buildings that stood stories high. He had stumbled into a metropolis, the likes of which he'd only seen in his father's books.

Here, Saleem thought with both trepidation and hope, *I can be lost.*

Saleem wandered through the narrow streets as cars and taxis zipped past him. A family walked by. The mother pushed a baby carriage while the father carried a young boy on his shoulders. Saleem looked away. For all the miles and months between him and Kabul, the hurt stayed close, no farther than the pigment in his skin. Would he ever look at a father and son and not feel the poison pulse through his body? Until the night Padar-*jan* had been taken, he'd never noticed fathers and sons. His eyes were drawn to them now, a self-inflicted thrashing that he could not resist because each time he hoped, with that part of a boy that refuses to stay beaten down, that this time would be the time the vinegar would turn back to juice.

Then there were mothers. And young girls of Samira's age. And healthy toddlers. More and more, Saleem had to turn his eyes away when he looked at the world. He was even more alone than he thought.

Saleem worked up the nerve to enter a small store. He traded a few euros for a sandwich and juice. The shop owner bagged his purchase and went back to his business.

He found a dimly lit children's park. He walked past the swings and the slide and the sandbox. He walked over to the carousel, a disk painted in primary colors. Saleem pushed the metal rail of the carousel and gave it a spin. It wobbled with a slow, hair-raising squeak. Night transformed play-grounds into ghost towns, empty of the redeeming sound of children laughing and giving chase.

Saleem lived in those voids. He lived in the uninhabited spaces of night, the places where bright, cheerful faces would not be. He lived in the corners that went unnoticed, among the things people swept out the back door.

With his knees tucked in, he slept the night behind the carousel and woke just as the sun came up. Horns were honking and the city was stirring to life again. Saleem made his way to the sidewalk. Today, he would plan.

Women with grocery bags and small children walked by. The shops looked familiar. The language sounded foreign. Things were different but the same. Saleem stayed alert for uniforms. With England as his destination, he needed to find the best route to get there. He'd managed to get by on buses in Turkey and thought he could try for the same here. He worked up the nerve to approach an elderly woman, her back hunched with age. He asked in a mesh of Greek and English for the bus station. The woman looked annoyed and waved him off, tapping down the road with her cane. Saleem continued down the block, his hands in his pockets.

He spotted a gray-haired man sitting alone outside a café. He had just folded his newspaper and was tucking it under his arm when Saleem approached and did his best to articulate his question again.

The man nodded, his face mostly covered by the wide brim of his hat. His voice had a soft rasp, weathered by the years.

"Dov'e' la stazione? Si, si."

With a series of hand gestures, the man pointed to a main road and a turn to the left. He repeated himself, speaking slowly and patiently until he was certain Saleem had a general sense of the direction he was to take.

Saleem put his hand over his chest and lowered his head in thanks, feeling much like Padar-*jan* in this gesture.

Street signs were not helpful. Saleem came to an intersection and wondered if this was where he was supposed to turn to the left. He walked for a few more moments and saw a wide structure, its entire façade a series of arched entryways and ornate windows. Two buses turned in to the road that curled around the building. Seeing a police officer sipping coffee up ahead, Saleem made a subtle, panic-stricken shift and veered off a side street. Two blocks later, he returned to the main road and, with the police officer well behind him, headed straight for the station.

Inside, the station was a bustling metropolis of its own. Saleem dodged travelers and meandered through until he found a wall of maps. There were four large posters of various scales on the wall. Saleem looked at the local bus routes and moved on. Next was a map of Italy.

But where am I now?

Somewhere close to water. Somewhere

close to Greece. His eyes zeroed in on the red dot on Italy's eastern shore.

Okay, so I am here. How will I get to England?

Saleem turned around to make sure he hadn't attracted any attention. Back to the map. To get to England, passing France would be the most direct route. But how to do it?

Saleem considered his journey thus far.

One step at a time. Major cities are easier to hide in. Don't get trapped in small towns.

Roma. Northwest from where he stood, it was the city labeled in the largest letters, and it looked like a series of paths led there and out. From Roma, he would have to make his way north to cross France and then the English Channel.

Saleem felt for the rope at his waist, his money pouch. Within it, he had tucked away the slip of paper with the address Roksana had found for him. A destination. That was all he had. No phone number, no map, no pictures. Just an address.

Saleem cautiously walked over to the row of desks with clerks sitting behind plexiglass windows. He stepped in front of an older woman who barely looked up. Saleem didn't understand a bit of what she said.

"Please? Bus ticket for Roma?" he asked,

praying the woman spoke English.

"Roma?" she asked, looking up from her computer. She peered over the top of her lenses.

He tried to read her and prepared to run.

"Eh, for Roma, it is better you take train, no?" Saleem nodded. She sounded casual, unsuspicious.

Saleem followed her directions to the train station, not too far away. There, he repeated his cautious surveys and waited until he was sure the scene was clear of police officers before approaching the ticket booth. He was able to purchase a ticket to Rome on a train that left two hours later and boarded it when he saw others embarking.

It was nearly ten o'clock at night when the train pulled into the Rome station. Before he dared step out into the night, Saleem took a moment to steel his nerves. Though he had taken one step forward, Saleem knew very well how quickly he could fall two steps back.

Chapter 47
Saleem

He reset his father's watch according to the clock on the station wall. Saleem walked into the familiar night of the unfamiliar Rome to find a place to rest until morning. He was anxious to find the best route to France but cautioned himself against rushing.

The air was chilly. Saleem stuffed his hands in his pockets, kept his head low and his eyes open.

People squeezed through the bottlenecked station exits with rolling luggage. Saleem chose a well-lit street much less crowded than the one most people walked down.

He had walked about ten or fifteen minutes when he saw them. Three women stood near the storefronts. They wore skirts that barely covered their backsides and tops that looked glued to their bodies. Two were dark skinned, African, one with hair that flared a bright orange under the light of the streetlamp. The third had skin lighter than Saleem's and auburn hair. They shifted their weight from side to side and walked a few steps up and down the block with arms folded, doing their best to keep warm. Saleem slowed his steps and watched.

Cars slowed as they passed. The girls would put one foot in front of the other and eye the driver with a head tilted to the side. Saleem watched the lighter girl. With the next car that approached, she glanced over her shoulder and ran her hand through her hair.

Saleem detected the all-too-familiar scent of desperation on them.

A small hatchback pulled up. One of the African girls walked over to the passenger-side window and leaned in. She put a hand on her hip. She shook her head and the car took off, barely waiting for her to pull her head out of the vehicle. She yelled angrily as his rear lights faded away.

The guys in the camps had talked about an area of Patras where men could pay women to be with them. Saleem smiled and laughed as they joked about it, but he had never seen such a place or such a woman. It was clear even to his naïve eyes that this was what they were talking about. But these were girls, young girls. Saleem wondered if he was wrong. He approached them, needing directions but also curious.

The auburn-haired girl saw him nearing and took a few steps back, leaning against the building's façade. The two other girls looked at him dismissively and chatted together a few feet away.

He could not help but stare. His eyes started at her thick, four-inch pumps and roved upward, tracing her bare legs up her thighs to where her black dress ended or began, depending on the point of view. The dress skimmed her thin frame, and a web of spaghetti straps crisscrossed her chest and back.

"Buona sera," she said. The streetlamp illuminated her delicate features, casting playful shadows across her face. She had a slim nose, pale green eyes that shimmered even in the evening light, and lips painted a garish red. Despite her made-up face, she looked no more than seventeen years old.

"Allo," Saleem replied bashfully. He searched for words. She looked impatient.

"Allo," she prompted. She'd gotten a feeling he was not a promising prospect, and her coy looks disappeared.

"I . . . I need help. How I can go to England?" It was as eloquent as he could be in this particular moment.

She rolled her eyes and turned her back to him. Saleem persisted.

"Please, I need go to England," he pleaded. "Somewhere I can sleep for one night? Do you know?"

"I cannot help you," she said abruptly. She spoke English but with an accent thicker and heavier than Saleem's. She took a few steps away as a car drove by, slowed, and then sped away. She looked back in his direction, annoyed.

"Go," she hissed. "Do not stand here!"

"Please! I come from Afghanistan. Do you know if I find more Afghans here?"

"I do not know."

"Where are you from?" he persisted.

"Albania," she said, her eyes wistful for a sliver of a second. "Now you go."

Saleem had never heard of Albania. He pressed on. They were so close in age. Maybe something about Roksana gave him hope that this girl would help guide him as well, though he knew there was nothing similar about them.

She turned her back defiantly. Saleem finally relented. He circled the blocks looking for anyone else he could ask for help but it was nearly midnight and he was exhausted. He rounded the corner and found her on the same block. The two other girls eyed Saleem from afar and crossed the street, shaking their heads. The Albanian girl stole a glance in his direction and threw her head back with a huff.

"I am sorry. I just want to ask you . . . please. I need to sleep, somewhere safe. No police."

"Please, you make problem for me. Go!" As if they had been beckoned by Saleem, blue lights twirled in the distance. The girls began to disperse.

"Police?" Saleem asked, as the fair-skinned girl hurried down the street.

"Yes," she whispered without turning around. Saleem moved closer to the building and away from the curb. The lights stayed at a distance. He watched her go, her legs pale in the darkness. She was awkward in her heels, and in her hurry, her ankle suddenly twisted in, sending her arms flailing. She stumbled a step or two before falling to the ground. Saleem ran over to her. Her knees were badly scraped, and she held her ankle, her face in a grimace. She tried to get back on her feet, but as she put weight on her right foot, she gasped.

Saleem held her elbow as she took off her shoe. The heel had broken off. She looked as if she might burst into tears. With her shoe in her hand, she began to hobble down the street. Saleem let her arm go but quickly caught up with her when he saw how she struggled to walk. "I will help you," he offered and quietly extended his hand. She looked at him with resignation and nodded.

"Here," she said simply and led the way. They made a few turns down slate-colored alleys. She led him to a rusted sedan parked on a back lot. She took a key out of her purse, unlocked the door, and slid into the backseat.

"Sit," she offered, pointing to the seat beside her. He followed, careful not to get too close. She was less standoffish now, but being alone in a car with her suddenly made Saleem uncomfortable.

"Your name?" she asked with mild interest.

"Saleem. And you?"

"Mimi."

There was a period of silence. Mimi fidgeted and rubbed her ankle. She looked at Saleem, her brow furrowed.

"Why you come here?"

"Here?"

"Italy. Why you come to Italy?"

"I want to go to England. My family is in England."

"Family?"

"Mother, sister, brother."

Mimi stared out the car window. Drops of rain fell silently on the glass.

"Where is your family?" Saleem asked. Mimi rubbed her arms and shifted in the seat.

"No family," she said abruptly.

"Oh."

Her answer left Saleem with many more questions.

"When you come to Italy?"

"Two years," she said. "Two years."

"You want to stay?"

Her lips pulled together in an angry pout. "There is nothing here."

"Where do you want to go?"

Mimi looked up as if no one had ever asked her that question. Something about the darkness made their conversation even more pleasantly anonymous than it already was.

"I do not know." The rain started to come down heavier, pelting at the roof of the car with a tin, staccato rhythm. Lulled by the dark and the rain, Mimi began to tell Saleem her story in a fragmented English that did not do it justice.

Mimi came from a poor family in Albania. She'd been the third daughter, and two more followed after her. When she was fifteen, her parents arranged for her to be married to a man nearly twice her age. She protested but it made no difference. She lived with her husband for nearly three months, picking up the empty bottles and suffering the rage of his alcoholic fits. After three months, she returned to her parents, but they refused to take her in again. Mimi went to live with her aunt.

She fell in love with a local boy who asked her to move to Italy with him where they would marry and start a new life. He arranged for them to travel by speedboat from Albania to Italy's coast. Mimi did not tell her aunt or anyone else about her decision to leave. When they got to Italy, they lived in a small apartment, and for a week or two, Mimi believed she was beginning the gilded life he'd promised her. But before long, the boy began to complain that they needed money. He could not find work, he'd said, and told his fiancée that her beauty could earn enough to support them both. He promised it would not be for long and that things would not change between them.

Saleem did not interrupt.

The boy took all the money Mimi brought home. He spent her earnings on drugs and went out with friends while she worked. One day, he took her to an apartment and unceremoniously traded her to another man. She'd pleaded with him, reminding him of the promises he'd made and all that she'd done for him, but he turned his back and never returned. The new man wanted her to work. When she refused, he beat her and locked her in a room with two other girls until they had no choice but to submit. That was seven months ago. He was not the kind of man to chance running from, she'd learned from some other girls.

"I have nowhere to go. I have no papers. My family do not want me. And if I leave, he find me."

Saleem had no words of comfort or encouragement. He was thankful the darkness hid the expression on his face. She was a used girl, the kind of shame people could not speak of in polite company in Kabul.

He had only one question, which Mimi answered without his having to ask.

"I do not know why I tell you. You say you need help. But you are boy. You are free. You do not need help."

Her assumptions angered Saleem. He wanted to hate her. Part of him did. He hated her for telling him things so horrible that his own troubles paled. He hated her for making him feel sorry for someone other than himself. He hated her for making him feel all the more helpless — useless to himself and useless to others.

Saleem took another sidelong glance at her. It was not hard to imagine that a family would turn her away. A girl who left her husband and then ran off with another boy, only to end up as a prostitute. In Afghanistan, she would have been put out of her misery long ago for the dishonor she had brought upon her family.

Saleem looked out the window. Out of the many, he watched one raindrop, followed it as it ran down the glass and disappeared into the night. He could not hate her. Despite her brusque tone and lurid exterior, she was just a girl. The best he could do was to say nothing.

"You do not have papers?" she asked.

"No."

"Hm."

Saleem toyed with his watch. He wondered if it was safe to be here with her, but it was raining harder now and he had no desire to seek other cover.

"Your watch . . . it is nice."

Saleem stopped playing with the wristband and sat straight up in the seat. After a few moments, he heard his voice break the silence.

"This was my father's watch."

As he watched the hands count the seconds and minutes, Saleem told his story. He said it plainly and quickly. It was surprising how many days and years mattered not at all. His story, the heart of him, was really made up of only a handful of seconds or minutes. The rest was empty road, an expanse that only prolonged the travel from one point to another.

He told her about his father. He told her about leaving and Polat's farm in Turkey. His voice softened when he talked about Madar-*jan*'s worries and Samira's silence and Aziz's broken heart. He talked about Attiki but left out Saboor and the stabbing, a moment he was still ill prepared to accept. He told her about Patras and Naeem's mangled body.

"You are just a boy," Mimi said finally. "Your family wait for you. You go to them."

"But I can go to France?"

Mimi was thoughtful.

"Maybe I show you — but maybe is bad idea."

"Tell me," Saleem urged. Any idea could be a good idea.

"People go to France every day. Some people, they take a box and go to France. Easy work, only important police not catch you because take you to jail."

"Only for taking a box? I can do this,"

Saleem said hopefully.

"I do not know. I take you to man — he know. I ask him for you."

He and Mimi made arrangements to meet again the following night. When the rain stopped, Mimi told him it was best if he left and found a place to sleep until morning. Saleem understood and walked into the night, grateful to have met Mimi, the girl-woman.

CHAPTER 48
SALEEM

Saleem spent the day wandering the streets of Rome. He watched tourists, cameras dangling from their craned necks. With glossy pamphlets in hand, they had a characteristic rhythm to their walk — stop, focus, shoot. A few steps more, then again — stop, focus, shoot.

He made a mental map to track his path. Cars honked and the sounds of a city drowned his morose thoughts.

Saleem rounded a corner and an earth-colored building loomed ahead, a relic rising above a crowded street. The lopsided building opened to the sky and looked oddly familiar to a boy who'd been in the country for only a day. He walked toward it, a flood of memories returning as he gawked at the structure.

He could not have been more than seven or eight years old, huddled with his family in the back living room of his aunt's home.

They were one of a few to own a video player and one of his cousins had borrowed an old copy of a kung fu movie from a friend. What was it called? Something about a dragon. This was the setting of one of the fight scenes, one that left Saleem chopping his fists into the air and flexing his spindly biceps for weeks.

He closed in on the Coliseum, his step quickened by nostalgia and curiosity. He followed the thick rope of people that circled the building. People were buying tickets to go inside. Saleem sat on a bench across the street. He could not afford to spend what he had on a ticket, nor could he bring himself to walk away. He could imagine those shirtless men, glistening sweat outlining their muscular forms — skillfully striking, ducking, and flying through the air.

Saleem thought of the truck drivers, the police officers, Saboor. His battles were nothing like those of the movie.

He wondered what Roksana was doing at that moment. Probably sitting in class, listening to the teacher with a skeptical ear. He went back to the day she'd taken him home. He pictured her leading him into the living room and talking over lunch. Her soft hand slipping his aunt's address to him. The way her T-shirt narrowed at her waist.

His mind jumped to Mimi, a very different girl, if she could be called that. Her skin, her legs, her chest. It was more than he had ever before seen of a woman. A woman of innocence and shame. Beyond the smoky eye shadow settled into the creases, the smell of cigarette smoke on her clothes, and the tossed-about look on her face, Saleem could see a sweetness to her. He saw it in the way she pursed her lips or sat with her chin propped on her palm.

Saleem had not known girls like these. Just thinking about them made him feel like more of a man, as little sense as that made.

Night came and Saleem found his way back to the dimly lit street. He did not see Mimi. He saw other girls, girls of all hues, wearing short pants or ruffled skirts, masking their ennui with coquettish postures. He kept his distance.

He sat on the front steps of an abandoned building. His watch read nine o'clock. A few cars drove by, slowly. From where he sat, he could see the streetlamp under which they'd met. He would wait, he decided.

Thirty minutes later, a car pulled up. The passenger-side door opened, and one pale leg after another, Mimi emerged. She closed the door behind her just as the car began to peel away. She adjusted her skirt and stepped back onto the sidewalk gingerly, her ankle still tender.

She wore a jade-colored top and white skirt that shimmered under the glow of the streetlamp. Saleem stood and walked toward her. She saw him approaching from afar but acted coolly.

"Mimi," Saleem said nervously. He kept his hands in pockets, not knowing what else to do with them.

"You come back."

By the way she said it, Saleem could tell she had not expected him to nor was she particularly thrilled that he had.

"Yes. Your foot. Is it okay?"

She nodded. Maybe she regretted telling him to return.

Saleem spoke quickly, before she could tell him to leave. "Can you take me to this man? The man who can send me to France?"

"It is bad idea. Sorry. Maybe is better you find your way."

The hope she'd kindled in him last night had grown into a full blaze. She was hesitant. Saleem was not.

"Please, I need help. I must go England . . . for my family. For my mother, my

532

sister, my brother."

Mimi winced at the mention of family. She put a hand on her hip and took a quick glance behind her.

"I do not know what happen. These people sometimes in dangerous places. You have come to Italy alone. I think you go now and find your way, like everyone. You can. No one watch you or hold you here."

"Mimi, please," he beseeched.

"It is not good idea," she said softly.

"I have nothing," Saleem said simply. "I need this."

He had more than she did, Mimi knew. She envied the chance he could take — the chance she, as a caged bird, could never take. She relented, having given him ample warning. Whatever happened after this moment would not be on her conscience.

"I show you. But you not say my name."

Saleem agreed readily. A ring. She hurriedly reached into her small handbag and pulled out a mobile phone. She spoke with someone briefly, her eyes roving the street as she talked. She sounded nervous, obedient.

"We go quickly."

He followed her lead. She told him she would lead him to an apartment building and, from there, Saleem would have to approach the man and ask for assistance on a passage to France.

Finally, Saleem thought, *I am getting somewhere.*

His relief was short-lived.

They had walked but a few moments when a steel-gray car whipped around a corner and screeched to a stop in front of them, nearly hopping the curb. They jumped back and Mimi went toppling over, her foot already unsteady. Saleem reached out to help her, and she took his hand.

"You are customer," she whispered quickly. Her voice trembled.

"What?"

But there was no time for her to clarify. A man in a black leather jacket stormed out of the car, slamming the driver's-side door as he came out. He grabbed Mimi's arm away from Saleem and asked her something in a language Saleem did not understand. Unsatisfied with her answer, he tightened his grip and tried to rattle the truth out of her. She pleaded with him.

"What are you doing with this girl?" the man snarled, turning his attention to Saleem. His dark, cold eyes narrowed. He stood a few inches taller than Saleem and was a good thirty pounds heavier. His unshaven face only intimidated Saleem more.

"I . . . I . . . I was talking," Saleem stuttered, before remembering what Mimi had whispered to him.

"Talking for what?"

"I want to ask her . . . because I want to . . ." Saleem faltered.

"Do you want her?" he said casually.

"Y-y-yes," Saleem said with as much conviction as he could muster. Mimi looked nervously from Saleem to the man.

"Good. Let me see money."

Saleem panicked. His money was in the pouch hidden at his waist. He could not take out a few bills to show this man without having the man see that he had more and he could not risk losing everything.

"I . . . I do not have . . ."

The man had let go of Mimi and was squeezing Saleem's chin and cheeks with a single, pressing hand, a viselike grip.

"No money?"

"No," Saleem squeaked through his mashed lips. The grip tightened.

"No money, eh?" He turned to Mimi and yelled something at her. Before she could begin to explain, his hand clapped against her face. She reeled backward. Saleem thrust his hands out toward her, but he now had the man's full attention.

"You wasting my girl's time?" He struck Saleem with the same vicious blow. Saleem staggered and tried to get his bearings, but the second and third blows came too quickly.

There was no arguing with his rage.

Pointed boots landed on Saleem's back, his stomach, and his ribs. He heard Mimi scream. He tried to cower, to cover his stomach from the blows. His breath was short. He felt pavement against his cheek, cold and rough. And then it stopped.

Saleem crawled away, coughing and sputtering on his knees. Mimi's cries faded. He dragged himself to a corner and lay behind a pile of cardboard boxes.

Please let it be over.

Saleem closed his eyes and gave in to the dark.

CHAPTER 49
SALEEM

Why didn't I fight back? What's wrong with me?

Saleem was almost as furious with himself as he was with Mimi's pimp. It was morning. His body screamed in protest as he hobbled his way to a corner store and bought something he could sip through his swollen, split lips. The store owner, taking him for a hooligan, took his money scornfully. He shook his head, disappointed in his country for not keeping the troublemakers out.

After finding his way to the train station, Saleem looked for schedules and routes that would take him into France. He felt the eyes of a police officer on his back. In a moment, Saleem had expertly melted into the crowd, leaving the officer to shake his head and return to the opposite side of the station.

Saleem grappled each day with the possibility that he might not make it to England. Taken with his experience within the first few days of arriving in Italy, he felt desperate to try something. But he was tired — fatigued as if his veins carried lead instead of blood. He was tired of having nothing to eat and tired of worrying about money. He was tired of watching over his shoulder. Leaving Kabul may have been a mistake after all. Things might have gotten better.

Saleem did not hear the click of heels nearing him. He'd nodded off with his back against the side of a building. In the recessed streets of Italy's capital, someone recognized his battered face.

"Saleem."

He opened his eyes to spy two knees with scrapes like skid marks. Mimi crouched beside him, her voice hushed.

"Are you okay?"

"I'm fine." His voice was low and insincere. He looked around.

"Are you alone?"

"Yes," she said. "Burim is not here."

His name was Burim.

"You are hurt bad? Oh, your mouth!"

"I'm all right. It's better now." Saleem admitted to himself that it was his fault he and Mimi ran into Burim that night and it was because of him that Mimi had been dragged away. From the looks of it, Burim hadn't let her off easy. There was a bluish hue below her left eye and a small scab on her lip.

"I . . . I am sorry, Mimi," he said. "I did not want for you to be hurt."

Mimi slumped to the ground and sat beside him. "I know. Burim is a crazy man. I know him. Nothing new."

"You need to get away from him." It seemed uncomplicated to Saleem. Why linger here when the money she earned was not hers and she lived in a perpetual state of fear? Why did Mimi not leave?

"I can do nothing. Not now. Maybe one day but now . . . now I have no choice."

They contemplated in silence, Saleem wondering why Mimi did not walk away today and Mimi knowing Saleem would never understand.

"I take you to the man now," she said. "Maybe you can leave. You have better chance than me."

"But Burim? What if he finds us again?"

"He is far now. He has two girls far from here. New girls. He go to meet them. We have time."

He nodded and followed. While he did not feel up to the meeting, he wanted desperately to leave Rome. Mimi led him down the same streets, watching to be sure he kept up the pace. They reached an apartment building with a broken knob and first-floor windows taped together. Saleem shook his head, knowing he was ignoring his instincts by entering.

"Inside door, press for apartment B3," Mimi instructed. "A man answer. He ask who you are and you tell him Mimi send you. Say you want to go to France and maybe he have job for you."

"Tell your name?"

"Yes. This man, he not Burim friend. But you do everything he say. Everything, understand? He is dangerous man but possible he send you to France. You come here in two days," she instructed specifically.

Saleem was relieved he had time yet before he was to meet Mimi's contact though it was disappointing that it would be at least another two days before he could leave this city.

"What's his name?" he asked. Mimi was already leading him back down to where they had come from. "What is this man's name?"

"No name," she said firmly. "No questions. He not like to talk."

"How you know him?"

"He work with Burim one year but they

fight for money. Now they not talk but I know man sends people from here to other countries. He tell you how you do."

Saleem nodded, understanding some but not all. Mimi was neck deep in a world of unsavory characters. Saleem wondered if he was one of them.

Maybe I am like her. Like the people she knows. Maybe I'm not an innocent boy on the run anymore. Maybe if I accept that, I'll be better off.

She walked ahead of him, her thin ponytail beckoning him to follow. Saleem, still sore, suggested they sit down and eat the half sandwich he had in his pocket. Mimi nodded up ahead.

"Come with me," she said and he followed.

She led him back to a dimly lit, one-room apartment in a building not far from where she'd found him. A simple sheet covered a twin-size mattress on a metal bed frame. A lamp sat on a wooden chair, and two other chairs were up against the opposite wall. The walls, painted what was surely once an inspiring red, had cracked with time. The galley kitchen was a few feet away, divided from the main room by a half wall. The appliances looked rusted and unused. The door to the bathroom was half open, and

Saleem could see a chipped porcelain sink and a narrow shower stall with blackened grout.

The apartment was in miserable condition and if Saleem had seen it before he'd left Kabul, he would have turned up his nose at it. But his perspective had changed. As Padar-*jan* often said, in the valley of the blind, the one-eyed man is king.

Saleem's more pressing concern was whether it was a good idea for him to be here. Mimi looked over and read his thoughts.

"He will not come. Burim has new girl. He stay with her and come back in morning. The first night is very, very bad." Mimi sat on the bed, and Saleem pulled a chair to sit across from her. He took the flattened sandwich from his pocket, unwrapped it, and offered her half. She took it from him with a soft thanks.

"You live here?" he asked.

She did. Her skimpy dresses and mesh shirts hung limply in the closet, looking as tired as she did. Mimi filled a glass of water from the kitchen tap, took a sip, and passed it to him.

The lamp did not provide much light, and the one window faced another building, not allowing for much street light to come in.

Saleem sat forward in his chair. His knee grazed Mimi's.

"I am sorry, Mimi. Burim hurt you too. You ask me to leave but I . . . I am sorry."

Mimi stared at the floor.

"Is okay. Forget it. He not change. He tell me I go free if I make money. I make money for ticket to Albania and I can go home. But now seven months and nothing. Other girls, they work two, three years. Nobody make enough money to be free. This is my life now. If you are here, if you are not here . . . it is same."

She looked up. Like the raindrops he'd watched on the car window, two tears slid down Mimi's makeup-covered cheeks.

"But you . . . you can go from here. Your family is wait for you and when they see you they will be happy." Her eyes widened as she pictured open arms welcoming Saleem. She wiped away her tears and smiled weakly.

Saleem wanted to offer her the same encouragement. He wanted to give her the same kindness. He faltered, then reached out and put a hand on her knee.

"You are strong, Mimi. You'll find a way. Something good come for you too. People help me to come here. You help me. God give the same help for you. Somebody will help you." Saleem heard the hollowness of his words.

"There is no one to help me. He take my money. I know he never let me go. He control everything."

Saleem felt his body tighten. Mimi, in all her frailty, still found a way to share. He could be more than what he was. Empty pockets did not mean an empty soul.

"He does not control me," Saleem said. "Help me find Burim, Mimi."

She covered his hand with her own and looked at him. She wanted to believe him, to believe every word of what he was saying even if only for a moment. She touched Saleem's cheek. His stomach dropped to feel her cool, thin fingers on his face. She touched his other cheek and his eyes closed. He imagined Mimi of long ago, a young girl who smiled and laughed with her sisters. He pictured a girl unsullied. He pictured the girl she'd been before the world had crushed her.

Mimi took his hands. Saleem sat on the bed beside her. He let his fingers intertwine with hers before sliding up her arms. He found her shoulders, the milky skin of her neck. Her hands pulled his face to hers, her breath teasing his cheeks. She brought her mouth to his.

She led, Saleem followed. He was timid and nervous but she reassured him with her whispers, the lightness of her touch. She coaxed him and he felt himself becoming a person capable of surprising things. He touched the bruises on her ribs lightly. Her eyes fluttered. There were other bruises, ones her clothing had hidden. He wanted to apologize a thousand times over. He pressed his face against her chest and heard her heart beat, slow and steady. His own heart pounded, untamed and eager.

He was riveted by her flesh. He hesitated, his hands fumbling for the right answers. His inadequacy did not seem to bother her. She welcomed him, making him believe that there was a way he could feel something other than loneliness and hurt.

Saleem turned to his side and traced the length of her arm. Mimi, the girl who needed saving, had saved him. It was only then, as his breathing cooled and slowed, as his muscles relaxed and regrouped, that he let his eyes drift upward to her face, expressionless and passive. It was only then that Saleem realized the bright and hopeful Mimi he'd pictured when he'd closed his eyes did not exist and probably never had.

CHAPTER 50
SALEEM

He waited in the dark. Mimi made fleeting eye contact with him from across the street. Saleem watched for her to pull at her skirt, the signal they had arranged. She stood apart from the others, purposely ignoring the cars that slowed near her. Not tonight.

Two hours later, she gave the sign.

They had planned it yesterday, while Saleem was still half naked, half intoxicated from her touch. It had to be fast and, like so much of Saleem's activities, it had to be in the night.

The signal. A surge of adrenaline raced through Saleem's body. There was Burim, sauntering down the street toward Mimi. Saleem waited, then emerged from behind the building's corner. He jogged, keeping his footsteps light, and crossed the street, half a block behind Burim.

You are not a coward.

Saleem said the words again and again,

egging himself on. It had been his idea and he could not turn back. He would make this happen. He was tired of things happening to him, as if he were an object instead of a man. The moment was here. Just as Mimi had guessed, Burim was coming to check on her.

Saleem was behind him, ducking away from streetlamps and staying close to the building fronts. Burim was talking to Mimi. She was fidgeting, her eyes darting nervously and her shoulders pulled together.

I looked just as weak to him. No more.

Saleem slipped behind an empty newsstand. His fingers tightened around the one-foot length of rusted metal pipe he'd brought with him. He could hear Burim speaking to Mimi. His voice rose. He was getting angrier. Mimi mumbled a reply. Burim snickered.

Saleem took a deep breath and stepped out from behind the stand. He swung and brought the pipe crashing down against Burim's ribs. Burim reeled and stumbled forward. Before he could spin around Saleem struck another blow and kicked behind Burim's left knee with just enough force to bring him down. Burim howled in anger.

Mimi had shrunk to the side, her back against the wall and her expression hollow.

Burim rolled onto his back and groaned. He looked up to see Saleem hovering over him, the pipe held with both hands, poised and ready. Saleem's chest heaved with each breath. Mimi approached and stood alongside Saleem.

"You . . . you . . . bitch," Burim spat.

Saleem saw the rage in Burim's face as his right hand reached into his jacket pocket. He withdrew a compact, black pistol, but before he could take aim, Saleem swung the pipe at Burim's hand and sent the gun flying. Burim cursed, holding one hand with the other.

"You are dead . . . you make mistake . . ."

He stumbled onto his hands and knees and looked up at Mimi. He hissed something in Albanian, words that pulled her blank stare into one of rage.

"Watch what I will do to you!" Burim was crouched, nearly up on his feet.

Saleem saw Mimi's outstretched arms. She said a few words and spat at him, her voice trembling.

Burim lunged in her direction with a growl. Saleem realized what was happening, and the pipe slipped from his fingers, clanging loudly to the ground.

"Mimi!" he shouted.

There was a pop. Burim stopped in his

tracks and spun around so that he was looking directly into Saleem's bewildered eyes.

Saleem jumped back. He looked from Burim to Mimi.

She was shaking. She dropped the gun
and covered her mouth with her hands. She
looked at Saleem.

The street was empty. The nearest cars
were two blocks away. Two or three lights
had turned on in the building windows.
Those who slept lightly were beginning to
stir. Mimi recovered first. She kneeled over
Burim and dug into his pockets, grabbed
his wallet, and snapped the gold chain off
his thick neck. He moaned softly but offered no resistance.

She stole a glance over her shoulder.

"Let's go."

They took off, weaving around buildings
and turning into dark streets to put distance
between them and Burim.

They were silent as they fled. Panting.
Looking over their shoulders.

"Wait," Mimi finally said. She put her
hands on her knees and leaned forward to
catch her breath. "I need to stop."

She looked ghastly pale, even under the
yellow glow of a lantern. Saleem knew he
must look the same. Things had gone terribly wrong. Burim was not supposed to

have seen his attacker. Mimi was supposed to look surprised and helpless at the attack. But Burim had seen their faces, had realized they had duped him, conspired against him.

"Mimi, we need to hide."

They went to her apartment. She quickly tossed a stack of folded clothes from the chair into a duffel bag.

She'd had no intention of staying here after tonight, Saleem realized.

Chapter 51
Saleem

Saleem and Mimi waited until afternoon to go to the apartment building she had pointed out.

"I wait here for you," she said and pointed to a bench half a block away. She pulled the sleeves of her sweater down over her hands and blew on them. The sun did little to warm her.

Saleem entered the old building. It was an uninviting warren of decay — cigarette butts scattered through the hallways, broken handrails on the stairs, and a flickering wall lamp. Radios and televisions buzzed behind closed doors, but there was not a person in sight.

He checked the apartment number, took a deep breath, and knocked. He took a nervous step back and waited. There was a click, and the eyehole cover slid open. After a moment, the door opened slightly, and a man stood before Saleem with a cigarette dangling from his lower lip. He wore an unbuttoned black shirt over jeans, his silver belt buckle a proud emblem on his waist. Somewhere in his late thirties, he looked the teenage Saleem over and concluded that he was unimpressed.

Saleem swallowed before speaking.

"I look for work, please."

"Who are you?"

"I want to go to France. I can work."

The man sucked on the cigarette he held with two fingers, then tossed it into the hallway. He squinted at Saleem as he exhaled.

"Who send you?"

"Mimi," Saleem said quietly. She'd told him to use her name, afraid he would not get far without it.

"Mimi, eh?"

"Yes." Saleem heeded her advice and kept his answers brief. The door opened a little wider and, with a nod, Saleem was invited in.

The apartment was larger than Mimi's but much filthier. There were clothes everywhere, crumpled food wrappers, and a coffee table topped with plates of food and several mobile phones. The television blared. Saleem reminded himself not to stare. The door closed behind them.

"Where are you from?"

"Afghanistan."

"Afghanistan?" he said, thick eyebrows lifted in surprise. "Why you want work?"

"My family is in London. I want to go there."

Saleem had second thoughts, his pulse racing. He had just caught a glimpse of a handgun tucked in between the cushions of the sofa. He stayed focused on the man before him.

"You have papers?"

"No papers."

"You know Mimi?"

"Yes."

"Every man knows Mimi." He chuckled, his mood lightening. He pinched Saleem's bicep between his thumb and forefinger and mumbled something to himself. His hands slid down, patting Saleem's trunk and then around his waist. He paused when he felt the hard sheath of the knife. He looked at Saleem.

"It is a knife," Saleem explained. He dared not move. He kept his arms extended. The man untwisted the sheath from the rope around Saleem's waist. He hadn't noticed the small pouch that bulged from Saleem's underwear. The pouch was safe for now.

The man pulled the blade from the casing

and whistled, impressed.

"Very nice. A gift for me, yes?"

Saleem opened his mouth to protest but caught himself.

"Yes," he said.

The man smirked. He tossed the blade onto the sofa.

"This is problem," he said coolly. "You want to go to London and you have no papers. You have money?"

Saleem shook his head.

"No money." He grinned snidely. "And Mimi tell you come here."

"Yes. I want to help you."

"Oh, you want to help me?" he said facetiously, bowing his head in mock gratitude. Saleem shrank before him.

"You not *help* me. You *work* for me."

Saleem nodded.

A second man emerged from the next room, the sleeves of his shirt rolled up past his inked forearms. He looked at Saleem curiously and said something to his roommate before taking a seat on the sofa.

"So you want to work for me, Mister *Afghan-i-stan*?" he asked, drawing out the syllables dramatically.

"Yes."

"What do you think, Visar?" He turned to the man on the couch.

Visar shrugged his bulky shoulders. He noticed the knife on the sofa, picked it up, and turned it over, admiring the casing just as Saleem had when he first found it.

"You like, Visar? Gift from the boy."

He motioned for Saleem to sit at the kitchen table. Saleem did so and waited. The man reached into a cabinet and tossed a square box onto the table.

"Open."

Saleem peeled off the tape and opened the box. Inside was a large stuffed bear, a children's toy about the size of a newborn. He turned it over, confused.

"You take this to France. I give you papers and train ticket from Rome to Paris. You talk to no one until you leave. In Paris, a man wait for you. You give him this. Understand?"

"Yes, I understand."

"Good. Now look here." He pointed to a small round lens sitting on the table and reached over for his laptop computer. Saleem stared at the ball, not sure what he was looking for or at. The man pressed a few buttons, grunted, and turned the lens away from Saleem.

"Train leave eight o'clock tonight from Termini. Change train in Milan and then go Paris. You have bags?"

Saleem shook his head. He had nothing.

The man stood and went into a hallway closet, dug out an empty backpack, and threw in three shirts, a pair of pants, and a magazine from the mess strewn about the apartment.

"Take. You must carry bag like tourist. Put inside," he instructed, taking the bear from Saleem and stuffing it in. "You leave here now. Come back two hours for papers and the bag. Do not be late."

Saleem took the bag.

"I said go now."

Saleem obeyed. He made note of the time so he would know when to return — not wanting to be late or early. He walked outside and into the bright but chilly afternoon. Mimi was not on the bench as she'd promised. He walked around the block, peering down alleys and into the small Laundromat on the corner. She was gone.

Had she planned it? Saleem had to wonder. So much had happened between them in the last two days. She'd been distant since last night, silent about what had transpired. She seemed neither shocked nor distraught, a melancholy calm to her voice.

At least she has the money, he thought. When they had finally stopped running, Mimi had pulled the bills and gold chain from her bag. She counted out four hundred twenty euros. She looked at Saleem.

Take it, he had said. *He took enough from you.*

She looked him straight in the eye, as if to gauge his sincerity. When Saleem did not waver, she stuffed the money into the pocket of her bag and kept a protective hand over it. There was no family waiting on her return. There was no one to smile as she walked into a room. Where would she go? Saleem shook his head knowing, by now, that freedom and four hundred euros wouldn't save her.

As promised, he went back to the apartment at seven thirty. Visar didn't bother to invite him in. He handed Saleem a manila envelope and the backpack.

"Hey, boy! Your train leaves in thirty minutes. Do not be late."

"Okay," Saleem promised.

Visar was about to close the door when he grabbed Saleem by the nape of his neck, his fingers digging into Saleem's flesh.

"If you not in Paris when the man wait for you, he find you and he kill you. You understand this?" His tone was icy.

Saleem swallowed the knot in his throat and nodded.

He was released.

Saleem made it two blocks down the street before realizing he was walking in the wrong direction. He checked his watch. He had twenty minutes to get on that train. He opened the envelope and pulled out an authentic-looking Greek passport with his picture and a false name. Saleem stuffed it back into the envelope quickly and looked to make sure no one was watching. Inside the envelope was also a train ticket. Saleem was on the move again, with no time to waste.

Saleem entered the station with a new dread. Taking inventory, he had some valid-appearing papers to show any inquiring officer, a handful of clothes, and a toy stuffed with undoubtedly illegal contents. If he were stopped and searched, the bear would surely draw suspicion.

Five minutes.

Saleem struggled to match the ticket in his hand with the gates listed on the announcement boards.

A tap on his shoulder. Saleem whipped around to find a police officer looking down at him with a frown. His stomach dropped. Before he could bolt, the officer spoke.

"Where are you going?"

"I have a ticket," Saleem blurted.

"Show me." He took the ticket from Saleem's trembling hand and looked up at the board. He pointed to the left. "Gate seven. Quickly."

Saleem mumbled an awkward thanks and did his best to walk, not run, to the gate. He fully expected to hear a voice call out for him to halt. He dared not look over his shoulder.

Keep moving. Keep walking. Look for gate seven.

He found the gate and turned back around quickly. No one had followed him.

One minute.

Saleem got on board and found the seat number assigned on the ticket. Just in time.

He took the stuffed bear from the bag. A woman sitting across the aisle looked over and smiled warmly. How odd he must have appeared — a boy-man traveling with a beloved stuffed animal. He gave the bear a squeeze. There was something firm within the stuffing, squarish in shape. Saleem pushed the bear back into the bag and warned himself against being too curious.

The conductor signaled the train to set off. Out the window, the adjacent train looked as if it were moving ahead. Then there were trees and tunnels. Green and gray. Alive and dead. Saleem was as safe as he was unsafe.

He handed the conductor his ticket and waited for an accusing look or at least a question. But Saleem, with his backpack, looked very much like one of the many students aboard this car of the train. The others sat in the seats behind him, laughing loudly and swapping magazines. The conductor moved to the next car, and the students, one by one, tucked headphones into their ears or fell asleep against a neighbor's shoulder, leaving nothing but the hum of the train.

Saleem thought of his childhood friends from Afghanistan. Had they been allowed to grow up together without rocket-rain, surely they would have been just as jovial and rowdy. But war had a taming effect. Kabul's children were not children for long.

Roksana was not like this group. She seemed to have absorbed some of the solemnity of her fellow Afghans without ever having stepped foot in the country. Her father's aloofness had sparked in her an obligation to delve into the struggles of her own people. He admired her for it, doubtful he would have had the same inclination.

Saleem wasn't sure what he would have been had he had a life like Roksana's. Two parents, school, a peaceful country. He would not have been this Saleem. This Saleem was the sum of a series of dreadful moments.

He turned the watch on his wrist. A few more scratches on the glass, probably from the night before.

*Look what's happened to us, Padar-*jan.

Had Saleem and his family left Kabul earlier, they could have had a better chance. They could have had a peaceful life in London, maybe near Khala Najiba's family. Saleem and Samira would be in school now, attending classes and struggling with home-work assignments, learning a new language. It was an image so perfect, so imaginary that it played like a cartoon in Saleem's mind.

But Padar-*jan* had instead chosen to keep his family in Kabul and hope for better days — despite the growing unrest, the killings, the droughts.

Why did you choose this for us? What good came from us being there so long after every-one else left?

Saleem awoke with a jolt. The train had stopped. He looked around and saw new passengers boarding; others had already disembarked. A man was loading his bag into the overhead area.

"Excuse me — Milan?" Saleem pointed out the window.

"*Si,*" he answered with a nod.

Saleem grabbed the backpack and bolted out the train door, nearly knocking over an elderly couple. He threw his hands up in a quick gesture of apology. He had only thirty minutes, he had been told, to find the connecting train that would take him to Paris. He hoped the train hadn't been stopped long. He dug the tickets out of the envelope and again tried to match it up with the information screens that flashed overhead.

Paris. Gate four. Ten minutes.

Saleem ran. He was in front of gate seventeen now. He dodged in and out of passengers and rolling luggage. He prayed no one would stop him.

CHAPTER 52
SALEEM

The train pulled to a stop in Paris in the morning hours. Saleem had made it into France, but before he could continue on in his journey he needed to deliver this package to the right hands. He hoped it would be easy to find this man.

Up and down the tracks, his eyes were dually focused on spotting uniforms as well as anyone who resembled the Albanians he'd met in Rome.

A hand grabbed at his arm. Saleem tried to jerk away, but the grip was tight. He turned around, and with one look, he knew his contact had found him.

He had yellowed teeth and dark, piercing eyes. The man wore a black polyester jacket over a gunmetal T-shirt with slanted graffiti print across the chest. His jeans were acid washed and slim.

"You are the boy. You come from Rome."

Saleem nodded. Same rules probably applied here, so he kept his mouth shut.

"Good. You bring something for me?"

He released his hold on Saleem's arm. Saleem slid the backpack off his shoulder and started to unzip it.

"Not here! Idiot! Come."

Saleem allowed himself to be led through the crowd, the overhead announcement system mumbling instructions to passengers scurrying in crisscrossing paths. They walked over to a bench near a bank of storage lockers. They sat side by side, as if they were waiting for a friend to arrive on the next train.

"Open the bag." Saleem had the backpack on his lap. He unzipped it slowly and pulled out the ridiculous-looking stuffed bear. He handed it over.

The man squeezed roughly, feeling for its contents. He looked at the bear's neck and legs to make sure no one had tampered with the seams. Satisfied, he took the backpack from Saleem's lap and sifted through it.

"Where is the passport?"

Saleem reached into his back pocket and pulled out the booklet. The man took it, flipped it open to the identification page with Saleem's picture. He threw the bag back onto Saleem's lap. "You are finished. You can go."

"But, the passport . . . please . . ." he began nervously.

"What?" he snapped. He was already up and ready to make a quick escape from the train station.

"I need the passport to go to England."

"Passport?" His accent was as thick and heavy as that of his friends in Rome. A haughty laugh gave Saleem his answer. "You want to pay for passport?"

"I do not have money. But I need it to go to my family," he pleaded. How could he negotiate with this man? The passport was in this man's pocket now, so close that Saleem felt the urge to grab it.

"Eight hundred euro," he said with a snide smile. "For eight hundred euro. Cheap price for you."

Saleem's depleted money pouch did not hold eight hundred euro. It did hold another purchase he'd made in Athens, but he was not willing to part with that.

"Please, mister, I have little money. Eight hundred is too much. Something smaller?"

"How much you have?"

Dare he admit how much was in his pouch? That small booklet with his picture and a false name could help carry him to London, to his family. It was worth everything he had, Saleem decided.

"One hundred fifty euro."

"One hundred fifty?" the man scoffed. "You are crazy!"

The passport was gone. He had already turned and taken a few steps when Saleem called out once more.

"Mister, please, tell me how I go to London?" The man considered Saleem for a moment, then huffed and took a step in his direction.

"London?"

Saleem nodded.

"Go to Calais. All you people go to Calais. From Calais there is tunnel." He chuckled, a hint that he was sending Saleem on a path with little hope for success. "Maybe you be lucky."

CHAPTER 53
SALEEM

With the help of a kind-faced elderly woman, Saleem located Calais on a map. The city, perched on France's northwest shore, sat directly across from England. A narrow channel of water ran between the two countries. He'd purchased a ticket immediately, having no desire to see any more of Paris and eager to continue on. By morning, uneventfully, he was in Calais.

Saleem wandered through Calais for hours, blending into its mixed crowds. He left the train station behind and explored the streets, eager to find his way to the port. On the way, he passed massive buildings with thick, tall pillars and balconied windows. Even the smaller buildings had ornate windows, chubby-faced figures draped beside the frames.

Familiar in Calais was the smell of seawater. Saleem followed the salted mist all the way to the port. The piers brought Saleem comfort, as he'd gotten to know the basic rhythm and culture that came from the slow moans of ship horns and the traffic of passengers and trucks.

This particular port was beautiful. Fingers of coastline jutted into the waters of the English Channel. Vertical sailboat masts intersected the horizontal expanse of water and sky. Farther along, giant ships were docked, preparing, like Saleem, for the next voyage.

Saleem left the street and walked through a gravel strip to get near the ships. He noticed two dark-haired men sauntering around in the distance — the thin, defeated refugee sulk.

I probably look the same. I just don't want to admit it to myself.

His instincts were right. They were Afghans, happy to welcome him to the camp. Already, Saleem was beginning to feel at ease. He walked with them to find the refugee camp known in Calais as "the Jungle."

The Jungle was Patras, transplanted. It was a wasteland within walking distance of the coast. From its limits, one could make out England, and its prehistoric-looking sheer, white cliffs.

The refugees of the Jungle languished,

their eyes fixed on the horizon and the promise of a better life. The Jungle was not a place to take root.

Surrounded by tall trees and bordered by metal fences, the camp was an open-air enclosure. Saleem entered via a dirt path guarded by three men. Though he was apprehensive, he noted that the other men were not. One of them, Ajmal, saw his curiosity and explained, with the satisfaction of one with wisdom to share.

"They won't disturb you. They're here only to watch for crime. We come and go as we please. But things are different at the port or at the tunnel. There, the officers are looking for us, and they won't hesitate to grab you by the neck if they catch you."

"The tunnel?" Saleem had set his eyes on the port but Ajmal spoke of a tunnel, the same tunnel that the man in Paris had mentioned.

"Yes, the tunnel. Oh, you are so new here!" He laughed. "The tunnel goes from here to England. It's about fifty kilometers. Many people have passed through it, sometimes on trucks or in the trunks of cars or just walking. But there are lots of police. I know one man, he walked through the tunnel twice, and both times he was caught just coming out of the other side! Can you imagine his bad luck? Twice!" The other man laughed with him.

Saleem could see the Jungle now. A colony of makeshift houses with sheets of metal as roofs and blue tarps for walls stood ahead, surrounded by a moat of refuse. The stench hit him as they drew close. Hundreds upon hundreds of Afghans lived here, along with some Iraqis and Iranians, Saleem was told. Aid workers came once a day to distribute a simple meal. Some of the men had constructed firepits though it was rare to be so fortunate to have anything to cook. It was worse than Patras.

The other man left, leaving Ajmal to introduce Saleem to the squalid conditions. Toilets, scattered here and there for the men to use, overflowed with human waste, and clouds of flies swarmed overhead. There were painted signs here and there in English.

WE WANT FREEDOM

NO LIFE IN THE JUNGLE

RESPECT FOR HUMANS

"The French government wants to close this camp, but most of the people here are seeking asylum. We are hoping they will not send us back. You have any family in England?"

"My aunt's family. And my mother, sister,

and brother are there now too. I mean, I hope they are."

"You hope?"

"We were separated on our way from Greece to London."

"Your mother went alone with two children?"

"Yes, but they had documents," Saleem explained. "I'm hoping they didn't get caught along the way."

"So you came as the rest of us did." Ajmal nodded in understanding. "Be thankful your family had papers. It's an ugly road to get here and definitely no way for a mother to travel with her children. God save our mothers."

Saleem let Ajmal's last words linger before he spoke.

"Do you have anyone in England?"

"Yes, my sister lives there with her husband and their children. And a few cousins too. I've been here five months. I came through Iran and Turkey, but then I was caught in Greece and sent to a detention center. They told me they would send me back to Iran and that I had to leave in thirty days, but no way was I going back. After what I'd paid to get that far! But now I'm stuck here with all the others."

"Have you tried to get across?" Saleem

asked the obvious question.

"The port is surrounded by high metal fences. You saw today, didn't you? The tunnel is the best way to go, but I've been caught twice. It's not easy."

Saleem understood. He had noticed the layers of fencing at the port. It was more heavily sectioned off than the other ports through which he had passed. He had to take the experience of Ajmal and the others into account. Only fifty kilometers of tunnel lay between him and England. Saleem smiled at the thought of being that close, finally.

"You can stay with me tonight. There are five of us living together, but we will make room for you. Tomorrow we can look to see who has more space. We all share here. That's how we live. Welcome to the Jungle, my friend!" Ajmal's outstretched arms facetiously presented the camp to Saleem in all its glory. Saleem laughed. He took his backpack and followed Ajmal to his hut.

Saleem was hungry, but there was nothing to eat, and he was too exhausted to look very far. Ajmal's roommates were young and good-natured, ranging in age from thirteen to twenty-one. Ajmal fell somewhere in the middle, the link between adolescence and adulthood. They shifted and shuffled themselves to make space for Saleem, giving him a battered piece of cardboard to rest on. He was able to get a good night's rest, lulled by the chorus of their snores.

The next morning, the camp buzzed with news from the outside.

"They're going to raze the camp. That's what they are saying. They're going to take everyone."

"What can we do?"

"We should move. We should leave this camp before they come in and send us all back to Afghanistan."

"Are you crazy? Where will we go?"

"We can all go through the tunnel. If we all go at once, they won't be able to catch everyone. Our chances will be better. We should do it tonight, the night of the holiday. There will probably be fewer guards there."

"As if one person does not draw enough attention! You think all of us should walk together into the police's arms?"

The debate went on for two hours. Just as the city of Patras had grown weary of its blight, Calais had tired of the Jungle. As Saleem listened to the sounds of their banter, his eyes were drawn to the sidelines. A white-bearded man sat on an overturned bucket. He watched the mass as they debated, observing without participating. Strange, Saleem thought, as it was rare for a man of his age to make the journey out of Afghanistan. Unless they found a legitimate way out of the country, people like him were destined to be buried in Afghanistan's blood-soaked earth.

The man looked oddly familiar, though Saleem could not place him. He stared, waiting for his mind to make the connection. He met Saleem's gaze and tilted his head to the side. Saleem looked away for a second, but his eyes drifted back again and he offered a tight-lipped smile in return.

Does he know me? Or did he just catch me staring at him?

Saleem kept his head bowed, and when he looked up again, the old man had vanished.

Several of the men went to explore a new part of town. The Jungle might close down, but that did not mean the displaced would be offered any alternative place to set up shelter. Some said the police were waiting for the right moment to storm in and sweep up the refugees. Saleem could not have arrived at a worse time.

They ate boiled rice with tomatoes. It didn't taste like much, but it was warm going down.

■ ■ ■ ■

In the early evening, two of Ajmal's roommates decided to leave the Jungle and set
up camp elsewhere. They believed those
who said the Jungle's days were numbered.
They packed their rusted frying pans, their
mugs, and their spare clothes into plastic
bags and headed off. Ajmal was disappointed to see them go but offered their
space to Saleem, who gratefully accepted.

The following morning, Saleem walked to
the fly-infested latrines. The camp was
quiet. It was just after sunrise and only a
handful of men were awake. As he came
around a cluster of tents, Saleem nearly
walked straight into the old man he'd seen
yesterday. The man smiled.

"Sohb-bakhair, bachem."

"Good morning to you, too. Pardon me
— I hadn't seen you standing here."

"The elderly become invisible sooner than
we would hope," he said, smiling.

"God forbid. It was my oversight," Saleem
said meekly. The man had to be in his
seventies, at least, with thin, olive skin and a
full white beard and mustache. The corners
of his eyes crinkled under heavy, snowy
brows. He wore a long beige tunic and

pantaloons of a slightly darker shade.

"You have come recently," he said. "What is your name and where are you from?"

"My name is Saleem Waziri. My family lived in Kabul."

"Everyone here says they are from Kabul. But I can hear in your accent that you were raised there. Walk with me. I want to know more about you."

Saleem followed, mesmerized by the soft rasp of the man's voice. They strolled away from Ajmal's hut and toward the far end of the camp, the side from which England's chalky cliffs could be seen.

I feel like I know you, Saleem wanted to say. But he resisted and followed the man's lead. They walked through the main pathway that crossed through the Jungle.

"A Kabuli family. Your father's name?"

"Mahmood Waziri." Saleem fiddled with the worn watchband on his wrist.

"Waziri. Mahmood Waziri? That name sounds awfully familiar. Let me see, do you mean Mahmood Waziri, the engineer? Worked for the Ministry of Water and Electricity?"

Saleem felt a tingle in his chest.

"Yes, yes! Did you know my father?" He stopped in his tracks and looked up at the old man's face. His thin lips parted in a half smile.

"Do you not see these white hairs, my friend? I am old enough to have known more than just a few men. I know generations of men. I dare to say, much of Kabul's history fills the space between my ears."

Saleem grinned.

"Of course I knew your father. He's not here with you." A gentle statement more than a question.

"No, he was . . . taken." Saleem said it quickly, not wanting the words to linger.

"A shame, a true shame. Such an intelligent man. And your mother? She was a teacher. Where is she?"

"She is with my younger sister and brother. I think they're in London. We were separated during our travels."

"Ah, I see. God willing, your family is safely in London and anxiously awaiting your arrival. You're brave to have made this voyage on your own. You must have seen many difficulties on your way here."

"No more and no less than anyone else," Saleem said, thinking of Ali. Naeem. The boys in Attiki. Patras. Pagani. The ones whose journey ended in the rocky waters. The ones who never made it out of Kabul.

"Wise of you to know this. We all cross a

hundred peaks to get even this far. And there will be more before we each make it to whatever destination God has fated for us."

"I worry about what God has fated for my little brother," Saleem confessed, digging in the ground with the toe of his shoe. "He has a bad problem with his heart. We were able to get him some medicine in Turkey, but after that we couldn't take him to any doctors."

"There are things beyond our control, but there is reason behind the system, whether or not we choose to believe it. Let's sit." He led Saleem to some small boulders a few yards away. "Let us talk of things more pleasant than the fate of the Jungle. Saleem-*jan,* I knew your father by his reputation. He was a brilliant engineer, one of Kabul's finest talents. Are you familiar with the work he was doing?"

"No, Uncle," Saleem said respectfully. His face reddened at his own ignorance when it came to his father's projects. "I only know it had something to do with water."

The man was forgiving.

"You were young, no doubt. Your father's area of expertise was bringing water to the outlying parts of Kabul and the surrounding areas. He had several ingenious irrigation projects that he pushed through the mountains of bureaucracy. And mountains of bureaucracy was when things were good.

"Later, there were much bigger obstacles in the way of his projects. There was no use trying to accomplish anything in Kabul at that time. People were scared. Nothing was happening. People were just trying to stay alive. When your father was killed, that left you and your mother to tend to the younger children?"

"Yes. We had no money. We weren't sure if they would come after us and we felt trapped. We had to leave Kabul."

"It's never easy to leave one's home, especially when there are only closed doors ahead of you."

"My father left us with nothing. It was useless to stay there. Most of our family had already left. My aunt and uncle have been living in London. A normal life. Not like . . . not like this. My cousins never saw things get bad in Kabul. That could have been our story too."

Saleem hadn't meant to sound as resentful as he did. It was a sentiment he tried to keep buried, but it resurfaced from time to time, especially when he felt exhausted by their journey.

"It is possible that if your father had led

his family out of Kabul earlier, maybe your story would be different. Perhaps you would be living somewhere in Europe, accepted as asylum seekers. But only if that was the destiny that Allah had in store for you. And there's something else you should realize. You think that it was futile for your father to stay in Kabul, to continue his work, but there are hundreds of people who would disagree with you."

"What do you mean? Which people?"

"Which people? Why, the hundreds of people who had *water* because of him. The hundreds of people were able to *survive* because of him. He was the only person insisting on these projects, demanding them. Other people looked for their own interests, money and guns fattening their bellies instead of helping to feed the people of Kabul. That is the difference that your father made. He changed people's lives. He never knew their names. He never saw their faces. But he saved their lives."

"I didn't know," Saleem said, his voice muffled with guilt.

"You would not have known," the old man gently replied.

Saleem stared at his shoes and blinked back tears.

It takes a lifetime to learn your parents.

For children, parents are larger than life. They are strong arms that carry little ones, warm laps for sleepy heads, sources of food and wisdom. It's as if parents were born on the same day as their children, having not existed a moment before.

As children inch their way into adolescence, the parent changes. He is an authority, a source of answers, and a chastising voice. Depending on the day, he may be resented, emulated, questioned, or defied.

Only as an adult can a child imagine his parent as a whole person, as a husband, a brother, or a son. Only then can a child see how his parent fits into the world beyond four walls. Saleem had only bits and pieces of his father, mostly the memories of a young boy. He would spend the rest of his life, he knew, trying to reconstruct his father with the scraps he could recall or gather from his mother.

But first, he had to admit the last year's worth of memories were tainted by a discreet anger he harbored for Padar-*jan* for keeping them in Kabul when they should have escaped. Now Saleem had learned his father had done so because he knew the importance of his work. When he'd realized his family was in danger, he'd made plans to escape but by then it was too late.

Reap a noble harvest, my son.

Saleem stuttered. "I . . . I loved my father very much."

"Of course you did. You are asking questions. You want answers. That is natural. That is exactly as your father would have done."

The old man had said something else earlier.

"You knew my mother as well?" Saleem asked, steeling his voice back to its normal cadence.

"Your mother, her name is . . . oh, my failing memory . . . what is it again?"

"Fereiba."

"Ah, yes, Fereiba-*jan*," he said. But to Saleem it sounded like he knew her name all along. "A delightful woman. As I said, I remember when she was a teacher. She made each student and each lesson important. You know, when she was young, the world treated her callously. But she did not let an unjust beginning spoil her. If you ever meet a former student of hers, you will be honored to hear what kind of teacher she was."

"How did you know her?"

"I guess you could say I was a friend of her grandfather's. He had a beautiful, bountiful orchard that was the envy of all in

582

Kabul. But as she became a young woman, I saw her less and less. I was pleased to hear of her happy marriage to your father. Their success made me proud. You know, my son, you're fortunate. I see both your parents in you."

"Fortunate" was not the word Saleem would have chosen if asked to describe himself. He had felt anything but fortunate in the last year.

"So, my boy, I can see in your face that you've traveled a rough road. But how will you get to England?"

"I don't know exactly, but this tunnel is probably the best route. I've been to the port and the fences are too thick. I just don't see how it's possible. Nearly everyone's been caught trying to get across there."

The old man stood up and stared off into the channel. From here it was easy to see the currents, linear streams of water a shade different from the rest of the ocean, like secret passages within the depths.

"However tall the mountain, my son," the old man said. "There is a way to the other side."

CHAPTER 54
SALEEM

For two weeks, the jungle boys lingered in the unknown, a more tightly wound time than the years they'd passed in covert transit. In those two weeks, the old man seemed to have vanished. Saleem asked Ajmal about him, but his roommate only shrugged his shoulders and said he did not know every one of the hundreds of Afghans in their settlement.

Every day, men in wind jackets and neatly pressed slacks came to the camp. From a distance, they pointed, made notes on clipboards, and snapped photos before they would shake hands with one another and head off in different directions. Something was in the works.

One group of boys had hatched a plan. A holiday was coming up in a few days. Two men had amassed quite a following of about two hundred refugees. The idea was to take advantage of the day. The skeleton crew on duty would be distracted, with conciliatory festive meals and a few libations on the job. No one in the camp knew exactly what the holiday signified, and no one really cared. All that mattered was that while the French guards were observing the holiday, they would be observing little else.

They talked about it every day, churning the theory into a hard plan.

"If we all go through at once, how many could they possibly catch? Maybe a few, but most of us will make it."

"You see! Even you say a few will get caught."

"Every day a few try to get through and how many actually succeed? Our chances will be much better. The Jungle is about to disappear. This may be our best chance."

Saleem debated the idea himself. It was a decent plan, he decided. But to brave the tunnel with hundreds of refugees seemed counterintuitive. All his other passages had been done alone, attracting as little atten-tion as possible.

Saleem listened from afar, wishing for an opinion from someone he could trust, but the voices he most wanted to hear were too distant to be audible.

Make up your mind. Time is running out. This money won't last much longer.

■ ■ ■ ■

With sunset, the buzz began. People fidgeted, legs were restless. Saleem and Ajmal watched from a distance.

"They look like they're going to mess themselves already," Ajmal said. "They're crazy to do this."

Saleem chewed his lip as he paced. Though he'd not yet decided if he would follow the others, his legs were restless too.

"Maybe they are. But maybe they're not," Saleem said. In a snap decision, he ran into the shack he shared with Ajmal, got his backpack, and pulled the straps over his shoulders.

"Wish me luck, brother. Who knows? Maybe I'll come back. But I need to at least try."

At quarter past eleven, with a pale, orange moon hanging low in the sky, the boys, a straggling crowd of a hundred, began their walk to the tunnel. They fractured into small groups, speaking in whispers and occasional laughs to break the tense mood. Most were grim and silent.

Saleem rushed to catch up with the stragglers. The path was familiar to him. He'd sat on the hilltop and stared at the tunnel entrance several times but never worked up the nerve to approach it. The boys reached a line of metal fences. The links were broken in two or three spots, inviting further trespass. Like the others, Saleem scraped through, wincing as the fence clawed at his back.

The tunnel entrance, concrete bored through the base of a grassy plain, was a valley flanked by verdant hillsides. There were openmouthed entries for trains moving in either direction, a network of tracks leading into the black holes. A narrow, graded median divided the train entry from that of the automobiles. The valley, as a whole, was a bed of metal, pavement, and concrete, set aglow by rows of sodium lamps.

There were few cars on the road tonight.

Saleem let the others lead the way. The walk here had been long. He rubbed his hands together to warm them. He was grateful for the parka he'd been given by one of the men in the camp. Dark shadows jogged toward the entrance, watching for guards, lights, or sirens. The night was still.

Go with them. They'll be in England soon. This is that chance.

Two or three at a time, they filtered into the tunnel and disappeared from view.

Saleem stood behind a tree and watched from the vantage point of a boy unnerved. Frustrated, he punched at the bark.

Enough of this. I am going to follow them.

And just as he resolved to push aside his fears and grab the low-lying fruit, the shouts rang out. White lights broke the soft orange haze. Three police cars peeled into view and screeched to a stop by the entrance. Flashlights led the way.

Saleem's heart dropped. There were so many. For hours, it continued. Men were led out, their hands tied behind their backs, their feet dragging with disappointment. The boys had considered the possibility that a few would be caught, but it was much worse. They'd rounded up at least half by Saleem's count. Everything those boys had done, all the money they'd paid and the risks they'd faced and the cold nights they'd endured — all of it had been in vain.

The others would likely be caught on the other side by the British authorities. What would become of them? Would they be given the chance to apply for asylum or would they be shuttled back to France?

Tonight had not been the right night to chase the moon. When all but one police car had finally left the scene, Saleem turned around and hiked back to the Jungle.

CHAPTER 55
FEREIBA

Najiba-*jan* has been good to us. I can see the look on her husband's face. Hameed would like nothing more than for us to be gone. Germany offers much better benefits to its refugees, he says, though he has no good explanation for why he does not want to move there himself.

I learned slowly, once I met them, that my sister had no idea he had discouraged us from coming to England. She'd even saved up some money and set it aside so that we would have something for food and clothing, until we were able to file the right papers and apply for asylum.

Her husband sees me as an intrusion. He wishes us to disappear. He cannot look me in the eye and fumbles for even simple conversation.

I want to tell him that he needn't be so anxious. Those days, when his flirtations and romantic promises filled my sky, are part of a time I can barely recall. So much has happened between then and now. Though Mahmood, my *hamsar,* no longer stands by my side, my years with him are larger than girlish dreams. I am grateful for the time we had together, short as it was, and for the children we raised.

Hameed, the boy from the orchard, played a role in bringing me to Mahmood. The betrayal I felt at the time melted away once I got to know Mahmood. It was not the straightest road, but it led me home.

Hameed does not understand that. And I cannot explain it to him because he is my sister's husband and I do not want to open doors that were rightly closed long ago. Najiba's heart is welcoming and wide. I do not want to stir any ill will.

Even KokoGul. Even to her I must be thankful for it was she who nudged Najiba under Shireen-*jan*'s nose. It was she who thought her prettiest daughter, her true daughter, was more deserving of our esteemed neighbor. And I know that when his mother told him of Najiba's beauty, he changed his choice readily and stopped visiting the orchard. He kept his choice a secret, too much of a coward to say anything himself.

I wept for days when I should not have.

We are too shortsighted to rejoice in the moments that deserve it.

Khala Zeba, Mahmood's beloved mother, saw what others did not. And my husband trusted his mother. How lucky I was to have both of them. Allah chose my *naseeb* wisely. In our wedding photograph I am solemn and unsure. Khala Zeba lifted my green veil and looked at me with warm, motherly eyes.

Mahmood's hand joined with mine that day, my mother's bangles delicately clinking against one another in their own private toast. My father had looked on somberly.

You look just like her, my daughter.

I remember the way my throat tightened, missing the mother I'd never met, the grandfather who had watched over me, and the old man in the orchard who promised to light the path before me. I was nervous about the man at my side, my new husband. But those people I missed so much, those faces I would only see in my dreams, whispered in my ear that all would be right.

Najiba's children have inherited their mother's delicate features and sweet disposition. From their father, only his restless nature. I watch them at the park, climbing ladders and laughing as they fall on their backsides or slip down a slide. Samira feels too old to play alongside her cousins. She's

591

nearly a young woman now and the only playgrounds of her youth were places of hiding on rainy nights. I wonder if that's what she sees when she watches the children on the swings.

She speaks now. Just short sentences, but she is coming along slowly. She waits, as I do, for Saleem to join us. I know when she sees him, she will be complete again, a whole and perfect child.

Aziz is too nervous to wander far. He watches the other children play and imitates their actions from a distance. His legs have thickened and hold his weight comfortably. He is thin but he smiles with pink lips and eyes bright enough to make mine water. Thank you, God. Thank you.

Something tells me my son is close. I continue to wait for him, and it occurs to me that's what being a mother is, isn't it? Waiting for a rounded belly to tighten in readiness; listening for the sound of hunger in the moonlit hours; hearing an eager voice call even in the camouflage of traffic, loud music, and whirring machines. It's looking at every door, every phone, and every approaching silhouette and feeling that slight lift, that tickle of opportunity to be again — mother.

I saw Saleem in my dream last night,

swimming across a brilliant, blue ocean with ripples that sparkled under a warm sun. The breeze blew a salty mist onto my cheeks as I watched him. There was water all around him, and he glided through, swimming in smooth, strong strokes as if he'd been raised by the ocean. From afar, I could see his mischievous grin, the proud triumph of a boy who'd found his own way home.

It was a good dream for a mother to have and I woke with a buoyancy I've not felt in a long time. Thank God for the water, for water is *roshanee,* water is light.

CHAPTER 56
SALEEM

"How many did they catch? Were they beaten?"

"I don't know. Maybe fifty . . . sixty. I've no idea what happened on the other end of the tunnel either."

It was morning and Saleem was telling Ajmal about what he had seen for the second time. Although he had recounted everything last night, Ajmal wanted to hear it again in the light of day.

"I knew it was a bad idea." Ajmal shook his head. "I would have been caught. I have no luck when it comes to the police."

"But we're not in much better shape. Look at us. How long do you think we can live here? People are getting sick. The town wants the Jungle gone. Even the Red Cross workers say trouble is coming soon."

"Where else can we go, Saleem? We have no documents. We have no money." Ajmal sat on the floor, his knees to his chest. His forehead touched his folded arms. "If I'd known how things were here, I don't know if I would have left Afghanistan. Maybe it would be better to die on our own soil than to be chased out of everywhere we go like stray dogs."

The same thought had crossed Saleem's mind, but now he quickly dismissed it.

"You're talking like the old and gray haired. We had to leave. If we don't plan for tomorrow, there won't be one."

Ajmal looked up. His ears tingled at the conviction in Saleem's voice.

The commotion began not an hour later. Ajmal and Saleem went outside to find out what was going on. A crowd of young French protesters had gathered in front of the camps. Some chanted. Some waved their fists in the air. Some carried signs.

BAN BORDERS
NO PRISON FOR IMMIGRANTS
HUMAN RIGHTS NOW

"Look at them all!" Ajmal exclaimed.

There had to be hundreds of people out there. Men and women. There were also at least thirty police officers with stern black uniforms and half-shell helmets, scrambling to surround the group and control the chaos. The situation was odd. The police were here because of the protesters. And the protesters were here for the Jungle.

"Their own people shouting for us!"

But Saleem saw more when he looked at the mass. They must know something. Maybe they had gotten word about that something. Saleem watched as more activists began to join the group, two or three at a time.

"Ajmal, this is not good. We should get out of here."

"Now? When we've just found hundreds of friends? I bet things will get better. We just have to wait and see."

"I don't want to see. We'll be caught in the middle of whatever this is. Just like in Afghanistan."

Ajmal sighed.

"Maybe we should set up camp somewhere else in town, like the other boys did."

"No," Saleem said. "I think we should make a run for the tunnel."

"The tunnel? Have you lost your mind?"

"I know . . . but look at where all the police are now. They are here! This might just be the perfect distraction."

Ajmal was as desperate as Saleem. His silence said as much.

"Listen, Ajmal. I've been thinking about it. There are two entrances to the tunnel.

The men all went through the entrance for cars and trucks. But there is the other entrance."

"You mean the train tracks?"

"Yes, the train tracks."

"That's a death wish. People have tried jumping onto the trains as they pass through. They've been electrocuted by the cables. And do you know how fast they roll through there? If you get hit by one of those trains — even your mother wouldn't recognize your body."

"I think it's worth a try. The fence is still cut open and we can go look. I don't see any other way. The lorries are nearly impossible to jump onto. And the ferries are so guarded. It's not like the other ports. I'm going to try to walk through the tunnel, along the tracks."

Ajmal took a deep breath.

"When are you going to go through with it?"

"This evening, once the sun has started to set. The dark will help."

Ajmal considered Saleem's reasoning. He nodded in agreement.

"Let's pray to God that this works."

Saleem ignored the hypocrisy of praying only when he was most desperate and hoped that God would too.

■ ■ ■ ■

When evening came upon them, Saleem and Ajmal said nothing to the others in the camp. They gathered whatever food they had stored in the hut and stuffed it into their pockets. With fifty kilometers of track to cross, they would need every last bit of sustenance. They made their way down the dirt path and out of the Jungle. Protesters came and went with their poster board signs. Saleem could not make out what they were chanting and averted his eyes. It was a strange thing to be running from, but the air was charged.

They arrived at the tunnel entrance, and Saleem led Ajmal to the opening in the security fence. The authorities either hadn't found the spot yet or hadn't had time to repair it. They crouched behind some trees and watched for guards. No one was in the vicinity, but there was a regular stream of cars. It wasn't completely dark so they decided to wait. No use in rushing the plan.

In an hour, all that remained of the sun was a purple glow on the horizon. The boys crept down the embankment and tiptoed toward the tracks, sidestepping the rails with caution.

Their first peek into the tunnel was intimidating. There was only about two feet of space on either side of the train tracks. They would have to keep their bellies plastered against the wall while trains passed by. Wavering or losing balance would be fatal.

"It will be dark," Saleem warned. "We should stick close together and listen for the sound of trains coming."

"Yes, stick together. And listen for trains." Saleem could hear the quiver in Ajmal's voice.

"Ajmal, you don't have to do this if you don't want to," Saleem said gently. He did not want to be responsible for what might happen if Ajmal's nerves got the best of him during their crossing.

"I'm fine, Saleem. I want to go."

The boys entered the dark. Saleem felt once more for Khala Najiba's address, tucked safely into his pocket.

They had walked about two kilometers into the tunnel when their feet sensed a light rumble in the tracks.

"Saleem!"

"Remember, up against the wall and don't move! Don't move!" Saleem yelled out. He pressed his cheek against the cold tunnel wall and tried to flatten himself. He closed his eyes, scared for Ajmal and scared for himself.

The train was upon them almost instantly, glaring lights announcing its arrival. Traveling at nearly one hundred miles per hour, the train slammed the boys with a hard blast of air.

One . . . two . . . three . . . four . . . Saleem counted as his fingers clawed at the concrete wall. Nine . . . ten . . . eleven . . . and the assault continued. Fourteen . . . fifteen . . . sixteen . . . until finally, mercifully, the deafening noise faded into the distance.

Saleem, unmoving, let out the desperate breath he'd held in. Slowly, his body, realizing it was whole, untensed. This could work!

"Ajmal?"

There was no reply.

"Ajmal!"

Silence still.

"Ajmal, are you all right! Answer me!" Saleem groped behind him in the dark.

"Yes, yes, I'm okay. I just . . . oh, Saleem, that was close!"

"But you are okay?"

"Yes, I am okay."

"Can you go on?"

"My friend, you've brought the donkey halfway up the hill, there is no use in turning him back around."

Saleem's laughter echoed through the dark tunnel. It ran ahead of him, leading the way like a beacon in the night. All he had to do was follow.

Saleem touched his pocket and felt for the pouch. He thought of his return to the pawnshop in Athens and the surprised look on the store owner's face when Saleem reached into his pocket and handed over money he could scarcely afford to pay.

Madar-jan, *I am just a few kilometers away. I will be by your side and show Padar*-jan *that I can be the man my family needs me to be . . . the man I want to be. I will not stop until I see these bangles back on your wrist, Madar*-jan.

His throat thick with the honeyed taste of promise, Saleem called out to his invisible friend.

"Ajmal, my friend, let's go!"

ACKNOWLEDGMENTS

My deep gratitude to my parents, who are a real-life love story and my biggest champions. For my *hamsar,* this story would not exist without you and your belief that I could make it happen. Zoran, Zayla, and Kyrus — my biggest critics — you make storytelling challenging and rewarding and I love you with all my heart. Fawod and family, your extraloud cheers feed my soul. Thank you, Fahima, for knowing me so well that you send all the right inspirations my way. You make my inbox happy. To my uncle Isah and the other family members who have shared details of their sometimes heartbreaking journeys, thank you for your generosity. Emine, my immensely talented Turkish advisor, your creative input was precious, and I hope the world gets to see the important moments you've captured (www.eminegozdesevim.com). For Laura, my overqualified Hellenic guide, *efxaristo koukla mou.* To my wise editor, Rachel Kahan, thank you for making my imaginary friends your imaginary friends and for taking such good care of them. Helen Heller, my astute agent, thank you for finding this story a home and for breathing poetry into the book's title (again). To the entire family at William Morrow/HarperCollins, thank you for your creativity, dedication, and enthusiasm. I am eternally grateful to all the friends who have supported my writing in many creative ways: the LadyDocs, the Queens crew, Professor Holly Davidson, the Warwickians, and others.

This story was inspired by the masses of people all over the world in search of a place to call home. It is a fictional story, meant only to represent the dilemma of the displaced in a small way. There are many out there documenting true human experiences, and I am grateful for the critical work they do. What do I wish for? Since I'm one part dreamer and two parts realist, I wish for a world that doesn't create refugees, but until then, I'll settle for the humanity in each of us that makes sharing and hearing these important stories possible.

GLOSSARY

Ameen Amen
aroos bride
aush noodle soup
azaan call to prayer
b'isme-Allah in the name of Allah/God
bachem my boy/child
Bibi-jan Grandma-dear
Boba-jan Grandpa-dear
burqa head-to-toe covering
chador head scarf
dokhtar daughter/girl
dua prayer
Eid holiday
espand incense used to ward off the evil eye
fateha funeral service
hamsar spouse
iftar evening meal to break Ramadan fast at sunset
inshallah God willing
jan/janem dear/my dear
jenaaza burial ceremony

Jumaa Friday
Kaka Uncle
Khala Aunt
Khanum Lady
khastgaar suitor
khormaa dates (fruit)
Madar-jan Mother-dear
mahram close male relative
mantu ground-meat-filled dumplings
masjid house of worship
moallim teacher
nakhod chickpeas
nam-e-khoda praise God
naseeb destiny
nazar evil eye
nikkah Islamic marriage ceremony
noosh-e-jan to your health
Padar-jan Father-dear
purdah veil/seclusion
qandem my sweet
roshanee light/fortune
sawaab spiritual reward
sheerbrinj rice pudding
shirnee sweets/a symbolic tray of sweets
  used to signify acceptance of a courtship
sura Qur'anic verse
tasbeh rosary beads
wa-alaikum and to you

ABOUT THE AUTHOR

Nadia Hashimi is an Afghan American pediatrician living in suburban Washington, D.C. She is the author of the international bestseller *The Pearl That Broke Its Shell.*